# THE RETURN OF THE EARL

# EDITH LAYTON

## THE RETURN OF THE EARL

AVON BOOKS

*An Imprint of HarperCollinsPublishers*

AVON BOOKS
*An Imprint of* HarperCollins*Publishers*
10 East 53rd Street
New York, New York 10022-5299

Copyright © 2004 by Edith Felber
ISBN: 0-7394-4542-1

*To Damaris Rowland,*
*for keeping the faith*

*Early one morning, just as the sun was rising,*
*I heard a young maid in the valley below.*
*"Oh don't deceive me, Oh never leave me,*
*How could you use a poor maiden so?"*

*Thus sang the young maiden, her sorrows bewailing.*
*Thus sung the poor maid in the valley below.*
*"Oh don't deceive me, Oh never leave me,*
*How could you use a poor maiden so?"*

—Old English folk song

# Prologue

*England
1800*

**T**he man paused at the brink of the door to the hold. He glanced up, narrowing his eyes against the sun. He breathed deeply, filling his lungs with the brackish air, as though he were about to leap into the sea around him and not just step down into the bowels of the ship.

"Take a deep breath," he told the boys at his side. "Hold it. Look at the sky. Remember all of it."

The three boys stood still and did as he said. Although they held up the line, the guards didn't react. No one in the long line of prisoners behind them complained either. Many of them were breathing deeply, too. It was, after all, the last breath of fresh air they'd get until the next day. In some cases, it might be the last they'd ever get, and they all knew that too well. The *Retribution* was bound for the other side of the world with its cargo of miserable souls, in condi-

tions so appalling that many would leave this world
before the ship reached its destination.

The guards allowed the man and boys their silent
good-byes. An extra minute in the weak spring sunlight was a small enough charity, and the last many of
these wretches would get, or deserved to have. They
were, after all, a collection of murderers, rapists,
thieves, frauds, cheats, and liars. That was why they
were about to be expelled from their native land like
the indigestible mass of filth that they were. Or so the
magistrates had ruled.

The man who paused at the brink of the stair that
would lead him down into darkness didn't look savage. He looked filthy and ill used. His clothing was in
rags. The once-fine ruffles at his wrists and throat had
long since been torn away. His breeches were ragged,
his jacket in tatters, his shirt might have once been
white, because gentlemen wore no other color. He
had been dressed like a gentleman, once. Although
gaunt, he still seemed fit, and moved with grace even
though he wore no shoes. His hands were fisted; he
looked ready to fight if he had to.

Tears cleared long trails down his smudged face as
he blinked, squinting up at the sun. Those tears could
have been from emotion or because it had been so
long since he'd seen the light.

Two of the thin and ragged boys at his side looked to
be about ten or twelve years of age, the third perhaps a
year or two older. They were so dirty it was hard to tell
if they were fair-haired or light-skinned. But it was
easy to see how worried they were. The man's face reg-
istered only anguish. Theirs showed fear.

Or so it seemed to those few onlookers who stood on the dock watching the prison ship prepare to set sail for the antipodes.

When prisoners were to be hanged there were always huge crowds to see them off, along with friends and relatives. Food and drink were sold, songs were sung, it was all holiday on topping day at Tyburn Hill. When convicts were sent to the ends of the earth they were seen off in silence, if they were seen at all. There was, after all, nothing interesting to watch. And no one, least of all the unfortunates themselves, knew when or where they were to go until they were already on their way.

England had too many prisoners to keep and far too many to hang, so many were banished instead. There were hundreds of offenses and only so many ways to punish offenders. Transport was as good a way as any and often just as permanent as hanging. It wasn't that prisoners weren't allowed to return from Botany Bay. It was only that few lived long enough to get there, and fewer ever returned.

"Time to move on," a guard said to the prisoner who stood at the brink of the stair.

He nodded. But then he straightened, eyes narrowed against more than the sun. He stared at a pair of men on the wharf. He couldn't help but notice them. They could be seen from a distance, especially on such a gray day. One of the men was fat, fair, and overdressed for such a sullen morning; he wore a long crimson cape and carried a silver-headed walking stick that glinted in the light. The other man was older, dressed drably, but well. Both looked back at the prisoner with interest.

One of the boys at the prisoner's side noticed who he was staring at.

He gasped. "Isn't that Sir Gordon?"

His father nodded.

"Who's 'e?" one of the other boys muttered, looking at the pair of spectators.

"The one who sent us here," the first boy said. "The one who said we stole from him. The one who lied!"

"Softly, softly," his father murmured as he kept staring.

"Who's the other?" his son asked.

"I don't know, though I should," his father said, his voice distant and troubled. "It seems important . . . I will remember."

"Here! I said time to move on," the guard said, brandishing the club he held.

"Remember his face!" the prisoner told his son. "Never forget it!"

"I will! I won't forget, I promise," the boy vowed.

The two other boys nodded, too.

Head high, the man stepped down the stair into the hold. He stopped, because his son held back. His voice gentled. "We will be back," he said softly. "That, I promise."

Then he continued down the steps, and his son followed. He didn't let go of his father's hand, nor did he lose his grip on the other boy's hand, and that lad held on to the last boy. Linked by circumstance and need, the four stepped down into the darkness together.

The day wore on, though the prisoners couldn't count the hours in the unrelenting darkness of the hold in the great prison hulk. But finally, even they knew it was night. Even so, many couldn't sleep.

"Don't worry," the man's voice said to the huddle of boys at his side. They sat on the rocking floor of the ship with the other prisoners, waiting for the morning, when their voyage into the unknown would begin.

Such was the power of his voice and the firmness of their trust in him that the boys obeyed, in spite of their fears. They curled close to him, closed their eyes, and finally slept. Only he sat awake through the night, as he always did, on guard. He was also busy planning. He didn't know where he was going or if he could get there. But if he did nothing else in life, he would see that the boys got there, and then one day, home again.

# Chapter 1

*England*
*1815*

The visitor was late, but he would have been unwelcome at any hour. Nevertheless, a stableboy came running to greet his carriage as it rumbled up to the manor house as the first star appeared in a purpling evening sky. Many more eyes watched from behind curtains on the dozens of windows of the great house. The oaken front door swung open, the butler and his footmen stood in readiness.

After a moment, a lean gentleman was seen in the doorway of the carriage. He bent his head, stepped out, and paused on the top of the little stair that had been let down. Straightening, he stood arrested, staring at the huge house, seeing the dark mass of it outlined by the last dim glow of sunset, punctuated by lights that twinkled in the dozens of windows facing the drive. It was too dusky for anyone to make out the expression on his face.

He stepped down and headed for the house, taking

the fan of stairs to the front door rapidly and with easy grace, as though he hadn't been confined in a rocking carriage for hours.

"I believe I'm expected?" he asked the butler in a rich tenor voice, as he swept off his high beaver hat and caped coat and handed them to a footman. "I am Egremont."

The butler bowed, expressionless. "This way, sir," he said.

The gentleman hesitated. A thin eyebrow rose. *"Sir?"* he echoed with cool amusement, slapping his gloves against his palm. "Maybe you didn't hear me. I am the new earl of Egremont. I'd believed I was expected."

The butler's expression didn't change, but his face grew ruddy. "Yes, sir," he said. "You were indeed expected. As to the other matter, I was led to believe it was not yet settled, sir."

The gentleman laughed. "So it hasn't been. I suppose I can't fault you for being precise. Announce me as Sauvage then, if you must. Lead on. Oh, and I'd like something to eat. Will you see to it? It's been a devilish long journey."

The butler bowed and led the gentleman into the front hall. The new arrival scarcely seemed to look at the house as he strode over the shining inlaid mosaic marble floors. He didn't pause to study the life-sized Grecian statues that lined the walls, or raise his eyes to the gilded domed ceiling of the great hall to see the rose-and-gold frescoes there. He had hardly a glance for the pair of separate twin staircases that wound their ways to the second level, where they met and embraced in a riot of carved acanthus leaves. He only followed the butler through the hall and down a corridor, seeming as cool and untouched by his surroundings as the servant who guided him.

"You're awaited in the red room, sir," the butler murmured. He threw open a door to an enormous room with crimson stretched-silk-covered walls, Turkey red carpets, red and brown settees and chairs. A massive fireplace with a leaping fire sparked reflections from the gilt edges on the furniture and many picture frames. But the fire only cast murky, ruddy shadows over the quartet of people there.

"Mr. Sauvage," the butler said, announcing him.

The four people in the room stared. The visitor looked back at them serenely, only his eyes showing animation, glittering in the firelight as he surveyed them each in turn.

He saw a stout middle-aged balding gentleman, the very model of a country squire, a young blond lady, delicate and perfectly dressed as a china figurine, an older woman, who was obviously her mama, and a square-faced, straw-haired, broad-shouldered young man. They goggled at him from out of the crimson shade.

Their first impression was of a dark, elegantly dressed, extravagantly handsome young gentleman. The high planes on his smooth face were exaggerated by dancing firelight, making him look as though he'd just stepped, smiling, from out of the devil's own dressing room. He was impeccably clad in a close-fitting black jacket, with a white neckcloth, dark skintight breeches, and shining knee-high boots. The gentleman's face was impassive. He had flawless skin, even features, and watchful eyes. The firelight made it impossible to make out the color of those wide, well-spaced eyes, but they were light, and shone with crystalline clarity. The most arresting thing about him was the cool expression on his smooth face. He looked as though no human emotion could touch him or ever had done.

The middle-aged man leapt to his feet. "What is the meaning of this?" he said. "You are not Geoffrey Sauvage!"

"No, I'm not," the gentleman said calmly. "Geoffrey Sauvage was my father. I am Christian Gabriel Peter Colinworth Sauvage, now the earl of Egremont, and master of this house. And you, sir? You have me at a disadvantage."

The older man opened and closed his mouth.

The others echoed his expression. It was the fair young man who rose to his feet and spoke.

"I am Hammond Sauvage," he said stiffly. "This is my fiancée, Sophie Wiley, and her father, Squire Henry Wiley and his wife, Martha. You must understand that this is difficult for us to take in all at once."

Christian nodded. "Of course, I didn't expect you to believe me right away either, Cousin. You *are* my cousin, aren't you?"

Hammond nodded curtly.

"But in time, you will believe me," Christian said placidly. He moved toward the hearth. "I've traveled a long way, and it's cold out there. If you don't mind, I'd like a seat by the fire."

The squire flushed, nodded, and sat again, obviously still struggling for something to say.

The new arrival seated himself and rubbed his slender hands together. "I only arrived in this country a few days ago, and came here straight from London—after I consulted with my men at law, of course." No one in the room spoke. After a moment, he went on, "I've asked for something to eat, and would be pleased to take it here, by the fire. I didn't stop for luncheon and am famished." The only sound was of the fire crackling in the hearth. "Does that offend?" he asked blandly. "Or is it only my arrival that does? I didn't expect to be met with joy. Yet although you'd probably prefer that I starve, and I don't blame you for that, I suppose, I really do need some food. Starvation's an inefficient way to dispose of someone, after all, isn't it?"

One of the women gasped.

"Yes. Inefficient," the squire finally said, harshly. "Unlike the way the sixth earl met his end. Falling off a cliff top is more efficient, I agree," he added, staring at the visitor.

"Squire," Christian said mildly, "you may believe almost anything of me and my father, but be reasonable. However wicked you think we were, I was only twelve years old at the time of the sixth earl's death, and my father and I were convicted felons on a prison ship on the way to the antipodes then. Evil has tentacles everywhere, no one knows that better than I do. But we had no power of any kind, criminal or otherwise, so we couldn't have hurt anyone here in England. Apart from the fact that I'd no reason to wish the man any harm until he refused to help us, and by then, there was nothing I could do but try to console my father about it. It's true," he added, to the squire's disbelieving stare.

Christian's smile was as cool as his words. "The earl believed the evidence against us without question. But then, he didn't know my father. You see, Geoffrey Sauvage wasn't in exile all his life, though so far as the family was concerned, he might as well have been. Right, Cousin?" he asked Hammond.

Hammond shrugged. "We never met, that's true. I don't know why."

Christian nodded. "Oh, but I do. The family wanted nothing to do with us, even before our conviction and sentence. My father was an educated man, but he worked for a living, doing accounts for wealthier men. That shocked and shamed the family. They didn't have to soil their hands with ink or trade. My father did. He was the younger son of a youngest son in a large family. Much smaller now, of course," he murmured, with the shadow of a smile. "There were several healthy heirs to the title. Even if there hadn't been, we were far from the direct line of succession. I suppose I had relatives who lived in expectation of even the remote possibility of inheriting this place one day. Did you, Cousin? Trust me, Father and I never did."

"But he did inherit, didn't he?" The squire said bitterly. "What happened? We hadn't heard of his death."

Now some flicker of emotion showed on the visitor's face, gone too soon to read. "You hadn't heard of his life either," he said gently. "Your sympathies are noted. Please, no apologies," he said, though no one offered any. "No one heard about my father because news takes a while to get from the other side of the world to England—even if someone was waiting for it. As we know no one was, we didn't send it. In fact, I didn't get the news of the inheritance immediately, though I came soon as I did. I'm sorry if that raised other expectations. It was you, Hammond, who expected to inherit, was it? Sorry. Ah, my dinner," he said, before Hammond could answer.

The butler entered the room with footmen carrying a small folding table and trays of meats, breads, and cheeses.

"Would you care to join me?" Christian asked, as the table was set up in front of him.

The squire waved off his offer. But as Christian picked up a plate, the older man spoke again, harshly. "So you're here to claim the title and the estate?"

"As I said. Yes. And the bank account and the stock holdings, the town house in Marble Arch, and the hunting box in the West County," Christian agreed, selecting a roll, a wedge of cheese, and a slice of beef. "The house in the Lake District, too. The mill in Sussex, the distillery in Scotland. The lot, and as soon as it may be done."

He looked up at the stricken company. "Mind," he said, pointing with his knife, "I realize it isn't the healthiest decision a man could make. Let me see," he said, ignoring the plate he'd just filled as he stared into the middle distance. "Have I got it all right? There's such a lot to get, isn't there? As I understand," he said slowly, "since we left England,

Charles, the sixth earl of Egremont, fell from a horse and down that cliff, striking his head on a stone not a year after succeeding his father, an invalid. The next earl, Godfrey, enjoyed good health for four years, until he, too, fell. But it was love he fell into—then a river, I heard. He drowned in a boating accident before his wedding day, didn't he? So the estate went to Frederick Sauvage, who held it for three years, until he suffered a heart spasm when his coach was stopped by a highwayman. Unfortunately, his pills, usually at hand, weren't. The highwayman was never caught.

"His only son, an infant, died suddenly soon after," Christian said as he buttered his roll, paying close attention to it as he did. "Now, let's see, his widow went to Ireland and stayed there, and who can blame her? The last earl was a bachelor. Well, but his ladylove was herself already married. As I calculate, that's five earls in a row, not even counting the infant, and in fairly close order.

"No," Christian said thoughtfully, answering himself, "being earl and master of Egremont isn't a very healthy occupation."

"There was no foul play," the squire said harshly. "Only a series of unhappy coincidences. Each tragedy was investigated, and each had sufficient cause. Charles had vertigo and refused to give in to it; Godfrey never learned to swim properly, Frederick was forgetful and didn't like to dose himself, as he called it, and so on. If the family suffered from anything, it was from stubborn pride."

"I'd heard otherwise," Christian said blandly, then

added, before anyone could speak, "I'd even heard talk of a curse."

"You have no hesitation about taking on the role though, do you?" Hammond asked bitterly.

Christian smiled. "No, because I don't believe in curses. And, too, I just discovered I have family feeling. I just never realized I did. Until I inherited, that is."

"The point is," the squire said, "we still don't know if you have inherited."

"Your point," Christian agreed. "You don't know. I assure you, I do."

"And we know nothing about you."

"More than I do about you," Christian said cheerfully.

"You don't speak with an accent," the squire's wife said sharply, speaking up for the first time.

"No, unless it's an English one," Christian agreed. "I was sent abroad on my grand tour of prisons when I was twelve. My accent was set by then. I speak as my father taught me, and he was insistent about my education—until it was stopped, by order of His Majesty."

"How did you get free?" she persisted.

"My father was a learned man in a land that knew the value of a fellow with an education," Christian answered calmly. "And he made friends quickly. In no time he was as appreciated by his fellow prisoners as he was by those who guarded him, and the man who hired him. When they realized that a man who works for his own improvement as well as his master's does a much better job, he was offered his freedom. Or rather, when he made them realize it. A wise man, my father. Except, of course, not wise enough to see whatever trap it was got him arrested in the first place."

Christian put down his fork. "He wasn't guilty of the crimes he was convicted of. Every felon says that, but in this case it was true. He didn't steal Sir Gordon's snuffbox or have me lift a silver candlestick. The thought is ridiculous. I went with him that day only because Sir Gordon summoned him to work on an error in his books on a Sunday afternoon. We weren't rich, but were doing well enough to have our own house, and food on the table. We had no need to steal. We certainly didn't need the money the pawnbroker swore we'd got an hour before we were arrested. By the way, the money we were supposed to have received was never found on either of us. Only in our house. And in a place we had never used for anything but storing ashes. You don't believe me?" He shrugged. "They didn't then, either."

"But that was a long time ago," Christian continued, pushing away his plate and rising. "And my weariness is very much today's. Would you excuse me? I'm deucedly tired and would appreciate a quiet room and a soft bed. We can continue this tomorrow if you'd like. If you'd just show me to my room, I won't keep you any longer tonight."

The other four exchanged glances.

"We've arrranged for a room for you at the inn down the road," the squire said gruffly. "It has excellent accommodations."

Christian's face showed no emotion, but he stood very still.

"Well, but you can't stay on here. No one does but the staff," the squire said. "And now no one else can, since ownership of the estate is in dispute," he added, scowling at the visitor. "We just came here to meet you. We live a few miles down the road. No one's lived here but staff since the earl passed away."

"The manor's been unoccupied for over six months?" Christian asked, turning to Hammond. "You hadn't moved in?"

Hammond's face turned ruddier than the firelight could account for. Sophie spoke up. "There were improvements to be made before we moved in, and they couldn't begin until the papers were signed. We are to be married in the autumn," she added proudly, puffing up her breast like a little white pigeon.

Christian sketched a bow. "Congratulations. So, where are you staying, Cousin?" he asked Hammond.

"He's our guest," the squire said. "Has been since he first came here to inspect the estate when he learned of his inheritance."

"Oh," Christian said, eyeing Sophie's blush. "And that's how the two got so well acquainted, no doubt? Sensible. But don't have regrets, Cousin Hammond. It wouldn't have mattered if you had taken up residence. It would only have been more uncomfortable all around. My claim's valid."

"It would have been harder to eject him if he was already here!" Sophie said truculently.

"I doubt it," Christian said. "Trust me. I have papers, more than you'd think. As a former convict, my life has more documents attached than most men have. I've presented all the papers to the lawyers. By the way, I've hired a legion of them myself. It costs a fortune, but I have one. My father was very success- ful in New South Wales, and investments made me more so. Now, please excuse me. I'd like to find that inn. I really am very tired. Good night," he said, bowed to them, and strode to the door.

They didn't start speaking until he'd left, then they couldn't stop.

The squire's wife turned on her husband. "Why didn't you have him tossed out?" she demanded.

"If it were only that easy," he said. "It will take time and money to get to the bottom of this. We can't discount him out of hand."

"You believe him?" his wife exclaimed. "No one heard from him for fifteen years. Yet now, just as dear Hammond here is about to take his legacy, he appears and claims his rights as heir? A man no one knows or has ever seen?"

"I believe anything until proven differently," her husband said heavily. "And so do the courts of the land. But it won't be easy for him. Most wretches who are transported don't even live long enough to return to England. He has to present some very com- pelling evidence."

"Oh, the villain," his wife raged. "How diabolically clever! If he'd claimed to be Geoffrey Sauvage, someone would have known the truth. A person can lose weight or gain it, grow bald or grow whiskers, have arms and legs lopped off, whatever," she went on wildly, her voice rising. "But there's no way a man can actually change his face, apart from cutting off his nose. So this fellow claims to be the villain's son—whom no one knows because he left this country when he was a boy."

"Is there nothing we can do?" Sophie cried.

"We'll need more than lawyers," her mother said furiously. "They can drag things on for years! More decisive action is needed."

Her husband nodded. "And we shall have it. 'Trust me,' he says. As if I would. Trust *me*, I'll soon give him a solution he deserves!"

"Sir!" Hammond said, shocked.

"No I won't kill the rogue, though he doubtless deserves it," the squire said hastily. "I leave that for the law to do. I only meant that I hired a Bow Street runner the moment I got word another claim to the title and estate had been made. The runner also undertakes private investigations. We'll get to the bottom of this, you'll see."

"I told you and told you to move in here months ago!" Sophie told her fiancé, stamping her foot.

"It wouldn't have made a difference. He was right about that," Hammond said.

"Yes it would have," she insisted. "Possession is a great part of the law, and if it's not, at least you'd have looked like the earl and he like the interloper if you'd already been master here."

Hammond's expression grew wary. "It wouldn't have been legal for me to move in. But the way you talk . . . you believe he *is* the rightful heir?"

"No," she said, "I don't. But I believe he's as evil as he is clever."

"We're at a disadvantage, and he knows it," her father said glumly. "If his father had come, someone might have recognized him. No one would know *this* fellow."

"No one?" his wife asked. "Are you sure? There must be someone, a close friend, a near neighbor, a relative . . . Isn't there anyone in your family who would remember him?" she asked Hammond.

"We're a small family, especially now. And as he says, no one was close to his father," Hammond answered, frowning. He raised his head, his expression brightened. "There is Sir Maurice, up north. He's the son of a younger son, and isn't in the direct line for the title, but he's the oldest in the family, and always was interested in its history. He collects antiques and loves anything about history, actually. So it's only natural that he'd become involved with the family geneology.

"He may even have met the real Christian at some time. He used to get about more. He's rich as he can stare, married a fortune. His wife died and left him more." He shook his head, glum again. "But he's practically a recluse now. I suppose if it were the eleventh hour, and we had no other option, we might try to summon him, but I don't know if he'd come. He lost his only son a few years ago and retired from society."

"Wait!" Sophie's mother cried. "Geoffrey Sauvage and his son lived near Slough, didn't they? I remember reading about what had happened to them and— the Wexfords . . . no! The Lowells! Your cousins, Henry," she told her husband excitedly. "They lived there until they inherited that farm. Yes, when the scandal broke, we spoke of them, remember? They had a son who was young Christian's best friend, and they were shocked by his arrest, they wrote to tell you so. We'll ask their son to come for a visit. He might not recognize Christian Sauvage after all these years, but he certainly could question the fellow better than we can."

"Jonathan Lowell fell at Salamanca," her husband said quietly. "He was a member of the Fifth and received honors. I saw his name in the reports, and wrote a note of condolence to his parents."

"But he had a sister," Sophie said excitedly. "She's my age. She and her family came to that ball we gave for my seventeenth birthday, remember? It was such an event, you invited everyone."

"Yes," her mother said eagerly. "They did come, though they didn't stay long. She was a nice enough young creature. The family's sound, but they aren't quite in our class, financially. She'd be thrilled to be invited to visit again."

"But she was years younger than her brother," the squire protested, "How much could she remember?"

"Enough," his wife said. "They said she used to follow her brother like a shadow. Any bit of information, however small, might help us."

"She was a handsome girl," the squire said reflectively, "I remember now. But since she's our Sophie's age, there's no telling if she's married with her own family by now. Five years ago, after all. Our Sophie was so finicking," he reminded Hammond quickly, "or she'd have been snapped up long before you came along."

"I know that, and I'm grateful for it," he said gallantly.

"I didn't keep up with the family," the squire said brusquely. "You never encouraged the connection," he told his wife. "I'd feel a fool suddenly asking the girl here now."

"Don't," his wife snapped. "Families have these little estrangements, the difference in our situations accounts for it. They aren't paupers, but they couldn't have afforded to give the girl a proper Season, and we weren't close enough to offer her one. Naturally we grew apart. This will merely be an invitation for a visit with us. If she's married, she can come with her husband. Likely she is, and married a farmer like her father, at that. They'd be glad of a chance to solder the connection between us. I'll invite her at once."

They left the room, busily making plans.

And so no one but the footmen who came in to clean up after them noticed that their unwelcome guest, for all he'd said he was famished, hadn't eaten a thing.

The inn was as comfortable as his reluctant hosts had claimed. Christian finished washing up and yawned. He opened the door and placed his boots outside in the hall for the innkeeper to collect and polish. Then he closed the door and propped a chair in front of it. He went to the window, pulled the shutters closed, and put a glass tumbler on the windowsill, placing it so that if the shutters were disturbed the glass would be knocked off and fall to floor.

He glanced around the room and nodded to himself. Dressed only in his shirtsleeves, breeches, and stocking feet, he padded over to a chair by the bed. He sat, reached into his shirt, and took a small pistol out of the concealed sling that he wore under his arm. He placed it on the table at his side, then bent and removed a leather sheath from under the stocking on his right leg. He slid out the knife that had been hidden there, examined it, slipped it back again, and placed it next to the pistol.

Only then did he sit back and pick up the glass of whiskey that was waiting for him. As he brought it to his lips, his hand shook so badly that the amber liquid spilled over the side of the glass. He carefully put the glass down again.

"Whoa, lad," he whispered in rougher accents. "This will never do." He laid his head on the back of the chair, closed his eyes, and breathed deeply. He sat a few moments, taking in long, deep, measured breaths. Then he opened his eyes, raised his hand, and looked at it again.

It was rock steady. He picked up the glass again and saw the liquid still as the surface of an icebound pond.

"Yes," he murmured. "Better. Still as death. Which is what you'd be if he knew what you were about." He raised the glass to his lips and swallowed, grimacing as the liquid went down his throat. "Better," he repeated. "No worries. Only the task ahead. Here we are, and here we stay. Trust no one, not even yourself, and get on with it. And stop talking to yourself like a daft old lag," he added, on a smile.

He yawned, picked up his pistol and knife, rose,

and turned his lamp down, but not off, leaving a slight glow that warmed the room. Then he slipped the pistol under his pillow, put the sheath and the knife at his right hand next to it, lay down dressed as he was, closed his eyes, and slept.

# Chapter 2

"**O**f course I'm excited," Julianne said. She shivered as she looked out the coach window and saw nothing but darkness. "I confess I'm also frightened."

"*You*, Miss?" her maid asked, astonished.

She nodded. "Well, I don't have that many adventures. And you must admit going to visit someone you don't really know is an adventure." She nibbled on the tip of her gloved finger. "If I only knew why they asked me, I might feel better. It's been so many years, why should my cousin Sophie suddenly want my company? We haven't corresponded, though I remember her, of course. Who wouldn't?"

"A very pretty young woman," her maid agreed. "But not a patch on you, Miss."

Her mistress grinned. "Take care you're not struck by lightning, Annie. Loyalty is one thing, blindness is another. Sophie was the prettiest little thing I'd ever seen, all blond curls and smiles. Charming, too, with never an unkind word. And I remember her house.

Lord! Who could forget? It beat Squire Hobbs's house all to pieces, didn't it? Don't pretend not, you queened it all over the neighborhood for weeks after we got back. 'Like staying in a palace,' you said. But the point is . . ." She stopped and made a face as she got a taste of the glove she was nibbling.

She put her hand in her lap, and went on, "Though they were wonderful hosts and Mother and I wrote to thank them, they never wrote to us again. And now, suddenly, they ask me to come visit and stay with them for a month! There's obviously some ulterior motive. I've wracked my brain and can't come up with one, and neither could Mother or Father. Which is why I'm here, I suppose. It's not just for the luxury of staying there again. I love a mystery."

She smiled, remembering her mother's words as they'd considered the invitation.

"You don't have to make excuses for taking advantage of a wonderful opportunity," her mother had said. "You'll meet interesting people and have a chance to enjoy yourself."

"You mean," Julianne had corrected her, "I'll meet interesting gentlemen there, don't you?"

"Well, yes, I do," her mother had admitted. "And it's important, because we can't help you with that. We're not poverty-stricken, you know. We do have a farm, and it's a mighty profitable one, there's not a thing about that to concern anyone of good breeding, because we don't run it with our own hands. Or at least, we don't have to. Your gardening and your father's horses are your own fancies. We come from a good family, too. But the thing is, we're not a well-connected family, at least we don't have many relatives in high places."

"And so though we try to provide you with everything you need, you haven't found a fellow who takes your fancy, and you're rising two-and-twenty. We have balls and parties hereabouts, but not one fellow you've met has ever suited you—at least, not above a few visits. And I don't see how we can attract more eligible men for you."

"Well, you could always hold a tournament for my hand," Julianne had said on a gurgle of laughter.

"That's closer to a solution than makes me comfortable," her mama had said. "Parents *can* see to it that their children have choices. Your father and I have the means but not the way to take you to London to choose the man you deserve. That is to say we have the funds, I think, but not the entrée to Society. We can't just take you to subscription balls and public masquerades; you need to be presented to a better class of gentlemen.

"And what better place than Cousin Wiley's house? It's not far from London, he's very well thought of, they entertain lavishly. Why, they're even on the best of terms with their famous neighbor, the earl of Egremont. Or were. He's passed on, but that means the estate soon should, too. Now, there's an estate! It's in every guidebook on the district. It would be exciting for you to see it, and you might meet the new earl and who knows what connections you could make if you were invited to a party at his house? Oh, Julianne, why not give yourself a chance to meet new people? Your father and I love you and would be happy to have you with us always, but we want you to have at least the chance to have your own family. If Jonathan were still here, of course . . ."

Julianne had covered her mother's hand with her own, and the conversation had ended so that it wouldn't end in tears. Five years, after all, was not so very long, not for a mother who mourned her only son, or for the sister who had adored him.

It was then that Julianne decided to accept her distant cousin's unexpected invitation.

She'd regretted it once her mother's tears were out of sight. How awkward to stay with a family she didn't know. The invitation, coming out of the blue, and couched in terms of "a chance for betterment for dear Julianne" had bruised her pride a little, too. "Betterment"? She wasn't a pauper or a peasant. And she wasn't ugly, awkward, or a fool, she simply wasn't married.

But in that moment, seeing her mother's unending grief, she'd longed to be able to give her something, ease her pain. And in a stroke of brilliant realization, she'd suddenly seen that she could! She could bring another son to her, a substitute son, in the shape of a son-in-law. And then one day, perhaps, a grandson, too.

Both husband and son could be like Jonathan. It shouldn't be that difficult to find such a fellow. She'd known many such, friends of Jonathan's, happy, outgoing, bold young men, who didn't think as deeply as they laughed—not that Jonathan had been stupid! But he'd been reckless and merry, happier riding than reading, unable to sit still, unwilling to ponder things too long. That was why he'd bought his colors and

gone riding off to war on a whim, thrilled with his decision, looking forward to action, adventure, and
laughter. He'd found only silence and eternal peace.

But now the world was at peace, too, so there was
less risk for such headstrong lads. If she could find
such an amiable, easygoing, uncomplicated sort of
fellow, she could marry him, and in one stroke give
her mother a lively lad to fuss over, her father a companion to fish and ride with, and herself a companion
who could bring sunshine back into her life.

She couldn't do that if she stayed where she was.
Jonathan's death had marked her. She'd been seventeen when she'd gone into deep mourning for him,
and it had taken a while to get over it. Her mother had
taken longer. They'd gone into seclusion, out of local
society, and by the time Julianne had been able to go
back into the social world, she'd grown into an altogether different sort of girl, a bit quieter, a little sad-
der. And the men who had been available to her no
longer were. Not that it mattered much. The local lads
bored Julianne.

She had nursed secret infatuations for several of
her brother's jolly friends. But they'd gone off to war,
too, and either married other girls or gone to their
own untimely deaths in battle. And now there was no
one she'd even consider for a life mate. It was hard
enough finding a friend. Her friends had married and
spoke of little but their husbands and children. New-
comers seldom came to their village, so she couldn't
even meet new women friends. But if she went to her
cousin Sophie's house . . .

"Well," Julianne said resolutely now, as the coach

rolled on to her cousin's house. "I don't know why I was invited but I mean to make the most of it, Annie. A month at a fine manor house, I'm a lucky woman."

And a month, she thought, would be over before she knew it, so if it was dreadful, she'd be home again soon enough. Only she hoped it wouldn't be unpleasant, and she prayed she could bring home a trophy from her adventure: a merry young man she could call husband, a fellow her parents could rejoice in, too.

Julianne stared out the window, the darkness making it into a sort of black looking glass. She surveyed herself in the dark mirror and patted a wayward strand of hair back into place.

"You look a treat," her maid said staunchly.

"Thank you," she said. But she wasn't worried about that. She wasn't a monster of vanity, but she knew she'd suit, at least for some men. Didn't she look like Jonathan? Her father had proudly called them his two bay ponies. Both Thoroughbreds, he'd say, sleek and wild, the pair of them with thick brown hair and big brown eyes that kindled gold in the sun.

Julianne was pleased by the comparison, but thought Jonathan had made a better-looking fellow than she did a girl. She had two straight winged slashes of brows over her eyes, just as he'd had. Though her complexion was clear and creamy, her nose straight, and her mouth plump enough to suit her, and her hair curled if she gave it half a chance, she thought her "look" was too vivid and strong for a proper Englishwoman. She was buxom though slender, and knew fashion preferred women with smaller attributes, whatever men said when they thought women couldn't hear them. But she'd do. She just had to find a lad who fancied her sort of looks. And now she might have the chance.

"I wish I could see," she murmured as she looked out the window. "Wait! Are those lights up ahead? Is that gravel under the wheels now? Are we slowing? Are we in a drive?"

"Aye, we're here, Miss," her maid said excitedly.

Julianne took a deep breath. She didn't let it out until she stepped out of the coach. She had to draw it in again when she stood in the front hall of her cousin's house and stared at her cousin Sophie as she fluttered forward to greet her. Sophie wore a fashionable rose-colored frock with a deeper rose shawl over her shoulders. Her hair was drawn up so it could tumble down in golden curls around her face.

"My goodness!" Julianne breathed. "You're even prettier than you were before, Cousin!"

Sophie flashed a smile at her, looking very satisfied by the comment. "Just as I remember," she said on a trill of laughter. "You were always so straightforward, you and your brother. Oh. I'm so sorry about him. Please accept my sympathies."

Julianne ducked her head and murmured a thank-you. It was hard to know what to say to someone offering sympathies five years after the fact.

"And here are my mama," Sophie said, "and papa."

Julianne curtsied to Sophie's mama, noting her resemblance to her daughter. The squire hadn't changed, except for having less hair than she remembered.

"And here," Sophie said with pride, motioning to a

broad-shouldered gentleman at her side, "is my fiancé, Hammond Sauvage."

Julianne's head went up. There'd been no mention of a fiancé in the letter. And moreover, Hammond Sauvage looked very like the sort of fellow she'd just been thinking of and not at all like the kind she'd have expected her cousin to marry. He was medium height and squarely built, with a thatch of straw-colored hair, an open, honest face, and eyes that didn't look as though they could hold a secret any more than they could a sneer. Though he was dressed correctly, he looked as though loose-fitted hunting gear would suit him better than the evening clothes he had on.

He bowed. "Miss Lowell," he said.

Sophie, having seen Julianne's momentary expression of surprise, raised her little chin, and added, almost defiantly, "Ham is actually heir to Egremont. He'll be the new earl, and is only staying on here until he can take possession of the estate and his title."

"Really, Sophie . . ." her fiancé began to say.

"Yes, really, Sophie, indeed," her mama interrupted. "What a way to greet your cousin after a journey of so many hours! Far better to offer her a room and something to eat by her fireside now. There's time for you two to get reacquainted later. You must be exhausted, my dear," she told Julianne, taking her elbow and leading her to the stair. "How were the roads? Is there still construction at the Applegate Tollhouse? What a bother. Is that your family carriage? How clever. At least that way your coachman didn't make you get out and walk up the hill at Torrance the way the public coachmen do. How thoughtful of your parents. I hope they're well? We'll see your coachman and horses housed for the night, and bring your bags right up. Come, I'll show you to your room."

Julianne followed, her maid in her wake. She didn't say anything, nor could she, because her hostess kept up a steady stream of polite chatter. But she wished she could turn around and hop back in the coach. Whatever had brought her to this house, she began to think that it would be far more complicated than she'd imagined.

Julianne's room was delightful, papered and painted in sunny yellow, so that even the night couldn't make it depressing. The big bed had a canopy with filmy gold curtains over it, the firelight made it seem to glow with incandescent light. A person would feel like a pearl in its bed, Julianne thought sleepily as she climbed into it.

She'd eaten and gotten into nightclothes. Her maid was snugged in her own bed upstairs. Julianne felt pampered, but ill at ease, and uncertain.

"Cousin?" a little voice called from the door. "Are you sleeping?"

*Surely the stupidest question in the world*, Julianne thought before she could chide herself for the unkind thought. But there was no way anyone could answer it by saying "yes." "No," she said. "Come in." She climbed out of her bed and went to greet her cousin. "I'm glad of the company," she told her truthfully. "It's a lovely room, but one always feels odd in a new place."

Sophie had changed her pink gown for an even

prettier white dressing gown. "So I thought," she said comfortably. "I came to keep you company. You didn't want to go to bed right away, did you?"

Her cousin had a way of asking questions that could only be answered in the affirmative, Julianne thought with amusement. But she was pleased. Maybe she could get some answers, then sleep easier tonight.

Sophie settled herself on a chair by the hearth, tucked her gown under her toes, shook back her head so that the firelight tickled the gold in her curls, and grinned at her cousin.

She really was adorable, Julianne thought as she took a seat near her.

"My, don't you look pretty," Sophie said. "That blue wrapper is charming. It's a lovely shade for you, it brings out the color of your hair. How lucky you are to have such hair, so thick and rich and earthy. But then, you're a very handsome girl. I'm glad my Hammond is the faithful sort. Don't worry, we'll find a young man of your own as soon as may be."

Julianne smiled but felt even more wary. Her blue wrapper was as old as the earth, and her hair looked like mud when she compared it to her cousin's fair tresses. And so far as she could tell, Hammond hadn't looked at her sideways. "Thank you," she said, and waited for whatever it was Sophie had really come to say.

"So, what did you think of him?" Sophie asked excitedly. "My fiancé," she explained. "My dear Hammond."

"He seems like a very nice young man," Julianne

said. "I hadn't known you were engaged. Has it been long?"

"Oh, months now," Sophie said with a wave of her hand. "He came here in September, and we were engaged by December." Her eyes grew wide, she looked as though she'd have clapped her hand over her mouth if she hadn't stopped herself in time. "Didn't you know? I was sure we'd sent your parents the announcement," she added quickly. "Didn't you see it in the *Times*?"

"We don't get it regularly," Julianne said quietly, feeling both offended and defensive; insulted because she hadn't been considered important enough to notify and inferior because she didn't scan the *Times* for the social news.

"Well, there it is." Sophie shrugged. "It hardly matters. You were going to be invited to the wedding, of course."

"Of course," Julianne murmured, suddenly not believing that at all. "Look, Sophie," she began, and hesitated, wondering how to say it. She couldn't spend a night in this house, however grand it was, without knowing why. She was too tired for intricate reasoning, so she decided to just be honest.

"Sophie," she said, "I guess I ought to have written to ask before I came. But Mama went on about your wanting to see me again, introduce me to society and such, and I wanted to believe it. That was before I knew you were engaged. Now it makes very little sense at all. You haven't seen me in five years, and here you have a fiancé, and I suppose more friends than you can count. So," she asked, cocking her head to the side as she studied her cousin, "why in the world did you invite me here?"

Sophie blinked. Then she giggled. "La! But you're so forthright! Just as I remembered."

"What a faradiddle!" Julianne laughed. "I'll bet you did no such thing. I was only here for a week, and we didn't spend that much time together. Oh, I liked you well enough, and I suppose you liked me, but cut line, Cousin, and tell me the truth, would you?"

Sophie looked dumbstruck. But Julianne felt the hard knot of tension in her stomach relax, to be replaced by a sad little lump of disappointment in her chest. This whole affair looked less and less palatable and very suspicious. She'd probably be going home tomorrow.

Mama would be disappointed, and so, come to think of it, was she. But all wasn't lost. Marriage to a suitable lad, even if only to heal her parents' hearts, wasn't a bad idea, and she wasn't ready to give it up yet. Maybe they could go to London, after all. Weren't there people you could hire to introduce you around? Mightn't there be some other long-lost relative they could ferret out?

Sophie's smile faded. She looked at her cousin and shrugged. "Very well. Mother wanted to talk to you, but I suppose it's best that I do first. But you know we never meant anything bad, and in fact, much good could come from this for you, too. Really. Because you can have a good time here with me. It's too bad we never got to know each other better. It isn't too late for that now. I mean, I'm engaged, but I don't intend to sit home and sew until my wedding day. There are parties we can go to, a wonderful round of social life we can share until I do marry. And after that, too. It wouldn't be the worst thing for you to be friends with a countess, you know," she added with a sly grin.

"But speaking of that, the thing of it is . . ." Sophie paused. She raised her cornflower blue gaze. The look in her eyes wasn't at all that of a giddy girl. ". . . Do you remember a boy named Christian Sauvage?"

"Christian Sauvage?" Julianne asked in surprise. "Of course I do! The scandal made sure of that."

"Do you remember him well? I mean well enough to know him if you saw him again?"

"My goodness!" Julianne marveled. "Christian Sauvage! I haven't thought of him in years. He was my brother's best friend before we moved away, so you can imagine how shocked we were to hear what he and his father did. It was so bizarre. My brother was sure it was a mistake. He wanted to leap on a horse and ride to London to talk with Christian and rescue him from what he was sure was some evil plot.

"But he was only a boy himself, and though he raged and ranted, he never got farther than the posting inn. He actually packed some things and ran away, hoping to make it all the way to London. My father found him at the local coaching stop and brought him home before he even left the inn yard. Jonathan went away to school soon after. I know he wrote to Christian when he heard he was in Newgate Prison, but then they lost touch, I think. At any rate, I never heard his name again, except the way you do when people rehash old scandals."

"Do you think you'd recognize him?" Sophie asked eagerly. "I mean if you saw him again?"

"Christian Sauvage," Julianne said pensively, re- membering. "He was a tall boy. So handsome, with such blue eyes." She opened her own eyes and fixed them on her cousin. "But I was a very little girl then, Sophie, and so for all I know he wasn't tall at all. And maybe I thought he was handsome because he was kind to me, or at least, he didn't torment me the way some of my brother's other friends tried to do. But Jonathan wouldn't have that, he always defended me . . ."

She felt sorrow welling in her heart again and brought herself back to the present with effort. "The truth is, Sophie, I don't know if I would recognize him now. But why do you ask? Why is it important?"

So Sophie told her.

# Chapter 3

"You see, I'm going to marry Hammond, and I wish to become countess and mistress of Egremont when I do," Sophie summed it up when she'd finished explaining her problem, and her cousin just sat staring at her wide-eyed. "Well, who wouldn't? It's the size of a small country. That's what Hammond said when he first saw it." She giggled. "After he succeeded to the earldom, he was going to remodel the manor according to my wishes; that's why he hadn't moved in yet. Who'd want to live in the dust and noise of a major renovation? It was to be ready for our wedding. We had the architects, landscapers . . . then, almost at the last minute, this *person* arrives and claims the estate as his? It isn't fair. And it may be criminal."

She lowered her voice and looked around the bedchamber, as though it was a ghost story she was telling by the fire. "After all, as Papa says, it may even be more than coincidence that so many heirs to Egremont died in such rapid succession, and so many from accidents. It is quite suspicious, wouldn't you say? Yes, Christian Sauvage and his father were halfway round the world, but who knows how long the arms of the criminal fraternity can reach?

"I'll say no more," she said primly, "because Hammond doesn't care for it. He's kind, and trusting to a fault. It's very lucky Papa convinced him to come stay with us while he looked over his inheritance. Luckier for me, of course," she added, dimpling again. "But for him, too. Because, never fear, my papa's hired Bow Street and private investigators, and crowds of lawyers, too. But Mama and I wracked our brains to think of someone else who might help. And we came up with you!"

"Don't be angry," Sophie concluded with a charming smile, seeing Julianne's stunned expression and reaching out to pat her knee. "After all, whatever else happens, nothing about this can hurt you."

Julianne suppressed her anger and her disappointment. She hadn't been invited for any purpose but to be used as a stalking-horse. Though the truth hurt, it made perfect sense. "I suppose you're right," she said, and couldn't resist adding, "but you may decide to put me on the next coach back home, Sophie. Because as I said, that was years ago. I've changed, he's changed, and I don't know if I can help at all."

"You'll stay for the month even if you don't know him from Adam. We'll have such fun," Sophie said, getting to her feet, "because we two did have fun together years ago, didn't we? And who knows? Your memory may be better than you know. Don't worry about it. Now, get some sleep. We've so much to do tomorrow." Smiling, she left Julianne to her muddled thoughts.

* * *

An hour later, Julianne sat upright in her bed. She felt cross and ill used, thinking of what she could have and should have said to Sophie. Her dignity was bruised. She was being used and had no way to protest, except with her feet. She should go straight back home.

But she wasn't sure she wanted to do that. Mostly she was angry with herself for being naive and needy enough to believe she'd been wanted for herself. She wished she'd been told why she'd been invited before she'd left home. She wouldn't have come . . .

No, she admitted, she would have. Her curiosity would have guaranteed it. It goaded her now.

Christian Sauvage.

She hadn't wanted to remember him. She supposed it was because memories of those days hurt too much, and so she'd buried them deep. But now they streamed back, and she realized that time had dimmed the pain. Remembering those long-ago days actually made her happy now.

They'd been good years, filled with long summer afternoons romping in meadows, gathering flowers while the boys flew their kites. Or catching minnows in a jar while they fished for fat lake perch. Or pretending to be a lady fair as they dueled with branches for her honor.

She remembered golden autumn hours spent riding her rugged little pony, trying to keep up with the boys as they went on their adventures, gathering nuts while they explored the deeper forests. There were rainy afternoons lying before the fire, listening to them dream aloud or watching them play chess, or sometimes, if she were very good, they'd include her in a game of jackstraws or charades.

And she remembered wailing, in any season, whenever her mama wouldn't let her go with them, or called her from play with them, so she could have her lessons and learn to be a lady. She only wanted to be one of them.

She'd been allowed to roam with them because, whatever mischief they got into, they always took good care of her. They read her stories and told her tall tales just to see if she believed them, and made her giggle by tickling her with straws or words, just to see how breathless they could make her with laughter.

Christian Sauvage had been Jonathan's best friend, but they hadn't been much alike, except in their love of mischief. Christian had been a quieter lad, more likely to slip a fish off the hook and watch it swim back into the stream than to stuff it in a creel. He'd been the one to memorize famous speeches to give their acting games more excitement, and the one who'd bring a book the next day to prove a point he'd made. And he'd been the one to caution Jonathan about danger. Yet he always participated in Jonathan's wilder pranks. In fact, it was his imagination that made them wilder.

His hands—she remembered his hands, she suddenly saw them holding a fishing pole, showing her how to use it—those thin hands were usually chafed and reddened from the cold, but skilled, and patient. And his eyes—crystalline, filled with light, blue and dazzling. Eyes too lovely for a boy to have, Mama had said. And his hair, thick, lighter than Jonathan's . . . she began to remember even more.

Jonathan had missed his friend badly when their family had inherited the farm and moved away, and had been making plans to invite Christian for a visit when the shocking news had come to them.

Christian's father had stolen a silver snuffbox from a client whose books he was working on. And Christian, with him that day, had taken a silver candlestick.

The goods had been found, the pawnbroker betrayed them, and the pair was thrown into Newgate. It was a hanging offense for both. Christian was only ten, but boys of seven were taken to the gallows for less, and it wouldn't have been the first time the rope claimed father and son together. But it turned out that the Sauvages were distantly related to the Earl of Egremont, and so their sentence was transportation rather than a noose. They languished in jail, then they'd disappeared from England as surely as if they had been hanged.

Now after all these years, Christian was back? Alive? And well? And wanting to be named earl of Egremont? It went beyond irony.

He'd avoided the wars, the battles, the wounds. Had he stayed in England, he might very well have gone to war with Jonathan and died along with him. But instead, he'd returned, in triumph. Julianne buried her head in her hands. Unworthy and unbidden, the thought struck her like a flash of pain: Christian had emerged from the past, unscathed. Where was the justice? Why should Christian, the criminal, be alive, and Jonathan, the hero, be dead?

Julianne raised her head. She had to meet this man who claimed he was the boy she'd known. If he were indeed Christian Sauvage, it would almost be like recovering a bit of Jonathan, a part death couldn't take away.

Her lips tightened. But what if it turned out the fellow was an imposter, raking up the past and all its pain in order to fill his pockets, just as the real Christian had supposedly done all those years ago?

Then she'd want to be the one to hang him.

"Today, we'll show you the wonders of Egremont," Sophie told Julianne at breakfast. They were sitting in a sunny dining parlor with the squire and Hammond. Her mama wasn't there because she kept Town hours and didn't rise until noon. "We'll ride over there after luncheon, when the sun's dried the dew. There's walking involved, and we don't want to get our slippers wet. Then you'll see what the fuss is about."

"They say Queen Elizabeth stayed at Egremont one summer and came back twice," the squire said, gesturing with his piece of toast. "But people have always lived in style there. There was a Viking hold on the site and records of a Roman fort before that. That was built over a mound from before even that. The manor sits on a rise overlooking the valley. It was popular because it was a defensible position."

"Not very, I don't think, if it was in turn Viking and Roman and all the rest," Sophie said, and giggled. "But we shan't have to worry about that," she said, with a smile at Hammond. "After all, no one will come at us with a battering ram."

"No," he said quietly, "only with a writ and a record of birth."

"I haven't seen them yet," the squire said. "*If* they exist, my solicitors will. We're pursuing every angle of this, my boy. In fact," he added as he rose, "I have to go. I'll be meeting with that fellow from Bow Street. He's arrived from London and sent word that he'll be here soon. I'd like you to speak to him, too. So, if you'd stop by my study before you go to Egremont?"

"Of course," Hammond said, getting to his feet in deference to his future father-in-law.

"Sit, sit, my boy, finish your breakfast," the squire said. "I'll see you later."

When he'd left, Hammond sank to his seat again, looking troubled.

"Never you mind, Hammond," Sophie chirped. "We'll unmask the fellow, and things can go on as they were."

"Have you seen much of him?" Julianne asked.

"Not since he first came," Hammond said. "I think that's been a mistake. The more he talks, the more chance we'll have of discovering the truth."

"Ah, he's been avoiding you," Julianne said, nodding. "That's a point against him. An honest man would have nothing to hide."

Hammond's face grew ruddy, and he slid a glance at Sophie. "No. He's not avoiding anything. He's been seen everywhere around the village. He's just not been invited here."

"Well, I can't bear the sight of him," Sophie cried, jumping to her feet and throwing her napkin on the table. "And I tell you it isn't right to force him on us.

You should be trying to dispose of him rather than asking me to talk to him. He's ruined our plans and is trying to destroy our lives, and I don't want to see his wicked lying face again!" She ran sobbing from the room.

"Excuse me," Hammond said heavily as he rose. "It's been a bone of contention. But now you're here, it will resolve itself." He left the room in pursuit of his fiancée.

Julianne was left sitting alone, looking at a plate of cooling eggs, trying to ignore the sympathetic gaze of the footman clearing the table. She felt sorry for Hammond, a nice young man, who seemed to be in love with her cousin. Sophie was acting as though she wanted him to challenge the imposter to a duel. Certainly, she mused, if a woman loved a fellow, it would be painful to see him lose a rich heritage. But wouldn't it hurt his feelings if all that carrying on led him to think that was all she cared about?

Still, maybe that *was* all Sophie cared for, Julianne thought, as she went upstairs to wait to prepare for what was bound to be a long day.

Julianne was disappointed; she'd thought a Bow Street runner would be dashing. She could have passed him in the street, town or country, and not noticed him. Mr. Murchison was a short, thickset middle-aged man; he dressed like a clerk and spoke in London accents. But then she noticed that his dark, deep-set eyes missed nothing.

As they stood in the hall waiting for a carriage that was being brought round, he studied her from under his bushy brows. Then he gave her his instructions.

"You're off to Egremont, eh? Well, now, if you should run into this fellow who claims to be the heir," he told Julianne, "because you may, as he's been poking around the manor, all you need to do for now, Miss, is get a good long decko at him. Look at him close, I mean. Don't try to be clever. Don't try to trap him or lure him, trip him or test him. He'd be better at that than you. Leave that to me."

She smiled. "I'd no intention of anything of the sort. As I told my cousins, I was just a little girl when I last saw him. I doubt I'll recognize him any more than he'd recognize me. I certainly won't challenge him. I wouldn't even know how to begin! And," she added, "there's been talk about how suddenly the succession came to him. I'm a great coward. I wouldn't like to anger a villain."

The runner shot a dark look at the squire. "I told you, no need for spreading such talk, sir! Only muddies the water. A great many heirs died in a row, but it happens in the best of families, and there's not a scrap of proof one way or the other. Mr. Hammond here is right, better relations with the fellow would make my work easier. It's easier to find out things about a man who thinks he's a friend than one who feels you're his enemy. Don't have to get under the covers with him, missy," he told Sophie, who gasped. "But there's nothing amiss with being polite. Oh, aye, sorry. My talk's a bit rough. But it's straight. Now, if anyone thinks of anything they'd like to tell me, anytime, I'm stopping at the White Hart, a message will always find me there."

"Isn't that where *he's* staying?" Sophie asked.

"Aye," he said. "And where we two have lifted a pint many a night since I got there. Well, here's your coach. Good afternoon." He clapped on his hat and stalked from the house.

Julianne was glad to step out of the house, too, and not just because it was a mild spring afternoon. But she'd noticed that there was increased tension between Sophie and Hammond, and she didn't know whom to speak to or what to say. So she got into the carriage, anxious to see the great estate that was the reason for her visit and even more hopeful of getting a glimpse of the man who had started all the fuss.

They drove off. Julianne sat back and enjoyed watching the countryside as it responded to the spring sunshine. They passed long green pastures filled with fat sheep and plump cattle, fields of sunshine-bright hops and rapeseed, and meadows teeming with poppies, violets, primrose, and pinks. She was so taken with the lovely scenery it helped relieve some of the tension. Because neither Sophie nor Hammond spoke a word, and Sophie's maid sat silent in a corner of the coach.

After a long while, even the beauty of the countryside paled. "How long until we get there?" Julianne finally asked.

"We've been there for the past ten minutes," Hammond said, glancing at his pocket watch.

Julianne stared. "All this is part of the estate?"

"Yes," Sophie said in a pinched voice. "And you haven't seen half of it. Wait until you get a look at the manor. And the dairy. And the buttery, and the orangerie, and the stables," she said, dropping each name like a bead of venom as she glowered at Hammond. "There was an indoor tennis court. The earl who built it was a friend of Charles II, and he was a fiend for the game, they say. But it's fallen to ruin. We were going to pull it down entirely," she added, glaring at Hammond.

"If you look to your right," Sophie went on, "you can get a glimpse of the lake. The music temple is to the right. The Parthenon—the white rotunda in the distance—is on that slope to the back over there. There's a maze around back of the manor, near the waterfall and reflecting pools. And there," Sophie said in a perversely satisfied little voice, "ahead. You can finally see the manor."

Julianne couldn't speak. She could only stare. She'd seen a few great houses, from afar. She'd never seen the like of Egremont.

Made of golden stone, tall and well proportioned, it sat atop a rise and surveyed the land around it. A columned front portico overlooked a leaping fountain in the center of the drive, where a larger-than-life-sized Triton ruled over a shoal of marble porpoises. Even the front drive was spectacular; the crushed seashells that they drove over were pink and gold. It was more than the obvious money the mansion signified that impressed Julianne. The place was gracious and beautiful. Now she could understand Sophie's despair at the thought of losing it, and even her fury at what she thought was her fiancé's less than vigorous defense of his rights to it. She could even begin to see why a man would lie and cheat to attain it.

"We'll take you through the house, then walk though the grounds," Hammond said, as the carriage stopped in the front drive.

"I don't understand," Julianne said, when she took his hand and stepped down. "Are you allowed just to roam here? I mean," she added, when she saw Sophie's affronted look, "since the place isn't lived in, can just anyone come visit?"

"The place is lived in," he said. "The staff's still here to keep the place running; a house of this size can't just be abandoned. The estate pays their wages while ownership is in dispute. I have access, as does the man who claims to be Christain Sauvage. But no one lives here but the staff. Come, this way."

A butler met them at the door, and Julianne was led through the interior of the treasure house that was Egremont. She was glad she'd worn her best straw bonnet and her prettiest walking gown, a confection of fluttering patterned yellow, because she'd have felt like a peasant in anything else. This house demanded the best of its guests.

She paced down shining corridors and gaped at ornate carvings, goggled at frescoed ceilings, climbed up one of the magnificent twin staircases and down the other. She saw state bedrooms and family quarters, studies and offices, a vast library that held books up to its domed and skylit ceiling, major and minor music rooms, withdrawing rooms and salons, great chambers and long galleries, and a kitchen the size of a barn. She saw masterpieces in gilded frames and mantelpieces carved from marble and mahogany over the many hearths. The artisans who had constructed the place had played with stone and wood, making them into exquisite shapes. She saw furniture made for kings and statues stolen from ancient temples. After a while she stopped exclaiming, because there was simply nothing left for her to say.

"Now you see," Sophie said, when they finally went outside again.

"I do," Julianne breathed.

But there was more. Most of the outbuildings were worthy of anyone's main residence, Julianne thought. At least, she'd have moved into the Orangerie, pitched a tent next to the little marble fishpond there, and lived happily ever after beneath the palms and citrus trees.

It was as they were strolling toward the ruined tennis court that they saw him.

He could be no other, Julianne thought. Not because she recognized him, but because of the way that Sophie stiffened, and Hammond paused.

Even from afar, it was plain to see by the set of the gentleman's dark head, the set of his shoulders, the way he moved with wary grace. He didn't exactly walk as though he owned the place, but as if he was ready to be attacked for defending it. He was with another man, but he was the only one she noticed. He was slender, immaculate, distinctive, only a little taller than average, but unique and unforgettable.

His face was remarkable. Even from afar the clarity of his complexion, the smoothness of his skin, the almost mannequin-like purity of those strict, even, masculine features, was striking. As they came closer, and he looked up to see them, his thin dark brows raised, and she caught the silver blue flash of his eyes.

Their eyes met, and Julianne's widened. She surprised a sudden look in his that made her think he recognized her. Those crystalline eyes lit with pleasure and rising joy . . . or was it the interest of a man for a woman he found attractive, as she'd been instantly drawn to him? But she knew she wasn't that stunning, and that gave her hope that he remembered her. Because now as she stared at him she realized she couldn't say she knew him, but she was sure she'd discovered someone she wanted to know.

She couldn't guess his reaction and couldn't try. She was struggling too hard to conceal her instant response to him. And that response was awe, gladness, and a sense of coming home—followed by dawning sensations of danger, mistrust, and fear.

She refused to be made a fool of. And yet, she was very much afraid this man, whoever he might be, was a man who could do it.

# Chapter 4

The two parties of strollers came to a halt face-to-face on the path beside the ruined building that had once held a tennis court.

"Sauvage," Hammond said, acknowledging him with a curt bow.

"Hammond," the other man said, as he too bowed, "Miss Wiley." But his eyes were on Julianne.

"Allow me to introduce you," Hammond said stiffly, "This is . . .

". . . the fellow who says he is Christian Sauvage," Sophie interrupted, speaking to Julianne.

"And this is Sophie's cousin, come to visit," Hammond said, when Sophie closed her lips tightly.

"Delighted, Miss—?" Christian said, leaving the obvious question of her name hanging.

Julianne opened her lips to answer and got a sharp pinch on the tender inside of her arm. Since she'd been walking arm in arm with Sophie, no one saw it, but it brought tears to Julianne's eyes. By the time she recovered herself, Christian had gone on smoothly. "Yes. And here is Mr. Battle, an architect, all the way from Manchester, where he's restoring a castle. A tennis court isn't such a grand commission, but since I could honestly tell him a king played here, he decided to take a look to see what can be done with it."

"We're going to tear it down," Sophie said.

Christian nodded. "I see. I am not."

There was an awkward silence.

"Obviously," Christian said after a moment, "neither of us can do anything at the moment." He seemed more amused than annoyed or disconcerted. "Which is just what I told Mr. Battle. But it's good to get ready for when things are settled. I thought the old tennis court should be restored because it's historic, and also because it would be a good entertainment on cold winter afternoons. That's how I liked to spend my long hot December afternoons."

There was another silence as they all remembered his exile, during which Julianne got the distinct impression that Christian was even more amused. *If,* she reminded herself, he was indeed Christian. The eyes were blue enough, and though his hair had been light all those years ago, hair often darkened with age.

But he was more than handsome—he was startlingly attractive in a disturbingly masculine way. When she'd last seen him he either hadn't been, or she'd been too young to see it. It had been his patience and kindness that had enthralled her then. Still, how could she have forgotten those astonishing eyes? Eyes that were looking back at her with the same interest and curiosity she was showing toward him.

She blinked and dropped her gaze. She'd been staring, gawking like the girl she'd been when she'd last seen him—if she'd ever seen him. Confused, Julianne looked away. When their eyes met, it had been palpable as a touch, and just as exciting and disturbing as she imagined a touch from a fellow like that would have been. It wasn't only that he was so striking-looking, he was so *aware*, as though he lived on tiptoe.

But how was she supposed to identify him if she couldn't look at him? If she couldn't ignore the warmer feelings he caused in her, she'd have to confess her ignorance and leave for home.

She definitely didn't want to go now.

"A shame we haven't had a chance to talk, Cousin," Christian told Hammond. He smiled, but the smile was wary. "So," he said, "are we going to go on with this dagger's drawn stuff? Mind, I don't blame you for doubting me, or being reluctant to cede the place. My God, when I first saw it I was knocked sideways! It's not just a manor, it's a kingdom."

Hammond laughed, unexpectedly. "Almost exactly what I said when I arrived. I was bowled over. I never came here as a boy, myself. Oh, once or twice, of course, for important family affairs, but I never paid it much mind. It wasn't in my future and so not in my plans. When I heard I'd inherited, I was staggered. So was the rest of the family."

"Oh?" Christian said, raising a thin brow. "There are many others?"

"Not many, but some." Hammond nodded. "Old Cousin Maurice, up north, Second Cousin Ferris in Scotland, and a raft of third cousins down in Sussex. We . . . *I* have a distant, but numerous family, at least, those who are a few times removed."

"I'd heard of Sir Maurice and Ferris," Christian said thoughtfully, "and the others. They were disappointed to hear of your inheriting? They should be thrilled to hear about me. But still, they're too distantly related to care that much, or at least, they should be . . . although they become less distant from the title every year, don't they?"

"You're thinking of saying one of them might have had a hand in shortening the succession?" Hammond asked. "Bow Street was far ahead of you. Sir Maurice hired them to investigate years ago when the last earl died. He could afford to, he's almost as rich as the earl was. Although he doesn't leave his own estate for more than a walk in his gardens these days—at least not since his son died in an accident three years ago—he's always taken the family seriously. Did you ever meet him, by the way?"

They all went silent, watching the man who called himself Christian Sauvage, waiting for his answer.

He seemed amused by their sudden attention. "No, as I said, we weren't considered part of the family then."

"In any case," Hammond said glumly, "Sir Maurice didn't discover a thing. And none of the family had the ways or means to commit mischief."

"Whereas," Christian said, favoring Sophie with a tilted smile, "I had both?"

"I never said that," Sophie said, drawing herself up. "I merely wonder if you are indeed the heir to Egremont."

"Well said," Christian said. "It's good to have things out in the open. I don't blame you for doubting me. But I am who I say I am, and I'll prove it. It's a shame I'll have to do that through attorneys and law courts, because that makes it hostile, but it will be done."

He bowed again and began to walk off, but Hammond stopped him. "Sauvage!" he said. "This makes no sense. We should talk."

"Why, yes," Christian said, as he turned around. "I'd like that. But I don't want to keep the ladies standing here in the open. Tell you what," he said, "the squire was right. The White Hart has a tolerable table. Would you care to meet me there for dinner?"

Hammond looked down at Sophie. She squirmed, frowned, but then raised her chin. "Should you care to come to dinner at our house, Mr. Sauvage?" she asked.

Whatever he had expected, it clearly wasn't that. The smooth bland expression gave way to obvious surprise. Then a sudden smile illuminated his face. "Why, thank you, how kind," he said. "I'd like that. Uhm, but would your parents, do you think?"

"It was in fact my father who suggested it," she said grudgingly.

The sparkling eyes lit with laughter. "I see. Well, then"—he slewed a glance at Julianne—"I'd be delighted."

"Tomorrow night then?" Sophie asked.

"Thank you. I look forward to it," he said. He nodded and, smiling, strolled away.

They didn't speak until he was out of earshot.

"That was well done," Hammond told Sophie, as they walked on.

"There wasn't anything else I could have done," she said bitterly. "You maneuvered me into a corner."

Julianne thought it was Christian Sauvage who had done that to both of them, but asked instead, "Why didn't you introduce me?"

"Ham and I decided it would be better not to. This way, he won't guess he should know you. When we do spring your name on him, we'll do it in front of others, so we can judge his reactions more closely. And this way, too, you can judge him without him trying to influence you."

"As for that," Ham asked, "any impressions yet?"

"Well," Julianne said slowly, thinking, "he doesn't sound familiar. But his voice would obviously have changed. He speaks well, but not like someone from another country. I'd think he'd have picked up an accent from where he'd been so long."

"He said his accent was set when he left," Hammond said, "and New South Wales is hardly a country. There've only been people there for forty years or so. Of course it was inhabited by natives before that," he corrected himself. "I mean civilized people."

"I'd hardly call criminals 'civilized,'" Sophie said with a sniff.

"Other settlers went there, too," Hammond said. "Not many, I grant you. I've read Captain Cook's accounts. It really isn't much more than a penal colony even now, so there wouldn't be a regional accent to the place."

"And so far as his face," Julianne said, thinking aloud, "the years change us all. No," she shook her head, "I'll have to talk to him." She wondered how she'd do that without that uncomfortable awareness of his attractiveness distracting her.

"That you shall," Sophie said gaily. "Who knows? A chance word, a slip of the tongue, a memory recalled, anything like that might tell us more than a coachload of Bow Street runners. You may be the one to unmask him. I'm so glad you came, Cousin," she added, giving Julianne a sunny smile.

Julianne was glad, too, though even now she didn't know if she wanted to be the one to unmask the man who called himself Christian Sauvage. She was already wondering if she might uncover more than she bargained for.

"Isn't this gown too elegant for a simple dinner?" Julianne asked as she gazed at herself in the looking glass. "If you really don't need it, maybe I could save it to wear on a more auspicious occasion? *Here*, of course," she added quickly, so Sophie wouldn't think she was a beggar looking for things to take home. "I'd have no need for something this modish at home."

"This *is* an auspicious occasion," Sophie said. "If you can addle his wits, maybe you can find out more. When men are swayed by their eyes they don't pay attention to their ears, or their brains." She laughed. "And that's definitely a wits-addling gown. I'm very glad my Hammond is constant as the sun in the sky. Actually, he offered for me the night I wore that gown, so if you're worried about *him* thinking you're out to entice him, don't."

Since that was the last thing Julianne had been

thinking of, she fell silent. And now the gown suddenly looked a little less magnificent, more like the castoff it was than the most beautiful thing she'd ever put on her body. But still, there was no denying it was exquisite. Simple yet luxurious, it was a column of deep, rich, crimson raw silk. It had long sleeves, a daring neckline, and golden ribbons that crisscrossed beneath the breasts. A line of embroidered golden rosebuds marched along the hems of the sleeves and skirt.

Julianne gazed at herself and was astonished at the transformation the gown and Sophie's maid had made in her. She looked sophisticated, exotic, and definitely erotic. And yet, even so, entirely proper. She didn't know how it was done although she'd paid careful attention to every step of the process, as had her own maid, who'd watched, wide-eyed.

Sophie's maid had brushed out Julianne's brown hair and drawn it up and tied it with a red ribbon so it tumbled down in one long glossy ringlet against her shoulder. Julianne had held her breath and closed her eyes as the maid applied a whisper of soot over each eyelid. When she'd opened her eyes again, they'd looked huge, deep brown, and exotic. A drift of rouge along her cheekbones made those widened eyes look tilted. Sophie had giggled as Julianne gasped when a fingertip of rouge was lightly drawn down along the cleft of her breasts. But that accentuated their fullness, called the eyes to their buoyant shape, and made the valley between them mysterious.

Julianne felt like an actress, or a fast woman, when the maid was done with her. But she also appeared so

deliciously appealing that she grew excited just looking at herself. She didn't know if the man who called
himself Christian Sauvage would be addled by her
looks, but she definitely was.

Sophie watched over the transformation, preening
a little herself. She looked like a charming cherub in
her gold gown, her curls dressed like a statue of a
Greek god and shining like an angel's. "A good lady's
maid knows all the tricks a good courtesan's maid
does," she told Julianne. "The only difference is that a
lady's maid knows when to stop."

"I've something good to work with here, too," the
maid said, looking at Julianne. ". . . As I'm accustomed to," she added hastily when she saw the look
that flashed in her mistress's eyes.

"Well, one thing's certain," Julianne murmured.
"He won't recognize me. I'm not sure I do!"

"Well, why should he?" Sophie said in an artifi-
cially bright voice, as she gave Julianne a warning
look. "You never met the fellow before the other day.
Unless it is my Hammond you're speaking of?"

Julianne winced. She'd forgotten no one else was
to know of her purpose for being here. "Of course
not, Sophie," she stammered. "I only meant I feel
transformed."

"Sukie, a very good job. You may go," Sophie told
her maid. "You too," she told Julianne's maid. "My
cousin and I can carry on now alone." She turned to
Julianne the second the door closed behind the two
maids.

"I know, I know," Julianne said wretchedly before
she could speak. "A mistake. I shouldn't have said it.

No one's to know my motive for being here. It's just that I'm not used to subterfuge."

"Well, get used to it," Sophie said angrily. "The fellow's a criminal, for heaven's sake! He has wiles, and money, at least enough to spend fostering his schemes. And you know that servants, even the best of them, are not only indiscreet, they can be bought."

"Not my Annie," Julianne said, straightening her back. "I don't know about London servants, but ours are practically members of the family . . ."

"Who don't have as much money as the rest of the family," Sophie said coldly, finishing Julianne's sentence for her. "And who have to sleep in the attics, do the washing and pick up after you. Even on a farm. Am I right?"

"Well, yes. But . . ." Julianne's voice dwindled. It was true, though she liked to forget it. Still, there were some things she had to establish here and now. She began to suspect that if she didn't show some spirit, she'd be run over and squashed flat by her cousin. Sophie might be small and adorable, and good company when she wanted to be, but she was also high-handed, arrogant, and possibly more conscious of class than any girl Julianne had ever met.

Sophie noted her silence with approval. "I also want to warn you that though I do think you look very well, I told you that so you'd be careful not to take his compliments to heart. I'm sure he'll have many for you. I saw the look he gave you when you met."

Julianne felt a flush of pleasure. So she wasn't wrong about that look he'd given her!

"He was trying to figure out where you fit in the

scheme of things," Sophie went on, treading on Julianne's fantasies. "Now, about that, tonight we must avoid using your name until we have to."

Julianne started to protest, but Sophie cut her off. "We'll tell him in due time, but we can find out a lot this way, even the runner said so. Be on guard. The imposter will be. Never forget he's clever. He probably knows there's a reason we didn't give him your name. So he'd try to charm it from you, and I'm afraid he may be able to do that. He's obviously a flirt and wouldn't stop at being a seducer to gain his ends. It's clear he's already impressed you."

Julianne bit her lip.

"It's not that you're not pretty," Sophie said in more kindly tones. "But he's a man trying to gain what few men have, and I doubt he cares what you look like so long as he thinks you can help him. I'm not trying to hurt your feelings. I just want to make sure you know the lay of the land. Think about it. He's a handsome rogue. I'm sure he can get women anywhere he likes; why, he may even have a wife. We'll never know, from him, at least."

Julianne's eyes grew wide.

Sophie nodded. "You didn't think of that, did you? Well, so it may be. Kings have wooed with less reason than an estate like Egremont. You're intelligent enough, Cousin, but you haven't experience with the world. You're an innocent, from a farm."

Julianne looked down at her crimson gown. Now she felt about as enticing as a sow with rouge on its jowls and a ribbon round its neck. The worst part was that Sophie was right. She was ill equipped to deal with a charming imposter—if he was one. But she also realized it would be disastrous to let Sophie think she had as little experience of the world as she did.

She drew herself up. "Perhaps I'm not as experienced with the social world as you are, Sophie. I never had a Season in London, true. But I'm nobody's fool, and," she went on, waving aside Sophie's hasty assurances that she knew that, "I wish you'd stop saying 'farm' that way, as though we lived in a barn or next to a sty, or took pigs into the parlor for the winter. We have a very fine house, not as fine as this one, maybe, but historic and well furnished, and quite sufficient for our needs. And we have acres of good land, with tenants on it as well. We have woodlands as well as pastureland, and extensive gardens, and for more than growing radishes.

"I don't have to milk cows or churn butter, and I've never worked in the fields. I grow flowers because I enjoy doing it. And, I'd like you to know, our family is highly regarded in the community. I don't have elegant clothes because I don't need them in my milieu. But I could, if I wanted them, I assure you."

"I never doubted it," Sophie said quickly. "The point is that I know more of the world than you do, and you must be guided by me in this."

"The point is," Julianne said hotly, "that *I* am the one doing you a favor, Cousin!"

Sophie started to speak and thought better of it.

"And I am unwed out of preference," Julianne added, "as I'm sure you are, too."

Sophie remained silent. Julianne was gratified. She began to think she'd been right in thinking that a lovely girl like Sophie had remained single through several seasons because she'd been holding out for the biggest fish in the social sea—which definitely would be an earl with an estate the size of Egremont.

"Very well," Julianne said haughtily. "And now, shall we go downstairs?"

"Yes," Sophie said curtly, and they left the room in mutual silence.

Julianne made her way down the long stair in the wake of her little cousin, feeling far less sure of herself than she wanted Sophie to know. She hadn't lied. She led a pleasant life at home, though she knew she'd have had a different one if her beloved brother had lived to share it with her. And she'd had beaux in her time, although that time had been ruthlessly cut short by mourning. But she'd never been courted for anything but herself.

Now she knew how an heiress might feel, never sure of any man's intentions. At least, she was unsure of one man's, and she realized she very much wanted his attentions. Sophie had ruined that. Because, of course, she couldn't be sure of a thing the man who claimed to be Christian said or even guess what he was thinking. That was what she was here to find out.

The rest of the company was waiting for them in the main salon, a sumptuously furnished gold-and-ivory room. Sophie's mama was there, in puce, wearing diamonds, and purple feathers in her hair. The squire was in formal evening dress, as was Hammond. But so far as Julianne was concerned, they were only background for the man who rose to his feet as she and Sophie entered the room. For the life of her Julianne couldn't see what he was wearing, because the expression on his face when he saw her blinded her. A look of such glad welcome warmed those crystalline eyes when she met them that it transformed his face. He looked younger, eager. Julianne got a fleeting impression of someone she knew and loved—it was almost like seeing her brother returned to her again.

Then, as though someone had snuffed a lamp, the look was gone, making her wonder if it had only been an effect of the shifting lamplight.

Again, she was faced with an impossibly handsome, immaculately clad stranger, who smiled as though he knew something she didn't. Julianne let her breath out in a deep and secret sigh, because likely, she thought sadly, he did.

# Chapter 5

The company made feeble conversation as they waited for dinner in the salon. Julianne, Sophie, and her mother sat and listened to the gentlemen as they talked about the weather, the ladies only making occasional polite observations. The mood was too uneasy for anything more spirited. The squire, Hammond, and the man who claimed to be Christian Sauvage carried most of the limping conversation. This gave Julianne the opportunity covertly to study the supposed imposter. At last, she had a chance to watch him without him watching her.

It must be damnably hard for him, she thought as she eyed him where he was standing silhouetted before the crackling fire. He stood with one arm on the mantel, his head cocked to the side, listening to his host describe how cold a winter it had been. While nothing in his manner was careless or discourteous, nevertheless his lean body looked relaxed. In fact, he seemed the most comfortable of them all. That surprised Julianne. It had to be difficult even to stand at ease in a room with a man you were trying to supplant, chatting amiably with another man whose daughter you might well do out of a title and a fortune.

Surely he knew he was in the midst of people who at the least suspected him and at the most wished him dead or gone? But he acted as though nothing could be further from his mind than what was obviously foremost on everyone else's.

The squire was too hale and gruff; it was clear how ill at ease he was. Hammond was quiet and seemed depressed. But the man who would be heir to Egremont appeared so urbane and charming that a stranger entering the room might have taken him for the host. It made Julianne wonder if the real Christian would be so confident, or whether this fellow's self-assurance was a telltale sign that he was a practiced cheat.

She had a better opportunity to observe him when they were called in to dinner. Because she was seated at his side.

The squire and his lady took the head and foot of the table. Sophie sat at her father's right hand, Hammond beside her. And Julianne was seated next to Christian, opposite Sophie and Hammond. It wasn't traditional. In Julianne's experience, the engaged couple would have sat opposite each other, so as to give guests a chance to speak to them. She quickly glanced at Christian as a footman pulled out her chair for her. Would he realize he was being seated next to her so she could test him?

He wore a bland expression. Nothing in his manner showed he thought the seating unusual. But then, she thought as she sat down, he might not know what was usually done. Even if he were Christian, he'd been in prisons so long he could have forgotten.

The conversation was general at first, the squire holding forth on the price of crops as a footman ladled hot brown soup into their bowls.

Christian hardly touched his.

"Is the soup not to your taste?" the squire's wife asked him. "I didn't think to ask, did you not have the same sort of food in . . ." she hesitated, then went on, ". . . the antipodes?"

He smiled. "In . . ." he paused. It was hard to say whether he was doing it to frame his answer or mock the question. Then he said smoothly, "In the prisons we ate whatever we were given. The food improved as our general condition did, and when we were free men we ate very well. Apart from some fruits, vegetables, fish, and animals that are found only in the antipodes, the cuisine is very much the same. We tried to make it so. After all, we all missed home, and tried to re-create it there."

No one said anything. They hadn't expected him to mention his criminal past. Although, Julianne realized, his avoiding discussing it would have been odder.

"The soup's excellent," he added. "It is only that I don't care for turtle, to tell the truth. Silly of me, really. But I had a turtle as a pet in New South Wales, and ever since I've disliked eating them." He smiled. "It would be rather like you dining on horse meat, or puppy soup."

Sophie put down her spoon and looked into her

bowl as though it was filled with poison. Julianne smothered a rising nervous giggle.

"The French eat horses, and puppies are a delicacy in parts of the East, I understand," he said conversationally. "But neither appeal to me . . . Oh, sorry. I didn't mean to upset you, Miss Wiley," he told Sophie. "It's hard for me to know what is or isn't appropriate table talk here in England. I've only been back a few weeks. Please feel free to tell me when I make a mistake. How else can I learn?"

"You do eat salmon, roast beef, mutton, and pigeon?" Sophie's mother asked. "That *is* what we are having for dinner."

"Oh yes, thank you," he said mildly. "I look forward to it."

"We'll be sowing soon," the squire said, changing the subject with a vengeance. "What sort of crops do you grow there in New South Wales?"

"I don't," Christian said. "That is to say, my father went into business rather than farming, so I have much to learn about agriculture if I want Egremont to prosper."

This caused another sudden silence.

It was like trying to make pleasant conversation on a battlefield, Julianne thought. This plan to get to know and learn more about him was ill-advised. He had every advantage. What could they ask him, after all? His future plans were a source of controversy. His past was suspect at best, and shameful in any event.

The squire cleared his throat and proceeded to

plow on in conversation as he meant to in his fields, launching into his spring planting schedule for Hammond's benefit. Sophie concentrated on her plate, occasionally stealing glances at the interloper who threatened her future, casting her gaze down if he caught her at it. Her mama was busy directing the footman to add more food to her guests' plates. But Julianne couldn't forget the warm breathing presence of the man next to her, and good manners and burning curiosity combined to make her decide to speak to him.

The difficulty was that she'd have to look at him, and it was hard to meet his knowing eyes. Plus, she wasn't supposed to give her name yet. He had to know it was a deliberate omission because he hadn't asked for her name. He hadn't asked her for anything. Maybe he was amused. He could be annoyed. His expression gave away nothing. She wished her cousins had been more subtle and at least hadn't seated her next to him. She wished she were more facile. But she couldn't just ignore the man. Especially when he was only an elbow's length away from her, and she was so aware of him she swore she could *feel* him next to her.

She turned her head toward him and saw him turn to her, as though he'd been watching her all along.

*Lord*, she thought, *he is such an attractive man!* Especially when she had his full attention, and those bright eyes were looking at her with interest. This close she couldn't help noticing how fine his complexion was. Surely a man who been sent to prison in London, then across the world in the company of murderers and to who knew what ghastly places would bear some scars? He didn't look as if he'd ever even cut himself while shaving.

She scrambled for something innocuous to say and noticed that he hadn't eaten much of anything on his plate.

"Aren't you hungry?" she asked, then added quickly. "The food is very good. Or maybe it isn't spiced the way you're accustomed to?"

"I'm sure it's excellent," he said in a low voice that didn't carry farther than her ear, "but I can't help but wonder what it's spiced with. My portion, that is. I wouldn't be surprised if there wasn't a sprinkle of poison to liven it up."

There were a dozen ways she could and probably should have answered that. But it was so near to what she'd been thinking herself that she brought up her napkin to cover a surprised gasp of laughter.

That seemed to please him.

"No, no," she murmured, when she could. "That would leave evidence. My cousins aren't fools. No, truly," she said when he smiled, "whatever they think of you, and you can hardly blame them for their suspicions, my cousins are straightforward, and Hammond seems to be, too. They might meet you in a court of law, or a court of fives, or even in a duel, but I think you can safely eat tonight, I really do."

"Well, if you're sure," he said doubtfully, eyeing his plate, then hers. "You urge me to eat. But as for you . . . you're sure you tried the beef? It does look very good."

She nodded. Clearly, he was joking . . . at least, she hoped so. As she watched, he cut a small bit of beef, slowly brought it to his lips, and, even more slowly, popped it in his mouth. He chewed, watching her carefully as he did. "Thank you," he said, after he'd swallowed. "It is good. And the pigeon? Have you tried it yet?"

Smiling, she nodded again.

He took a small bite of that, too. Then he looked at the tiny peas on his plate, then at the ones on hers. "But you haven't eaten any peas, have you?" he asked softly, his expression wistful as he stared at them. "I wish you would."

"You *are* teasing me, aren't you?" she asked.

He smiled, a true warm smile. "Of course. But I had to find something to talk about that wouldn't make you turn to stone, which is what I seem to have transformed everyone else to this evening."

"It *is* difficult, isn't it?" she said quietly. "I hope you understand that my cousins aren't rude or cruel. But you have to admit that your sudden appearance upset their plans. What are they to say? What can they think?"

"I know exactly what they think, and I do understand," he said as softly. "There's not much I can do about that. Now, tell me please, since you didn't expect to inherit the estate or marry the heir, what has my sudden appearance meant to you, Miss Wiley?"

Her smile froze. She wasn't Miss Wiley, but her cousins hadn't wanted her to mention her name yet.

"Oh, I see," he said gently, when she didn't answer, his interested expression turning cool and polite. "You have an issue with me, too. Maybe," he mused,

"I shouldn't have tasted that pigeon, after all." This time, he didn't seem to be joking.

Julianne felt his withdrawal and the loss of his approval, and hated it. She struggled for something to say and, in that moment of silence, realized that their quiet banter had stopped other conversation at the table. They were the focus of everyone's attention. Her cousins and Hammond were watching and straining to hear what they said.

Her cheeks grew hot. Julianne suddenly decided that she could and would not play this game. She didn't know who this man was, but she really didn't know who her cousins were either. One thing she did know. Her cousins were trying to use her, and if this fellow was trying to do the same, there wasn't much to choose between them. In fact, though he could be an out-and-out villain, in the few moments she'd been speaking with him she'd felt more of a connection than she had with her cousins since she'd gotten here.

When she came right down to it, it hardly mattered to her who did inherit the title. It would suit her if justice were served, whoever was served up the estate. And if those dunderheads couldn't think of anything to say to him, then what did they expect? she thought angrily. They'd seated her next to their quarry, after all. She'd been used as a hunting dog, and that was demeaning and unfair.

Mostly, she realized she didn't like deception for a very good reason. She was terrible at it, as well as roundly ashamed of herself for trying to be a sneak.

"We weren't ever properly introduced, were we?"

she said loudly and clearly enough for everyone else
to hear. "My name isn't Wiley. I'm Sophie's cousin
on her mother's side. Nor do I live near here, or even
visit often. In fact, I only just arrived the other day,
and only for a short visit. I should be going home
very soon, in fact."

Well, there was truth! she thought, as a triumphant
flush heated her face. She'd ended the game and
would probably be told to pack her bags tonight.

"And so your name is . . . ?" he asked.

The others in the room seemed to be holding their
breath.

"I am Julianne Lowell," she said, holding her head
high.

"Julianne . . . Lowell?" he said slowly, his gaze traveling over her. His eyes slowly warmed, lit with brilliant light, and widened. "From . . . Little Slough?"

She nodded, holding her breath.

"Julie, the tag-along?" he asked, incredulous. "The
little pestilence, as Jonathan used to say? Julianne,
*Jonathan's* little sister?"

Now she couldn't breathe. Her hand flew to her
breast as her eyes searched his.

"Where is the dratted fellow, anyway?" he asked,
half-rising from his seat. He looked around with a
dawning smile, as though he expected Jonathan to
come laughing from out of the shadows of the now
deathly silent room, as he'd have done so long ago if
he'd been discovered at one of his pranks.

"Jonathan . . . died," she managed to say. "At Salamanca, in battle, five years past."

"Ah!" he said, sinking to his chair as though she'd dealt him a blow. "I'm sorry, I didn't know."

But for the first time since her brother had died, Julianne didn't feel like weeping when she talked about it. Instead, her heart leapt, and she found tears of joy blurring her vision.

"Christian?" she asked, putting out a hand to him. "Christian? Is it really you?"

So they'd gotten Julianne Lowell to come and inspect him, Christian thought as he rode back to the inn where he was staying. He was glad he'd ridden horseback rather than taking a carriage, he wasn't used to this soft and misty weather, and he liked it. He also felt more able to defend himself this way. Still, he doubted he'd come to harm here. After all, if he wanted to dispose of an inconvenient relative he wouldn't do it in his own backyard either. Too incriminating. There were better ways.

Julianne Lowell, he mused. Now, that was interesting. He'd wondered who she was, and hadn't doubted she was there for a reason. It was obvious from the first, from exchanged looks and sudden silences, that the woman was part of some plan. But Julianne Lowell? He hadn't expected that. How should he have? There was a long list of people to remember, and though the name Jonathan Lowell would certainly have gotten his attention, he'd forgotten about her.

Now he was glad they'd remembered. This was very good. She was exactly the sort of woman he appreciated. He smiled. That admittedly, wasn't a hard standard for a woman to measure up to. But though he liked most women, he wouldn't have wanted to pass any time with her if she'd been prissy or toplofty or put on airs—like her cousin. Sophie was a dashing little baggage, but not his sort at all. This Julianne was not only appealing, with her charming face and buxom figure, but seemed as candid and honest as the women he was used to, even though she had manners and morals and breeding. No. The morals, he thought, was a thing he'd yet to find out about. He looked forward to it.

Best of all, she laughed when something struck her as funny and not just because she was expected to, the way her cousin and the ladies he'd met since he got here did. And she was definitely interested in him, and for more than finding out who he was. He was never wrong about that.

He frowned. Her brother was gone, which was a tragedy. He wouldn't think about tragedies now, he couldn't. But he could consider how to find out if she really was who she claimed to be. That was doubly difficult if a man's senses were involved, and his definitely were. His opponents weren't stupid. He could never forget that. Interesting though, he thought, as he rode into the courtyard of the White Hart. This adventure was getting more interesting every hour.

He swung down from the saddle, handed the reins to a stableboy, and strode into the inn, headed for the taproom. The architect, Battle, had left, but he wasn't ready for the solitude of his room just yet. He didn't like being alone, wasn't used to it, and only went to his bed when he knew he would sleep.

He paused at the door to the common room and looked in. He never entered a room he didn't survey first. The taproom was like dozens of others he'd seen in the countryside here, with a low-timbered ceiling, dark wood floors, a long wooden plank of a bar with chairs drawn up to it, and a few tables at the sides of the room. As his eyes adjusted to the dim light he saw three locals at the tap, holding forth on the state of the world, and another solitary traveler at one of the tables. He smiled. Even if no one spoke to him, he'd be far from alone and unnoticed.

He took a table by the wall, signaled the innkeeper for a pint, and sat back. He was approached before he'd finished half of it.

"Evening, sir," the heavyset man said as he drew out a chair and joined him.

"I'm surprised," Christain said softly. "I wouldn't think you'd speak to me so openly. You don't care if your employers know it, Mr. Murchison?"

The runner shrugged. "It makes no never mind if they do. I've ways of doing my job, and they'd best accept it. You took your mutton with them this evening, did you?"

"You know I did. Mutton, beef, and fish, and none of it poisoned, to my relief."

"They wouldn't be such fools."

"But someone would?"

The runner looked at him from under his thick brows. "Aye, that's why I'm here. You're being studied by someone else now, lad."

"The longlegs crouched over there, in the corner?" Christian asked smoothly. He raised a brow, indicat-

ing, with the smallest tilt of his head, the table in the
darkest corner, where a lanky fair-haired man sat in
the shadows, huddled over his pint of ale.

The runner gave a crack of laughter. "Awake on all
suits, aren't you? Aye, he's the one. There's muscles
there, though he's lean, and he favors one of them
long legs, but moves light withal. He's been your
shadow for a day now, but not shadowy enough, is he?
There's the rub, sir. I'd almost believe you were who
you claim to be if you didn't know shadows as well as
you do."

"Survival knows no class or rank," Christian said
with a wry smile. "I assure you, if you raised the
Prince where I grew to manhood, he'd be a master of
shadows too."

The runner nodded, acknowledging that.

"And your investigations on my behalf?" Christian
asked.

"Nothing new. You met the Lowell female?"

"Yes. Interesting that you didn't tell me her name."

The runner shrugged. "I never said I wasn't working two sides of the street. Sometimes not giving information tells me more than giving it."

"I congratulate you on your industry," Christian
said with a wry smile. "What have you learned by
having me discover her name myself?"

"Nothing," the runner said with another shrug. "It
don't always work, but it's always worth a try. You
could have done a heap of research. You might even
remember her. That's for me to find out. What did you
think of her?"

"The obvious. She's lovely, charming, kindhearted."
He smiled. "We got along very well."

"She's an innocent," the runner said.

"I agree. Don't worry. I'm not going to kill her."

"It's your pleasuring her, not killing her outright,
that would do her in. She's a good girl, the kind that
can't play with a gent. Her being easy with a stranger
is manners, the mark of a real lady, even if she don't
have a title. She doesn't expect nothing but the same
from a fellow, neither. I'm only telling you this because I don't think you're used to such, where you
come from."

The younger man's smile faded. "Sound advice
coming from such a moral fellow," Christian said
with heavy irony. "But we all have weaknesses,
don't we? Different priorities, I expect. You may be
prim as regards the ladies, but you have no com-
punctions about taking my gold as well as the
squire's, do you?"

"No," the runner said easily. "Because I'm not
working at cross-purposes. The answer I find will
only make one of you happy, but I'm not diddling either of you while I'm at it. It's only when I find the
truth that one of you will have cause for complaint.
And never doubt it: I will find the truth. I charge for
my inquiries, but the truth can't be bought. At least,
not from me."

He put both hands on the table. "I'm a Bow Street
runner and proud of it. In the end, the law is my only
employer. If you're the earl, I'll be pleased to say I
worked for you. If not? The penalty for imperson-

ation's heavy, and if you take the title and move into Egremont and they discover you're not who you say you are, I don't doubt it would be the rope for you this time. Not a silken one like they have for the nobility, neither, not that it makes much difference to your neck at the drop, I don't suppose. And much as I like chatting with you, it's all the same to me. It's work.

"Good night, sir," the runner said as he used his hands to push himself upright. "And watch your back, because I do enjoy working for a double fee and would like to keep doing it for at least a little longer."

"Oh, no worries," Christian said. "I don't trust anyone, Mr. Murchison, including you."

Murchison bowed. Christian gave him a sour smile and watched him leave. He sat in silence a while longer, then, after yawning and stretching theatrically, he also rose and strolled to the door. One seemingly casual glance back before he left showed the tall man in the corner pointedly not watching him. He smiled and went up the stair to his room.

He was glad he hadn't had time to hire a valet; he didn't like the idea of anyone waiting in his room.

He eased open his door and stood silent a moment. When he was sure there was no one breathing there, he went inside. He locked the door, set a glass at the window again, stripped off his shirt and removed the sling that had been wrapped around his chest. He looked at the perfect deadly imprint of itself the pistol had left in his flesh and rubbed it. Then he washed from the bowl and pitcher on the table.

Clad only in his breeches and hose, he went to the bed and sat down. He slid his knife from his boot before he drew them both off, then after putting knife and pistol in their nightly places, turned the lamp down and lay down. Only then did he relax.

It was going as well as could be expected, but he wished it would go faster. They'd sent a man back home to make inquiries, and he'd guess a dozen more letters, too. He'd expected that. It would take time to get answers. But they'd accepted all the papers he'd given them so far. Now he only had to wait. He put his hands behind his head and smiled. Things were looking up. This Julianne would make the waiting easier.

She was a good girl, Murchison said. That was something he'd have to discover for himself. What he already knew was that she had shining brown hair and big brown eyes, a pretty mouth and very fine breasts. He was very partial to those. No question, she attracted him, body and soul, and sex was about more than the mechanics of the thing; at least, so it was for him.

His plans were filled with danger, and there was nothing more he could do about them tonight. His dreams would be uneasy, as always, because his past was easily as lurid as his future could ever be. So he tried to put off his memories and forestall his dreams by thinking of nothing but the pure pleasure that would come to him if he were clever and lucky enough to accomplish what he'd set out to do.

He thought of the magnificence of Egremont, its riches, treasures, and honors . . .

But his last thoughts as he drifted to sleep were of Julianne Lowell, the woman sent to unmask him.

# Chapter 6

Julianne and Christian walked slowly through the squire's rose garden in silence. Then, in mutual unspoken agreement, they went out the gate to the road. Julianne's maid paced a distance behind them, but otherwise they were alone as they made their way along the lane, so intent on their thoughts they were blind to the beautiful early-spring morning.

It was a mild day, fragrant with the heady flowers of spring, the birds almost as mad with song as the bees were at their work. But neither human made a sound except for crunching the gravel underfoot. They were a handsome couple, he the epitome of a gentleman in his slate trousers and dun jacket, high beaver hat, shining half boots, neckcloth, and linen fine as any fashionable fellow on a stroll through Hyde Park. She wore a pretty peach gown enlivened by green ribbons at the waist and a straw bonnet to shield her complexion from the sun

Christian turned his head to the side, watching his companion. "I'm ready," he finally said. "What are your questions?"

"That's just it. I don't know what to ask." She turned her face fully to his, and he saw that her eyes were as troubled as her voice. "This whole thing . . . It was awkward, the way my cousins left us together just now, awkward and embarrassing. I apologize. I mean, to invite you in, then have everyone suddenly remember all the things they had to do so they could leave us alone."

"Not entirely alone," he remarked. "They didn't throw you to the wolf. Your maid is in easy calling distance if I decide to ravish you."

"You know what I mean," she said with a scowl.

"Too well," he said, snatching a lilac blossom from a bush they passed. "As well as what they mean. They want to know if you can discover who I am." He looked down at the blossom, tore a tiny floweret from it. "What's wrong with that? I'd do the same if I were they, if maybe a little more cleverly. But as for you, I wonder . . . last night you seemed so sure of me, of who I am. What changed your mind?"

She looked stricken.

"They did, did they?" he asked, answering his question. He shrugged. "Again, I don't blame them. But I'm surprised at you. To change so drastically in a night . . . Still, we didn't have much chance to talk. Now we do. So what do you want to know? How can I restore your faith in me?

"Julianne," he said in a softer voice, dropping the blossom to the path and concentrating on her, "don't worry. What you think won't mean much in a court of law. It's unfair, and not something I believe, but it is the way of the world. Firstly, because law's a man's game, and a woman's testimony is always suspect. Men don't trust your sex because of your gentler emotions, as though having a soft heart meant a soft head."

He shook his own head in disgust, "As though Elizabeth wasn't a wiser, sterner monarch than most men who came before her!. And I could tell you about some women I've met . . ." He smiled. "But I'd best not. They were brave and bold, but bolder, I think, than you're used to hearing about. Speaking of which," he said on a sigh, "many men think it's easy to seduce women. That counts against females, too, although if it were true, the world wouldn't be filled with whores, would it? There'd hardly be a need for the profession . . . Oh!" He scowled. "Not a word for polite company. Forgive me. I'm not used to polite company. But what *is* the right word to use if you're talking to a lady?"

"There isn't one," she said, wondering if he could possibly be serious. There was such a thing as essential manners, and the antipodes were, after all, on the same planet. But Christian, she remembered now, had always had a sly dry wit. Her pulse picked up, along with her hopes.

"Right," he said, "I remember. The unnamed profession. At least, it's a woman's occupation that men can't mention in front of women. Strange, that, isn't it? Oh well, I'll get used to it, I suppose. I'll have to. Forgive me again."

"What do they call them where you came from? . . . Oh. Never mind," she said, realized the trap. She tried not to smile, which made him smile.

"I'd tell you, but it's probably worse. Now, as I was saying about women and the law," he went on. "You don't have to worry about your testimony. But even more important, if something isn't on paper, it doesn't really matter much who says it, man or woman. It can be argued and challenged, and in the end means little. So what I'm trying to tell you is that whatever you decide about me, it won't decide my fate. Unless, of course," he added, "you catch me in a lie that you can prove. But there's little likelihood of that, isn't there?"

She looked at him curiously.

"You don't have any letters from me," he said.

She couldn't tell if that was a statement or a question. "No, but he did write you letters, though. You never answered him."

"Letters?"

She ducked her head. "After. When he heard you were in . . ." She paused, it was hard for her to say the word to him. She'd never known a criminal before. Naming his prison seemed more offensive than his mentioning prostitutes to her. But there were no adequate euphemisms. "When you were in Newgate Prison," she went on quickly, "he wrote to you. You never wrote back."

"I never got any letters. But that doesn't surprise me." He straightened his shoulders. "Well, if you don't have any questions for me right now, I have one for you. What happened to Jon? Tell me more please. Unless it's too painful. I'd understand if it is."

"Oh no," she said. "Actually, it's important to talk about it. He died, he didn't vanish from all human

memory. At least I don't want him to, he's gone, but I
want others to know who and what he was."

She looked at him. The sunlight made her eyes
glow gold as they studied his face, her expression
suddenly deadly serious. "I don't know if you're who
you say you are," she said. "I don't want to be a fool."

"I don't blame you. Tell me about Jon, then I'll tell
you about myself. And then you can try to trip me and
trap me to your heart's content."

She winced.

"Julianne," he said softly, "I remember you as a
child. You remember me as a boy. Neither of us are
those people anymore. I've already assured you that
whatever you decide won't settle my fate. But maybe
I can tell you something to make you easier in my
company. Jon was my best friend, and you were his
sister, his charge, and so mine, too. I discovered that a
little sister was as much of a treat as a pest, or at least
you were." He smiled. "It wasn't always lovely,
though. Especially when we wanted to be off without
responsibilities and had to drag you along. And you
wailed like a banshee at the drop of a hat. We didn't
dare let you carry on because your mother would
have killed us. So you got your way. I hope that's
changed, by the way," he added.

The glow of warmth she'd felt the night before
reignited.

"But you were also amusing," he went on. "You
were easy to tease, a boy likes that. And you were
wonderful for my self-esteem, because it was clear
you wanted to be with us every minute. I had no
mother and was an only child. With you and Jon I felt

as though I'd another family. Then my life suddenly changed. Friends and family deserted me and my father. England threw us out. That was shocking. But we were lucky, because otherwise we'd have been killed."

She was astonished that he could say that and continue to stroll along, nothing in his face or voice hinting at the pain he must feel.

"So for a very long while I tried not to think of England or those old days at all. Then I heard about the inheritance. After I got over the surprise—and the instant reaction of wanting to throw all of it back into their faces—I came back. Now that I've returned I find I want more than the estate and title. I want to find whatever little bits are left of my old life."

She reached out to him before she realized what she was doing, and snatched her hand back. One did *not* try to smooth the lines of pain from a strange man's face. They were gone in a second anyway, and he wore his usual faintly amused expression as he looked at her.

He gazed at her with interest, his eyes showing nothing else. That was what she found so disconcerting. One moment it was like talking to an old friend, and in the next she was confronting a stranger, an attractive and somehow dangerous stranger

He was right, she had to ask questions. She *yearned* to ask them. She picked up her head. "I do have a question," she said.

"Yes?"

"You were in prison, then sent to the Hulks. And from there to New South Wales, where you were put in another prison. That must have been terrible. But, none of it shows. That is, there are no marks of it on you." She fell still, embarrassed. It was a terribly personal thing to say, and she felt ashamed of herself for it.

It didn't seem to bother him in the least. "That's true," he said, "I've few visible scars. That's because my father protected me, and my . . ." He paused, and went on, "fellow prisoners tried to protect the younger lads. I *do* have a few scars I'd love to show you, though," he added brightly. "But since I'm trying so hard to be a gentleman, I can't do that . . . now."

Her eyes flew to his, and she saw his dawning smile. Christian had always loved to tease her.

"Come, there must be more questions," he said.

"There are, hundreds more. But what can I ask? What was the name of our dog? What was Jon's favorite food? How did I wear my hair? Lord," she said, shaking her head, "so many more questions I can't think of them right off."

He grew silent. She continued to walk alongside him, but her hands grew cold, and her heart sank. It was one thing to go for a stroll with an attractive gentleman who might very well be a dear old friend. It was another to find herself practically alone on a quiet country lane with a man who'd been a convict, and who now had a fortune to gain if she could vouch for him, and perhaps, no matter what he'd said, a harder time gaining it if she denied his claim.

"Scrubby," he said, "Your dog was called Scrubby. He was a terrier who dug holes. Jon loved most sweets, but he especially liked pancakes with jelly, and you, your hair was always braided." He looked for her response.

She tried to subdue her elation, and succeeded. Bad questions! she chided herself. Anyone could have known Scrubby's name, the dog followed them everywhere, just as anyone could have known she wore braids, and most boys loved pancakes.

"And our cousin Jerome?" she asked brightly.

He grew quiet, obviously thinking. "I'm sorry," he finally said. "I don't remember him."

Her face flushed. She'd just invented him.

"Oh," he said, watching her. "Does that sink me entirely?"

She shook her head. She thought he knew as well as she did that it didn't.

"So. Any more questions?"

"I don't know what to ask," she said, avoiding his gaze. It wasn't wrong to try to trap a thief, but she felt like a criminal herself for doing it. Or rather, for doing it so badly. She must have insulted him. Nothing in his expression implied that he thought so. But he was as good at keeping his thoughts to himself as she was not.

"You can always ask more later," he said. "Will you tell me about Jon now?"

She looked at him.

"How did he come to join the army?"

She was happy to change the subject. "He wasn't a political fellow, though he opposed Napoleon, of course. Still, he was content to read the news and follow events, until a recruiting officer came to the village, and he heard the music and saw the flags and colors. Then he could talk about about nothing but the war. My parents tried to cool his enthusiasm. But then they took us for a visit to London, and Jon saw the massing of the troops outside the palace. After that, there was no holding him back. As my father said, Jon fell into step with the pipes and drums and never walked normally again. He couldn't rest until he could buy his colors, and though my father was against it, no one could ever stop Jon from having his way, not when he got the bit between his teeth. You know Jon," she said, with a wistful smile, before she could stop herself. "I mean . . ."

"Yes," he said with the warmest smile she'd yet seen from him. "I do, and I did. And if I'd been here then, I'd probably have gone off to war with him. I'm sorry."

"For what?"

"For being here now, when he is not."

She dropped her gaze and bit her lip, unable to answer. It was too close to what she'd been thinking, and now, too unfair to contemplate.

"He was a genius at convincing people to do what he wanted," he went on. "Remember when he wanted to go to the Gypsy Fair? No one had time to go, no one wanted to take us. But Jon was adamant and had our parents talked into it in a week."

She stopped in her tracks. "You remember the Gypsy Fair?"

"Would I be likely to forget?" His eyes sparkled. "The green was transformed, it bloomed with tents and banners. I suppose now I'd think it tame, but then it was spectacular. We didn't often have such entertainment. Remember the fried cakes, hot pies, gingerbread? The oysters and ices?"

She laughed. "I made such a pig of myself! But it was wonderful."

"Yes, and so was the entertainment. Gypsy dancers, music, trained bears, conjurers, fire-eaters, tumblers, and fortune-tellers. The tents where ladies couldn't go, and a boy had to be older to be let in. That really annoyed Jon and me. We tried to sneak in, but were caught. And, of course, there was the acrobat, the one who fell. I'll never forget. I thought he was dead. But he got up and bowed, and walked away. Forget the man who made cards disappear up his sleeve and reappear behind my ear. That was my first experience of magic."

She stared at him. There were always fairs in the summertime. A boy would have gone to several, and certainly one in his own backyard, so talking about it wasn't proof he'd been to that one with her. But that fair and that day stood out in her memory. It was the first time she'd seen that Death didn't confine himself to old people and sickbeds; it was the day the acrobat fell.

The acrobat had been up on a rope that stretched between two tent poles, a limber young fellow dressed in fool's motley, a yellow-and-red tunic and yellow tights. He capered above the crowd and transfixed the eye. He'd been dancing on his rope, making the crowd laugh. She'd stood, neck bent back, looking up at him.

And then he'd tottered and tried to regain his balance, his arms waving madly, his body arcing to and fro. Everyone gasped. They stopped talking, the noise of the fair slowly ground down to silence as they all looked up to see him struggling to right himself. And then, he'd fallen, like a spinning top, all the way down to the straw-covered ground beneath. She could still hear the awful sound he made when he hit the ground.

The crowd had gone as deathly still as he lay there, crumpled in a heap. She'd been so afraid. But before any of his shocked fellow performers could reach him, he'd stirred. He'd groaned, and staggered upright. She'd held her breath as he'd looked around. And then, he'd given the transfixed crowd a shaky bow. They'd gone wild. She'd never forget how her emotions had soared with the acrobat, fallen with him, then miraculously risen again.

This man remembered, too.

She stared at him. "You are *really* Christian?" she asked, incredulous. "Oh, stupid, stupid," she asked herself in frustration before he could answer. "What should I expect you to say?"

"Hello, Little Jewel?" he asked.

And then she closed her eyes to keep in the tears. Because no one but her parents had called her that for so many, too many, long, lonely years.

They couldn't stop talking after that. He told her about the land he'd come from, about little green birds that could speak like men, about animals with pockets, and sharks big as trees that patrolled the seas around that alien land. She told him about Jon's life after he'd left, then, when he asked, about her own.

"I'd no heart left after Jon died," she said. "We

were so close, and when I understood he was never coming home, I took it badly. Dr. Raines said it was because it happened at a melancholy age for a girl, as I was entering womanhood. He said that was when females are particularly emotional. But I think it would have happened however old I was."

"And that's why you haven't married?"

Her eyes went wide. "I'm single at an age when many women are married, but I'm not in my dotage."

"I know," he said. "But you're so lovely and charming it's strange that you're still alone. Or am I being stupid? Have you a beau?"

"No," she said. She pretended to look around. "My goodness! We've walked a long way. We'd better turn back before they begin to worry about where we've gone."

"Too far, too soon, I suppose," he mused as he turned in step with her. They went in silence a while before he spoke again. "We've talked about where I've come from, and what you've done, but there's so much we haven't touched on. Would you walk out with me again, so we can talk some more?"

She nodded. "Yes, I'd like that."

"Good," he said. "But before we do, and before we get back to your cousins, would you like to ask me the most important question so we can have it out of the way?"

She looked at him.

"Whether or not I'm a thief, of course," he said mildly.

She gazed at her toes. "I didn't know how to ask that," she whispered.

"I thought so. Well, I'm not a thief, and neither was my father. You'd expect me to say that, so let me explain. The thought of theft was so far from our minds we didn't have a defense when we were 'apprehended,' as they said then. Think about it. Would you have a ready excuse if you went back to your cousin's house now and found them confronting you, accusing you of stealing a ring, or pin, or brooch? Of course not. Innocent people can only keep protesting their innocence, they don't have excuses. Neither did we.

"My father was a very smart man, Julianne. Other men trusted him to correctly tally their life savings and investments, after all. And what would I want with a silver candlestick?" he asked. "We weren't rich, but we had everything I wanted. I can't prove that even now, of course. The man who accused us is long dead. But why we were accused? That's a different story. I always meant to return and find out. Now that I'm here, I will. I don't ask you to believe me, but I have to ask you if you'll try."

"Why?" she asked, her eyes searching his. "What does it matter if my testimony in court doesn't mean anything?"

"Isn't it obvious? Julianne, life took a lot of things from me, and from you. I think its time we take back what we can, put things back the way they could and should have been. Don't you? So I'd like to know now, before more time goes by, will you give me a fair chance?"

She took a deep breath. "You know why my cousins brought me here?"

He laughed. "Of course."

"And yet you trust me?"

"As much as you do me. No, more than that, I'm sure." His smile was warm, intimate, beguiling. "Julianne, I'm only asking you to give me time."

She wanted to be as candid with him as he seemed to be with her. She tried to find a way to allow herself this dawning joy. "Why aren't *you* married yet?" she finally blurted. "Or are you?"

"Yes, I am, and with three children," he said. He laughed at her expression. "Don't look embarrassed! That's a good fair question. No, I'm not married. I wasn't in a position to marry for a long time. Then, when we made our way up in the world, I didn't find any woman I trusted enough to love with all my heart, much less marry." He grew serious again. "Women sent to the antipodes aren't all depraved, some were innocent, too. But not for long. I'm not saying that made them unlikely candidates for love, only that if I loved any, it was never for long. And understand, there aren't many females there. They're still so scarce they're a valuable commodity. At first, I wasn't rich enough to interest many, then, when I understood that, I was too wary."

He bent his head to her ear and lowered his voice. The sound of it, soft and husky, made Julianne shiver. "But I wasn't a monk," he breathed, "and I don't want you thinking I'm claiming to be one. It's just that I never found anyone I wanted to stay with. Come, Julianne, don't worry. I'm not asking you to trust me yet. I'm only asking you to give me a chance."

"Why?" she murmured.

"I'll swear you know that," he whispered, glancing

at the maid walking behind them. "And if you don't, that's an answer I can't give you here and now. At least, not the way I want to."

He looked sincere. He also looked devilishly handsome. Of course he wasn't a monk. He might be a cheat and a conniver, able to convince people of a great many things, but he'd never convince any sane female of that. He was also intelligent, he'd just inherited a vast fortune, and if he could be believed, he already possessed a tidy one. And yet he was plainly making up to her.

She didn't believe it. She didn't believe him. She didn't want to doubt him.

"I'd like to know you better," she said.

His smile was wide and warm. "Then you will."

He took her hand and placed it on his arm. They walked back to the squire's house that way, although Julianne wanted to skip along the path, the way she hoped she had with him so long ago.

He said good-bye to her at the garden gate. Annie, the maid who had accompanied them, ducked a curtsey and went back into the house.

"Tomorrow then?" he asked, holding her hand.

The way he looked back at her made her catch her breath. "Isn't tomorrow too soon?" she asked.

"Not for me."

"For my cousins," she said, hoping he'd argue with her.

"They'll be delighted. You're hot on the case. Lord, I hope you are," he breathed, and bent and brushed his lips against hers.

It felt like a shock, it felt like velvety sweet, it felt like she had to taste more. But he only stepped back, smiling that cool smooth smile.

"Yes," he said, "I thought so." He bowed. "Tomorrow. At noon? We'll ride or walk, but we'll talk. Until then," he said, and strode to the stables to collect his horse.

And left her to try to collect her thoughts.

They were waiting for her in the parlor when she came back into the house, and for a moment, Julianne wondered if her cousins *were* going to accuse her of stealing a pin or a ring or a brooch.

"We asked you to question him, not fall in love with him," Sophie said angrily the moment she walked in.

"I beg your pardon?" Julianne said. Her cheeks were burning. They must have seen that kiss.

"You were out an hour, and you come in looking dazed?" Sophie sneered. "I believe you know just what I mean."

They *hadn't* seen. Julianne let out her breath. Her cousin would certainly have more to say if she knew. "You asked me to get to know him. Would you rather I wrote him letters?" she asked haughtily.

"Now, now," the squire said, "Julianne's right, Sophie. She does have to lull him."

"I wondered from the first if it was right to ask an innocent girl to do such a thing," Hammond said with concern. "If he is a rogue, we've done her a grave disservice leaving her in his company for so long."

"Oh, good heavens!" Julianne said, honestly angry. "I don't know if he's a rogue, but he hasn't done me half the disservice you're doing now. We walked, we talked. I discovered nothing to discredit him so far. Do you want me to continue with this or not? I can always go home." She waited. She didn't know what she'd do if they told her to leave.

Sophie's mama shot her daughter a furious look.

"Please stay," Sophie said grudgingly. "And forgive us. We were only worried about you. The fellow's too handsome and smooth by half."

"I said I'd do as you asked," Julianne said. "Now I find I want to know just who and what he is for myself as well as you."

"I can understand that," Hammond said with sympathy.

"So can I," Sophie said, watching Julianne closely. "But don't be misled, Cousin. If he really is going to be the next earl, the knowledge of who he is will be the only thing you'll get. An earl will look higher than a farmer's daughter for a wife."

"I know that," Julianne said, because she did. "But if he's really who he says he is, there's something else for me, too. I'll have more memories of my brother, and you cannot know how much that means to me."

"We do," Sophie's mama said. "But so does he. Be very sure he's counting on that. So. Did you discover anything new?"

"I did," Julianne said, keeping the enthusiasm from her voice. "Some things that seem to point to his telling the truth. He remembers our dog and Jon's favorite food, even going to a Gypsy Fair at home with us, with too many details for him to have made it up."

"Dogs and favorite foods," the squire scoffed. "Such could be learned secondhand from anyone in your village. I'd expect him to have researched things that the true Christian Sauvage would have known. And the Gypsy Fair, what's that to say to anything? They're all over England. One comes here, too. It's the one with the fortune-tellers and fire-eaters, the living skeleton and suchlike, isn't it? And that acrobat? Ho, Sophie, remember? We thought she'd weep her eyes out when he fell and pretended to be hurt," he told Julianne. "The next year she couldn't wait to see him do it again."

Julianne closed her eyes. She felt, she realized, very like that acrobat who fell. Because she'd been so high, and the wind had been knocked right out of her.

# Chapter 7

The lone horseman clattered into the courtyard of the White Hart as the sun began to move from its zenith. He slid down from the saddle, handed the reins to the stableboy, and walked into the inn, looking thoughtful.

"Good afternoon—Softly, softly, sir!" the Bow Street runner exclaimed, flinging up both hands as Christian whirled around and dropped to a crouch, his hand snaking inside his jacket. "If I'd wanted to have at you, I'd not have spoken first, would I?"

Christian stood up. He tugged at his waistcoat to straighten it. "As for that, I think 'Death to Tyranny' was the last thing Caesar heard before he was stuck like a pig. Some assassins like to get in a last word. No hard feelings, Murchison? My fault entirely, but I don't like being surprised."

"No offense taken. Don't blame you for wool-gathering, though," the runner said. "She's a lovely piece."

Christian's eyes turned icy, his voice was as cold. "I didn't mind seeing your shadow all day, but I do mind your language. She's a lovely lady, and please don't forget that in future."

"Aye, 'lady,' then," the runner said, unperturbed. "But here I was, brought up to think only females with titles was called such. Well, live and learn."

The younger man checked. "Oh, right. That's true. I'd forgotten. Well, at least, I think of her as a lady because she has the manner and manners of one. Whatever she's called, she's not what you implied."

"I don't imply. I'm here to prove. If you say she's a lady, so she is in my book. Speaking of which, I've a few new notes in mine. Do you have time to talk?"

"I have nothing but, until tomorrow," Christian said. "But not here, let's go into the taproom."

The runner hesitated. "Mebbe this needs talking about in your room?"

Christian laughed. "No, I don't think so. Much as I trust you, whatever we say can be said at a table with my back to the wall and my eyes to the front."

"My feelings are hurt," the runner said. "But I don't blame you. That's what I want to talk about."

"Oh?" Christian said with interest, as they went into the taproom.

They took the same table they had the previous day. Two local men were at the tap, and the same man sat huddled at the farthest table in the darkest corner.

The runner put his hands on the table. He raised a thumb toward the man in the corner. "Him," he said. "Just thought you'd like to know you had two shadows today while you was out on your stroll with the . . . lady."

"Oh, I knew that," Christian said, signaling the

innkeeper. "Make it two," he called the man. "Like the number of my shadows," he told the runner. "You know who my other admirer is, Murchison?"

"I wouldn't be worth my shilling if I didn't." The runner took his well-thumbed occurrence book from out of an inner pocket. "Captain Anthony Briggs advertises himself as a retired army officer who does private investigations, for a fancy fee. Leastways, that's how the squire got his direction when he went to London to put in his inquiries about you."

"Makes sense," Christian said. "The squire would be a fool not to take double precautions. So he hired a runner and a private party. Wise of him. I'd do the same."

"Aye. He says yon cove was a decorated officer, invalided out of the service. He don't act sick, nor look it, 'cept for that limp, and a nose that looks like he went a round or two in his days. His hands must be mincemeat, too, he never takes off his gloves. So here we have a fellow who looks like a pugilist but carries himself like an officer, and rides like the devil. So it makes sense that he was one, though there isn't a trace of him or his commission in any of the records I've had my sources sorting though."

"That makes sense, too," Christian mused. "It's probably not his real name. He's obviously down on his luck and has to work for his porridge now, and the upper classes are funny about admitting that. I think my new family minds my history of working as much as my having been a convict. Breaking rocks or making bread, it's all the same to them if you do it with your hands. Gentry don't use their hands for anything but playing cards, collecting rents, and patting horse's rumps and women's arses."

"Well said!" the runner chortled.

"So, have you spoken with him?" Christian asked.

"No. I tried a time or two, here and in the road, but he answers in one word and don't give another. Aye, thankee," he said, pausing to take his pint from the innkeeper. He downed it in long swallows and wiped his mouth with his hand. "Excellent brew! These locals know a thing about the heavy wet, don't they? Well, I'll leave you now, sir. Just thought I'd tell you to watch your back. Yon captain's watching you right enough, and I don't know enough about him to be sure it's all for the squire's sake."

"I'm obliged," Christian said. "And so to save you time spent in lurking, I'll tell you my plan for the rest of the day. I'm going to write letters, then go for a ride to shake out my fidgets. I'll dine here, then to bed. I'll be going to the squire's at noon tomorrow, so you can save your energy until then."

"Thankee," the runner said, rising, touching a finger to his forehead, as if he were a peasant saluting a lord. "Mighty considerate. Damned if I wouldn't like to see you turn out to be an earl, at that."

Christian chuckled and watched him leave. Then he finished his pint, and left the taproom, and the man sitting in the darkest corner.

\* \* \*

Christian put down the pen, and read over what he'd written.

*"I'll keep you informed of events, but it is going as planned. See to events at your end, and all will be well."*

He frowned, then added, *"Don't worry, and don't lose faith in me. I can do this, and I will. My love to you all, C."*

He reached for the box of sand and prepared the sheet of paper for the post. When he was done, he took it and the two other letters he'd written and left his room. He went quickly and quietly down the stair, but when he got to the main room of the inn, instead of going out the front door, he went to the kitchens. He slowly pushed the door open and looked around. As he'd thought, it was quiet because it was the hour when the innkeeper and his wife were napping in their room. The scullery maid dozed in her chair by the hearth; the inn's old yellow dog raised its head and looked at him. Christian didn't disturb either of them as he stole through the room and slipped out the back door.

The ostler was sitting in the sunlight in front of the stable, head back, eyes closed, enjoying the spring sunshine. Christian didn't disturb him either. He quietly saddled his own horse, put his letters in his saddlebag, and led the horse down a back path to a meadow. Only then did he mount, and ride, going over the soft grass so his horse's hoofbeats wouldn't be heard. When the inn was far behind him, he turned toward the main road. Then he galloped.

It took him less than an hour to reach the coast. He

smelled the salt air and smiled when he came to a rise and looked down to the sea. Egremont was indeed a treasure. It not only was worth a king's ransom, it was wonderfully located to boot, a few hours from London, yet near the wide sea.

He rode down to what had been a sleepy fishing village until the recent wars. Now the snug cove had become a thriving port. Naval families lived in the hills overlooking the crescent-shaped harbor, and all sorts of ships visited its busy docks.

Christian tethered his horse by the docks and went in search of the sea captain he'd been told to find. He found him in minutes, gave him the letters and payment, along with a brief, humorously phrased, but serious warning. Then he left him.

With one last regretful look at the sea—*By God*, he thought, *if I win all, I will buy me a place by the sea*—he got back on his horse and rode off. He didn't want to be missing for long. Murchison would be mad as fire as it was to find he'd left the village—that was, if the fellow had believed him in the first place. Still, Christian hadn't sensed the runner at his back. It hardly mattered now. He was sure his letters would be on their way safely, by the next fair tide. He wasn't sure about king and this country, but one thing he would and did stake his life on. There was honor among thieves. At least among the ones he knew.

He rode on at a more leisurely pace, never looking back. And so it was odd that he turned off the main highway halfway back to the inn. He went onto a one-lane path that some farmer had made to separate his pastures. There he stopped, dismounted, tethered his horse by the edge of a fence near sweet new pasture. Then he leaned back against a stile and waited.

The rider he'd been waiting for appeared a few minutes later. The man was dressed like any traveler, but nevertheless looked dangerous because of his size and his crooked, obviously once-broken nose. Even so, he was not unhandsome, although his face was a mass of contradictions. He was still fairly young; but his thick honey brown hair had been streaked with umber by the same foreign sun that had obviously gilded his skin. The nose gave his long face an interesting aspect, saving it from prettiness because his mouth was full, well formed, and oddly sensitive, and his long, sky blue eyes were framed by starry black lashes. But his expression was forbidding, and deadly serious.

He rode straight to Christian and swung down from his horse. Now that he stood instead of being hunched over a table at the inn as he usually was, it could be seen that his shoulders were wide and straight.

He flung his reins over the fence as Christian had done and offered Christian his gloved hand. "When did you see me?" he asked, as they clasped hands.

"As soon as you left the inn," Christian said.

"Liar," the man said, a crooked grin creasing his face. "You didn't catch wind of me until I left the docks just now, but let it be if it makes you feel better to pretend you know it all."

"But I do," Christian said comfortably. "How are you? How are you faring?"

The man smiled widely, transforming his face, making him look raffishly attractive. "I haven't found anything new, or I'd have got word to you. The squire's still throwing money to the winds trying to pin you down. Murchison's a canny one, and honest, after his fashion—or at least honest as any damned redbreast can ever be. As for me? I've no worries."

"You never do," Christian said. "That's what worries me. So watch your own back, you don't have to be concerned about me."

"I shouldn't worry about you, and that's a fact," the man agreed. "You've got them scrambling. And what a little honey you found yourself right out of the gate, to while away the time until you take all! Pretty as she can hold together, and smart, but not smart enough, poor lass. Like all the others, she's ready to fall. You can see it in her big brown eyes when she looks at you." He clasped his gloved hands to his heart in a mockery of an enraptured girl. "I don't know how you do it." He shook his head.

"I'm not doing it," Christian said blandly. "She's Jonathan Lowell's sister. She sees me as a link to her brother; there's where the warmth comes in."

"Oh, I know her name. But I don't doubt that warmth is in other places, too, if you'd a mind to find them," the other man said easily. "It would be a waste if you didn't. Seems to me she's just full of warm places. Wait, Lowell—Jonathan Low . . ." His eyes lit. "Now I have it! He was the best friend from the past. From the home village. Where's the boy?"

"Dead, in the wars," Christian said simply.

"Ah, it makes sense. So that's why the squire sent for her."

"She's also Sophie Wiley's cousin. Making it easier for them to send for her."

"Sophie, now there's a pretty piece," the other man said with approval. "The kind I particularly like, as sly as she's delicious. The kind you have to disarm in more ways than one. I ran into her, although, sadly, not literally, the other day when I made my report on you to her father. He introduced me, though you could see he didn't want to. He may believe I'm respectable as houses, and a retired army officer to boot, but hired help is hired help, after all. Still, she eyed me like I was a roast pig on a platter and greeted me as though that's what she wanted for dinner."

"She's engaged," Christian said.

"But I'd wager that engagement is a ball in play now that there's a chance her beau might not get the title. Don't worry, I know her kind. Since I have nothing she knows about, I'm only for the eyeing. I will survive. Mind, the Lowell chit's a treat for the eyes, too, and no airs or graces, neither. It's too bad for me that she only sees you. I wouldn't toss her out of my blanket. Nor should you. Not only because of the sport; your being warm with her would be a fine way to convince the world of who you are."

"I'll never convince them. I can only prove it in a court of law. I will, then be damned to the lot of them."

"And Mistress Lowell?" the other man persisted, watching him closely.

"We'll see. Now," Christian said, "enough about wenches."

"There's never enough about wenches," the other man said plaintively.

Christian smiled in spite of himself but went on, "We don't have that much time. Where are you staying? I thought I'd swallow my tongue when I first saw you sucking up the innkeeper's brew calm as you please at the White Hart. I never guessed you'd come so close. And bowing to the beauty at the squire's house? You're a mad thing, and one day it will be the death of you."

"Hasn't been yet, and I'm not counting on it," the man said placidly. "I'd been a bit more cautious at first. I had let a room at a cottage, about a mile from the White Hart. It was a snug spot, and a snug dimpled little widow my landlady was, too. Put your eyebrows down. She was too old for sport and too young for me to tarry without danger of making a mistake I'd have had to pay for with my single life. I'm highly eligible, doncha know," he said mockingly, raising his broken nose in the air. "I put it about that I was a traveling peddler, hanging about waiting to see if there was any custom for me when the new owner came to Egremont."

Christian laughed. "It may have done you good with your widow, but Murchison told me you are Anthony Briggs, late of His Majesty's army, now pursuing private investigations. He knows the squire hired you."

"Investigations of a private and delicate nature, I'll have you know," the other man said prissily, then grinned. "Aye, he's a knowing one. So, when I found out I was bubbled, I reckoned I might as well take a room at the White Hart. Anyway, my widow was tempting, and you know I'm no good with temptation."

"You're good enough if you have to be. But, 'Anthony' now, is it?" Christian mused.

"*Captain* Anthony Briggs, if you please, sir. Good, isn't it?"

"Yes," Christian said. "The truth is it feels good just knowing you're near. But we can't stand here much longer. As it is, I'll tell Murchison you and I spoke, because for all I know he's watching us right now. I'll tell him you came too close, and I lured you in and confronted you."

Anthony ducked, and came up with his fists in classic boxer's stance. "Want to pot me one, to show you meant business?"

Christian put up his own fists, then straightened, and smiled. "God, it's good to see you! Stay safe, and watch yourself. But let me know if you find out anything. I'd like to have this settled in a matter of weeks, and I begin to think I can."

Anthony straightened and gazed at him seriously. "And this Hammond cove? He seems right enough. But you want me to pursue that line of inquiry too?"

"No," Christian said. "I think he's what he appears to be—or at least, as much as I ever let myself believe anyone is. He came here thinking he'd get Egremont, but I don't think he'd ever make a move to be sure of it. Though, God knows, he's got enough good reason. Now he's got nothing but a fiancée who could spit tacks because he may be cut out of the succession, and prospective in-laws who are looking at him twice because he doesn't look so fine without that title and estate. Anyhow, he appears to be lumbered with honor. Go now. Stay at hand. The game is sure to change soon, and I feel better for knowing you're nearby."

The tall man nodded. "As for me, I don't sleep unless I know where you're sleeping, and who's nearby." He hesitated. "You sent letters today. Did you get any or hear anything?"

Christian shook his head, momentarily looking troubled. "Nothing. So we still have time. I hope to have it all done before anyone hears a word. Then it will be too late." He swung up on his horse. "Mount up and go first. I'll wait at a distance and watch from afar."

"And who will watch you?"

Christian threw back his head and laughed with genuine humor. "Why, everyone, old son. I thought you knew that. Everyone."

Christian waited until the tall rider left the lane and watched him ride off into the distance. Only then did he steer his mount back to the highway, and when he reached it, he rode slowly, lost in thought.

It was all going according to plan, as he'd said. But he hadn't told Anthony all.

Such schemes always invited the unexpected, he supposed. That didn't mean he had to like it. He hadn't expected Julianne Lowell. The problem was that he already liked her too much, and that complicated things. Women always did. In this case it wasn't just her looks. He was used to pretty women because women liked him. That had been one consolation in his life, child and man. Women civilized a man, his father had always said, and he'd found it true. Even the uncivilized ones did that. There was something about a feminine influence, however malign, that made a man feel more complete. His smile was crooked as he realized he'd known more malign females than good ones, but had cause to appreciate them even so.

On balance, he'd been lucky, he supposed. He'd lost his mother early on and had always longed for a female influence in his life, and had always gotten what he'd longed for, even in the most unlikely places and circumstances. Other men thought it was because of his looks or wiles. But he thought it was because women could tell when you really enjoyed their company. He did. A man could lie about almost anything and be believed if he was skillful enough, but never about how he felt about women. That was something that was part of a man, it showed no matter how he concealed his thoughts. He ought to know, he was very good at concealing his own, sometimes, even from himself. But not today. Because the thought of Julianne Lowell troubled him.

She fascinated him. With all the women he'd known, he hadn't known many like her. Sophie was pretty and feminine, but manners and station aside, he could understand her because he'd met so many like her. Julianne was different. She acted like a lady, yet spoke to a man as directly as another man, which he could never forget she was not. It was a beguiling combination. The only women he'd known to act that way had been those who had absolutely no interest in sex with men, either because of their advanced age or unusual personal preferences. But though she was straightforward as a man, Julianne obviously fancied men, and himself, in particular.

It showed in small ways. She couldn't keep from glancing at him under her eyelashes. She ducked her head and fluttered her eyes to avoid looking directly into his when he looked back at her. It wasn't flirtation. He knew what that was. This was more exciting because she couldn't seem to help it.

Lord, he'd like to make love to her. He could have her, he thought, if he tried. He doubted she knew it. He had, from the moment they'd met. The thought kept nibbling at him. He thought her face was lovely, with those brown-gold eyes and that adorable mouth. He absolutely loved the look of her body; she really did have exceptionally fine breasts. He didn't think she knew it either, and while that made his conscience twinge, it did even more to his physical parts. Though it was true he didn't have much experience with respectable women, females were females, after all. He doubted he'd have much trouble bedding her. That wasn't arrogance. It was simply his experience.

She was also smart, which he appreciated. And lonely, which drew him. And she trusted him, without knowing if she should. There was the problem.

He did possess a sense of honor. Much of it learned in dark places at great cost, yet nevertheless, a kind of honor. He knew it was wrong to corrupt the pure, not because the Bible said it, but because innocence of mind or body was such a rare and fragile thing in his world.

Nor had women been included in his plans. But then she'd come on the scene. He hadn't been able to ignore her since.

The horse slowed to a walk, and he didn't notice.

Finally, Christian blinked and looked around. Had he lost his mind? He'd been riding without looking or thinking of where he was. What folly! Hadn't he learned that if a man relied only on his five senses, he'd be butcher's meat by evening? Yet that was just what he'd been doing.

He was worried about Julianne Lowell? How could he be sure she could even be trusted? She'd been sent to spy on him, she'd even admitted it. How much of what he saw of her was real, and how much was what she wanted him to see? Was he even certain *she* was who she claimed to be? He couldn't trust anyone here. How could he have forgotten that? Madness.

But a fellow could certainly have a woman without giving her his trust. Whatever his own preferences, most men he knew did just that. He could find pleasure so long as he remembered to keep his head and watch his back. That was his first priority. He must never forget that, or his mission, or his present danger, ever again.

Christian spurred his horse to a gallop to clear his head and get back to the White Hart faster. The future would come, and if he could have Julianne Lowell as it approached, that would be fine. If not? He wouldn't worry about that. It was enough that he looked forward to seeing her tomorrow. He'd see what happened after that. He was tired of looking back. It was time to move on.

# Chapter 8

"I'm not sure I approve this," Hammond said, eyeing Julianne's pretty gown and the prettier blush on her cheeks as she tied her bonnet strings.

"I appreciate your concern, Hammond. But there's nothing to disapprove of." Julianne closed her lips before she could add, "and it's none of your business."

"Nothing to disapprove of?" Hammond asked. "There's a great deal, I think. You're doing something that's not done: going off by yourself with a strange man. A man, moreover, who claims to be someone we can't prove he is. And you say it's nothing?"

*And it's your fiancée who'd kill me if I didn't go,* Julianne thought, *not to mention the fact that I'd want to kill anyone who made me stay home now, after I've nerved myself up to go all night.*

"He's hardly likely to do anything disrespectful if he's eager to prove he is who he claims to be," she said. "And how can I find out anything if I can't talk with him?" She hoped she didn't ruin this perfectly reasonable statement with a giggle. But giggles kept bubbling up in her throat, and it was all she could do

116

to hold them in. She actually felt she was filling with fizzy air. It was ridiculous, and lovely, and a joy to feel this way after all her sorrows. Whatever else the advent of Christian Sauvage meant, she hadn't felt this vividly alive for years.

Christian was taking her to see Egremont again today, and he promised he'd have a hamper of food for lunch. The sun was shining, and they'd picnic at Egremont, he said. She hadn't done anything like it since she and Jon had been children. The prospect made her feel like a child again. The idea of being alone with Christian made her feel her own age—and excited to her eyebrows.

But Hammond was scowling as if he could see all the secret thoughts and longings she had tied up in today's excursion, including the ones she hadn't even admitted to herself yet.

"I know you must meet with him," he said. "And I don't think he'll attack you. But I do think he knows how to charm and manipulate, and I don't think you're safe against that." His honest face looked deeply troubled. "I argued against your going today, Julianne. I only ask you to remember, that as *I* am the one most directly involved in this, I don't want you to sacrifice your comfort or safety in the push to discover the truth. We have other means of doing that, so you don't have to go with him, and certainly not alone."

"But everyone felt he'd be less guarded without a maidservant hanging on his every word," she said. "Servants do listen, you know. They can hardly help it. I know the upper classes think they're furniture, but they're not, and that's not how I was brought up to think either. I wouldn't feel comfortable making some poor girl sit there and pretend she was a tree while I talked and joked with someone. So this way he'll feel freer, and who knows what will be said?" Or done? she thought on a spike of excitement that made her blush even more rosily.

Hammond noticed, or at least, he frowned again. "Well, if anything happens to upset you," he said, "I want you to promise me you'll come back at once. You may not have a maidservant with you, but I'm sending a groom, and he'll be within calling distance at all times. *That*, I insisted on," he added with emphasis.

Her spirits fizzled, just a little, but she silently conceded he was right. It was one thing to be daring, another to be foolish.

"Would you stop plaguing her?" Sophie asked as she came into the hall.

"I'm merely ensuring her safety," Hammond said stiffly.

"No, you were trying to change her mind. I thought we were done with that."

"*We* were done with it," he said pointedly. "But *I* had never discussed it with *her*."

Julianne frowned. They sounded like a much-married couple now, not like engaged lovers. When she'd come here Sophie and Hammond had been constantly smiling on each other. Now they were glaring and had obviously been squabbling. Julianne wondered how much of this particular quarrel had to do with her fate, and how much the growing possibility that Hammond might lose Egremont. If he did, he might lose Sophie, too. Julianne didn't know if Hammond thought, as she herself began to suspect, that Sophie's love for him was dependent on his future fortunes.

As if to illustrate that, Sophie leapt to battle. "Oh, and so I suppose you're willing to give up Egremont and the title if it will spare my cousin some discomfort? Lud, Ham, I didn't think you such a fool."

Julianne gasped.

Hammond's face froze, and his ears turned brick red.

Sophie realized she'd gone too far. "I'm sorry, Ham," she said, laying her hand on his sleeve. "I didn't mean to snap at you. This whole thing has turned me topsy-turvy. Just the other week we were picking out new silks for the wall of the grand salon at Egremont, and now we don't know if we'll have to live"—her voice broke—"in rented rooms, instead!"

"I'm not as fabulously wealthy as the earl of Egremont," Hammond said with awful dignity, "but I'd hardly ask you to live in rented rooms, Sophie. I think, though, that it would be best if we talked about that future now. If you'll excuse us, Julianne?"

"I was just leaving," Julianne said, and fairly flew out the door. It wasn't the thing to wait for a gentleman caller on the doorstep, but she'd rather wait in boiling rain than stay inside a minute longer.

She was standing lost in thought, wondering if she'd witnessed her cousin's engagement breaking up, as Christian's sporty curricle came rattling over the pebbles in the drive.

He stopped the curricle and looked down, his head

to one side. "Is something wrong?" he asked. "You're still coming today, aren't you?"

"Oh. Yes," she said, startled, glad she'd had something to occupy her mind, because he looked so fine she thought she might have been overwhelmed if she'd been watching for him. He wore a high beaver hat and a many-caped greatcoat. He wore it open to show his dark brown jacket and mustard waistcoat. She could hardly help noticing his tightly fitted buff breeches and high, shining, brown boots. He looked dashing, fashionable, unapproachable, and utterly desirable.

"But there's a problem?" he asked, looking at her intently.

"Family business," she said on a weak laugh. "You know the sort of thing."

"I can guess," he said grimly. "They've ordered you to find me out by sunset, or you're out on your ear?"

"Lord, no!" She reluctantly smiled. "Shall I, do you think? I mean, find you out?"

"Oh, yes," he said, matching her smile. "I hope so."

She gave him a tremulous smile because she couldn't manage a more confident one, picked up her head, and the hem of her skirt, and accepted his hand as she put a foot on the wheel and stepped up to the high driver's seat where he sat.

It was a soft day, and if the sun wasn't brilliant, it was at least out, which was rare for an April day in England. The pinks and yellows of blooms from the towering shrubs that lined the drive to Egremont looked like those in a pastel painting. As they approached, the manor seemed suddenly to appear from out of the mists.

"It's magnificent." Julianne sighed, taking a deep breath of the flower-scented air. "But that's such a cliché, isn't it?"

"Because it's only true," he said. He slowed the horses to a stand so they could look at the mansion on the hill. "God! I mean, Gad! Pardon me, I'm still trying to remember how to speak to a lady. But I can't get used to the fact that this place will be mine. Just look at it! I never knew it existed, except in a distant sense, the way you know about an old relative you never expect to meet again. It was never part of our plans, certainly not when we lived here, of course not when we were thrown out of England. Not even when we won free. When I think of how many people had to die to make it mine, I'm boggled. The coincidences are as staggering as the place is overwhelming. But I'll take it, and gladly. Wouldn't you?"

"Of course," she said, and dared a look at him. She'd been gazing at the scenery all the way here, but now felt comfortable enough to look at him while they spoke. When she'd first tried, she'd felt her stomach grow hollow, and she got dizzy. She still felt that when she looked at him, but now she rather liked the experience. She liked it so much she had to remind herself that she had work to do. "Does it bother you that so many of your relatives perished so . . . precipitously?"

He laughed, and shook the reins to get his team moving again. "You mean do I think there's a curse on the place? No, and damned . . . deviled if it would matter to me if there was. There were curses and spells on every inch of the land I've come from—or so the natives say. They said the whole place was sacred, wrapped up in a story in the dreams of their god. Sometimes I believed it. And I lived with enough ghosts at Newgate . . ."

He frowned. "No, I'll take Egremont, curses and all. The only thing that bothers me is that my relatives don't believe in curses. They think my father and I had something to do with the vanishing earls, though damn . . . deviled if I know how they think we could have done it in chains, from halfway round the world."

"Still," Julianne persisted, "you must admit it was strange the way so many of the previous earls met accidents. By the way, speaking of which, how long, do you think," she said carefully, "before the matter of the succession is finally resolved?"

He gave her a sparkling look that made her stomach feel as though she stood on the edge of a steep precipice. "Back to work, eh," he asked. He laughed at her expression of guilt.

"Tipped your hand, luv," he explained. "Three's a number that can't be denied. 'By the way.' 'Speaking of which,' and 'Do you think,' is two too many. If you put that many qualifiers in front of a question, you're telling me exactly how nervous asking it makes you. Don't look ashamed! That's a good thing. Shows you're not a practiced sharper. I just came from a place filled with practiced—and convicted—Captain Sharps, so I know."

He'd grown more careless in his speech, she realized. His accents remained the same, but the longer they were together the more slang and cant he used. She liked it. That showed he was able to be a perfect gentleman as well as a casual friend, the way he'd been when they'd been young . . . No. He wasn't that, either.

"Don't worry," he said gently, watching her. "You'll reckon it out sooner than later, trust me. A great many things happened to me, Little Jewel, I'm not the boy I was. But I'm not a bad man, either."

There was nothing she could say.

They rode down the lane to the lake.

The lake was so perfect in its design that Julianne was sure it was artificial. Artful plantings of trees and shrubs along its banks enhanced it, making it lovely at every angle it could be viewed from.

They drove to a huge building that stood on a grassy slope overlooking the lake. It was a copy of the Parthenon, a round marble rotunda with high white columns, open on all sides. A wide tier of stairs fanned out from its entrance. Christian stopped the phaeton, tied the horses to a plinth so they could crop the grass, took down a hamper, and held out a hand to help Julianne down. She alit and looked around. The building nestled in the embrace of enormous shrubs on three sides, so its primary view was its own shimmering reflection in the lake.

It was quiet except for birdsong and the sound of the slow hoofbeats of the groom who had followed them. As they watched, the groom tethered his horse in a copse of trees a few hundred feet away, within earshot, if not easy reach. He ambled over to a tree and sat on the ground beneath it, very ostensibly looking toward the lake and not at the couple who were walking up to the Parthenon.

Christian hoisted the picnic basket. "I appreciate your cousins' trust in me."

"It's only that they didn't want to send me alone," she said, embarrassed because they hadn't trusted him, as well as because she knew they shouldn't have sent her if they didn't, and she oughtn't to have come knowing that.

"I know," he said. "It wasn't irony. I appreciate the fact that they trusted me enough not to send a maid-servant to hover over us."

She didn't know if he was being sarcastic or not. That was one problem with this man, she could never tell if he was serious or teasing. That was one of the things that made her begin to believe he was Christian. It would be the sort of joke he and Jon always played on words, and people.

"I could have had a footman along to lug this," he went on, raising the hamper, "and to wait on us. But I didn't want to make it a formal luncheon. No, the truth is that I did. I wanted to entertain you at Egremont in high style. They won't let me. Only the staff lives there now, and they're the only ones who can dine there, too. Isn't that absurd? The servants live like earls, and the earl dines out of doors. I've eaten in worse places, but I apologize to you." He waved off her assurances that she didn't mind. "We'll make do in the summerhouse, if you don't mind, as the butler suggested. Summerhouse?" he murmured, looking at the false Parthenon. "It looks big enough to house three families."

They took the shallow stairs and entered the rotunda. Christian stopped in the chill shade of the place and looked around the bare stone building. "Brrr," he said. "Looks more like it's meant to house three dead families. The thing feels like a mausoleum."

She giggled. "It looks like one, too."

"This is no place to have luncheon," he said with a frown. "Maybe in the summer, when it's so hot the lake starts boiling, but not now."

She looked at him curiously. "It never gets that hot here."

"Ah, caught out the imposter, have you?" he said with a wry grin. "Afraid not. It's just that I forgot. It's hard to remember I'm no longer in a land where you either bake off your ears in summer or freeze off your . . . extremities in winter. Funny, how you cling to memories of little things, like happy moments and favorite dogs, but forget the main events." He frowned. "We can't stay here, it's bloo . . . blasted chilly. Are you game to have luncheon in the sunshine, on the grass? There's a blanket in the curricle, we can dine overlooking the lake."

"I'd like that," she agreed.

In the end, he found a patch of sunlight on the close-cropped grass, near a thick stand of rhododendrons to the side of the summerhouse. He spread the blanket, and they sat. She noticed, not without amusement and a delicious sense of danger, that they sat in a place where the groom wouldn't see them unless they—or he—stood up.

The innkeeper of the White Hart had done them proud. They lunched on pâté, cold chicken, sliced beef, cheese, bread, and little tarts, and had a bottle of a fruity red wine to drink. All the while they lunched, they chatted. He was happy to tell her about the wonders of the antipodes. He spoke of little green birds and animals with pockets again, adding some bits about opals, gold, and pearls. But he never mentioned prisons or chains, punishments or other prisoners.

She sat upright with her legs tucked under, her skirts carefully arranged, and listened with sinking spirits. She'd read much the same about the antipodes in the *Gentlemen's Magazine*s she'd found in the squire's library, and heard nothing she hadn't read about. Apart from the fact that she had no more proof that he was really Christian Sauvage, she began now to wonder if he'd even really been on the other side of the world. Nor did he say anything more about their common past.

"You're very quiet," he finally said. "Haven't given you much chance to talk, have I? And how are you to know who I am if I don't talk about the past you remember?"

She blushed.

"No, don't be embarrassed," he said. "Of course you want to know. And I want you to. You probably won't believe this, but it isn't so much about Egremont now as it is about you and whether you believe me."

That she did not believe. Not when they sat on the grounds of one of the finest estates in England. Not, when no matter how he protested, he knew that her opinion might have even some small bearing on his ownership of it. But she said nothing. This was not about her desires, she had to remind herself. This was about discovering who he was.

He sat on the blanket, one leg extended, one knee bent, his arm resting on that knee, the wineglass dangling from his hand as he studied her. His eyes were clear and transparent as the shimmering lake as he looked at her. "Julianne," he said on a sigh. "Shall I tell you about the time we flew the kite and you wailed for hours because the wind blew the string out of your hands and whipped it away over the treetops? Or the time Jon and I decided to try to make invisible ink and ended up making such a mess I was forbidden your house for a week? Or the time Jon fell down the abandoned well and we both nearly had heart spasms, until his head popped up and we realized it was boarded over and he was standing on wood and not water? And laughing like a madman, because he'd crouched down in order to terrify us?"

"I don't remember the invisible ink."

"And so then I'm a liar?"

She gazed at him, all her hope in her eyes. "I don't think so. I don't want you to be. Oh, what am I to think? How I wish Jon was here; he'd know in a minute."

"Would he? It was a long time ago, and I've changed. It isn't only the years, it's the quality of those years." He looked at her steadily. "You remember my father?"

"Oh yes," she said eagerly. "He was such a nice man, always working at books and balances, but he always had time to talk to us."

"I remember something else now," he said. "He once said you were like a kite yourself, in that you were always attached to Jon's sleeve and trailing after him. Do you remember that?"

"No," she said in frustration. "But you said it didn't matter what I remembered. You said no one would care."

"I never said that," he said seriously. "I only said it wouldn't matter in a court of law. It matters to me."

"Why?" She waited for him to say it was because she was beautiful or some such, not because she wanted to hear it said, but because that was the sort of thing a deceiver would say.

"Because you bring back good memories, Julianne. Because you and Jonathan and the life we led was a pure, untouched part of my life, one of the few parts of my youth that I want to remember. And also because," he said with a gentle smile, "you are a beautiful woman, and I can't resist wanting to please you."

That wasn't quite what she'd feared he'd say. But the flattery was close enough, and so that counted against him. She gazed at him and wished she could read his mind.

He studied her in return, then suddenly leaned in toward her, and never touching her otherwise, laid his lips on hers. Only that. But she sat very still, and felt her heart leap up. His mouth was firm, yet soft and sweet. It only lasted a moment. Then he leaned back and looked at her.

She couldn't think of what to say, or do. But she licked her lips because it had been so very sweet.

He carefully put his wineglass down, rose on his

knees, pulled her into his arms, and kissed her, thoroughly.

She gasped, and he used the moment to slide his tongue past her lips. That made her gasp again, and she heard him chuckle, and he did it again. She'd been kissed before, of course, but none of her beaux had ever taken such liberties. At least not for very long, because she hadn't liked those kinds of kisses. They were wet, crude, and unpleasant. Or so she'd thought, before. But this? This was an invitation, not an onslaught, a tentative inquiry. And even more, everything about this man felt good, even the texture of his tongue.

The kiss felt odd to her at first. But then she grew involved, and soon her pulses beat in time to the rhythm he set as his tongue moved in her mouth. She leaned in toward him. He tasted of good red wine, dark and sweet. He held her gently, yet even closer. She relaxed against him, marveling in how his lean body felt so wonderfully warm. Now he wasn't remote or reserved, she could feel his heart hammering under her opened hand. Unlike other men she'd kissed, he neither hesitated nor forced her to more. She felt safe and yet daring, as though she were greeting an old friend, yet dazzled by the feelings this amazing stranger brought to her.

He finally pulled back only so far as to spread soft light kisses along her cheekbone until he reached her ear and whispered, a smile in his voice, "Come, Little Jewel, do the same for me." Then he kissed her again, and without thinking, without allowing herself to think, she slipped her tongue into his warm, opened mouth, and felt the warmth of his gratified sigh.

His hands spread against the sides of her face to angle her for his kisses as he deepened them. He caressed her back and her shoulders. His hand moved to her breast, and cupped her. He stroked an aroused nipple to make it peak the more, as his mouth went to her neck, to her collarbone, and traveled on. She clung to his shoulders and shivered. She caught her breath. And then suddenly, it all felt much too good.

She pulled back, astonished and embarrassed in equal measure.

He let her go at once, but frowned. "What is it?"

"You . . . I—we . . . should not."

"Why?" he asked.

"You know."

"But I don't."

"I can't," she managed to say, looking anywhere but at him.

"But why not?"

She stared at him, because what he asked was too bizarre. "Because," she finally said when it appeared he wasn't joking, "what we did could lead to more."

He smiled, and drew closer again. "Well, yes. That's the point."

She put up a hand, her amazement winning back her sanity. "I don't know what they do in the antipodes," she said, "but surely you remember that a well-bred woman doesn't do such things with a man unless they're promised to each other—and I don't expect that!" she added quickly.

"In fact," she said, jumping to her feet, shaking out her skirt and looking around anxiously, "doing *that* with a woman of any reputation would ensure your

having to marry her. Even doing less. Even just kissing. *What was I thinking?*" she asked, her hand going
to her forehead. "Lord, I'm lucky that groom is doz-
ing with his eyes open."

He'd gotten to his feet when she did. "Wouldn't do
him good if he weren't; he can't see us from here; I
made sure of it," he said calmly. "I know I've con-
sorted with some irregular females, but you mean to
say a fellow can't cuddle with a respectable female
here in England? That can't be so. It's true that we're
freer where I come from, but men and women can't
be that different."

"Well, they are," she said in a less certain voice.
Because she knew very well that many girls at home
married and delivered perfectly fine fat babies five or
six months later. But they were local girls of no particular degree. She'd heard all the gossip about the
wild ways of the *ton*, too. But that was a rackety set,
and she knew who she was. Or at least, she thought
she had. She didn't know what to say, then remembered she was an enlightened female and not missish. And besides, how could she be after what they'd
done?

"If women do such things in the antipodes," she
asked, hardly believing she was having this discussion—any more than she believed she'd allowed what
just happened, "what do they do if they conceive
from such . . . doings?"

"Then the fellow would be responsible and do the
right thing, I'd hope."

She eyed him narrowly, as her sense returned.
"And you'd risk that? You hardly know me. But you

were raised here, you know our rules and morals. You must be joking." Her eyes widened. "Or did you think my morals were light because I came here by myself? Or that I'd do anything to discover who you were? They aren't, and I'm not, and I wouldn't!" she said, feeling chilled to the soul. She stood tall as she could. "I agreed to tell my cousins who I thought you were. I also thought I could rediscover a piece of my past. But I have no interest other than finding the truth. I'm sorry if I gave you the wrong impression."

He reached out to take her hand. She stepped back. He frowned. "I wasn't joking," he said. "And yes, I was taught those morals, too. But I was a boy when I left your world, if not this island, and I forgot. Or, at least, I'd hoped what I was taught was only like the fairy stories they also told me then: fanciful tales just for children, to shape their character, not necessarily the truth. The world they sent me to was very different. That made me think what I'd been taught wasn't true. I see my mistake. I'm sorry if I offended you."

He bowed his head. When he raised it his eyes glittered. "If I'm supposed to marry you now, Julianne, and you want me to, I'm at your service."

"Oh no!" she gasped. "In the first place you'd think I was after your fortune, and in the first place I don't know you."

He smiled a more natural smile. "That's two first places. I didn't mean to addle you. Or if I did, not that way. And I want to know you better, too. So if you won't have me, please forgive me, and let's let it be. And then, too, there's my wife and three children's feelings to consider."

She smiled. Her smiled faltered. She finally just shook her head. "I don't know what to make of you."

"That's why you're here isn't it?" he asked blandly. He began plucking up their picnic things. "It will all come clear in time, Little Jewel." He paused and looked up at her. "You will give me that time?"

She only nodded, bent, and helped him gather plates and cutlery. She didn't trust herself to speak. Christian had always liked to tease, but surely not about such an important thing? What would he have done if she were a stickler for propriety? Or if she'd been trying to trap a husband? He'd taken a huge gamble. Or had he? He didn't have Egremont and its treasures, yet. For all he claimed, he mightn't have two pennies to rub together. He might actually be married, after all.

She'd never done as much with any man, and never anything so intimate so quickly, willingly, unthinkingly. But it had been so easy and felt so right. It had been as natural as laughing with him. She bit her lip. Now, at last, she was worried. Whoever this man was, she liked him much too much, and soon it might not matter who he was, as long as he was with her.

# Chapter 9

Julianne sat silently, her hands clasped in her lap. She'd held them like that since she'd realized they were shaking, and they had been since she'd climbed into Christian's curricle for the ride back to the squire's house. She couldn't believe her behavior with him. She'd acted like a positive *trull*, she thought in despair. What had come over her? Well, she thought, not knowing whether to laugh or cry, she certainly knew what almost came over her! And he was sitting right next to her, occasionally glancing her way.

Drat and blast the man. She wasn't loose, and he'd made her forget that with just a kiss. He was an enigma and a problem, and she wished she could just lean over and kiss him again. Worst of all, now she knew she couldn't trust herself any more than she could him. She stole a glance at that smooth hard face, and yet felt a thrill, remembering how warm he'd felt, how impassioned he'd been.

He hadn't said a word to her for miles, had let her maintain her silence, but he saw her steal that glance at him.

"So, you'll never talk to me again?" he asked pleasantly. "That will make your inquiries difficult, I think. Or do you plan to submit them in writing?"

She tried not to laugh.

"Julianne, I said I'm sorry if I offended, but it was nothing, really. I don't mean it was nothing," he said quickly. "It was something delicious. But it was only a kiss or two. What was it after all, but a few minutes of pleasure? No harm done, no risks run, nothing to thunder from the pulpit about, no worries, really, unless you insist on it. Do you?"

"Of course not! But I shocked myself. Beyond that . . ." She hesitated, then decided to be absolutely candid with him, "I wonder what you think of me."

He checked, and looked at her searchingly. Then he smiled. "I think you're delightful, but couldn't you tell? Don't throw anything at me. I mean that in other ways, too."

"It's just that I felt like you were an old friend," she said, her head to the side as she tried to puzzle it out aloud. "I suppose that made me more comfortable with you, the way we used to be. I forgot we were grown-up. But I discovered that soon enough," she said ruefully.

"Ah. So you recognize me, at last?"

She shook her head, and stared at her fingers. "Sometimes I do. Sometimes I don't. You know things I've forgotten, and when you speak of them I remember. You don't know other things I think you ought to. I wish I knew." She turned and stared at him, frowning fiercely. "If you'd come back to England just as Christian Sauvage, home to show the world how well you'd done for yourself, I wouldn't have doubted you. But there's a fortune and a title awaiting the heir to Egremont. That changes everything."

He nodded, his eyes serious. "I see. But I wouldn't have come home if I hadn't heard of the inheritance. And don't you think the fact that you can tell me this means you trust me just a little?"

She laughed bitterly. "Oh, but the problem is that I trust you more than that."

He didn't laugh in return. "We'll have to do something about that," he murmured.

"I think," she said, "you've done enough for a while. I think it would be better to let things go on by themselves for a space."

"But you're willing to keep seeing me?"

She looked out at the road ahead and nodded.

"Good. Then don't let them send you to me like a . . ." He paused, and changed what he was going to say. "Make sure they treat you with respect, Julianne. As they would if it was your cousin they were sending to me. Let them surround you with chaperones, or with however many they'd send along with a proper English lady. You deserve no less. And don't worry about me," he added, chuckling, "I love a challenge."

Her head snapped back. "Oh, you're saying you won't treat me with respect unless they do?"

"I have enough trouble with temptation as it is. I told you, I'm never sure just what you consider proper over here. *Now* what have I said to upset you?"

"Are you saying that to win my confidence or do you mean it? Oh, blast! Even if you're joking, there's doubt! Do you see what I mean?"

"I do. But think of this. Would you even tell me your fears if you didn't trust me on some deeper level?"

She looked down at her hands again. "To tell you the truth, Christian, I no longer know what I do!"

"Good," he said. "That's a beginning."

They didn't speak again until he drove up to the front of the squire's house. He leapt to the ground to help her down and paused for a moment in the drive, holding her hand. "Tomorrow?" he asked.

"I'd like to," she said, "but maybe that's too soon?"

"I'd think the more you see me the happier your cousins will be," he said. "I'd wish the more you see me the happier you would be. Tomorrow then?"

She nodded. Then she grinned. "Better bring a bigger carriage. I'll have a legion of maids with me."

He smiled. "Better bring an appetite, too. I thought we'd lunch at the inn this time. Tomorrow, then," he said, and climbed back up to the driver's seat, took the reins in one hand, saluted her with the other, and drove away.

She watched until he was gone, then turned to go into the house, knowing there were questions she'd have to answer but not particularly caring what her cousins thought right now. She knew what Christian was, if not who he was. He was a man who made her realize she was alive again.

He might well be a liar and a cheat. But if he really were Christian Sauvage, he'd soon be an earl. And so then it was altogether possible, actually probable, that once he achieved his goal he'd give her a smile and maybe a kiss on the cheek, then go find himself a rich, titled woman to marry. If, she corrected herself, he didn't already have that wife and three children, after all. But at this point, she told herself, it didn't matter.

What mattered was that his presence was a challenge and a dare. She had to get to the heart of it, even if it took her own heart from her again. Because whatever else the man who would be Christian tried to make her remember, he'd reminded her what life was all about. Soon enough she'd be home again. Once the mystery of the heir to Egremont was settled, she didn't think anyone would have a use for her here. Her cousin certainly wouldn't, the fiction of their friendship was already wearing thin. And if Christian turned out to be a cheat, he'd either be gone in the dead of night or carted off in chains. She didn't want to think about that. If he was the earl, he'd remain a friend, she did believe that. But she couldn't see him pursuing their friendship if she left.

When she returned home, she thought, she might accept her parents' offer of a trip to London, or to Brighton, or somewhere where she might meet eligible men. She hadn't known enough of them. She might only be a gentleman farmer's daughter; but like that bespelled princess she'd heard about at bedtimes when she'd been a child, she felt she'd been aroused from a deep sleep by a kiss. It was time for her to find someone to live her new life with, someone to love.

For now, she was being courted. Even if it might be for all the wrong reasons, it was opening her eyes to her opportunities again. If she were smart enough to keep remembering it, she'd fare well. If not? She shivered with remembered pleasure, laced with thrilling fear. Well, she'd just have to make sure she was that smart. But she'd start living again, that she vowed.

Julianne was humming under her breath as the footman opened the door for her, and it was all she could do not to waltz into the house.

"Here she is!" squire's wife said, rising as Julianne entered the salon.

Her cousins were all there, as were Hammond and a tall, elderly gentleman, who got to his feet with difficulty, leaning heavily on his walking stick.

"Sir," Hammond said, "this is Sophie's cousin Julianne Lowell, the young woman who grew up with Christian Sauvage, as we told you. Julianne, here is my cousin, Sir Maurice, the baronet Sauvage. His title was awarded by the king, for services rendered," he added with pride.

"Merely for my help in matters of acquisition," the old gentleman said in a surprisingly strong voice. "I have a certain expertise with antique paintings, porcelain, pottery, and other items of virtue. He appreciated my help in their selection."

"The baronet honors us with his visit," the squire's wife added with a trill of excitement. "He seldom leaves his home. It is one of the foremost castles in the north, filled with treasures remarked upon in every guidebook on the region."

"My late wife's contribution to the family," the baronet said with a dismissive wave of a hand. "It is true that I seldom travel, or at least have not in the

past few years, but I do when I must. My concern for
the family and its honor outweighed my creature
comforts. I grew impatient with written reports. If
there is a long-lost cousin returned to us, it's my duty
to come and see him. If it turns out that he's a charlatan, the more so. Good afternoon, Miss Lowell."

Julianne dipped her head as she bowed.

"A pretty child," the baronet commented with approval as she did. "Yes, she is lovely, Martha, you
were right. And you sent her out alone with this fellow who claims to be my cousin? Fie, Henry," he told
the squire. "That wasn't at all well done of you."

"As I said," Hammond said triumphantly.

Julianne felt warmed by the old gentleman's concern for her.

"Of what use was it?" the baronet went on. "If anything, it might have muddied the waters. Young
women's heads can be turned so easily."

Julianne's eyes narrowed, she was glad she still had
her head lowered in a bow.

When she lifted her head she found the old man
looking at her keenly. He was thin, and not unhandsome for his age, his face creased with strong lines by
his eyes and mouth, but otherwise unwrinkled. What
hair he had left was silver and cropped close to his
head. He had a long nose and gaunt cheeks, but his
eyes were clear and blue as the sky. He was dressed in
black, his clothes hung on his lean frame rather than
being fitted as tightly as fashionable young men wore
them, but he was scrupulously clean and immaculately dressed. And mercifully, Julianne thought, unlike many gentlemen of his generation, he smelled of

lavender water and not camphor, or more distressing scents.

"So, Miss Lowell," he said, "what do you make of the fellow? Is he your childhood friend, do you think?"

"I don't know as yet, sir," Julianne said. "But I can tell you I begin to think he might be. He remembers things a stranger wouldn't, things too insignificant for anyone else to know." She glanced at Hammond and, seeing his pallor, felt her spirits sink, and added, "But I was only a child when he left, so my impressions mightn't mean much in any event."

"Oh, I believe they are meaningful," the baronet said. He gripped his walking stick and used it to lower himself slowly back into his chair. "Sit, child. I've a thing or two to ask, as well as tell you."

Julianne took a chair opposite the old gentleman and looked at him curiously.

"Does he ask you about your childhood?" the baronet asked her.

"No, not really," she said. "He asked about what happened to his friend, my brother. But he never asked about me—except, of course, to ask if I remembered things he and my brother did."

"And did you? And what sort of things was he talking about?" the old gentleman asked.

She thought back. "I remembered many things, not all. But . . ."

"He told her about the Gypsy Fair," Sophie said with a bitter laugh. "She was astonished that he remembered it. But I told her everyone knew about that. The truth is, he's very beguiling."

"I never doubted that, whether he is or is not who he claims to be," Sir Maurice said. "An imposter would trade on charm, and the men of our family are known for it. Your own cousin Simon was just such a fellow."

The room went still, everyone remembering that charming young Simon, Sir Maurice's only child, had been drowned in a boating accident three years before.

"But I was talking to your cousin Julianne," the baronet went on mildly. "And I should be pleased if you did not interrupt, Sophie."

Sophie hung her head. Her parents looked embarrassed.

Julianne was impressed at the easy command the baronet had taken of the room. She wondered what Christian would make of him and how the two would deal together. The more she thought of it, the more she realized they were very much alike in their calm, effortless air of command. It made her feel more comfortable, and she looked at the baronet with growing interest. He smiled his encouragement at her.

"He told me about several incidents in my childhood," Julianne told him earnestly. "He knew the pet name only my family called me. He knew about my dog, my brother's best pranks. So many little things that, in truth, sir, I do begin to believe he may be who he claims to be."

"I see. And what did he tell you of his crime? And his punishment?"

She looked down. "Nothing. That is to say, he denied he committed a crime, but said little else about it." She looked up at him again and explained, "I didn't ask more because it's obviously a painful thing to him. Well, why wouldn't it be?" she asked, seeing Sophie looking at her with disgust. "What purpose would it serve except to embarrass or cause him pain? I don't know anything about that part of his past, so what could I discover? I wouldn't know if he was lying about that."

"Exactly," the baronet mused. "But I would. I heard the evidence. Charles, the sixth earl, sent to me, and I came to do what I could to protect the family. After I heard the evidence about what Geoffrey Sauvage and his son had done, I was deeply shocked, and shamed that we shared the name. Christian and his father were convicted and sent to the antipodes instead of to their deaths. It was no less than they deserved. And that charity, I may add, was only because the late earl had a soft heart. And see what it cost him," he murmured.

"Miss Lowell," he said, holding her gaze with his unwavering blue stare. "*Whoever* this man who claims to be Christian Sauvage is, I believe him to be a liar and a cheat. I doubt he is the liar and cheat that I knew. I have reason for this belief. I was just about to tell your cousins what I've discovered.

"I may not leave my home very often, but I do keep apprised of my family's doings, sad though they have been in recent years. Precisely because of that I've paid dearly for information. And because I've done that, I know even more than Bow Street and the pri-

vate investigator your cousin just hired," he added
with a nod at the squire.

He looked at Julianne again. "Let us look at the
facts. Geoffrey Sauvage and his son were sent to
Newgate. The place is a hotbed of disease; fevers kill
many before they come to trial. The Hulks, where
they stayed before transport to the antipodes, were
perhaps worse. And the less said about Botany Bay,
the better. Most don't survive the ordeal. But this fellow who claims to be Geoffrey Sauvage's son says he
has! Survived, and survived again, and yet again? The
odds are long against it. Still, his would be better than
most," he added with a thin lipped smile. "If only because I have discovered that Geoffrey Sauvage had
three sons."

"What?" the Squire and Hammond cried in unison.

The squire's wife looked astonished, Sophie's eyes
went wide. Julianne sat still as death.

The baronet nodded, pleased with the effect of his
announcement. But his gaze grew sharper when he
saw Julianne's reaction.

"The reason Geoffrey survived so long," he went
on, watching Julianne carefully, "was because he and
his son were befriended in Newgate by a pair of hardened criminals. They may have been boys his own
son's age, but they were already steeped in crime.
They'd been street arabs, living in gutters, picking
pockets, stealing from shops and carts and engaged in
too many other criminal endeavors to even list in polite company." He waved a thin white hand, "There
was no limit to their sins. And so, from having been
there before, they knew how to get on in prison. They

helped Geoffrey avoid pitfalls a more naive man would have faced. In turn, they received the protection of a strong grown man, who also had access to money.

"Geoffrey used that knowledge to survive and go on to New South Wales. He won his freedom there. That I do know. When he became a free man, he adopted the two boys, that is, took them as his wards, and called them his sons, too. Now, I ask you," he said, leaning forward and looking at Julianne, "what odds that Christian survived the wretched deprivations of such a life? In the end, it appears that even the wily Geoffrey didn't." His lips curled. "But there were two other boys, both about his own age, who enjoyed Christian's father's protection. Neither can inherit, of course, but either could impersonate the heir. And who better to know what a boy's previous life was like than another boy who shared his life and his stories with him during all the long years of their captivity? I haven't discovered what became of those two boys, but believe me, I shall."

Julianne sat rigid, listening, her eyes blank with shock.

The baronet thumped the floor with his walking stick. "Yes," he said, "I believe this fellow is one of those boys. Or, and this may also be the case, he could be yet another felon from that penal colony. Think of it. A letter comes telling of a vast inheritance. Geoffrey Sauvage is dead, even this fellow admits it. Perhaps Christian Sauvage and the other two boys are now dead as well. But there's still a fortune to be seized. This fellow knew the men who should have inherited, as well as their history. He sees an opportunity, and he grasps it. I am here to see that he does not."

He sat back, triumphant.

Julianne felt sick.

"So what are you going to do?" Sophie said eagerly, "Have the man arrested? Oh see, Hammond, it all will be well again!"

Hammond didn't smile. Neither did the baronet.

"No, not yet," Sir Maurice said. "I haven't enough proof, yet. And there's more to be proved. Think of the succession to Egremont. So many able men dying in such rapid succession in a series of accidents? I've always wondered about the evil coincidence. If what I suspect about this man is true, I'd like to find out if his father or his confederates here had a hand in some of those accidents. Surely this fellow would know about it, and so also be culpable. He wasn't an infant in the eyes of the law. Twelve-year-olds regularly meet their maker at the gallows, and for good reason."

Sir Maurice's eyes glittered as he went on, "Crime knows no age. Nor does tragedy. My Simon was only two-and-twenty, and in robust health. But even a healthy man can't survive a burst boat on a raging river. They said he hit a rock going over a rough patch of rapids and tore a hole in his boat. It's true, he loved paddling over the rapids, and had been warned about such dangerous sport. But who could warn him against perfidy? After all, if all men in the direct line to Egremont should die, then even my Simon would have been a candidate for it."

The squire's wife gasped, the squire looked grim. Sophie sat frowning, watching Hammond, who looked unhappy.

"But what if this man *is* Christian?" Julianne asked.

The baronet studied her. "You already care for him?" he asked.

Her face grew hot. She remembered Christian's embraces. She tried to compose herself and remember the reason she allowed those embraces, apart from Christian's devastating attractiveness.

"I have a care for the truth, sir," she said. "What if he *is* telling the truth? Some people do survive against all odds. And if he were innocent, then his life would then be in danger, too, wouldn't it? I'm not just speaking about a possible murderer. You're also acusing him of impersonation. The penalty would be a heavy one. Shouldn't we take care to be sure of the truth?"

The baronet nodded. She thought she saw a gleam of appreciation in his eyes. "Indeed," he said. "The penalty for impersonation would be prison for him, again. If he was actually awarded the estate and title, and accepted it, and deception was discovered, the penalty would increase, of course. Then it would be death."

Julianne's hands grew cold, she held them tightly together. "And so, then, a lot of evidence would be needed, of course," she said.

"Of course," he said, watching her with what looked like amusement.

"And so," she went on, trying to hide her anger at

that amusement, "am I still needed to meet with him to discover what I can?"

"Oh, yes," he said. "If you are willing to continue to help us, we would be grateful. Though I tell you right now," he said, looking at the squire and his wife instead of at Julianne, "I will not serve you up to him as a sacrificial lamb, as has been done."

"I never wanted that," Hammond said, with a scathing look at Sophie. "I protested it."

"That was correct," the baronet said. "A young innocent woman is hardly equipped to deal with such a villain. There are historical precedents for such impostures. Some have been amazingly successful. There was a famous case in France, when a man came back from the wars and convinced a grieving widow that he was her husband, returned to her! He was eventually found out. But if a widow was won over, just think of how easily a childhood friend could be swayed. Are you engaged to meet him again?" he aked Julianne.

"Yes, tomorrow," she said, privately thinking that widow must have been very lonely or a total clunch. "We were going to lunch at the inn where he's staying."

"Good. I'd like Hammond and Sophie to join you."

He didn't ask her, he told her. Although Julianne was a good obedient daughter and used to obeying the voice of authority, she felt her hackles go up. This man wasn't her father, nor even, strictly speaking, a relation, except by marriage. And yet he commanded her the same way that he gave orders to everyone in the room. She wanted to rebel. And then she remembered she wanted to see Christian again, and soon.

She nodded and didn't say more. Instead, she listened to them all talking about Christian and his claims, rehashing what she'd heard until she grew tired of hearing it. Besides, she was thinking of more important things. "May I be excused?" she finally asked. "I'd like to write a letter to my parents before dinner."

"Of course, my dear," Sir Maurice said.

Julianne rose. She couldn't help seeing that the baronet watched her thoughtfully as she left the room.

As Julianne went upstairs, her thoughts twisted around each other like mating snakes, each one birthing another.

They were going to try to set a trap for Christian. Surely, he expected that. What worried her was that they didn't seem to care if they caught an innocent man in that trap. They had money, position, knowledge of the law, and friends and acquaintances in power in England. And Christian had no one on his side.

But if he really was a cheat and liar?

Even so, she thought, surprised to find tears pricking at her eyes, he hadn't committed a crime in decades. If he was one of the adopted boys, hadn't he already suffered enough? And most of all, should a man be stripped of his freedom, not to mention his life, only because he'd planned to do something?

But an attempted crime *was* a crime.

And someone might well have murdered the previous earls and made it look accidental.

By the time she got to her room, Julianne's head

was aching. She sank to a chair and tried to think reasonably, without remembering clear light eyes, warm hands and breath, and soft kisses.

It was altogether possible this man wasn't Christian. That he wanted to claim a fortune and a title that wasn't his. She could believe that of him. But she refused to believe he'd kill for it. It was true she'd never met a murderer, but she'd been brought up to believe in herself and her innate good sense. No, she thought, on a soft, relieved sigh, whatever his sins, she wouldn't believe he was a killer.

He was intelligent, quick-witted, charming, and only possibly a liar. Even so, she couldn't think any of those things was a hanging offense. And so then, whoever he was, he deserved to know what they'd discovered.

At worst, if he were a cheat and a schemer, he'd cut and run. If he did, then Hammond would take all. Justice would be done without blood being spilled.

At best, if he really was the heir and knew what the baronet had discovered, Christian would stay on and fight for his rights. He deserved that chance. And the choice he made, Julianne realized, could in itself be a fine test.

She'd see him tomorrow, but she doubted she'd have a chance for a word alone with him. She dismissed the idea of sending him a note to tell him what she'd discovered. Notes were too easy to intercept, at least they were in all the novels she'd read. She had to speak to him. But when?

Julianne came to a decision. It was a dangerous one, at least for her reputation. But these were desperate times, at least for him. And she'd been asked here to resolve matters, hadn't she?

She'd rise early. It wasn't hard; she might keep fashionable hours here, but she lived on a farm, where everyone rose with the roosters. She'd dress without calling her maid, slip out while everyone was sleeping, and go to the White Hart. She'd tell the man who claimed to be her childhood friend what she'd found out. And then, devil take the hindmost—or the foremost. It would be up to him.

# Chapter 10

It was three in the morning and the countryside slept, except for prowling foxes and gliding owls, and the man who claimed he was the new earl of Egremont. He looked nothing like the calm, collected gentleman who made that claim. Because he sat bolt upright in bed, eyes wide, expression contorted with horror, face drenched with perspiration and tears.

Christian saw nothing but blackness and still heard nothing but the thundering voices that had woken him. He didn't know if he was sleeping or not. There was only one way to find out. He stumbled from the bed and staggered to where he thought the window was, flung back the curtains, and pulled at the shutters. The drinking glass on the sill fell and landed on his foot. He welcomed the pain as he stood, head out the window, taking in great gulps of cool night air.

It took a while for his heart to stop racing. But slowly, he felt the grip of panic ease. The moisture on his body cooled until it only felt clammy. He shivered. He refused to think about the dream he'd just had, it was enough that he'd dreamt it again; he would not revisit it willingly.

Finally, he turned from the window and drew the shutters closed again. He went to the pitcher and bowl on the bureau, stripped off his nightshirt, washed the cold stink of nightmare from his skin, and dried himself. Then he drew on another shirt and a pair of breeches. He would not face his pillow again, and not just because it was dank from the residue of his dreams. He wouldn't risk sleep again just yet.

He pulled on hose and boots, and left his room, taking the stairs on his toe tips, so as not to rouse anyone in the sleeping inn. The kitchens were cold and empty. Even the dog on the hearth only beat his tail on the hearthstones as Christian went through the room, drew open the door, and walked out into the night.

He stood in the kitchen garden and let out his breath. It was a clear night, the stars above brilliant, the moon only a thin sickle as it slowly sailed west. The night smelled of earth and damp grasses and faint pungent odors from the stables. Christian breathed it in as if it were perfume. It was fresh, and cool, and real.

He heard footfalls behind him and his shoulders leapt. But he didn't run, or spin around to fight. The footsteps weren't made by anyone creeping up on him. Whoever it was wanted to be heard. But still, because it was ingrained, he ducked and turned, his hand sliding down to his boot.

"Another?" a low voice asked.

Christian nodded, rising to his full height, "Yes, but it's almost gone now. How did you know?"

"Ah, well," Anthony Briggs said, "I'm a knowing one. And I heard you cry out."

"Damnation!"

"Be easy. No one can see your dreams but you, and you didn't wake anyone else. They sleep like dead men here in England, their stomachs full, their heads empty, and their consciences free. Amazing, ain't it? Must have been a bad one," he commented, "seeing as all you have with you is the knife. Left the pistol, did you? Just as well. The way your hand's shaking, I might have had my liver aired."

Christian slid his knife back into its sheaf and said nothing. But he frowned, because he realized his hand was still trembling.

"Come," Anthony said, "let's sit there, under the tree. There's a seat, and it's far enough from the inn so we can talk without worrying about waking anyone but the birds in the tree."

"You ought to get back to bed," Christian said.

"Oh, I will, in time," Anthony said on a huge yawn, "But I'm awake now, and the stars are so bright we could almost play a hand of piquet here, if I'd the cards with me, that is. What I do wish we had is a bottle, but I can get one from my room, if you want."

"No," Christian said. "In time, maybe, so I can sleep again, but not yet."

"I'm not sleepy yet, either," Anthony said. "Come on, let's sit and chew over things together. It'll settle your nerves."

"You've done this too often," Christian said, frowning.

"No, I just know the way of it," Anthony said. "Are you coming?"

Christian nodded and followed him to the round rustic bench that encircled the heavy trunk of the old elm.

"Ah," Anthony said with pleasure, sitting down and stretching out his long legs.

Christian looked at him and laughed. "Lud! I really did wake you suddenly."

"Always dress like this at this hour," Anthony said casually, glancing down at himself. He wore his gloves, and carried a long-nosed pistol in one hand. But his chest was bare, as were his feet. Otherwise, he wore only a pair of breeches. "Never mind. I'm not cold. I'd have dressed proper if I'd the time, your earlship," he added with a smile in his voice. "Your room's always protected, and I didn't see anyone creeping about the place tonight, so I guessed it was the nightmare plaguing you. Still, I'd never risk your life on a guess. I couldn't risk your neck by delaying a minute. I came running. But it got quiet too fast, there were no sounds of a scuffle or anyone moving about after. So I knew what it must be. I waited outside your door just in case, though. Then when I heard the sounds of washing up, I knew for certain. A bad one, eh?"

Christian shrugged. "The usual."

"Bad enough," Anthony commented.

A companionable silence fell between them.

"So," Anthony finally said, "nothing new happened to provoke it?"

"Nothing," Christian agreed. "Dreams come in their

own time and for their own reasons. The Bible says they're portents, but that rules out mine, because mine have all happened. I'm a boy again in them, and whatever else the world throws at me, *that*, at least, can't happen again, thank God. They're not symbols, either, like Daffyd said the Gypsies believe, because they're too damned clear. I know what they mean. I suppose I'm just doomed to live some things over and over again."

"Aye, but you don't have them as often lately, do you?"

"No, there's that."

"So," Anthony said, "no telling if they won't just stop one day, and never come back."

"No telling," Christian agreed.

They sat in silence again until Anthony spoke. "Say," he said heartily, "want to go back to my room and have that hand of cards now? Because," he added on the merest breath of a whisper as he leaned over, making it look like part of the stretching he was doing to uncoil his long body as he began to rise, "there's something moving at the back door, so how about we get up and you go left and I go right?"

Christian stood. "A good idea. I'm not sleepy, and I'm feeling lucky. Shall we?"

"Nay, lads," a voice said softly from the darkened garden path, "don't go on account of me. And put your skewers and cannons away, I'm not looking for trouble either."

"Murchison," Christian said, peering into the darkness. "What the devil are you doing out here?"

"Same thing the captain here is, I expect, sir. I

heard you cry out then I heard captain come pelting down the hall, so I followed. But at least I dressed for the occasion."

The two other men laughed. The runner was wearing his long coat open over a nightshirt and had on only one boot.

"Have a seat then, if you wish," Anthony said generously. "We were admiring the night."

"I will, at that," the runner said, and sat between them. He dug a pipe out of his coat pocket, and as the other two sat in silence, lit it, and puffed it into flame.

"I suffer from the nightmare," Christian said into the darkness.

"I should think so," the runner said. "What with the way you and your father were handled—if that is what truly happened, sir," he added fastidiously. "In my experience, it ain't uncommon for those who suffered in youth to experience it again in their dreams. Time, and a good wife, can cure it, they say."

"A good toss, certainly," Anthony commented, with a straight face. "Or so I hear."

"It can delay the onset," Christian said, as seriously. "But it's no cure."

"Myself, I sleep light, because of my trade, y'see, and it don't give dreams a chance to get a good hold of me," the runner added. "Bits and pieces is all I remember."

"Not bits, but pieces is what I get," the captain put in. "My dreams are of an erotic nature more often than not."

"Lucky fellow," the runner said, blowing out a long puff of smoke that concealed his expression. "An

army trait, is it? I mean, from being away from females so often and for so long."

"Just so," the captain said after a pause.

"Didn't know you two had made friends," the runner said to Christian eventually. "I mean you and the
captain, sir."

"I woke him, the least I could do was to be pleasant
to him," Christian said without missing a beat. "And I
find that he's an agreeable chap. Don't look surprised, Mr. Murchison, you and I have lifted a pint together, haven't we? I never blame a man for the
business he's in, so long as it isn't dirty business, and
yours and the captain's is only gathering information.
Anyway, why antagonize either of you? Though you
both may be looking for a stick to put in my spokes, I
know you're only trying to earn a decent living. I respect that. I've known too many men who tried to
earn indecent ones. In fact," he said, "though you follow me like shadows, I suppose you two have even
more in common with each other than with me."

"Why, I suppose we do at that," the runner said.

"Very true," the captain agreed.

There was another moment of silence.

"Lovely night," Christian finally said.

They talked about the weather for a while, then
about the innkeeper, who they all agreed was a good
fellow. Then Christian stood.

"I really am tired now," he said, "I know from experience that the dreams can continue if you go right
back to bed, but after a lively conversation such as
this one, I think I can safely go back to sleep. You fellows don't have to hurry in. I'm not going anywhere

tomorrow. I plan to sleep late, then lunch here with Miss Lowell."

"You may be going somewhere sooner than you think," the runner said, taking out an implement and tamping down the bowl of his pipe.

Christian paused. "Indeed?"

"Aye, the squire has company." He put the pipe back in his mouth, drew in a puff, and when he exhaled, said, "It's the baronet. Sir Maurice Sauvage."

"Maurice? Well, well," Christian said, his head to the side as he considered the information. "That *is* interesting. The old gentleman left the north to come see me, did he? I suppose it was meant to be a surprise. I'm glad it won't be. I wonder if Miss Lowell will still be allowed to come here tomorrow. Thank you, Mr. Murchison, that was considerate of you. At least I know what's afoot. Good night then, gentlemen. I'll doubtless see you both tomorrow, whether I'm ready or not."

"Count on it," the captain said.

The runner only smiled.

The two men watched Christian until he went into the inn.

"It was mighty generous of you to inform the earl of the grand surprise planned for him," Anthony finally said.

"Ah, well, I've taken a liking to him. Anyway, I've got no reason to put his neck in a noose, excepting if he insists on it. And you?"

"Me? I like him, too. I'm gathering information, but I don't like playing hangman either."

They sat in companionable silence.

"Although," the captain said slowly, "it's not such a

revelation if the girl was coming here tomorrow. She'd tell him about the baronet, surely."

"Oh, likely. But who knows whom they'll send with her to watch his reaction when she does?"

The captain nodded. "Very true." He waited, then asked, "So what do you make of this Christian Sauvage?"

"If I knew, my job would be through."

The captain sketched a bow from where he sat. "Well said."

"One thing I do know," the runner said. "The position he's dying to take up may help him do just that. Being earl of Egremont ain't a healthy title to hold."

"Not so far," the captain agreed.

"It's a fact that the man who finds the truth in all this can catch himself a murderer. Not just a villain who killed once, but who did it again and again, maybe, who knows?" The runner took his pipe out of his mouth and pointed with it for emphasis. "I mean to know, though. And not just because it's my job. But topping nobs, now that's serious business. Leastways, one that would make folks take note. Money's fine and no mistake, but there's a thing that would do a fellow's reputation proud."

"It would get him more trade with the gentry, too," the captain commented. "But for myself," he said carefully, "I don't care about my reputation, not once I have enough to line my pockets. Then, I'm off, going home, to Cornwall. I've been in foreign parts too long. I'm hoping to cut line and sink roots back home at last. If I make a success of this inquiry, I'll finally be able to. Now, I'm not bragging, but only saying true that I think this job will do it for me. So I'd take my share of the money, and be gone, for good, letting some other clever fellow take the praise and the credit, no matter what I'd done to help."

They sat listening to a newly sprung night breeze ruffling the tree above them. The wind had shifted, and a fine mist was blowing in, throwing a thin gray veil over the stars and moon.

"Well, I don't know about you, Captain," Murchison said, slapping his knees, "but it's getting too damp for my bones out here. Still, I ain't one whit tired. Wake me up thoroughly, and I'm ready to go for hours."

"As am I," the captain said. "Mind, if I had to sleep, I could. The army teaches us that. But once up, I can stay that way until I fall down. Would you care to repair to my room? I've a dandy pack of cards and a bottle or two. I think," he said carefully, "it might be to both our advantages to get to know each other better."

"So it might," the runner said, as he stood, "so it might. But mind your purse, Captain, I'm a dab hand at cards."

"As am I," Anthony said. "This ought to be interesting then."

"That," the runner said, looking up him sidewise, "is bound to be true indeed."

The two strolled back to the inn, shoulder to shoulder, and went inside.

Now, at last, as dawn neared, it seemed everyone at the White Hart was finally asleep. The Bow Street runner and the investigator from London had put away their cards and found their separate ways to bed. But in that last and darkest hour before dawn, even before the barnyard rooster blinked open his mad red eyes, one man was stirring at the White Hart. He stood in the inn yard and stared into the swirling mists as though it was a crystal ball that would tell him what the new day would hold for him.

Christian hadn't gone to sleep again. He'd heard Anthony and the runner go up the stair and into Anthony's room. He'd waited until he heard the runner leave and walk unsteadily back to his own rooms, and the inn fell silent again.

Christian waited until he could no longer endure hearing his own heartbeat. Only then had he left his room again, this time dressed properly. He had to go outside to greet the clean promise of a new day.

It had been a bad night, but he'd had worse. Now he had only to wait for rising dawn to show him the road, and he'd walk until he'd erased the last of the night. A long walk down country lanes in the cool silence of a new morning would be like balm to his soul.

But he didn't know the roads and had to wait for the light to rise. He stood in the darkness, watching the mists turn gray. And so he blinked when he thought he saw a single horseman appear out the vapors, riding down the road toward the inn. His interest was caught, and he watched warily, waiting for the figure to emerge from the fog, wondering who it could be.

If it were a traveler, it would have to be a mad or a

desperate one to risk his neck riding through the night. A peddler wouldn't visit when even the lowest kitchen maid was still asleep. It could be someone bringing news, or fresh eggs, or someone employed at the inn, coming to work. But still, Christian's hand slid inside his jacket as he waited for the horseman to come closer.

If the fellow had reason to be here, Christian's pistol would never be withdrawn. But there were too many other reasons for a man to come stealthily toward a sleeping house. It was also true that the figure might only be a phantasm of the mists, born of lingering nightmare and fed by constant apprehension. Christian knew, too well, that he couldn't kill his nightmares. But the feel of his pistol in his hand steadied him.

Now he heard sound of muted hooves on the road and knew it was no product of imagination. He prepared himself as the rider came near.

"The devil!" Christian exclaimed when the mists parted again.

"Christian?" a soft voice asked incredulously, as the rider bent low to try to look at him, "Is that you? Oh, what luck! But what are you doing here? How did you know I was coming?"

"My God, Julianne," he said in astonishment, catching her horse's reins so he could look up into her face. "What are you doing here at this ungodly hour?"

"I came to see you. I had to see you before anyone else did."

He reached up to help her from the saddle. She put

out her own arms and slid straight down into his.

And then he caught her up in his embrace, and she went willingly. She only made a soft sound when their lips met; but, by then, neither was listening to anything but the blood that was beating so loudly in their veins.

# Chapter 11

She'd been so anxious, so afraid. Julianne's boldness had dwindled with every fearful minute as she crept, caped and soft-footed, out of the squire's house.

If she hadn't been more worried about what would happen if she didn't warn Christian than about what might happen if she were caught at it, she'd have stayed in bed. But she couldn't sleep because she kept thinking of the danger he was in, and knew she couldn't live with herself if she didn't try to do something to help. And, after all, she kept reminding herself, in the unlikely event that anyone saw her, she'd simply explain that she thought she was doing it for the best. Let them think she was foolish. The worst they could do to her would be to send her home. They meant to do a lot worse to him.

She'd waited until the night was almost over, but it was still murky outside and a lot quieter than she'd imagined. It had been a long time since she'd been out of doors, alone, at that hour. It had been never, actually, she realized as her horse's ears had gone back

165

at a shrill whistle made by some unknown creature in the misty night.

At first, she'd been afraid her horse would stumble, but that was less of a fear as her own eyes adjusted to the dying night. Then she'd been fearful of every sound. When the breeze picked up and flapped a branch near her face as she rode by, she'd had a lively moment trying to avoid all the bats she imagined were winging home, headed straight into her hair instead.

Then, as she'd neared the White Hart at last and seen a figure standing solitary and lost in the shredding mists, she'd wondered whether to go on. She did, deciding it would be a servant she could tell some faradiddle about getting lost on her morning ride. Who else but a servant would be up at such an hour?

And then, against all sense and reason, she'd seen that it was Christian himself rising from the mists like a man in some romantic dream. She'd come close and looked down at him. He'd raised his hands to her, she'd seen his pale handsome face clear, reached out to him, and lost all her sense and reason when she found herself slipping into his arms.

He kissed her, with her willing cooperation. His lips were cool, but they soon warmed against hers. She forgot herself, the dank dawn; she was enveloped in the heat of his kiss, his body taut against hers. She reached up a hand to touch his face and felt how cold his cheek was, how damp with chill dew, his hair. He shuddered at her touch, and she didn't know if it was from passion or cold. It broke the spell.

She stepped back, bewildered and afraid—for him. "Are you well?" she asked.

Because now she could see his face more clearly, and he looked hollow-eyed and haunted. It made him even more desperately attractive to her, but she wondered why he looked so raddled and weary, his eyes searching her face as though he thought she had an answer he'd been urgently seeking.

"I'd be better if you came close again," he said.

"But I would not," she said, eyes down, shaking out her riding skirt for something to do. "I don't know why I did that, and I wish you'd forget it," she murmured distractedly.

"Oh, never," he said. "What in God's good name are you doing here?" he asked, tilting his head to the side.

Now his voice was as low, calm, and amused as ever. It brought back the wits his kiss had scatted for her. "I'll tell you. Can we walk a way?" she asked nervously, looking around. "I don't want to be seen."

"Of course. Good. You *do* want to be alone with me."

"That is *not* what I meant," she said. She saw his teasing smile and how it restored him, and felt her heart unclench. "Look, I came to tell you something," she whispered, "but I don't want anyone to know. Please?"

He took her horse's reins and walked down the lane and into the rising mists with her.

"Tell me," he said.

"Wait until we get someplace where we can't be seen from the inn. I haven't long. I have to be back before the household wakes."

They walked in silence until they came to a meadow, round a bend. Then he stopped. "They won't see us here. What is it, Julianne?"

"I had to tell you that the baronet, Maurice Sauvage, came yesterday and is staying with the squire now."

He nodded. "I know."

Her shoulders slumped. "*You do?* Oh, Lud. I came all the way here, sat up half the night in a fever of apprehension. I was so frightened." She spoke more to herself than to him. ". . . faced bats and who knows what, and risked my reputation to tell you something you already knew?"

"Thank you," he said. "I appreciate it. And don't forget the kiss, that was lovely, too."

"Forget the kiss," she said quickly.

"Not likely. But why did you do all this for me? I was going to see you this afternoon. Julie?" he asked suddenly, urgently. "I *am* still going to see you? Or have they forbidden you?"

"No, I mean, yes. I'll see you, but Sophie and Hammond are coming, too, so I won't be able to talk freely."

"And my cousin Maurice? Will he be there?"

"No. He's going to invite you to dine with him at the squire's."

"I see," he said. "So why the urgency?"

She looked away from him, staring out into the meadow, absently noting that she could now see the fences standing like ghostly sentinels in the swirling mists. "Because the baronet told me what would become of you if you aren't really Christian. And I don't want to see that happen." She turned to him again, her voice low and earnest. "I don't think a man should be punished just for something he plans. The punishment would be very harsh, you see. Imprisonment, and maybe, if you were successful in getting the title and they proved you lied, maybe even . . ." She couldn't go on.

"Death?" he said, sparing her the effort. "Well, that would be better than imprisonment, actually. But you think that would be my fate?" He asked, bending his head, trying to see her expression. "You don't believe I'm who I say I am?"

She shook her head. "I don't know. Honestly, I do not. You seem to be, then I'm not sure. I do know that whoever you are, I don't want to see you cruelly punished. After all, you haven't *done* anything yet. That's why I came. Because the baronet believes you aren't Christian. And from the way he speaks, he either has or expects to have evidence of that soon."

He didn't move. "Really? What makes you think that?" he asked in an altered voice.

She lowered her gaze.

"You came all this way, and you've nothing to tell me?" he asked with what sounded like amused affection.

"He said," she hesitated, and then said in a rush, "he said he'd found out your father, that is—I mean, Geoffrey Sauvage, adopted two brothers around the same age as his son when he was in the antipodes. He took them as his wards, said they were also his sons." She raised her eyes to his. "Is that so?"

"It's a matter of record," he said evenly.

"Oh," she said in a small voice.

"Why should it matter?"

"He wonders if you're one of them, instead of be-ing Christian. Because he doesn't believe you are Christian, and he thinks boys would share stories, and that might be how you knew so much about my brother."

"Do you think that's what happened?" he said, his voice even and expressionless. "Do you think I'm one of those boys?"

She shook her head, and said miserably, "I don't know."

"I see." He smiled. "So then, nothing's changed, has it?"

"Of course it has!" she said, astonished. "If you aren't Christian, that means that the net is tightening around you, and you must leave now! Look," she said anxiously, "I came to warn you. Maybe you ought to cut loose now, leave before any harm is done."

"And you, Julianne?" he asked, looking at her strangely. "What do you think?" He watched her closely, seeing her face dreamlike in the swirling mists, the mist bedewing her hair, her eyes wide and innocent looking. His mouth tightened. "I suppose," he said softly, "I should know that already. After all, it's very strange that a well-bred young woman, or at least one who keeps protesting that she is, would go flying off into the night in order to confront a possible criminal by herself. And all to warn him to be gone or he'll be hurt. Are you such a Good Samaritan then? Or is it possible you were moved by something I can more easily understand?"

She stared at him with incomprehension.

"Or could it have been done out of lust?" he mused. "For money? The baronet has full pockets, and he'd love me to disappear so he could keep scandal from the name. And whatever I did or did not, my name is scandal. The squire's well larded, too, if not a Midas, and he has better reason to pay well to see the back of me, because he wants his daughter to marry Egremont and have all its treasures. Either of them, or both, could have come down heavy to finance this little mission of mercy of yours."

"You could think that—of me?" she asked, taking a step back, as though he'd run mad and she was afraid he'd turn violent.

He shrugged. "I could believe that of anyone, especially now, when there's a ripe plum for the plucking, and my giving it up would benefit so many people."

"How would it benefit me?" she asked furiously. "I don't need money. And no one could pay me to do anything! I'm not rich, but I'm not needy."

His smile was not merry. "So my father and I said, so long ago, when we were accused of stealing. No one believed us then, or it seems, even now. So you may be telling the truth. But you did seem to need my kisses. Aye, that makes even more sense. Money may not be it after all.

"Is that it?" he murmured, as if to himself. "There are women who are drawn to danger, God, I know that well enough. The guards at Newgate often made a good haul out of a man's last night. There were females who paid great sums to spend those final hours in the condemned man's arms, no matter what the poor cove looked like. He could have had a face like the back side of a shovel, and a body only good for crow bait, still often as not he got a chance to bed a wealthy mort his last night on earth—some of them highbred, too." He hitched a shoulder in a tic of a shrug. "Some females get a thrill out of making love to a man they know will soon be a corpse."

The increasing light showed his lips set in a crooked smile that was almost a sneer. "I didn't think you were like that, Julianne," he said. "But then, you say you still don't know me. And so it stands to reason that I really don't know you either, do I?"

She slapped the sneer from his face.

Then she stood wide-eyed, staring at him, as horrified by her action as he'd been surprised by it. "I'm sorry," she whispered, aghast.

"I'm not," he said, and pulled her in his arms.

He only held her. She buried her face in his shoulder and trembled with shock. "Shhh," he said into her ear, "don't fret. I deserved that. In fact, thank you. Whatever you think of me, I do know you, Julianne. I just forgot that because I've known too many women who aren't like you."

He stroked her hair, and put his lips on her cheek.

"No," she said quietly. "Don't kiss me, please."

She felt his lips turn up in a smile. "I can hardly do that now, can I? After what I said? I've ruined that chance for myself now, haven't I?"

She pulled back to look at him, winced when she saw his reddened cheek, and opened her lips to tell him: No, he had not. Then she realized: Yes, he had.

But then he kissed her, and she found she had nothing to say.

It was a sweet, almost innocent kiss, with nothing of heat, or tongues, or searching hands, only all their hearts.

He raised his head and smiled at her. And then she lost her head and pulled his down to hers again.

This time their kiss was intense. It was cool and damp in the meadow because the sun was still only a promise. But his body was warm as she pressed against him, and his hand on her breast was warmer. He ran a hand through her hair; he traced the shape of her face and measured it with soft kisses. His hands caressed her back from shoulders to hips as he pulled her closer still. He lowered his head, and his lips trailed shivery fire on the breast he bared as he slipped one button after the other from their fastenings on her gown. His mouth was hot as the center of the sun as it closed over the tip of her breast, and the touch of his tongue spread flames to ignite the very center of her body. He kissed her lips again, and they breathed in rhythmic concert so they wouldn't have to stop.

He finally exposed both breasts to his gaze. He leaned slightly back and sighed. And his smile was as soft as his gaze was intent when he gently cupped one breast and lowered his head to the other.

And then, with a shudder, she pulled away.

He resisted her for a heartbeat, and she realized how strong his slender body was, because she couldn't move. But then he let her go.

"Why stop?" he asked, hands at his sides, his eyes half-lidded.

"Why?" she echoed, flustered, trying to straighten her gown and her thoughts at the same time. "My goodness, Christian, have you never known a decent woman?"

"Few," he said, "but still, why? You wanted to."

"I can't, we can't," she said in an agonized voice. "Don't you know?"

"No one will know, no one has to if we don't want them to."

"But I will," she said. "Oh, Christian, I'm not the sort of woman I always am when I'm with you." She stopped, hearing herself.

"I can't do such things," she said, looking down as she continued to fasten her gown. "Lud!" she muttered. "I don't know why I even did that. I think it's because I somehow feel I know you. Or because I'm far from home and find myself so alone . . . I know men have a word for women who let them think they will and then will not. I'm sorry, because even if you have every right to use that name, you haven't, and I thank you for it . . ."

She muttered in agitation as she tried to do up her gown again. The rising light showed her so rosy and well kissed that he clenched his hands to keep from dragging her back into his arms. But he was expert at dampening his urgency, he was practiced at restraint, and best of all for that restraint, now he was amused.

"You don't find me at all appealing?" he asked with a straight face.

She was too flustered to see the joke. "It's that, of

course, too. But I'm not the sort who lets that matter—or at least I didn't used to be." She stopped fussing with her gown. Now she began to straighten her hair. "I don't want a babe out of wedlock, it would ruin my parents as well as me. To say nothing of the poor child. And don't say you'd marry me, because that's a poor reason for a marriage, though I know it's a common one."

Her arms were raised as she pulled her hair back, and he saw how that made her breasts rise against the fabric of her gown. He took a deep breath and ran a hand over his own hair to smooth it.

"I don't understand," he said, with honesty. "Where is the objection? I'd make sure there was no babe. There are ways, you know, and if you don't, I do. So, no one would know. What's wrong with that?"

He knew she'd say no, knew a discussion never seduced a woman, but was fascinated by her reasoning. She'd been all fire in his arms, he'd tasted her surrender on her lips, and then she suddenly rejected him. That had never happened before. He knew a woman's willingness too well to mistake it. And he'd thought he knew her. Were the women in England really so puritanical? Or was it only the unmarried ones? Then they truly were like none he'd ever met. But then he remembered the only women he had met in his scrambled life: the convicts, whores, sporting ladies, and began to realize how badly he might have erred. He wanted her badly, but never wanted or expected her to be hurt by his desire.

"What's wrong with that?" she echoed, lowering her arms and staring at him. "Oh, my. We come from different worlds, all right. I couldn't. Or rather, I suppose I could, but I shouldn't, and I always do what I should. It makes life easier. Because don't forget, *I'd* know. And I have to live with myself after you're gone—one way or the other." There were better arguments about morality she could cite, but looking at his grave, handsome face made them seem inadequate.

But it seemed to settle the matter for him.

"Yes," he said. "So." And then he was the calm, cool man she'd first met again. "Do you want me to apologize?"

"Oh no," she exclaimed. "It was my fault as much as yours. I'd just like you to forget it."

"I won't," he said. "I hope you won't either. But no one else will know. Thank you for the warning, Julianne. I do apologize for doubting your reasons for giving one to me. But I'm staying here. I'm not afraid of the baronet or what he might prove. In fact, I hope he does find something. It may help me. I've come to claim Egremont and to hold it. But I've also come back to find out why my father and I were falsely accused and sent away. I'm staying to do both those things, and more," he added, with a warm smile for her.

"Be careful . . . If you were arrested, I couldn't bear it," she blurted. "I'd grieve, I would. It goes beyond the effect you have on me, which is obvious, and which embarrasses me. I'd protect you for my brother's sake, if nothing else. And if you aren't really Christian—well, at least I warned you that they might know it. We can still be friends, I hope. It's just that I won't meet you alone again."

She turned on her heel to go to her horse, then looked back at him. "I have to tell you that those kisses only showed my feelings, not my mind," she added. "I still don't know who you are. But one thing I do know, I don't want to see you come to harm."

He took her hand. "I won't ask you to trust me. I have to earn that. But don't worry about me either— although, you know? It's very good to have someone doing that—aside from myself."

She gave him a wavering smile, and he stood looking at her. Then he let go of her hand.

"Look at the light!" he exclaimed. "Back you go, then." He made a cradle of his hands to help her mount her horse again. Once she was up and settled in the saddle, he handed her the reins. "Go home. If they notice you've been gone, tell them you couldn't resist the fine morning," he advised her. "I'll see you at luncheon. I know you won't be able to say a private word to me, but don't worry, I'll content myself with guessing what they would be if you could."

She hesitated. "Don't imagine too much," she said.

His smile was wide and winning.

"And don't think about those kisses, please," she begged him. "Because if you do, I'll know, and I'll blush. And then they'll know; and *then* my word will be good for nothing, and I might as well leave this place and go home right now."

"I'll think about what I will, ma'am," he said. "But don't worry, I never show what I'm thinking unless I want to."

She frowned. "That's what I'm afraid of," she said.

She kicked the horse into a gallop and rode off into the awakening day.

He stared after her, aching with unfulfilled desire, sorry he'd let her go, though he knew he'd had to. He could have detained her in spite of her objections. He knew women well enough to be sure of that. Whatever he was or was not, he was a good lover, and experienced enough to know she had no experience. He'd have known when she was at the end of that long slope he'd been pushing her toward, and by the time she knew, he'd have had her over the edge and plunging toward ecstasy. There was no bed, there was nothing but the grass, or the wall of the inn, but that was better than he'd often had to deal with, and that would have been fine. Though he was sure she didn't know that either.

A few more minutes in his arms, and it would have been too late for her, and he supposed, for himself. So he'd let her go.

He could have eased himself, and given her something fine to remember. He knew he was a good lover, that wasn't just vanity. He'd been taught by the best. The women he'd known may have started out in life being as virtuous as Julianne, but they'd had to trade every item of virtue they'd possessed in order to survive. So when at their leisure, they felt it was their due to take their pleasure, and so they'd told him— especially when they'd showed him what their pleasure was.

It had always been a mutually beneficial arrangement. He'd never loved, but always loved the pleasure he could share with women. He hadn't lied to Julianne. The world he came from didn't see virginity as a thing to treasure, maybe because, he realized now, they didn't see virginity that much at all. Instead, it was a thing to barter, because sex was a thing either to make money or take comfort from. He could see that it might be a way to show love as well as passion; he even wished that was something he'd done in his time. But as he hadn't loved, it was a moot point. Sex itself had always been good enough for him.

Even so, he hadn't really wanted to take Miss Julianne Lowell tonight, though he needed to and could see that though she didn't know it, she'd wanted him to. Because he'd realized it would trouble her, at least, later. And it just might be that he really cared for her. More than that, it was entirely possible, he thought, that he might have found love, at last.

And so he knew too well that actually making love wouldn't be good for either of them right now, or maybe, ever.

# Chapter 12

❦

"**S**uch excellent food," Christian told his guests when the innkeeper had closed the door to the private dining room, "but no one seems to be hungry. I think I should try to clear the air and restore your appetites. Item one: I know my cousin Maurice has arrived. I received a note from him this morning," he added, glancing casually around the table.

Julianne breathed a silent sigh of relief. Her tension eased, but she didn't dare meet Christian's eyes. Since she'd arrived at the White Hart with her cousin and her cousin's fiancé she'd been quiet as the maid who came with them. Christian had greeted Sophie and Hammond calmly and blandly ordered more food and chairs, as though he thought they were there to chaperone her and he didn't know they were only trying to learn more about him.

Julianne felt the shoe was on the other foot; she was terrified they might guess how she felt about Christian if she so much as looked his way. She was sure she couldn't keep the memory of his kisses from her eyes. So she studied her plate and listened closely.

Christian went on. "Item two: I've been invited to Egremont tomorrow to meet Sir Maurice. He tells me he's an expert on antiquities, and feels honor-bound to show and explain the treasures of Egremont to the prospective heir, so that nothing of value gets overlooked or ignored in the transfer of the estate. It's very kind of him to go to such trouble for me."

"It's not just for you," Sophie snapped. "He wants Hammond to know what's valuable and what's not, too."

"He's really doing it for the sake of the estate," Hammond explained. "He's very proud of the family name and heritage."

"I never said otherwise," Christian said smoothly. "He also invites me to tea after the tour. Now that puzzles me. I was denied access to anything at Egremont, so I assumed everyone else was, too."

"Oh, true, true," Hammond said immediately. "I wasn't allowed to do anything but take measurements. We were only there to meet you when you arrived because your note said that's where you were going."

Christian frowned. "So you've said. But now, here's Sir Maurice, not even next in line, a mere baronet, and he's able to open the house and order the servants, and even have company for tea? How can that be?"

"Well, I suppose the staff is glad of a chance to do something," Hammond said, shifting in his chair, looking vaguely hunted. "They must be dead bored with so much inactivity since their master died."

"Oh yes," Christian agreed, "servants hate having all their days off with nothing to do but make themselves comfortable." He glanced at the maid, who now wore a studiously blank expression.

"I think it's because it's so hard to ignore his wishes," Julianne quietly said. "Sir Maurice has such an air of command."

"Fiddle," Sophie said, "it's because they *know* Sir Maurice. He used to visit the earl often in the old days. And he said there were treasures he wanted to show us, things he was afraid the new owner might pass by because they didn't look valuable to the untrained eye. So, of course, it would look shady if the staff didn't let him in."

"Really?" Christian asked. "And how does he know my eyes are untrained? We've never met."

"Well, maybe he doesn't think you're going to *be* the new owner," Sophie said triumphantly.

Hammond winced. Julianne bit her lip.

But Christian laughed. "That's the daisy! That's showing me. But what will you do if I am?" He leaned forward, not smiling now. "Look, Miss Wiley, let's have some plain speaking. I'm tired of this nipping and pinching. I never meant to upset your applecart. I don't bear you and Hammond any ill will. But I am who I am, and I'll be damned if I'll go away because it doesn't suit you. I'm here, and here I'll stay, and I'll prove my right to do it. So you should accept it because you'll only make yourself unhappier if you don't.

"I'll prove my father's innocence as well as my own," he went on. "And I will be the master of Egre-

mont. I know I have enemies, that's why my father
and I were imprisoned. But I also know Hammond
was too young to have been one, and so were you. Besides, you had no reason to hate me until I snatched
Egremont from you. And so I also tell you I'd like to
be a friend as well as a neighbor. But that's entirely up
to you."

He sat back. "You really should try the fricassee,
it's the best thing the landlord has done."

He hadn't raised his voice once, but he'd spoken in
such a voice of command that even Sophie fell still.
Julianne sat openly staring at him. She was enor-
mously proud of him, and yet curiously found herself
a little frightened of him as well—until he turned his
head a fraction and dropped an eyelid in a wink at her.

And then she was only worried again.


They were all assembled in the great hall at Egremont the next afternoon, waiting for the man who
called himself Christian Sauvage to join them. Even
the squire and his wife had asked to come along on
the tour Sir Maurice was going to give Christian and
Hammond.

Julianne stood with her hands knotted together, just
the way her stomach felt. Because she didn't know
how Sir Maurice would greet Christian. He hadn't
said a word about him last night at dinner although
his thin face was eloquent whenever Christian's name
had been brought up. Then it had been a study in con-
tempt. Now, at last, they'd be meeting face-to-face.
Julianne doubted that Christian would be anything
but cool and charming to the older man, as he was to

everyone he met. But she didn't know Sir Maurice.
She didn't think she could bear it if the old gentleman
was rude or cruel to Christian, and didn't know what
she'd do if he was.

It was one thing to have been a spy for her cousins
before she'd met Christian. It was quite another now.
He might be an imposter; she still hadn't made up her
mind about that. He might also be a seducer, but she'd
already spent the day chastising herself for her part in
that. But she was sure that, whatever the man who
would be earl of Egremont was, he was also a man
who had suffered greatly. And, she admitted sadly,
she was rapidly losing her heart to him, much good it
did her.

Julianne had worked it out during her ride back to
the squire's house at dawn. She'd been weary, yet ex-
hilarated in that febrile way that weariness begets.
She realized she wasn't reasoning perfectly. Lack of
sleep didn't encourage rational thinking, but sometimes it helped a person leap over barriers. Her part in
all this business finally made sense to her. It didn't
make her happy, but it made sense.

If Christian Sauvage were really the boy she'd
known, it would be wonderful. It would mean he carried the living memory of her brother in his heart and
mind. But even if it were true, it wasn't likely he'd
carry more than that of her in his heart or mind.

His heart and mind was one thing, Christian's body
was another story—a more adult one. Julianne repressed a shiver, just thinking about it. But there was
no sense in thinking about it. If he really was an earl,
he couldn't offer her much more than that lean body,

and probably a lot less. A rich, titled gentleman would look much higher for his bride. As well he should, and she knew it. So she couldn't take so much as another one of those wondrous kisses.

A fine thing if she made love to him! It wasn't so much the loss of her maidenhead that troubled her, although she was practical enough to see the dangers in that. It was that she knew the loss of her heart would be even worse. She reasoned that if she'd suffered so long from the loss of her brother, she'd probably exile her heart much longer if she lost a true lover. And she'd be little more than a slut if she gave herself to any other, even if he was the man she eventually married.

Christian the imposter could offer her pleasure, but there was no future in that, even if he did marry her. He'd either come to an end at the end of a rope or fly the scene one night while she lay sleeping. Even if he were faithful to her and escaped punishment, making love to such a man would be like running off with the Gypsy Davy, like in the old song. She didn't want to end up sleeping in haystacks, an outcast and a rover, the way that poor lady had.

It wasn't likely. Even if he asked her to flee with him, and she didn't expect that he would, she wouldn't go. Because that would mean he was a liar. She'd almost given her body, and that shocked her; but she wouldn't give her life to a liar.

So that was that. But she couldn't help being spellbound; it was like being part of an enthralling play. She had to know how it all turned out.

Now she waited for Christian to arrive so the second act could begin.

The great hall at Egremont was filled with light that shone in through the high windows above the twin staircases, so the expressions on every face of the waiting players could be seen with pitiless clarity. Sophie, a vision in a primrose gown, had an expression that reminded Julianne of a spoiled child at a sweet shop, one of smug, expectant greed. Hammond was dressed for a day in the country; but though his clothing looked comfortable, he didn't look as though he felt that way. The squire looked uneasy, too; his wife's expression was strained. Sir Maurice, dry and proper as a vicar at a wake in his neat black-and-gray attire, wore no discernable expression. He just kept looking at the big gold watch he held in his thin, long hand.

When the tall clock in the hall began pounding out the hours, the old gentleman closed his watchcase with a snap. "They teach prayers and handicrafts in the better prisons," he commented dryly, "but I see they don't teach promptness there."

Julianne frowned.

The baronet saw it. "Punctuality is a gentleman's trait," he explained. "I doubt even a man sent to the antipodes for his crimes would forget such a basic tenet of good breeding. Further proof of what I suspect, my dear. Because those of our class are taught from childhood that when one is expected at a certain hour, the least one can do . . ."

They heard the great front door swing open. "Good morning," Christian's voice rang out, even as the last chime of the clock faded away.

He gave his coat to a footman and came into the

hall where they were waiting. Julianne's pulses picked up at the sight of him. He was dashing in a dark brown jacket over a mustard-and-gold-patterned waistcoat. His neckcloth was tied casually but correctly, his breeches were dun, his polished boots, brown with small gold tassels. He wore no other ornaments. But his eyes were luminous as any gemstones and blazed with dancing light as he looked at her, then at each of them, and bowed.

"I give you good morning," he said, "I hope I didn't keep you waiting long. My horse wasn't saddled as I'd requested, and that ate up a few crucial minutes."

He didn't introduce himself to the baronet, but looked straight at him with interest. The baronet gazed back at him with no expression. They were like a pair of cats, Julianne thought uneasily, staring each other down before they decided when to pull each other's fur off. And then she realized how alike they were in their silent appraisals of each other, and her mood lifted. They might be jockeying for position; but in poise, at least, Christian was showing he was the baronet's equal.

No one else in the party spoke. As the silence dragged on and threatened to become embarrassing, Julianne remembered her role as a minor player in his drama. That gave her the courage to speak up. "Sir Maurice," she said, breaking the silence, "may I present Christian Sauvage?"

The baronet inclined his head.

"Sir," Christian said, bowing. "Though we're related, we've never met."

"*If* we are related," the baronet corrected him. "But yes, in any case, that is true."

Christian's calm expression didn't change. "You did meet my father, though," he said pleasantly. "He mentioned it to me once, when he was telling me about all the family members who didn't answer his letters asking for help."

The baronet raised an eyebrow. "Yes, Geoffrey Sauvage did write to me. And I did investigate the charges against him and his son. They seemed valid. So I did nothing to help him. My poor cousin the earl did, however, and it is his house and treasures that I feel honor-bound to explore with the heir this morning. There's much of value here, as I'm very sure you know. I have an obligation to the family, and that's why I suggested this tour. I would add that the staff has been apprised of all these pieces I will show you, and they have been and will be well guarded. Well," he said, turning to the others. "Shall we begin?"

*Neatly done on both sides,* Julianne thought. She was relieved that their ill feelings were so politely expressed. She took a deep breath and followed the baronet as he led their little group out of the hall and into the great house.

"Many would pass this up," the baronet went on, holding up a small brown-and-yellow vase, "but it's worth more than the oil painting that hangs above it. Note the glaze. Very similar to the urn I showed you in the long gallery, remember?"

He looked at Julianne.

"Yes, it is, very," she lied, because she didn't remember the urn he was talking about.

It pleased him. He smiled, and carefully placed the

vase back on the table. "Now, if we proceed to the blue drawing room that adjoins the Queen's chamber, I think you'll find the hangings there of interest."

"But isn't that a Van Dyck hanging above the vase?" Christian asked.

Sir Maurice paused. Christian stood next to Julianne, and it was she whom the baronet looked at as he answered.

"It is a Van Dyck," the baronet said curtly, "but a very inferior one. The vase is some three hundred years older, and in this case, age is superior to youth. Especially if youth is imperfect and the article of antiquity is rare and fine." He smiled at Julianne, and added, "Now, shall we go on to the Queen's chamber?"

Julianne nodded. But she no longer knew what he was asking her to admire. It was, she thought as they followed in the baronet's wake, like having to smell too many perfumes. She couldn't tell the difference between them anymore. She didn't think she was uneducated, but she felt like a savage dragged in from the wilderness to look at and praise Edgemont's treasures. She'd seen so many riches, heard so many new terms used, been shown so many things like marble therms and pedimented doorcases and Venetian windows, that she was dizzy.

The names of kings' famous plasterers and woodcarvers, esteemed architects and artists had been dropped as the baronet pointed out chimneypieces, ceilings, friezes, screens and moldings, columns and bas-reliefs. And those were only some of the major architectural features. Lectures about them had been interspersed with discussions about tinier treasures in every room. Julianne had gazed at important boxes, plates, mirrors, and urns, spoons, thimbles, and presentation cases, and more that she'd forgotten. She was numbed by the splendor and her own ignorance.

But each thing the baronet showed them was beautiful, or at least interesting the way he described it. He clearly loved many of them. That could be heard in the unusual warmth in his voice and the tender way he handled each item. And though Julianne knew she was unimportant in his scheme of things, Sir Maurice had been kind enough to take the time to see that she saw and understood each piece. The old gentleman looked forbidding, but he had impeccable manners. From the first he'd treated her with courtly grace.

True, the others' reactions to his lectures weren't encouraging, and so Julianne could understand the baronet ignoring them. Sophie was wide-eyed and mute, and, like her parents, seemed so staggered by the magnificence of the treasures and in awe of Sir Maurice that she didn't say a word. Hammond looked fascinated, but didn't seem to know what to ask. Christian did. And he asked often. But since he managed to remain at Julianne's side throughout the tour, Sir Maurice had to look at her in order not to speak to him.

She'd seen so much that all she could do was to keep nodding and smiling—very like the tiny Chinese mandarins embroidered on the hanging he was showing her.

And they'd only gotten through a dozen rooms. Dozens more awaited.

The baronet picked up a miniature enamel box and

held it on his palm to show his audience. "This charming bibelot is recent, Limoges, and only from the last century but . . ." He looked at Julianne, and hesitated. Then he glanced out the window, put down the box, and exclaimed, "I'm afraid I got carried away. Only see where the sun is. It's time for tea. I believe we should leave our tour for now."

Julianne ducked her head, embarrassed. He must have seen the glazed look in her eyes.

"Thank you," Christian said. "That was informative."

"Yes, thank you," Hammond said quickly. "I wish I'd brought paper and pencil. I won't remember half of it."

"You must hire an antiquarian and have the whole of it cataloged," Sir Maurice told him, as they walked toward the salon where tea was waiting. "I begged the previous earls to do so, in turn. And each put it off. You see the folly in that, I hope."

Hammond, walking at Sir Maurice's side, nodded. "Yes, certainly. Would you do the cataloging, sir?"

The baronet laughed. "Me? Oh, no. You must hire a professional antiquarian for that. It's merely my hobby."

Julianne, trailing behind them and the others, frowned. Her eyes glowed with repressed emotion.

"What is it?" Christian, still beside her, asked.

"That's wrong!" she murmured, unable to stop herself. "He's only speaking to Hammond, and Hammond hasn't been named the heir. And if it isn't wrong, it's rude!"

"I'm used to it," Christian said softly. "Both the wrongness and the rudeness. But I'm not used to anyone here defending me. Thank you again."

"Again?" she asked, looking at him directly.

He smiled. "Good. I was beginning to think you were taking your cue from Sir Maurice."

Her eyebrows swooped in a frown.

"You haven't looked me in the eye all morning either," he explained.

She bit her lip. She couldn't possibly tell him he affected her too strongly; she didn't dare look into his eyes for fear she'd be lost in them. Anyway, she suspected he knew it.

He smiled. "Although," he went on, "in Sir Maurice's case, I could understand it. A gentleman who's courting a young lady should keep his eyes on hers every minute. It convinces her that he's smitten, and that way he can see if she's eyeing any other fellows."

"The baronet—and me? Ridiculous!" she snapped. She stopped, and glanced around. Then, seeing no one had heard, lowered her voice even further, and added, "He was just being polite."

"No, he refuses to acknowledge my existence," Christian said blithely. "And you are prettier. But he could have looked at any of the others. In fact, he should have if he wanted to avoid me, because I made sure to walk with you. But he couldn't take his eyes from you, even though you aren't an 'item of antiquity,' " he added in a perfect mimicry of the baronet's dry tones.

She'd imagined she'd be too embarrassed by her wanton behavior earlier that morning to talk normally to him ever again. But once they'd begun, their conversation seemed as natural as breathing. "Be serious," she said. "What are you going to do about the way he's treating Hammond, as though the thing was already decided?"

"I am serious, and it's not decided, and I'm not going to do a thing about it," he said. "The lawyers are doing it for me. I've already hired someone to catalog the treasures of Egremont. I hope he can get to it soon, because I'm beginning to think Sir Maurice might be tempted to slip a spoon or a patch box up his sleeve before he leaves. He has every chance to. He runs tame here."

"Sir Maurice?" she squeaked, appalled, and then covered her mouth with her hand. "How can you say such a thing?" she whispered.

"I've seen the work of those who covet before. And my old cousin has the look of a prime coveter, believe me."

"He doesn't need to take anything from here," she scoffed. "He has a treasure house himself."

"A collector never has enough. He wants to possess everything rare and beautiful. Did you see how he held that Meissen jug? A man could get himself arrested for looking at a woman that way. He looks at you that way, too, by the way. Beware, Julie. Be careful that he doesn't try to steal you away, too."

"Don't be silly!" she said, both flattered and amused by his warning. "He's just a mannerly gentleman. And lecturing on art isn't wooing."

"It is to some men," he said seriously. "Especially those who have little else to offer—at least to a women who isn't ready to fall in love with their money or title. And anyone can see you aren't."

"Oh, nonsense," she said with a laugh. "I mean, of

course I'm not interested in that, and he's not interested in me."

But then she couldn't say anything else to him. They'd reached the salon where tea was ready to be served, and the squire's wife made sure Julianne was seated next to her and Sophie, far from Christian.

"That," Sophie told the baronet, as the company rose to leave Egremont House, "was delightful."

*That*, Julianne thought as she got up from her chair, *was an ordeal*.

Sir Maurice had held court all through tea. The things he said were intelligent. But he didn't let anyone else speak. There wasn't even a chance to whisper a word to someone else, not with his eyes on everyone. She'd wanted to ask Sophie if everything was all right between her and her fiancé. The hostility her cousin showed toward Hammond was so obvious now that Julianne felt *not* asking about it would be rude. But it would have been like having a conversation with your neighbor in church during a sermon, at a funeral, when you sat in the front row, next to the bereaved, and right under the minister's nose.

The baronet dominated the conversation. He *was* the conversation, prosing on about art and art history. Even Hammond, who hung on his every word, looked relieved when tea was over. Julianne hadn't paid much attention to what the baronet had actually been saying. She couldn't. She'd been too embarrassed by the way Sir Maurice had concentrated on her. Or at least, since Christian had mentioned it, the way she thought he had been.

She looked well enough in her saffron gown, she
knew, with her hair done the way Sophie's maid had
showed her. But she knew very well that she wasn't a
raving beauty. Nor was she a titled lady. So there was
no reason for Sir Maurice's interest in her, though she
wracked her brain to find one. He couldn't be courting her goodwill to find out any information she
could give him about Christian. He didn't even want
her consorting with Christian, the way her cousins
did. And she seriously doubted if dry old Sir Maurice
was even capable of romantic feelings toward a female. It certainly bordered on obscene to imagine the
dignified gentleman harboring any lustful ones.

Still, it did seem like he was always addressing her,
even though he was talking to everyone. Probably because she looked like an attentive student, she decided. Or had been. Since Christian had planted the
worm of doubt in her mind, she found Sir Maurice's
observation of her discomforting. And every time
she'd looked away from his gaze, she'd seen Christian's calm, amused eyes on her. So she'd ended up
staring at her plate until she was sure she'd be seeing
tiny puce roses in her dreams.

"When can you tell us about the rest of the treasures?" Hammond asked Sir Maurice, as they prepared to leave.

"Soon," the baronet said. "When everyone is free."
He smiled at Julianne. "Perhaps in a day or so?
Would Saturday suit?"

"I hope not," Christian said.

It was the first time he'd spoken since they were
served tea. They all turned to look at him.

"There will be a fair in the village, it's all the talk at the inn," he went on. "I'd thought we'd go again, Julianne, for old times' sake. Miss Lowell, her brother, and I, went to a fair years ago," he told the company. "We both have fond memories of it. Would you like to come with me again, Julie?" he asked gently. "We could try to dig up some more memories there."

"Are you talking about the fair where you saw the falling rope walker?" Sophie asked. "Julianne was *so* impressed that you remembered him," she told Christian spitefully, "until I told her that particular fellow fell from his wire at every fair in the area for years. It was part of his performance."

"Was it?" Christian said, unperturbed. "Well, I'm glad to hear it. It bothered me for years. I was afraid he'd cracked his head and didn't know he'd done it until afterward. Come to think of it, he had to be a crackbrain to do that for a living. Shall we see if he's still at it?" he asked Julianne.

The squire, his wife, and Sophie, looked at each other, clearly torn. Sir Maurice obviously hated Christian, and they didn't want to displease him, but if anyone could find out anything more about the fellow, it was Julianne. Hammond frowned. And Sir Maurice stood rigid and still as he waited for Julianne's answer.

She'd been asked to choose between being entertained by a titled and respected gentleman in one of the finest manor houses in England, or go with a possibly dangerous criminal to traipse through a country fair. Her answer came easily, for it was the simplest thing she'd had to say all day.

"Oh, yes," Julianne told Christian. "I'd love to!"

# Chapter 13

〰

"**D**on't pretend you're asleep," Julianne whispered to the doorknob as she rattled it. "If you don't open this door, Sophie, I'm going to pack and go home tomorrow, instead of to the fair, because I'll see that's what you really want me to do."

She waited, shifting from foot to foot. It was late, the corridor was dark, but there was a glow of light showing from under Sophie's door—the door that hadn't moved since she'd knocked on it and called to it long moments before. Julianne heard nothing stirring behind it either. But she knew she had her cousin's attention, she'd swear the silence was a *listening* one. "You've avoided me for two whole days now," she went on, "and I won't have any more of it. Either talk to me now, or off I go!"

She waited. "Very well," she finally said, her voice firm but her heart sinking, "so be it. I'll be leaving first thing in the morning. You can explain it to your parents and Hammond and Sir Maurice. I choose to avoid embarrassing moments. After all, what does it matter? I'll never see any of you again."

She turned, biting her lip. Now she'd done it. She had to go, and she didn't want to.

"Who'll tell that villain who calls himself Christian?" Sophie asked. She stood in her doorway in her night wrapper, glaring at Julianne.

"Oh, Christian?" Julianne said as lightly as she could. She marveled at how easy it was to be an actress once she'd decided that her whole role here was a charade. "No need to worry, I'll tell him."

"I'm sure you would," Sophie said with a sneer. "Come in. No sense letting the whole household hear."

"Hear what?" Julianne asked as she went into her cousin's room and the door was shut firmly behind her. "All I want to do is talk to you about why you don't want to talk to me. Although all I originally wanted was to find out what was happening between you and Hammond. You were April and May when I arrived, and now you don't even talk to each other."

"Yes!" Sophie said triumphantly, spinning around to confront her. "You want to know if the way is clear for you, don't you? Well, I can tell you that it is. If you want him, and he wants you, you can be sure I won't stand between you anymore."

Julianne had been absently admiring the new coverlet on her cousin's high bed, but that made her turn to stare at Sophie. "What are you talking about?"

"The fact that he defends you like a ... mother tiger. 'Don't send her to Egremont to meet with the fellow,' he says. 'Don't send her to be a cat's-paw.' That's all he ever says these days. And then today, I come down to find you deep in private conversation again. If you want him, you may have him with my good wishes and best of luck to him with you, too. Although why he'd want a female who flirts with everything in breeches, I do *not* know."

"What?" Julianne exclaimed. "What in blazes are you talking about?"

"I've said too much already," Sophie said piously, and plumped herself down in a chair by her vanity table. She snatched up a brush and began stroking her hair with it, forgetting that her hair was up in a night braid. Her grimace of pain as the brush caught in the braid brought tears to her eyes, but she kept on.

"I don't want Hammond," Julianne protested. "He doesn't want me. We talk about events, nothing more. And what's this about me flirting with everything in breeches? Who am I going to flirt with here? The butler? The footmen? Your *father*?" She fell still, the ludicrousness of that last making her speechless for a minute.

"Hammond. Sir Maurice. And that fellow who calls himself Christian Sauvage," Sophie said, tears now trailing down her cheeks.

Julianne paused. "Well, you asked me to get into Christian's good graces," she said feebly, and added with more conviction, "and since I begin to think he may be my old friend, of course I enjoy being with him. But Hammond? He's a very nice young man, but I don't feel a thing for him that way—even if I did— which I certainly do not," she added hastily, "he's yours, and anyone with half an eye can see it. He adores you. If he's trying to protect me from possible danger, that's only a masculine response to the situa-

tion, I think. Because he must feel inadequate about
this whole matter of the inheritance. He can't do anything but rely on lawyers and Bow Street. He certainly can't do what I do with Christian . . ."

Her voice trailed off. Her cheeks felt hot just thinking of what she did with Christian. So she went on
quickly, "As for Sir Maurice! Really, Cousin! He's
old enough to be my grandfather, and he's been nothing but kind and gallant, as gentlemen of his generation were taught to be toward females. He's nice to
me because I'm a guest here, and if not of his class,
then acceptable to it. And as for your *father* . . . Me
flirt with him? Sophie, have you run mad?"

She saw her cousin's mouth begin to turn up at the
corners. Their eyes met. Julianne couldn't hold in her
giggles, and soon Sophie was joining her. "Oh, Lud!"
Julianne said, wiping her eyes. "Can you just see it?
Can you imagine what your father would do if I so
much as winked at him?"

It took a while for them to stop laughing. When
they did, Julianne grew serious again. "Sophie, please
tell me I'm not the cause of your problems with Hammond. And don't tell me there are no problems, because anyone can see it. I'll leave here instantly if I
am," she added, and felt sick, because as she said it
she knew she meant it.

Sophie put down her hairbrush and cast down her
gaze. "No," she said in a small voice, "No, you're
not." When she looked up again, there were new tears
in her eyes. "I might as well be honest," she said dole-
fully. "I've been trying to be that with myself. What
am I going to do? Most of my friends are already

married; but I was holding out for a prince, a fellow of worth and means and charm. I didn't find anyone like that in London, but I wasn't on the shelf yet, so I waited . . . maybe too long. At any rate, I was going to return to London this spring. I'd be there right now, in fact, if Hammond hadn't come along."

Her eyes grew a dreamy distant look as she went on. "He was like a prince out of a fairy tale. He came riding up on a fine horse to introduce himself to my father as his new neighbor: the new earl, heir to Egremont. Egremont! The place has dominated our thoughts forever. We wondered who the new earl would be, and here was Hammond: young, handsome in his way, and clearly taken with me. Father told him he could stay with us until he took possession of Egremont. And so he did, and in the meanwhile, he took possession of my hand and heart.

"We walked together and talked together for hours," she said dreamily. "In no time he asked me to be his countess. I was thrilled. I said yes. But now . . ." She lifted tear-dewed eyes to Julianne, her face pale. "It isn't you, Julianne. I know he's not interested in anyone but me. But as for me? Now I don't know. If he isn't the new earl . . . The truth is I don't know if I want him without the title and Egremont. I'm not superficial or mercenary, I'm not! I could have married wealthy men. It's just that I never *thought* of Hammond without Egremont. Why should I have? The inheritance and the man were one; it's hard to separate them even now. What shall I do?"

"Oh, Sophie," Julianne said, falling to her knees beside her cousin and taking her cold hand in both of

hers. She'd never liked her half so much as she did at
that moment. "I think you should wait and see.
There's no point in breaking off with him now."

"Yes, there is," Sophie said, sniffling. "That way it
doesn't look like I'm casting him off because he isn't
the heir. That would look dreadful!"

Julianne let go of her cousin's hand. "Well, yes, but
if it turns out that he is, there might be some diffi-
cultly mending matters."

"With Hammond? Never," Sophie said, reaching
for a handkerchief and blowing her little nose. "He's
smitten."

Julianne rose to her feet. "Then I guess you'll have
to do what everyone else is doing: wait on events. But
in the meanwhile, why be mad at Hammond? It only
makes everyone uncomfortable."

"Everyone sees it, do they?" Sophie asked.

"You hardly speak to him, you treat him even
worse than you do Christian."

"The man who calls himself Christian," Sophie
corrected her. She glanced at Julianne, then away. "As
for that fellow . . . What does he think of me?" she
asked in a carefully neutral voice. "He's always polite, he answers my anger with jokes. But he conceals
his emotions. Does he see that Hammond and I are at
odds now? Does he blame himself for it?"

"Why no, we don't discuss it. Do you want me
to . . . ? Sophie," Julianne said, her eyes widening as a
sudden notion came to her, "you're not thinking of
breaking it off with Hammond now so you can be free
to make a match with the new earl, are you?"

Sophie turned her head and looked at herself in her

mirror, suddenly fascinated by a nonexistent spot on her cheek. "Of course not. Odds are the man is a thief or worse. But one never knows what the future holds, does one? After all, you seem to believe he is who he says he is. But isn't he the most attractive man?" she asked eagerly, swinging around to face her cousin directly. "And he has excellent manners, wherever he got them. If he is the heir, his years in prison mean nothing; in fact, it will make him even more glamorous to the *ton*. He'll be accepted everywhere. You're right; I've been horrid to him.

"That will change!" she said with decision. "I'll try to be civil, starting tomorrow, at the fair. We're going too, you know—as if we'd let you ride off with him alone. Sir Maurice would *slay* us if we did."

She looked at Julianne's dumbfounded expression. "So, you see? There's no reason for you to be upset. It will all work out. Don't worry about me and Ham. He'll take me back in a minute if things should turn out differently."

Julianne found herself with nothing to say. But she forced herself to say all she could. "Oh, I see," she murmured. "Well, then, Cousin. Good night."

The morning dawned clear and mild. Julianne wasn't tired in the least, even though she'd sat up extra hours after her meeting with her cousin. At least, until she'd decided there was nothing she could do about anything but wait and see, and had escaped into sleep.

Now she sat in the small salon at the front of the squire's house and waited for the rest of their little party to join her. She'd prepared herself for a day at a country fair as though it was a presentation at court.

She wore her prettiest day gown. Dark gold with pink rosebuds, and low at the neck, it gave her both color and a certain elegance, she thought. She'd put on a pair of soft kid half boots, because the fair was on the green, and she remembered how she'd romped through it last time. She had a rose-colored shawl to wear over her shoulders and a parasol to match. Her hair was drawn up like a sophisticated lady's, but tied by a ribbon and left to hang down in back like a schoolgirl's, which was fitting since she felt caught between childhood and maturity. In all, she decided she looked as good as she could.

Still, she knew brown hair didn't glow in the sunlight like flaxen curls did. Nor did doe brown eyes sparkle in the light like azure ones could. And a gentleman's farmer's daughter didn't hold a candle to a squire's in any light.

If this Christian were a false one, he'd prefer a squire's daughter as an ally because of the influence such a connection could provide him. He might prefer Sophie anyway, Julianne thought sadly, even if he were really Christian Sauvage. She'd find out today. She'd primped and worried, fussed and fretted. Now all she had to do was wait and see. She heard footsteps and looked up.

Sir Maurice stood in the doorway, neatly dressed all in gray. "Ah, good," he said, "I have a chance to speak with you alone. I asked the servants to let me know when you left your chamber and asked my cousins to wait until we'd spoken. My dear," he said as he came into the room, leaning on his walking stick, "I hope you know you don't have to go out today with this charlatan. Not for your cousins' sakes, no matter that they brought you here for that purpose."

Julianne began to protest that it was not why she was going, but he held up his hand to silence her. "I know you're a good, dutiful girl, but I want you to know there's no longer any need to jeopardize yourself on their behalf now that I'm here. You can let me, and Bow Street, do the work now. We can continue the investigation."

It would pain Julianne to lie to the old gentleman. He'd shown her nothing but grace and decency. But she found she didn't have to. "I'm not doing this for my cousins anymore," she said truthfully. "I need to know for myself. I'm not interested in Egremont or its treasure, sir, beyond the appreciation for great art, of course. My interest is personal." Her eyes begged him to know what she said for truth. "If there's any chance the man is Christian Sauvage, I must know. It will be like having a part of my brother back again."

A gentle smile lent tenderness to that austere face as he looked down at her. He was a tall man, she realized, but it also seemed that he looked at everyone from a great height. "Innocence herself, she is," he murmured. "A face that would credit Raphael, and the soul of an angel he might have painted. You aren't acquisitive, are you? Astonishing. You're a little treasure yourself, you know. I wish my son had met you years ago." He paused and closed his eyes for a moment. "But there's no sense grieving over what can't be changed, is there?"

"That's what you must learn, too, my dear," he said, looking at her again. "Then go and see for yourself, but don't get your hopes up. I've every expectation of proving who the imposter is, and soon. I become surer every day that whoever this fellow turns out to be, it will not be your old friend and playmate. But go on to the fair. I'd come, too, were I young. Hammond will be there, and I'm also sending a footman. And it is broad daylight, after all. You can't come to harm."

Julianne lowered her gaze. He had no idea of the harm she could come to, and she didn't want him to see it, or her shameful longing for it, in her eyes.

Sophie wore a cherry red gown, a dashing straw bonnet, and a warm and welcoming smile for Christian as he stepped out of the carriage in the drive. Sophie's unstinted smile made his eyes narrow, fractionally, for a moment. Julianne knew, she was watching that closely. It made Hammond look miserable—she didn't have to look closely to see that. And it made Julianne herself blink and swallow hard.

"Good morning," Christian said in his usual even tone. "Are we ready to leave?"

"We are," Sophie practically sang. "And we can't wait." She took Hammond's hand without looking at him, stepped up and into the carriage, arranged her skirts, and gave Christian a dimpled smile. "Now," she said, "about that acrobat you remember from the fair, we'll all look for him. But you must tell us. Was he fair or swarthy?

"Well?" he asked Julianne, as she took her place

beside her cousin. "First test of your memory. What was he? Do you remember, Julianne?"

"Now, now," Sophie said gaily, "that's a leading question. It's not Julianne's memory we're here to try, is it?" She said it so lightly it was hard to tell if she was teasing or testing.

But Julianne's stomach tightened. Whichever it was, it made her uncomfortable.

It didn't seem to bother Christian. "True," he said. "Very well then. I remember a yellow-thatched fellow. A very improbable shade of yellow, at that. Doubtless he colored it so it would show better from far away."

"Yes!" Julianne said, her eyes growing wide. "It was a clown color. Maybe he was a clown, too?"

"His name was Sparrow and he was a clown, a contortionist, and an acrobat," Hammond said as he seated himself opposite them. "We've made inquiries," he added when they all looked at him. "The falling acrobat was a famous act, performed at every fair that would have him, Gypsy or not, in spring, summer, and autumn, for fifteen years. Greenwich, Camberwell, St. Ives, Bury St. Edmunds, the lot. Horse fairs, horn fairs, May fairs, he was a busy fellow. He even performed regularly at St. Bartholomew's Fair, in London," he added, staring at Christian. "The fellow tumbled from his wire every time. But he died in bed two years ago."

"Pity," Christian said levelly. "Shall we go see who's replaced him?"

Julianne smelled it long before she saw it, and heard it even before that. She sat up straighter when she heard the far-off sound of trumpets and drums and fiddles, and the tinny whine of hurdy-gurdies mixed in with the hum and babble of voices and laughter of a great crowd.

As they rode on toward the village, she rolled down her window farther, raised her nose, and caught the scent of roasting meat and the sweet-sour wild smell of some enormous barnyard. "There's a menagerie!" she told Christian excitedly. "I'd forgotten that!"

He smiled. He could see her eyes lighten with surprise. She was very like a child again in her excitement. Except that children's bosoms didn't swell like that when they took deep breaths, he thought, and damned himself for his preferences. A friend didn't stare at another friend's breasts; he was having a hard time remembering that.

"Yes, tigers, monkeys, a wild hyena, and a lion, too. Remember?" he asked her.

"And a kangaroo, that should interest you," Hammond said. When Christian merely looked at him, he added, "We asked what the attractions would be. Sir Maurice wouldn't have let the ladies go if there'd been bear baiting or such."

"Very proper," Christian said.

"And dwarves," Julianne said, as though speaking in a trance. "A giant man, and a fat woman. A man like a skeleton . . . Roundabouts! One you didn't have to push, because they'd a man and a boy who cranked it. I remember. And a wheel studded with seats that moved around, taking you up into the sky and down again. Huge swings, the kind that can hold men and women and children all together. Remember? And

THE RETURN OF THE EARL                209

Punch and Judy, and people in costumes, and on stilts, and trained dogs that dance on their hind legs, and so many toys to buy, some so little you can slip them right into your pocket . . ."

"And lads who'll slip their fingers right into your pockets, too," Christian said, smiling. "We aren't children anymore. Watch your purse and your pockets."

Hammond frowned. "This is a local fair. There'll be none of that here. There won't be any gin shops or loose women, peep shows of an unseemly nature, gambling or such. That sort of thing is for the bigger fairs."

Christian laughed. "It's a fair, my friend, and a fine fair day. There'll be hundreds if not thousands of people here from miles around. And with a crowd like that there'll be almost as many sharpers and dips, negotiable women, peep shows, gin shops, and *such*," he mocked the word with the emphasis he put on it, "as there are people here. There'll be plenty of crime. Believe me," he said with a crooked grin. "I should know."

Hammond's jaw clenched.

"But then you'll be the best one to protect us," Sophie told Christian warmly, not a trace of spite in her voice.

"Of course," he said, with no expression.

It did look as though a thousand people were there, Julianne thought dizzily, gazing out the carriage window as the coachman jockeyed for position in a long row of coaches. The place they finally stopped was on a rise, overlooking the crowded green. She could see rude tents and shelters thrown up everywhere. There were impromptu stages on stilts with huge banners fluttering over them, and enormous signs with pictures and prose promising all sorts of bizarre wonders and delights. Little clearings between the tents had cook stands, the fragrant smoke rising from them advertising their wares even better than their shouting proprietors could.

Everywhere, people were on the move, in a confusing welter of noise and movement: The green positively boiled with people. Julianne held back a moment after she stepped out of the carriage.

"Changed your mind?" Christian asked.

She shook her head. "No, but I didn't remember— or maybe I did, but children are excited by crowds, and I've lived a quiet life since I was here last. This seems so . . . much," she said, at a loss for words. She raised her voice so she could be heard over the sounds of music and the crowd. "But I want to go. It's like being young again."

She didn't say that here on the brink of the fair she felt her brother's presence more strongly than she had for years. She could almost feel his warm hand closing over hers, and hear his admonition again: *"Now, if you get lost, I'll murder you. So stay close. Hear?"* There'd been another boy by her side who had smiled, and taken her other hand. With a strong stout lad on either side, she'd walked into the fair. She'd never felt so protected and honored before, and never since. She glanced up at Christian and hoped he remembered. And prayed she'd know if he really did.

Christian told his coachman and the footman to enjoy the fair for a while, but to be back in an hour in case they wanted to leave early. Then he offered Julianne his arm and, with Sophie and Hammond following, they strolled down the grassy rise and went down into the crowd.

# Chapter 14

"They're gone!" Julianne exclaimed.

Christian turned his head. There were masses of strange faces in the roiling crowd behind him, but not a glimpse of Sophie or Hammond. "So they are," he said, putting his hand over Julianne's where it clutched his arm. "When did you last see them?"

"Somewhere between the giant swing and the dwarf horses . . ." she said. "No, just after we left the roundabout."

His hand tightened over hers. "Don't worry. I won't lose you. Hammond's a strapping lad, he can take care of Sophie. And wherever they wander, they know where the carriage is. We'll all meet there later. Or do you want to turn back and search for them?"

She turned a troubled face to his. "Do you think we can find them?"

He had to bend until his lips almost touched her ear to be heard over the music and shouting. "I can hardly find my own nose in this crowd," he said, laughter in his voice. "And I don't think it matters, but if you feel uncomfortable alone with me, we can go back and look for them."

Uncomfortable? She hadn't felt so good in years. "We're hardly alone!" she said. "You're right. They know where the carriage is, we might as well see the fair. Maybe they'll find us."

She didn't really care. All she could think of was the fair—and the man at her side. As they walked on, it did seem as though the years fell away, but she was too enraptured by the man to think about the boy. She knew she was there to try to remember, but couldn't think of anything but the present. And what a present it was!

She hadn't seen so many people in one place for years. There were men, women, and children, whole families that had taken off a few hours of work to go to the fair. Hardworking folk out for a day's pleasure: farmers, shopkeepers, laborers, even servants. Their class could be told by the clothing they wore. There were some people of higher quality present, too; Sophie had nodded to them.

Everyone had noticed their little party, the squire's daughter was by way of being a celebrity in the district. It seemed from their curious stares that everyone had heard of Hammond, who might possibly be the new earl of the finest manor in the region. Julianne wasn't sure everyone knew about Christian, but it was clear that women of all classes and ages noticed him. She preened a little at how the men were noticing her as well, but that wasn't the reason for her utter delight.

She and Christian had privacy in the midst of many.

Pressed close by the crowd, they had to walk hip to hip and talk into each other's ears, and yet she never had to worry about impropriety. It was delicious.

As they strolled on into the fair, the years fell away from each of them. Christian loosened his neckcloth, as every man there did. It simply was too warm and too rustic an occasion for fashion. Julianne folded her parasol; there was no room for it. They became more casual with each other, too. There was no point to formality, not with the crush of the crowd and the wonders to see and exclaim over.

It was as though she were a child again, and yet better. She could see and understand more than she had on that long-ago day. She could definitely appreciate the man at her side better, too.

They stopped, without consultation, at all the places she wanted, and exchanged smiles or comments that showed they were of a single mind, too. They paused to watch the Gypsy dancers and the locals cavorting to the wild music. He asked if she wanted to dance, and though she did, she knew she shouldn't because it would be a common thing to do. And so she said no. "Chickenhearted?" he asked, as the boy Christian might have done to dare her. But he smiled as though he understood, and they went on.

They paused whenever they heard a trumpet blaring to announce some new wonder. They stood listening to the barkers who urged them to come and be dazzled. Julianne watched a stream of fairgoers putting down their coins and pouring into a tent. She looked at Christian when the barkers implored them to pay to see fantastic freaks of nature.

"No," Christian said to her inquiring look. "Most of what they show isn't real anyway, and those poor souls that are would upset you. Anyway, most of them aren't meant for the eyes of well-bred young women."

"Can we pretend I'm not?" she asked plaintively,

"Gladly," he said, "but not here in front of all these people."

She colored a little and walked on.

There were plenty of other things to stare at. They watched Punch and Judy swatting each other until the end of their playlet, then they applauded the lumbering bear that danced on his tether.

Christian teased Julianne unmercifully when she refused to let him lift her into the great scale so that the Gypsy could guess her weight and laughed at her amazement when she couldn't find the pea under the thimble another fast-talking fellow kept moving around a board.

She applauded when Christian stripped off his jacket, raised a mallet, and thwacked a stump until the lever fastened to it hit a bell. She thanked him prettily when he gave her the whistle he'd won, as well as when he bought her an ugly little doll from a persistent vendor. She grew sad when they entered the stifling menagerie tent and saw the moth-eaten lion in his inadequate cage, and held her breath because she was too well bred to hold her nose when they passed by the scruffy-looking hyena's cage.

She said nothing when they saw the kangaroo, all the way from the antipodes, as the sign proudly proclaimed.

"Yes, they are from the land where I've been, as I

told you," Christian said, answering her unasked question. "But I don't have much firsthand experience with them. I didn't have free time . . ." He laughed at his own inadvertent pun, then added, "And when I finally did, I didn't have much time to explore, as you may well imagine."

She turned a grave face to his. "But I can't imagine, can I? And you never talk about that part of it . . . at least, you never speak of the trials you endured."

He paused. "Do you want me to?" he asked, watching her expressionlessly. "I thought you were here to find out about my distant past, not my recent one."

It seemed to her that the tumult of the crowd faded, that there were only the two of them standing there. "Yes," she said honestly. "I want to know about those days, too, because I want to know everything about you." Then she bit her lip and glanced away. That was, she knew, far too much for her to say.

He hesitated. "Then I'll tell you," he said gravely. "But not here, and not now."

" 'Ere! You done looking or what?" an aggrieved voice said. "I means, paint a pitchur o' the beast and have done. There be others what wants to ogle 'im, y'know," a red-faced man behind them said.

"He's all yours," Christian said, and led Julianne away.

"Thirsty?" he asked, as they left the tent, and he saw her eyeing the line in front of a lemonade seller dipping her ladle into a big wooden tub.

"Oh yes," she said

"Ale? Gin? Beer?" he asked.

"That lemonade would be fine."

"*That* lemonade would not," he said firmly. "Just look at who's putting down the ready for it. There's not a lady in the line, and the coves guzzling it are already a few sheets to the wind. If there isn't more blue ruin in it than lemon, I'm a noddy, and I'm not."

She grinned. His speech was becoming as casual as his neckcloth.

"Now, there's a lass selling frumenty. I'll have a sip and let you know if you dare," he said, and led her over to a vendor doing less brisk business.

He bought a penny cup, sipped, and grimaced.

"Does it have gin, too?" she whispered.

"No," he said. "Just fruit. You'll like it."

She laughed, drank it, and they wandered on.

"Do you want something to eat?" he asked her, as they passed cook fires, where sides of pork and beef were being turned on spits.

"No, thank you," she said, eyeing a woman working at a great cauldron, dishing out a greenish lumpy soup. "The baronet said we oughtn't dare, and that he'd have tea for us when we returned."

"Good," he said. "I'd hate to see you poisoned. They'd blame me, you know."

As the sun passed its zenith, the crowd began to thicken. The noise increased to a roar, the food smells grew less enticing and more stifling, and the press of the crowd increased until they were being pushed through the fair instead of walking at their leisure.

"Have you seen enough?" Christian asked. "Do you remember anything you want to ask me about?"

"No," she said sadly. "I thought so when I got here, but no." She had to raise her voice to be heard. "I remember the smell and the sounds, and some of the sights. And the acrobat, of course. He was there, I think," she said, pointing to the place where she thought the acrobat had fallen on that distant day. "Or maybe there. Who can tell? That's just it. I don't remember exactly. And I don't recall anything else important. It may be because I'm too tall now and seeing it all from a different angle."

"Do you want to walk on your knees?" he asked with interest.

She giggled.

"So, then, I think it may be time for us to go," Christian said into her ear, his warm breath sending shivers up her spine. "Unless there's something else you want to see?"

"No, I've had enough," she said gratefully. She hadn't wanted to complain, but the pleasure of the fair was fast fading into a jumble of noise and smells.

"There's just one more thing we have to do," he said, raising his head and looking around. "Ah, there. That seems to be as good a place as any."

He led her to a tent with a sign above it promising the wonders of the educated pig. But there was no one in front of it but an old man.

"Next show ain't for an hour," the man said when he saw them. "But I could let you in fer half price now," he added hopefully.

"I'll give you full price, if you can give me some information," Christian said.

The man's eyes narrowed. "I don't know much."

"Aye, I'll bet," Christian said. "And your pig's my uncle, too. Listen, I'm not a redbreast or a noser, all I need to know is what became of a cove who used to work here years ago. He was an acrobat, and took a header from a wire here, on this ground, some seventeen years past. Looked as though he'd snapped his neck. But up he came a moment after, to amaze the crowd. Yellow-thatched he was, and dressed in red. Remember him?"

"Oh, well," the old man said with relief. "Hand over the gelt, my man, I knows him. Knowed him, that is. He ain't with us no more."

"Yes, I heard he passed over," Christian said.

"Him? Nah, he's still above ground. It were the Sparrow what stuck his spoon in the wall two years back. He's the bloke who fell to rise again, like the advertisements went. Made a pretty penny at it, too, until he cocked up his toes. It weren't the act what done for him, it were a cough, not the fall, because he knew the way of it. No, what you seen *here* was Alfie Brogan, the poor sod . . . pardon, lady," he said to Christian's sudden frown.

"Alf's sprightly enough," the old man continued. "Pure luck. He guv up the act after that day, the first and last time he done it. See, he was trying to do what Sparrow did, but almost broke his neck. Scared him as much as the crowd, and he couldn't straighten up for a twelvemonth. If you needs to talk to him, he's in Coventry now, making saddles for his bread 'n butter."

Christain smiled. "You relieve my mind as well as my purse. I saw him that day, and didn't think I was such a flat as to fall for an act. Thank you." He handed the old man his coins. The fellow took them and touched his hand to his hat.

"Now," Christian told Julianne, "we can go. I'm satisfied. It was a point I had to make."

She looked at him curiously.

"Your cousin said I saw the acrobat in London," he explained. "I wanted to prove her wrong. What we saw was a one-time-only show."

Julianne smiled and walked away with him. She only glanced back when Christian turned his head. He looked back at the old man they'd just spoken with. The old fellow grinned and gave them a wink.

She almost stumbled. "The ground's uneven," she said quickly, to cover her doubt and confusion. Was it a wink to show a job well-done? Or was the old man just being friendly now that he'd coins to warm his pocket? She looked down at her feet to avoid Christian's eyes. "Do you think Sophie and Hammond will be at the carriage waiting for us?" she asked, to divert him.

"Likely," he said, "but they can wait a minute more."

He stopped. She looked up and around, to see that they were standing behind a tent, alone. He'd gotten them out of the crowd.

"At last," he said with satisfaction, "at least, this." He bent his head and kissed her lightly on the lips.

She knew she shouldn't have leaned in for his kiss. Knew very well it was wrong to wrap her arms around his neck and press close to him so she could kiss more thoroughly. Understood entirely that it was

foolish and fast, and folly and not what she ought to
do at all. But she knew even better that his mouth was
warm and delicious and that there'd never been anything like what she felt when his arms closed tightly
around her.

She also knew that though she'd closed her eyes
the sun was shining brightly, and that there were hundreds of people around them who might discover
them at any moment. And knew even better that she'd
be sorry later, when she thought about it. And so
though her heart was beating fast, she was as glad as
she was sorry when he let her go.

"I'm sorry," he said, "but I refuse to perform for an
audience."

She blinked, and looked around. She saw no one.

"Come on," Christian said wearily as he raised his
head. "Show your ugly face. I saw your long shadow,
and I swear I could hear you breathing."

A tall, fair-haired man with a bent nose stepped out
of a shadow and grinned at Christian. "Well, I'm that
surprised you could hear me breathing over your
panting, sir. Give you good day, ma'am," he said politely to Julianne, as he bowed. "Whoever you are.
Because believe me, I don't know and won't tell."

"Better not," Christian muttered. "Nameless lady, I
give you Captain Anthony Briggs, a blasted rogue
whose job it is to watch my every move so as to keep
the general public safe, I suppose. The squire is his
employer, and the Devil is his master. Don't tell me
the redbreast is lurking behind another tree," he said
to the captain.

"Dearie me, no," Anthony said, looking around

with mock fear. "Last I saw of him he was tracking after your cousin, lady, to see she's safe as houses. He knows what side his bread is buttered on."

"As you should," Christian said. "But if Murchison is on that trail, there may be reason." His lips tightened. "You go back to the fair and see what's up with them," he told the captain. "I'll be along presently— if they're not already at the carriage. I'll take you there," he told Julianne. "If they're waiting for us, we'll go back to the squire's. If they aren't . . ." He took Julianne's hand and led her up the slope again.

Only the coachman was waiting for them.

"Go in, and stay there," Christian told Julianne, his voice suddenly clipped and cool. "No matter what. I'll be back. Wait for me." And then he was off, striding down the long slope to the fair.

Christian knew exactly where to go. The crowd had clustered like a legion of ants around a bread crumb. He used elbows and boot tips to make his way through, leaving exclamations and threats—which ceased the minute those who uttered them saw his expression—in his wake. He saw no sign of Sophie or Hammond, or Anthony Briggs. But there was too huge a crowd massed tightly together to make out much.

They were watching a fight. Two Gypsy women had faced off six feet apart, in a ragged circle in the center of the crowd. They were screeching at each other. Both were dark and exotic, as Gypsies were supposed to be, but also young and uncommonly pretty. Their faces were rosy with anger. One had her

blouse pulled down from one shoulder, exposing a
very shapely breast that could be clearly seen by
every man who pushed and shoved his way far
enough up front to see. She didn't seem to notice. The
crowd did. They watched with breathless anticipation.

"So last time I'm warning you—you stay away
from him, hear?" one shapely Gypsy woman
screeched at the other. She pulled a long, shining
knife from her skirts and brandished it. The crowd
gasped and tried to draw closer.

"Aye, and who's to make me?" the other said, with
a smirking smile, as she tossed back her long shining
hair from her naked creamy shoulders.

"Very neat," a voice filled with admiration said at
Christian's ear.

"Yes," Christian said, without turning his head. "It
is a pretty sight. Firm as an apple and twice as tasty-
looking. The ken they're working is, too. Never fails.
Two lovely tarts about to go at it, stripping down before they do, always enough to make the crowd forget
good sense. If they ever had any. Hand on your wal-
let, Mr. Murchison, and hold on to your handkerchief.
It's a fancy act. By the time they're rolling in the mud
with their skirts up to their ears, their friends the dips
will have their paws on your watch fob. They'll be
working the crowd until the play's over."

"Think I don't know that?" Mr. Murchison said in
surprise. "What do you take me for?"

"A knowing one," Christian said. He looked at the
crowd. "So where are the lovebirds, Miss Wiley and
Hammond?"

"Lovebirds?" Murchison scoffed. "They're more

at dagger's drawn like the pretty Romanies are right now. They're just across the way, near the stout fellow with the white whiskers. She's behind Hammond and trying not to be. The clunch shoved her behind him so she don't see nothing a lady shouldn't, and she's ready to tear his head off, wanting to get a better eyeful."

"Ah, yes," Christian said, when he saw Sophie and Hammond across the impromptu circle from them. He smiled as he saw Sophie trying to pull away from her protector. "Looks like she'll do more damage to him than the Gypsies will, at that. I'm going to get them out of here. Fun's fun, but you never know when a lay like this will turn serious. One too many a push can come to shove, then to mayhem. It's late enough so louts in the crowd are soused, a lark like this can turn to riot."

"You're the knowing one," Murchison said in admiration. "I'll help."

Christian was elbowing his way through the mass of people when he heard the first furious shout to come from the crowd, and not the fighting Gypsy women. By the time he managed to force his way three more paces, he saw the first punch being thrown by a red-faced drover at an equally angry farmer. Soon Christian was ducking and twisting, shoving his way toward where he'd last seen Sophie and Hammond.

As he'd feared, there were too many fairgoers who'd drunk too deeply, tempers had flared, and a melee had started.

Christian ducked a punch and had to land two others. He pulled his coat from a drunken oaf's clutches and kicked the fellow's leg from under him to keep him from coming on. He forged on, the screams and shouts of the crowd ringing in his ears. He pushed, and his head was smacked with something hard. He reeled back. He shook his head, touched it, and felt wetness on his fingers. He hoped it was just spittle from the drunken lout screaming in his ear, pushed him away, and fought on. There was no time to look at the damage; to halt would be to be stopped in his tracks until the riot wound down. Because that was what it had become.

Christian kicked, prodded, and, at one point, bit his way toward where he'd last seen Sophie and Hammond. She'd been wearing red, he remembered that. He saw a drover's crimson kerchief, a clerk's red plaid waistcoat, a brave cherry feather in a farm girl's bonnet, the bright cardinal splash in a Gypsy's swirling skirts . . . and Sophie, a few feet away, cringing behind Hammond.

Hammond stood legs apart, fists clenched, facing the crowd, making himself the best target at the fair, Christian thought with annoyance as he kept fighting his way through the crowd.

The mass of people swirled around him, changing places as though in some mad dance, but Christian focused on Hammond and moved in his direction, trying to reach him and Sophie. One of the Gypsy girls who'd started the melee was very close to them now, Christian noticed. He thrust forward, pitched toward

Hammond, and reached his side—just as onlookers saw the silver flash of a long knife plunge into Hammond's chest.

Hammond gasped, clutched his chest, stared at it, then at Christian, and fell.

# Chapter 15

"Clear the way!" Mr. Murchison bellowed, swinging a stick to enforce his words, as Christian lifted Hammond and carried him out of the melee.

Christian, breathing hard, laid Hammond down on the first clear grassy patch he found and straightened with difficulty. "The fellow's solid muscle, he weighs a ton. He's breathing, but he's bleeding," Christian said. "Is there a doctor around?"

"No need for a sawbones, let my woman have a look at him," a swarthy man said as he came running up to them. "You lads," he ordered a group of hard-faced men behind him, "what are you waiting for? Get in there and break some heads if you must, but get this stopped, and now! They'll tear my tents down, then where am I?" he asked bitterly, not expecting an answer.

"I'm Smith, I run this fair," he told Christian, "My woman's good as a sawbones. I've sent for her." He squatted and looked at Hammond, frowning at the blood that stained the front of his shirt. "Must have missed his heart, or he'd be dead. There's a mercy, at least. Ah, Francine," he said as a wild-eyed Gypsy woman came running to join him. "Have a look. The bloke's in trouble. If he dies, we'll be, too. Don't matter who done for him. Everyone knows Gypsies is murderers and worse."

The woman stared down at Hammond. She nodded, pulled a long knife from her skirt, and in one swift fluid movement, knelt. Murchison cursed and moved toward her, but Christian put a hand on his shoulder to stop him.

"Think, man," Christian hissed. "She doesn't mean to harm him. Likely it's just to get his shirt off so she can see the damage."

The woman turned her head and looked up at him. "Want to give me a hand, sir? If one of mine helps, they'll blame us if he snuffs it. But if a gent's in it, we might be able to get out of this with a whole skin."

"Then I'm the last man you want laying a hand on him," Christian said with a sour smile. "If he dies and I'm beside him, it would be like saying you're in league with the devil, believe me. Murchison, assist her, will you?"

"You're letting her touch him?" Sophie shrieked, as the runner bent to help the Gypsy woman.

"Captain Briggs," Christian ordered, staring at the man who stood behind her, "take the squire's daughter to the carriage and stow her there. Miss Wiley," he told Sophie, "the fellow behind you is the man your father hired to watch everything I do. He'll see you safely to your cousin. She's waiting in the carriage. There's nothing you can do here now but be in the way. I won't let them hurt Hammond," he added in a gentler voice. "After all, whatever you think of me, remember that if anything bad befalls him, I'm the one sure to be blamed for it."

She stood rigid, then nodded. "I'll stay here," she said, lifting her head. "At least until I know how he is . . . please?"

"Then be still," Christian said. "How does he?" he asked the Gypsy, who with the runner's help had gotten Hammond's blood-soaked waistcoat and shirt away from the wound.

"The man must have been born under Virgo, because it would be his planet that rules the day," she muttered as she stared at the blood that sluggishly oozed from Hammond's bared chest. "Good fortune was his, whatever you think. The thrust was deep. But it was a nice clean one, and missed his heart and lungs. He'll ache and he'll groan, but if the wound doesn't go putrid, he'll live as long as his Maker intended."

"That's a relief, indeed," Christian said. "Can he be moved?"

"After I stop the bleeding and pack the wound, aye, take him away from here . . . please," she added in a mocking look at Sophie, where she stood, ashen-faced.

"It's as good as done," Christian said. "Did you know who struck the blow?"

"I'm a Rom, but no fortune-teller, nor one of the wenches running the stripping lay," she said contemptuously. "I told you it was the wrong day and place for it," she told the swarthy man, then turned to her work with Hammond again. "I saw nothing until I got here," she said as she did.

"Of course you didn't," Christian said. "And I suppose that goes double for every man and woman in your clan? So I supposed. What did you see?" he asked the captain.

"You running to him," Anthony said, jerking a finger at Hammond. "And then, him falling like a felled tree."

"Wonderful," Christian muttered. "And you, Mr. Murchison?"

"A knife struck, I saw the sun glinting on the blade before it was buried in his chest. But not who held it," the runner said. "There was too many milling around him. I'm willing to go bail it wasn't you, though. If only because it would have been a damned stupid thing for you to do, with everyone watching."

"I'm touched at your faith in me," Christian said. He took a deep breath. "All right, let's get him stoppered and bandaged. I'll see him home. But then I have to leave. Don't get your hopes up. I'm not running for the antipodes again. But I'd rather not face that lot at the squire's again just yet."

"They can't hold you accountable!" Anthony said with a fierce scowl.

"They can do anything they damn please," Christian said grimly. "And they know it well. They've done it before."

The sun was setting when Anthony entered the White Hart again. He looked into the taproom, saw Christian sitting by a window staring out. There were two glasses in front of him, one empty, one half-full. The captain sauntered in and took a seat at Christian's table.

Christian turned and raised an eyebrow. "Is this wise?"

The captain shrugged. "Don't matter now, does it? At least anyone listening to us at the fair would know, and I'll bet my last pair of boots there was at least one someone listening aside from the squire's daughter and the runner."

Christian drained his glass and raised his hand for another. "The one who stabbed him, do you think?" His voice was only slightly slurred.

"What are you drinking?" Anthony asked curiously, looking at the glasses on the table.

"Started with the light blue. Now? The landlord's best brew."

"You jug-bitten?"

"Not enough."

"Oh, well then, let's see if I can catch up. They think you did it, of course."

Christian, head down, and studying the rough tabletop, nodded.

"But Murchison don't, and his word has weight. And though the old gentleman hates you right enough and wouldn't trust you enough to ask you to drown his kittens, I don't think he really believes you did, neither. Because it would have been a stupid thing to do, and, whatever he thinks of you, he knows you aren't that."

"And Julianne?" Christian asked slowly.

"What do you think? But still, I think it would be best if you cleared out."

Christian's eyes widened as his head came up. "He's dead then? But he was doing well."

"Hammond? No, he isn't ready to dance, but he's happier than he's been in weeks. See, his almost being killed settled the squire's daughter down. She's cooing over him like a mother bird, and he's loving every minute. Yes, and a pint for me, too," he told the innkeeper, when he came to collect Christian's empty glass.

"Someone tried to kill Hammond because I was there," Christian said.

"Don't give yourself airs. It would be a neat fit; but like I said, there's too many holes in it. Hammond could have enemies, too, you know. If they think that you're not the heir, it would be Hammond, right? Maybe someone wants to prevent that. Maybe it was just a mistake. It was a riot. Tempers flare. The wrong man's been snuffed in a crowd many a time, you know that. Maybe you were the one they were trying for, did you think of that?"

Christian stared at him.

"Thought not. There's so many reasons for his being skewered, we could be here all night discussing them. But as for what it means to you? It will keep you away from Hammond and the rest of them. Maybe someone wants that."

"Won't work," Christian said.

Now Anthony raised a tawny eyebrow. "You run mad?"

"No. Just that it doesn't make any difference, does it? They hated and mistrusted me before this. This only means they'll keep at it. I just have to keep away from places where someone could be killed in my company," he said, on a twisted smile.

Anthony sat silently while the innkeeper delivered the drinks to them. He waited until the man had gone, took a long swallow from his glass, put it down, and bent closer to Christian. "You don't have to stay here, you know. It won't make any difference in the inheritance. Papers are papers, and they're all under lock and key. You've seen the place, they've seen you. You've even gotten a tour so you could count the silver, now no one can slip it out from under your nose. Think, man. You can *leave* now. I think you should."

Christian shook his head. "No one is going to frighten me off. You should know that."

"I do, well enough. If you've good reason, nothing would turn you aside, but I fail to see . . ." Anthony gave his companion a searching look. "I'll be damned for a fool!" he suddenly exclaimed. "It's her, the gentry mort, ain't it?"

Christian swirled the ale in his glass and stared at it as though he could read his future in the bubbling amber liquid. "A female's a female, pretty though she is. They've tempted me to many things, but never to put my head in a noose."

His companion didn't speak, only stared hard, his brilliant blue eyes looking deep. "So your mind's set?"

"It is."

"Then there's no sense my wasting my breath," Anthony said, and began to stand up.

"Yes, she's lovely," Christian said, low. "And gentle and kind. Smart, too. I wouldn't pass an extra hour with her if she wasn't."

Anthony eased down in his seat again.

"I'm not getting anything on the side," Christian said seriously, so seriously his companion realized again how much he must have had to drink. "She's proper as a parson—well, not quite. She's too honest for that. But she's no merry leg, you know. You shouldn't even think of her in those terms," he added censoriously.

"Sorry," Anthony said. "Although, if you remember, I never said such."

Christian seemed lost in a reverie. His eyes were bright but unfocused, the only other sign of his intoxication the increasingly careful way he chose his words. "She's pretty, and clever, and she has the most amazingly beautiful . . . But I'm too much of a gentleman to mention them, you know. The thing is, she's also kind," he said with wonder. "I haven't known much of that . . . God! I am jug-bitten," he said with loathing, looking down at his glass as though it were a serpent. "My fault. I tried to get drunker than a sow. There was nothing I could do but wait and see what happened to Hammond. But I wanted to leave, but only for a little while. The thing is . . ." He struggled for words, his cool expression gone. He looked younger, and in pain. He ran a hand over his hair, and frowned, trying to find the right words.

"We saw the Gypsies today," he finally said. "That was what reminded me. The thing is, Amya . . ." Christian stopped and looked at his companion owlishly. "I mean, *Anthony*, I'm so very tired of being treated as though I were a Gypsy rover myself. No matter what I say or how I act or dress, everyone's ready to run me off. They watch my every move, waiting for me to pocket the silver, or steal their babies, or God knows what else. She isn't like that. Or rather, when she does distrust me, she tells me so. And then, when I explain, I think she believes me. The thing is that I no longer know if that's good or bad. Can you believe it? *Me?* Now there's something to worry about. But don't worry. I know what I know, and who I am. Blast, I'm not making sense."

"Too much sense," Anthony said softly.

"Don't worry," Christian said again. "I know what I must do, and I'll never forget or spill it." He closed his eyes, and took a breath. His face cleared of expression. "But oh, aye," he murmured softly, "she tempts me sore. Still, the thing is that no man runs me off—not anymore. I've rhymed that," he said in wonder, opening his eyes. "So it must be true. Isn't that what the Romany say? Gads, I wish Daffyd was here!"

"It's what a man with a bellyful of booze says. You need sleep, and I don't feel like hitting you on the head so you can get it. You've a damned hard head. And a punishing left. So let's have another round, and then I'll see you to bed if I have to carry you up the stair," Anthony said, drained his glass, and signaled the landlord again.

"All right. But don't let me dream," Christian said earnestly.

"Oh, lad," his companion said.

Hammond was propped up in bed on his pillows, Sophie at his side, anxiously watching his every exhalation. His face was ashen, his arm was in a sling, his chest was wrapped round with thick bandaging, and he was beaming with happiness.

"I'm fine," he said again. "I wasn't happy when the doctor bled me, and I'm weak as a kitten now. But I've got my kitten back," he added, giving Sophie a look of pure adoration, "and that's all that matters."

"I should say not," Sir Maurice said impatiently. "I'm glad you and your lady have reconciled, but what matters is who struck you. Again, was it that fellow who claims to be Christian Sauvage?"

"And again, I can't say. I didn't see," Hammond said with a trace of impatience himself.

He seemed to have lost a lot of blood but recovered his spirit, Julianne thought. She stood beside the bed, along with the squire, his wife, the Bow Street runner, and the doctor. The past hours had been terrifying. Julianne had been caught in a whirlwind of conflicting emotions from the moment Christian had appeared at the carriage with the blood-drenched, stricken Hammond. She'd worried and wondered all the way on the mad ride back to the squire's house, while Hammond lay across the seat, his head in Sophie's lap. Then she'd fretted for hours more, after Christian had left, worrying about why he'd gone, wondering if she was keeping a deathwatch, waiting for the doctor to come out of the sickroom to say how Hammond was. Only Sophie had been allowed in his bedchamber during those desperate hours, and only because she'd carried on like a banshee, refusing to stay out until finally they'd said she might come in.

Now came the glad news. Hammond would live; he'd escaped death by inches but would recover by leaps and bounds. Now he could meet with the others so they could continue the inquiry, trying to discover who had actually struck him.

"But he was seen running to you and was right beside you when you were attacked," Sir Maurice persisted.

"I said I saw him coming toward me," Hammond said. "And he was beside me when I felt the blow. It felt like a punch in the chest, not a knife, at all," he added with wonder. "I didn't know what had happened, others knew it before me. But there were a lot people around me all that time, I could hardly breathe there was such a crowd. So I don't know if he did it. I must say I doubt it. If he was out to kill me, I think there have been better opportunities than having at me in front of all the world."

"Aye, and so said I," Mr. Murchison said, rocking back on his heels.

"So everyone would say," Sir Maurice said. "That is why it was a perfect time for him to strike."

"That's very rococo!" Julianne exclaimed. "I mean it's too elaborate. The attack seemed made at the spur of the moment, and so I think it was!"

She fell silent when the baronet turned and stared down his long nose at her, his thin nostrils pinched. But she'd thought about it all this time. Whatever the man who claimed to be Christian might be, she knew in her heart that he wasn't a killer. She also knew that wasn't a thing she could say aloud because it sounded weak and foolish even to her own ears.

But she knew what she knew, she thought stubbornly, as she raised her chin and looked back at the baronet. If she couldn't trust her own insight, whose could she trust? Certainly not anyone's in this room; they all had their own aims in the matter. She had a right to her opinion.

Unexpectedly, the baronet smiled. "Please don't look daggers at me, Miss Lowell," he said, with that ghost of a smile on his thin lips. "We've had enough to do with sharp blades for the day, don't you think?"

The others in the room traded their shocked expressions for weak chuckles, as the baronet continued to smile. "I'm not sure I agree with you, my dear," Sir Maurice went on. "But it's obvious I wouldn't able to get the local justice of the peace to disagree, at least not in court. No one saw the imposter attack. That doesn't mean he didn't have a hand in it. He could have had someone in his employ do it, and likely did. The difficulty comes in proving it. We'll continue our interviews at the Gypsy camp and investigate the performers and workers who were at the fair. They're a bad lot; most of them hardened criminals, no doubt. Any one of them could have done it."

"As could any visitor at the fair," Mr. Murchison added. "We couldn't hold them all for questions, sir. But those we think have a personal interest in the matter will be questioned. I'll speak to the fellow who claims he's Christian Sauvage soon as I leave here."

"If he's still in the vicinity," Sir Maurice said dryly.

Julianne's eyes widened. With all her worrying about what might happen to Christian, she hadn't thought of that.

Sir Maurice slid a glance at her, as he added, "I'll have to leave it to you, Mr. Murchison. I certainly don't want to deal with him. You continue your line of inquiry, and I'll pursue my own. If you remember anything else, Hammond, I'd ask you to send for me immediately."

"*I'd* ask him to sleep now," the doctor said testily.

"Of course," Sir Maurice said.

"And I'll stay with him until he does," Sophie said, in a voice that brooked no opposition.

Julianne was smiling as she left the bedchamber. Sir Maurice saw her expression, and paused outside the door. "You are amused?" he asked.

"Oh, no," she said, embarrassed. "I'm only happy that something good came from such a terrible thing, because now at least Sophie and Hammond are together again."

"I am not sure it is such a wonderful thing," Sophie's mama said bitterly. "Hammond has a neat competence, but nothing to what we imagined he'd have if he was the new earl of Egremont."

"Martha!" the squire said nervously. "Take care what you say. Hammond will likely be our son-in-law. And," he added on a weak laugh, "I'm not at all sure it's wise to be heard saying anything against him after that attempt on his life."

"Very sound advice," the runner said.

Sir Maurice added, "Sound advice, yes, Mr. Murchison. But my suspicions do not fall on my hostess. You will speak to the imposter as soon as possible?"

"I'm on my way now," the runner said, sketched a bow, and strode down the hall to the stair.

"Too much excitement," the squire said. "I think we'll have a bit of a lie-down before dinner. See you then," he said, and escorted his wife to their own bedchamber.

"So then, it is only you and I," Sir Maurice told Julianne. "Unless you have letters to write?"

Since that was exactly the excuse she was going to give, Julianne colored and shook her head. "No," she said. "I'm too upset at what's happened to write a straight line."

"Good," he said. 'I could do with some tea. And you?

"Oh, yes, thank you," she said, and, taking his proffered arm, went down the stair with him, though her mind was already trying to follow the runner and imagine his conversation with Christian, if—indeed—Christian was there to have one with.

"Beg pardon?" she asked, when she realized the baronet was waiting for a reply.

He patted her hand. "I understand, this has been a stressful day. I only asked if you were looking forward to London?"

She missed a step and might have tumbled down the stairs if she hadn't been upheld by the baronet's surprisingly strong arm. "London?" she asked stupidly, stopping where she was to gape at him.

He clucked his tongue. "They didn't tell you? I'm not surprised, everything is at sixes and sevens. But your cousins and I met this afternoon after the doctor pronounced Hammond out of danger. We've decided to remove to London, where he would be safer, as soon as he can travel. The late earl's solicitors and bankers are there; Bow Street is there, the courts are there. So that's where we are to be."

"But not me," she managed to say. "They won't need me there."

"Of course we do," he said, laying his cool dry hand on hers again. "You'll be asked to testify at some point. Don't worry. It will be brief, and can be private. And you won't be required to see the imposter again. The game has obviously changed, and it's too dangerous now."

She looked at him with all the doubt and confusion she felt.

"You were wrong, you know," he said gently. "I didn't want to make an issue of it, but an assassination can be very rococo. It is very like a chess game. You're a player in the game now, my dear. The imposter obviously thinks so, too, or he wouldn't have played on your tender sensibilities. No, don't look guilty. I don't blame you, your compassionate feelings do you credit. But they are not to be relied upon.

"You're young and trusting," he told her, his blue eyes alive in his cool, pale, expressionless face. "Utterly inexperienced with the ways of such a criminal mind. I am not. He knows you miss your brother and seek a connection to him again. For him to play upon that most natural wish is vile, but not surprising, at least not to me. I'm a man of experience and have encountered his type before. His sort of charlatan is no better than a Gypsy, and twice as dangerous because he can pass as a gentleperson. You haven't seen his like before and so must be protected from danger. Those dangers include your own laudable sensibilities.

"Don't be vexed with me," he added with a sad smile. "You think I don't know the ways of the female heart. But I do. I may not be young and handsome, but I do know." She tried to murmur weak denials. "Please," he said, cutting her off. "I beg you at least to think about the sense of what I'm saying, because I've no ulterior motives, only a wish to restore my family and ensure your safety. As for the imposter? He has everything to gain and nothing to lose. And now he's getting desperate.

"You see," he said, lowering his voice, though they stood in the middle of the stair and there was no one to hear them, "the end grows near. He knows it, too. Otherwise, he wouldn't have attempted such a reckless act. I can't prove it yet, but I know he showed his hand today. So now more than ever we can't have you influenced by such a villain. You need never see him again."

"But surely," she stammered, "if we go to London, so will he."

Sir Maurice smiled. "I am counting on it. Now, shall we take our tea?"

# Chapter 16

"**H**ammond is still doing well?" Julianne asked, as Sophie dressed for dinner.

Sophie beamed. "Very well, and I am, too. It took almost losing him to make me realize I didn't ever want to lose him. Ham says that was a costly lesson, but he was willing to pay every part of it. Wasn't that sweet?" She twirled in front of her mirror, smiling at how her leaf green gown fluttered around her. "Do you like this one? I was saving it for something special, and I want to look especially good this evening, even though I'm not dining with Ham. But I'll be in his room the moment we're done with our dinner."

"It looks lovely, and I'm very happy for you," Julianne said. "But I wonder if we could have a moment alone?" She smiled at Sophie's maid. "I've something personal to discuss with my cousin," she explained.

"You may go," Sophie told her maid, and as the girl left, added, "My goodness, Julianne! You don't have to ask a servant's permission. What is it you wanted?"

"I wanted to say good-bye," Julianne said. "I've packed and will be ready to leave in the morning.

Now that Hammond's on the mend, I can go."

"Good-bye?" Sophie asked in amazement.

"Why, yes. I've just heard that you'll be going to London. My purpose here has been fulfilled. I miss my parents and want to get back to my own life. I'll go to London if I have to testify, but now, I'm going home."

"You're joking, of course," Sophie said. "You must come with us."

"No, I mustn't. I don't want to."

"Who would not want to visit London in the Season?"

"Me. I haven't the clothes, for one thing," Julianne said lightly, citing the only thing she'd thought her cousin might understand. She certainly couldn't tell her she hadn't the heart to take part anymore in this matter of the true earl of Egremont, not if she could do nothing to save Christian. The baronet had seemed sure of his destruction. A young man she'd loved had been destroyed once before, and she refused to experience such a loss again. If she couldn't help, better to go home and try to forget. She certainly couldn't take part in a round of merriment with the very people who would celebrate Christian's ruin.

"You don't need many new clothes . . ."

"I do if I go with you," Julianne said on a forced laugh. "You, my dear Cousin, will be going to all the best parties, at all the right houses. Attending operas and soirees and routs and who knows what else? Besides, I've served my purpose, haven't I? You invited me here to identify Christian Sauvage."

"The man who calls himself Christian Sauvage," her cousin said.

"Right," Julianne said. "I met the man and can't help you there, because I don't know who he is. So though I'm flattered you asked, why should I go with you to London now? Invite me to your wedding, and I'll be happy," she added. "And please believe I am very happy for you, and not because I'm angling for the true heir to Egremont—whoever that may be . . .

"See?" Julianne shook her head. "I'm doing it already, defending myself and my intentions. I can't put a word right because the whole affair makes me uncomfortable. I hope it works out well for you, but I think I'm well out of it now. I'm ready to go home. Thank you for a lovely time, and," she said, taking her cousin's hand, "I do mean that."

"I know," Sophie said. She didn't release her hand. "I do like you, Cousin, and so do my parents—and Hammond. In fact, he likes you so much that I was most vilely jealous of you for a while. Until, of course, I realized he didn't like you like *that*. The point is that we all feel wretched for having used you and worse once Sir Maurice pointed out that we had. And the other thing is," she said in a rush, "that he wants you to come with us, and we do what he asks."

Julianne frowned. "Sir Maurice? He's not my relative. I don't have to do as he asks."

"I know, but he could be your relative, and without much effort, I think." Sophie tittered. "He's old, but he's not dead yet. And he's very, very rich. Oh, come," she said, with an arch look, as Julianne stared at her, frowning. "You know exactly what I mean."

"I hope not!" Julianne said in revulsion. "He's nice to me, but you've got the wrong sow by the ear. I'm sure he doesn't mean anything like that. I know I don't!" She dragged her hand away from her cousin. "If you wanted to say something to really keep me away from London, you've done it. I wish you well, Sophie, but I'm going home now!"

"I don't see why you should act so insulted," Sophie said in annoyance. "He hasn't a direct heir anymore, and he has a vast fortune, it would be only natural . . . Oh, forget I mentioned it. You're probably right. It's Mama who puts all these matchmaking ideas in my head. Why," she said slyly, watching Julianne closely, "she even said she thinks you've fallen in love with the imposter! She believes you defend him because you've lost your heart to him, and I might add, she hopes that's all you've lost."

Julianne's face grew pale.

Sophie tilted her head. "Oho," she said. "For once Mama is right. Is that why you say you don't know who he is? That puts the whole matter in a different light, doesn't it?"

"That is absurd," Julianne said, the color rushing back to her face. "And insulting. I'm very glad it's time for me to go home." She lifted her chin and began to march toward the door.

"So everyone can say that Mama's right?" Sophie asked sweetly.

Julianne stopped, turned, and stared at her.

Sophie nodded. "They will, you know. Mama's a

dear, but she gabbles, and she'll be going a great
many places in London. I hear that the case of the
true identity of the earl of Egremont is already fabu-
lous gossip there. Doubtless your part in it will be a
wonderful tidbit to chew over, especially if you're not
with us. Your absence will give credence to the rumors. Why, they'll likely even get back to your little
village."

Sophie traced an invisible circle on her vanity's top
with one finger as she spoke. "You don't want to go to
London now. I'm sorry for it. I suppose you must do
as you wish. But if you don't go, with us, you know
you'll only have to go later, as a witness, and perhaps
stay even longer then. Doubtless the lawyers and Bow
Street will hear the rumors, too, and they'll want to
know much more from you. I know our solicitors
will.

"Sir Maurice says the imposter should be in irons
before the month is out. And if it's said that you were
in sympathy, or more, with him . . ." Her eyes flashed
as she looked up and saw Julianne flinch. "Think!"
she said angrily. "Who else would profit from Hammond's death? The imposter as much as signed his
death certificate with that blow, Sir Maurice says.

"If you're not in London with us, your reputation
will be ruined," she went on. "If you come with us,
however it ends, we'll see the matter is settled, at least
for you."

"That," Julianne said furiously, "is blackmail!"

"I suppose it is," Sophie said, with a shrug. "But it
won't harm you. Mama will see you have the clothes
you need, and she won't ask you to pay a cent of it. In

fact she'll be insulted if you try. Anyway, the baronet would probably skin her if she accepted funds from you. He's mad enough that we had you meet with the imposter alone, so he could 'work his wiles on you,' as he said."

Sophie smiled. "So you see, you absolutely must come to London. And whatever you think of me now, I think one day you'll thank me for it. This is the best thing for you, know it or not."

"The baronet asked you to do this to me?" Julianne asked, her nostrils now as pinched as that gentleman's on his highest ropes.

"Oh, no," Sophie said innocently. "It's only that he asked that you come with us, and I know what he asks is best for us. And some people need to be pushed into what's best for them."

*And some people*, Julianne thought feverishly, *will need to be told about this as soon as possible.*

She'd done it before and she could do it again, Julianne told herself firmly. They hadn't caught her last time, and they wouldn't this time either. She didn't like deception, she hated feeling furtive. It wasn't like her. But it was necessary. She hadn't any other choice. When else could she speak to him alone, or for that matter, at all? Twist and turn as she might, she didn't see any other course of action, and it was action that she had to take now. She'd grown up with boys, perhaps that made her braver than most women. But she was a woman now, and she thought that made her even braver still.

So Julianne rode on alone through the night again,

this time more troubled by what she didn't see than by what she did. She stopped her horse every now and then and paused to listen for anyone following. All she heard were the innocent sounds of the night, and her own wild heartbeat. Because this time she was riding to meet a man who might be a killer as well as a swindler. Whatever he was, she wasn't afraid of him, only for him. And she had to say goodbye to him.

She doubted she'd have another chance. She was going to London, and now she knew she was under suspicion. They suspected her allegiances, and once they heard Sophie's story of her reluctance to go to London, they'd probably keep a watch on her. After the attack on Hammond, they'd be watching the house like hawks as well. But they weren't just yet. She had manged to leave the house without the hint of a shadow to prevent her. She supposed it was because they were all still in shock. She knew she still was. Best then to strike while the iron was hot, and she had enough bravery born of anger to send herself out the door. Because after tonight she might not have the courage, and after tonight she might never see him again.

She didn't know if he'd be arrested or made an earl. She couldn't bear seeing him in chains, and if he was indeed the rightful heir, it was almost certain she could never have him for her own.

Well, there it was, she thought sadly, she'd admitted it. She cared for him. Very much. She wasn't sure that was love, because she'd never been in love. When he touched her, she wanted more. That, she knew, was lust. And he made her remember those good, long-gone days. That, she realized, was longing for what could never be recaptured. He made her laugh, and that she knew was what a friend ought to do, and he was certainly becoming that. But she knew he might be an imposter, and he might be playing her for a fool.

Still, she had to talk to him, tell him she'd be leaving, and let him know what the baronet had predicted. The worst they could do to her if they found out was send her home. *Well then, good,* she thought unhappily, and rode on. She supposed they could ruin her reputation, too. But although the thought pained her now, she didn't think it would matter much later, when she was safe at home, where they would love her no matter what someone else might say she'd done.

She had a few hours until dawn. It was a clear and starry night, but the moon wasn't full. Julianne's eyes had adjusted to the darkness, she could see the outlines of trees and make out the turns in the road. She breathed a sigh of relief when she saw a fiery glow of light ahead, like a grounded star before her in the night. She rode to it. The inn had a lantern over the front door that they kept lit through the night just in case some lost traveler needed a beacon.

Julianne halted her horse in front of the door. And then she sat staring stupidly at the inn sign, realizing the one thing she hadn't thought about.

Tonight there was no tormented man standing in the swirling mists in the dooryard, miraculously looking for her. There was not one person abroad, not a living soul stirring. Christian must be sleeping, as everyone else in the dreaming world was now. So how was she going to find him?

Well, Julianne thought, as she slipped off the horse's back and threw the reins over the fence in front of the inn, she'd just have to, somehow. She had a vague plan of slipping into the inn, creeping up the stair, and whispering his name. Nothing else came to mind. If she was seen, let them think it was a tryst she was keeping, she thought fiercely as she went to the door. What was that to a man's life? It was no less than that which spurred her on.

She had to see Christian immediately. The urgency of her message was what had propelled her from the house in the midst of the night, finally sending her up and out of her bed like a crab popping out of a pot of scalding water. Sophie had said the baronet had promised that Christian would be in irons before the month was out.

She reached the door, put her hand on the latch . . . and discovered that the door was bolted fast. The guests must all be sleeping. A prospective lodger was supposed to rouse the landlord.

There was nothing for it but to creep around the house and try the door to the kitchens. The only person who might be woken there would be the lowest kitchen servant. At any rate, she couldn't stop now. If she did, she'd get on her horse and go back; her courage was evaporating with the dying night.

Julianne gathered up her skirt and began to walk around the inn. As she did she formed the nebulous idea of telling the kitchen wench some tales and promising her coins for her silence and for telling which room Christian was in.

She stepped into some soft gooey muck, and grimaced. Pulling her boot free, she went on, trying to avoid the mess in the stable yard. Once on firmer ground she stealthily approached the back door.

And gasped when a gloved hand clapped over her mouth.

Julianne bit down hard and struggled as an iron hard arm locked around her waist. She was pulled back against a hard body. She kicked out for all she was worth.

"By God! A female!" a masculine voice hissed in her ear. "Ouch! Stop that! Do you want to wake the whole town?"

She stopped, though her heart was hammering so loud she could scarcely think. She was pleased to hear he was breathing as heavily as she was. And then not so pleased, as the other implications of that sank in. She tensed.

"Now then," the voice growled in her ear. "No screaming when I take my hand away, or I swear I'll give you such a dunt you won't remember anything until next week."

She nodded. The hand left her mouth. She took a deep breath, felt the body behind her tense, and then, as she remained still, relax.

"Now let's see what's afoot . . ." he said. "Miss Lowell! What the devil are you doing here?"

He was a tall fair-haired fellow with a kink in his nose, and eyes so blue she could make out their color even in the scant light.

"Captain Anthony Briggs, retired, at your service," he said, when she didn't answer. "Remember me, from the fair? With Christian? I was hired by the squire to investigate the matter of the lost heir to Egremont."

She took a steadying breath. "Then why didn't you cry out an alarm when you saw me?"

"Good question!" he congratulated her. "Knew Christian wouldn't care for a nodcock," he murmured. "Thing is, I wasn't sure who you were, and a canny officer never cries rope on anyone until he can see what flag he flies. Now, what are *you* doing here?"

She moistened her dry lips with her tongue as she tried to come up with an excuse.

"Oh," he said, with a peculiar smile, "I'm the nodcock, ain't I? Go right on up. Don't think he's expecting you, but he'd have to be dead not to welcome you to his bed. Third chamber to the left at the top of the stair."

*"Mr. Briggs!"* she gasped as she realized what he meant. "It is certainly not that!"

"Captain Briggs," he corrected her absently. "Then what is it? You're not carrying cutlery or a cannon, so I don't think you're out to kill him. And if it is pleasure you're after bringing him at this hour, why the devil are you? You're a proper young lady, aren't you?"

"I am," she said. She hesitated, and then, since he hadn't exposed her, went on quickly, "I'm here to tell him something. I have to talk to him. It's a matter of . . ." A horrible thought occurred to her. "Are you working for the baronet as well?"

He nodded. "And a few others."

She closed her eyes and her mouth. Her shoulders slumped. Now she'd done it. When the news got back to the manor, at the least, she'd never be trusted again. They'd think she was a trollop, at best.

The man watched her in silence, then seemed to come to a decision. "I work for everyone, but I owe allegiance to only a few. Christian is one of them. Your visit is your secret, and his. If you don't want to go upstairs, I'll tell him you're here. Give me more than a moment," he warned her. "He'll need to be woken, and quietly. He had a pint too many last night. My fault entirely, I thought he needed some rest after his day at the fair. Wait here. Don't make a sound."

Julianne paced the kitchen garden for what seemed a half hour, then started silently singing verses to an old song in her head to pass the time. She frowned when she realized she was singing about a woman lamenting how she'd been deceived by her lover. Still, the song was lodged in her mind, and it had a great many verses. She'd gone through three renderings when she saw the back door to the inn open.

"The devil!" Christian exclaimed. "He spoke truth. I thought I was still dreaming." He reached her side in a few strides and caught her up in his arms. Her hood fell back as he buried his face in hair. "Lord, Julie. Why are you here? How did you know I needed you here? I'm so glad you're here."

His hair was wet, his face was cold, he smelled of soap and coffee. "I was drunk as a wheelbarrow last night," he muttered, "and dead to the world when Anthony woke me. But I'm not a drunkard," he said quickly, pulling back to look into her eyes. "The problem is that I can drink too well, it takes a lot to stagger me, and I tried for oblivion last night. That was stupid. And I'm well paid for my idiocy. It felt like being resurrected from the dead. My head aches, I won't tell you what my stomach feels like . . . but why are you here?"

"I'm going to London," she blurted. "The baronet insists. There are to be inquiries, Sophie says. The matter of the earldom. I didn't know when I could slip out again to tell you. But Sir Maurice said that you'd be in irons before the month was out. I had to tell you, warn you."

"Oh, is that all? Thank you. But I knew some and guessed the rest. You'll like London. And I'll be there, too."

She stared at him as he ran a hand over his hair in a gesture she was coming to recognize meant that he was thinking.

"You're going to London?" she asked, her own stomach feeling hollow. What a fool she was. He'd been planning to leave and had never said a word about it.

"Yes, I was going to tell you when it was settled. I have to. That's where the final inquiries into the title are being held."

"But Sir Maurice said you'd be in irons before the month was out."

"Oh, don't look like that," he said, pulling her back into his arms. "I've no plans to go to prison. Sir Maurice is thinking wishfully. I'll be earl of Egremont when I return. Mmm, you're warm, and it's a cold,

cold dawn. But we can't stay here, right under everyone's noses," he said, looking up. "The stars are the wrong way round, but I can read them anyway. I can't ask you up to my room, even if I meant nothing but conversation. Anthony would be scandalized." He grinned. "And you're right. We won't be able to see each other for a while, I suppose. Care to come for a walk with me?"

"In the dark?"

"We won't go far, but I'm tired of whispering."

He took her hand, and she stepped to the bottom of the garden with him. They walked until they came to a circular bench wrapped around a huge tree.

"There," he said, as they sat down. "Shelter from the dew and the eyes of the inn." He put an arm around her and took a deep breath. "What do you want to talk about? Come, Little Jewel," he said, when she didn't answer. "You've got dozens of questions in that pretty head of yours; when I put my ear to yours I could hear them buzzing there. Ask me anything."

"Who are you?" she said.

He laughed, low. "I told you who I was. Either you believe me, or you don't. Nothing I say will change that."

"You told me who you were," she said carefully, "but not who you've become. You never said a word about . . ." She paused, discovering that the darkness gave her the false courage of anonymity. "You never really spoke about Newgate, or the Hulks, or your imprisonment there or in the antipodes."

"No," he agreed. "I didn't. I don't like to talk about

it. And I don't think it's good for a proper young woman's ears. Why is it important?"

She closed her eyes, trying to hide in a deeper darkness. "Because anyone could have found out about my childhood, Sophie said."

"True, true." His voice came soft and slow. "But any old lag could tell you about prison, love. What would that prove? Only that I've lost my soul some-where along the way and am trying to find it again. And how would that help? But if you wish . . .

"Newgate is hell," he said. "The rich do well enough there. They have separate quarters, good food, and clean water, even visitors. We weren't rich, we had some funds, but the lawyers ate up our house and property. We were thrown into a cage with twenty men where there was adequate room for four. Vile men and good men, dying and desperate ones, men and boys, and they preyed on each other. My father was strong, but not wise to the ways of men with no morals. If it weren't for the two boys I met on our first day, I don't believe we'd have lasted a night, much less a week. But the boys traded their prison wisdom for my father's strength, and we looked after each other. Against all odds we somehow survived. We en-dured a year before we were sent to the Hulks.

"The Hulks," he said softly, "made us want to re-turn to Newgate." His voice became expressionless. "They were once ships of the line, warships. They lie at anchor, out of sight and mind. Most of them take you nowhere but to your grave. You're sent to the low-est deck first. There's no light or air. If you live long enough, you rise to the next deck. If you survive the fevers and fights, you may be lucky enough to be let out to work on the roads or in the muck of the river-bank each day and be locked up again every night. If you eventually rise higher, you may finally sail away—to Botany Bay. Then if you can survive the voyage, you reach land and work in the sunlight again. If you're clever and lucky, you live out your sentence. Not many do. We did."

The night was still. Julianne didn't know what to say. He'd told her everything and nothing, and she couldn't ask for more.

"So you see," he said on a breath of sound, "it's very important that I become the rightful earl of Egremont. Not much can change the laws of the land or the way England treats her prisoners, not in a year, or maybe even in a lifetime. But a man of funds and influence can do more to change things than any man can, and few, if any of them, are trying. I will. I shall. That's why I'm here. The title has power. Egremont has riches that make men like the baronet drool just talking about them.

"I don't care about cloisonné snuffboxes or Van Dycks or da Vincis," he mimicked the baronet's dry tones, "or any damned item of *virtu*, as he put it, that Egremont holds. I care about the power of the name and the title, and the way it may work for change.

"Although," he added, his voice becoming his own again, "I do like the thought of owning all that silver and gold, of course. And so, there you have it. By the way," he added, "I spent most of our time together talking about our shared past, not because I was try-ing to convince you of who I was, or at least, not entirely. And certainly not because I learned about it from others. But because I enjoy doing it. And you're right. We've discussed those days enough. So now what shall we talk about? Because if we don't talk, I'm going to kiss you."

"That would be a mistake," she said breathlessly.

"I thought you knew," he said as he took her into his arms. "I'm famous for my mistakes."

Their kiss was long, full of heat and yearning, and desperation. She was crying when they were done.

"Ah, Julie, my jewel," he said, touching the tears on her cheek. "Are these for me? Then don't. I will endure. Now, time to get you home again. It may well be that you'll be called to testify for or against me. Being found wandering home at dawn from a secret meeting with me, wet with tears and dew, won't help either of us. But never doubt it, we will meet again."

She was moved so deeply she couldn't speak. And even worse, in spite of what he'd said, she began to doubt she'd ever see him again, however it all turned out.

# Chapter 17

⌍⌌

Hammond healed quickly; the household was packed up in no time at all, and Julianne's parents were ecstatic to hear she'd been invited to London. So it wasn't very long before Julianne found herself in a carriage on her way there.

"One of the best things about Egremont is that it isn't far from London," Sophie burbled, as the coach moved out of her drive. "We'll be there by dinnertime, and this time of the year that means before dark. So if you get weary," she cautioned Hammond, in the seat opposite her, "just say something, and we'll stop."

"I feel right as rain," Hammond assured her with a grin. "I'm taped up tighter than a dead Egyptian king, so nothing jars, and nothing hurts."

Julianne sat up straight. Sophie had said that Egremont wasn't far from London, and yet they were leaving from the squire's house. Were they now that sure that Hammond would inherit? Why? She'd tried to avoid her cousins in the days since the night she'd met Christian in the dark, and wondered if she'd missed anything.

She decided it had been a slip of the tongue. Old dreams die hard, she certainly knew that. She relaxed and tried to sit back again. That was difficult, as she was sandwiched between Sophie and her mama; Hammond had the seat opposite to himself, since the squire had chosen to ride horseback along with the outriders alongside their coach. And Sir Maurice had departed some days earlier, after making the shocking announcement that he'd see them in London, too.

The others at the table had gone stone still and stared at him.

"But you never leave the north!" Sophie's mama had gasped.

The baronet gave her a thin smile. "Patently untrue, my dear Martha. You see me here before you right now, do you not? It's true that I don't like to leave the comforts and beauty of my home. But I do what I must for the family and always have done. I'll be needed in London. And so I'll be there." He'd given Julianne a warmer smile as he explained, "My family is always uppermost in my mind. How could I be comfortable thinking of Egremont in the hands of a usurper?"

She'd ducked her head, not wanting to show how upset she was by the question. He took it for modesty, she supposed, and was glad he didn't ask more. She'd been trying to avoid conversations with him. She doubted the old gentleman entertained any romantic notions about her. But since Christian had joked about it, and her cousin had mentioned it, too, it had poisoned any pleasure she'd taken in the baronet's company. Now every gallant courtesy he offered was tainted by the faint suspicion it might be more than that. And so though she was uneasy about this trip to London, she was glad that at least she probably wouldn't be seeing Sir Maurice as often there.

Now, Julianne gazed out the window and soon was farther away, in her mind. Instead of sitting rump to rump with two perfumed ladies, she was back in that cool dark night in the inn's kitchen garden, the only warmth that which she found in Christian's embrace as she tasted the blazing heat of his mouth. Lord, but the man's mouth had held delicious secrets, and made her yearn to discover every one of them . . .

But Sophie's mama began talking, and that ended any daydreaming.

"First thing we shall do after we get you settled comfortably, Hammond," Sophie's mama said, "is to leave our cards at all the best houses. We have to let the *ton* know we are in town, *and* with the future earl of Egremont."

Julianne hoped Sophie and her mama didn't feel her squirm. "But surely," she asked meekly, "that's a bit premature? I mean, to tell them Hammond will inherit when it isn't decided yet?"

It seemed to her that the others in the carriage exchanged more than a look as they glanced at each other. Then Sophie spoke. "It's as much as decided, Julianne. Or so Sir Maurice said. But I suppose you're right. Much better to say he is the heir presumptive, then let them discover the truth when the news is made public." She exchanged another silent look with her mother and Hammond.

That was when Julianne realized they must have

spoken about a great deal more than she knew these last days, when she'd thought she'd been the one avoiding them. She didn't have much to say for the rest of the journey. But then, ominously enough—at least to her, neither did they.

"London, in all its glory," Sophie said happily, when she saw how her cousin was staring out the window at the city they were driving through. "You'll like it here, Julianne, once you get used to the noise and the crowds. Don't worry, it's terrifying for a country girl, but you'll soon find yourself accustomed."

"I *have* been to London, you know," Julianne said a little gruffly. "although not in years. We were here to see Jon before he went abroad. We saw his regiment drilling in Hyde Park; they looked so brave and splendid . . ." Her voice tapered off, and she added quickly and too brightly, "To think! It was so long ago and yet seems like yesterday. We stayed for the week, and saw everything: Astley's horse circus, the Tower menagerie, we heard a concert in the park and saw the palace, too."

Sophie laughed. "You haven't seen anything. We'll go to dances and parties, the theater and restaurants. Good. We're finally leaving the riffraff behind. Now we'll make better time."

Julianne looked out the window again. They'd passed through slums teeming with foot traffic, swarming with people with dogcarts and handbarrows further clogging streets full of running children and throngs of adults. But now they drove freely down a broad avenue that ran alongside a green park. This was obviously a wealthy district: it was cleaner, the traffic thinner, the horses and the coaches were of a finer class. The few people she saw were either dressed splendidly or were clearly servants.

They finally slowed as they approached a half circle of tall, imposing town houses. The coach rolled to a stop in front of a handsome gray house at the end of the quiet street. As the coach rocked and settled, the door was pulled open. The squire stood there, fresh-faced from his riding, and beaming. "We're here," he said. "How are you faring, Ham? Feeling good enough to use your own pins to get down, or do you need some help?"

"I can do it myself," Hammond said, "and I'd rather, thank you. But it will take some time. Let the ladies go first."

After Julianne got out, behind Sophie and her mama, Hammond edged his way stiffly down the short coach stair to the street. "I feel fine," he said, as they watched his slow progress. "I'm just getting out the knots after sitting for so long."

The door to the town house opened.

The squire looked up and smiled, his wife beamed and curtseyed, as did Sophie. Hammond nodded a stiff bow. And Julianne gaped.

"Very good, you're here," Sir Maurice said as he came down the steps to greet them. "And well before the dinner hour. Welcome."

Three liveried footmen came running out to retrieve their baggage.

"Sir Maurice is staying here, too?" Julianne asked Sophie softly.

"I should think so!" she exclaimed. "It's his house, after all."

Julianne was not happy, although she had every reason to be. Or so her cousins said. It didn't make her any happier to know they were right.

The baronet's house astonished her with its luxury. Four floors high and with a garden in the front and back, it was elegantly designed and furnished with taste. "I've my own room in the attics," Julianne's maid had reported with awe. "I don't have to share a bed with nobody, and I've got a window, too."

Julianne had three windows in her huge bedchamber, her own bath, and a toilet. And it flushed! She was embarrassed by how fascinated she was by it, and was glad no one could see her testing it again and again. She'd expected the fine paintings she saw on the walls throughout the house, the objects of art on display. But she hadn't anticipated, or experienced, all the modern facilities and little elegancies that made life so incredibly comfortable here. There were gaslights in the downstairs rooms, fresh flowers everywhere, and her bed was wide, soft, and always fitted with fresh, clean-smelling sheets. It staggered her that an austere gentleman as Sir Maurice would live in such luxurious style. She told Sophie so the first evening they arrived, as they waited in the salon for the rest of the family to gather before dinner.

"Oh, but his wife was a rich woman, and she pampered herself," Sophie explained, picking a porcelain shepherdess from a nearby table and turning it over to see who had made it. "And I expect he keeps to such style in her memory."

"And for my guests," the baronet's dry, amused voice added.

Julianne and Sophie swung around to see that Sir Maurice had arrived. Julianne blushed. Sophie grinned.

"My own needs are less demanding," he went on. "But I suppose one becomes accustomed. So, you like my town house, do you, Miss Lowell? And careful with that, my dear Sophie, it is Sèvres, and from Versailles."

"It's a beautiful home," Julianne said, as her cousin hastily put the figurine down. "But you said you stay most of the time in your home in the north. So is this house always empty? It's hard to believe, it seems so lived in."

"It is lived in," he said. "Since I haven't been in London in the past three years, I rented it out. To responsible persons, of course. But there's no sense letting a valuable property go unused; money makes money, that's sound practice. I've a clause in the lease that says the tenants must vacate when I come to Town." He saw her expression, and his smile became wider. "Don't risk a penny at whist, Miss Lowell, your opponents will know every card in your hand. You mustn't feel so sorry for my tenants, my dear. They're staying in a fine hotel now, I believe, and at any rate, are seldom so inconvenienced.

"But now that I'm here again, I quite like the idea," he mused, looking around the room. "I can inspect the property to see how it's being kept up, entertain, and take care of family business." He frowned. "But alas! I'm a bachelor again, and have no idea of how to entertain you young ladies as I wish to."

"Oh, don't worry, Sir Maurice," Sophie's mother said breathlessly as she entered the room at a trot. "We do!"

"And so how do you find London, Miss Lowell?" the tall gentleman drawled, as he looked down at her through his lifted quizzing glass.

*Where it's supposed to be*, was what Julianne longed to answer. Instead, she smiled, and said, "Fascinating. I know I'm not supposed to be enthused about it, but I am a country girl, after all." She hoped that would be enough to make him move on. He was too immaculately turned out to be interested in a bumpkin. His perfection actually made her anxious and a little too aware that though her gown was lovely, it was made-over. She was sure he'd never owned any item of clothing that had been refurbished. In fact, she wondered if he ever wore anything twice, except for his golden fobs and signet ring.

He was a handsome man with even features. But what one noticed first was how well dressed he was. His neckcloth was so high Julianne wondered if he used the quizing glass because he couldn't lower his chin. His fair hair was brushed to perfection in a style Brummel had made popular. Doubtless, he was a member of the Dandy set.

Julianne was coming to see that men in London society all belonged to some sort of set, and they showed which one by the clothes they wore. She supposed it saved them time and effort. They didn't have to say a word to let other men know what their conversation would be, and it made it simpler for a woman to decide if she was interested in anything more than conversation with them.

There were several members of the Dandy set at Sir Maurice's house this night. There were even more gentlemen in dashing, but more casually cut clothing. Their jackets, though snug, were just loose enough to move their broad shoulders in, and their breeches were tight enough to show the muscles in their legs. Most of their faces were not fashionably pale, but lightly tanned, and those that still had their hair wore it in a short Brutus crop. Sophie told Julianne they were members of the sports-mad Corinthian set.

There were also a few long-haired young men wearing dandified clothes, but just rumpled enough to show they didn't care for fashion as much as poetry. Sophie claimed there were even a few stars of the literary world here tonight at her soiree—Sir Maurice's soiree, in fact. The old gentleman had agreed to host a party in order to introduce Hammond and Sophie to polite society.

Those men and others filled the baronet's drawing room, and to Julianne's amazement, many seemed interested in her. She decided it was because of how low her gown was, as well as because of her novelty. She was a stranger to them, and everyone else seemed to know each other.

"It is mid-Season," Sophie had told Julianne before the party. "Half the unattached young women have made their catches. But that leaves the other half free, and so who knows whom you might attach?"

Julianne hadn't expected anyone to take an interest in her and was surprised and a little awed at first by how many gentlemen had. But she wasn't shy for long; it wasn't in her nature. Soon she'd had introductions to half a dozen gentlemen, all of whom promised they'd be calling on her.

"And so what have you done here in Town?" the exquisite gentleman she'd just met persisted.

Julianne decided to be kind, because for all his affects, the fellow really did have lovely blue eyes. They reminded her of someone she'd never see here tonight. "So far, I've seen the inside of a dozen dressmakers' establishment . . . oops, I mean modistes," she corrected herself. "But though I'd like to see more, I've been well entertained. We haven't got modistes at home, you see . . . only dressmakers," she added with a smile.

"I'd be happy to take you to see the sights," he said.

"Oh, I wasn't angling for that!" she exclaimed.

"I know," he drawled. "Which is why I should like to. I must toddle on now. Whitworth is the name. Please don't forget it. I'll see you again, soon, I hope." He bowed, and left her.

She wasn't alone for long.

The rakish-looking young gentleman who had been eyeing her all evening appeared at her side. She was pleased to see he was just as attractive from near as he'd seemed from afar. He had a bold, strong face with remarkable cheekbones, and his mouth was full and sensual. His dark eyes danced with light as he looked at her. "Bored to flinders yet?" he asked.

"Oh, no!" she said. "Just the reverse. I find this all fascinating."

"Not supposed to say so, you know. Or rather, you don't. Someone should show you how to go on. I'd be delighted to. The baron Hawthorne, at your service." He bowed, but not low, only far enough to be able to stare down into her gown, not bothering to hide that he was doing so.

He might be handsome, and a baron, and from London, but Julianne relaxed even as she grew annoyed because she knew his sort too well.

"I know how to go on, thank you," she said coolly, drawing back. "If I don't hide my enthusiasm it's because I don't chose to do so."

"As candid as she's beautiful. Even more interesting," he said, with a twisted smile that bordered on insolence. "And Lord knows I find you interesting enough. Do you know what a relief it is to meet someone so fresh and sweet in this jaded company?"

"How could I? That's illogical. Look," she said, deciding to make short work of him, "sorry to disappoint you, but being from the countryside doesn't make me uncivilized, or inexperienced."

"Fascinating," he said, moving closer. "A girl who admits it!"

"Do excuse me," she said. "I see Sir Maurice wishes to speak to me."

It was a lie, but the old gentleman had been looking her way, and she was glad of an excuse to leave.

"How delightful this party is," she said, when she

reached the baronet's side, so the leering lord she'd left could see her in conversation.

"Was that fellow bothering you?" he asked. "I'll have him shown the door if he was."

"Oh no, nothing so drastic," she said, smiling. "I just didn't choose to pass any more time with him. Not that I'm using this encounter just as an excuse!" she added hurriedly. "I'm having the best time, and I wanted to thank you."

He took her hand in his cool, dry one and patted it. "That pleases me. Now, shall we go in to dinner?"

She hesitated, wide-eyed. Going in to dinner with a gentleman showed a preference in companionship. Then she relaxed, embarrassed by her own foolishness. Sophie and Christian had indeed muddied the waters with their speculations. After all, whom else should he ask? The baronet was not known in London anymore, and of his two female cousins here, one was married and the other, engaged. Julianne was the only single female of his acquaintance, as well as being a guest in his house.

And whom else could she go to dinner with, when the one man she wanted to sit with, talk with, and be with, was the last man on earth who'd be allowed to set foot in this place?

Julianne smiled at the baronet, put her hand on his arm, and went in to dinner. And silently promised herself that if he didn't turn up soon, she'd think of a way to find that other man here in London, and soon. Because though she hadn't seen him in two weeks, not a day passed when she didn't wish she could.

# Chapter 18

*He isn't here. He must have decided not to come to London after all,* Julianne thought in despair. Because she never once caught a glimpse of Christian. She didn't see him at the opera or the theater, though dozens of gentlemen of the *ton* were always there. She never saw him at any of the many soirees and musicales, levees and balls where she went with her cousins almost every night. She didn't even glimpse anyone who looked like him in the fashionable shops or restaurants they frequented.

Of course she couldn't go where the gentlemen went, their clubs and boxing salons. She couldn't go to places like Tattersall's to buy horses either. She certainly couldn't visit gaming hells or bawdy houses, or cockfights and boxing matches where gentlemen lost their money in fashionable but less mentionable ways. Still, she'd been in London for three weeks, and hadn't seen or, more ominously, heard a word about him.

The baronet's thin nostrils no longer pinched together at the sound of his name, because no one spoke it. Nor did the squire's color rise at the mention of his prospective son-in-law's rival. His wife had no reason to frown, and Hammond and Sophie were April and May together again. No one any longer mentioned even the possibility that Sophie wouldn't be mistress of Egremont.

It was as if Christian had disappeared, as though he'd never been.

And though Julianne yearned to ask her cousins about him, she didn't dare. Her interest in him would be taken as rude or threatening; or worse, she feared, it might be taken for what it was. She missed him. She wanted to see him, hear his voice and his laughter. She needed to know what had happened to him—although, as time began to pass, she didn't want to know. Because she was afraid he'd done the right thing, and cut and run. And never told her. But then, why should he? He owed her nothing, really, after all.

That would mean he'd been a liar and had no part in her past or future, and she'd never see him again. Or kiss him, or touch him, or see the look in his eyes that told her he wanted the same.

She might despair for him, but she didn't lack company. Nor did she lack suitors, only any interest in them.

Her cousins had made good on their promise. Julianne now had a wardrobe they thought suitable for London, though privately she thought it would suit a princess. Tonight she was dressed in a gown of gold cloth, with a sheer pink overnet on the skirt. Her hair was dressed with fresh rosebuds, and she knew she'd never looked better. But though the ballroom was crowded with the *ton*'s most fashionable ladies and gentlemen, there was only one man she yearned to have see her in her splendor. She began to believe he never would. She realized she was a fool and had been played for one, and yet, though she knew it all, she ached to see that cool, handsome face one more time.

"Know it's probably been said before," the gentleman standing next to her said, interrupting her train of thought, "but not by me. You look very well tonight." He laughed. "Like saying the Coliseum's a nice building, aint it? But I'm no poet. Accept my compliment on your great good looks, Miss Lowell. You outshine all the ladies tonight, if not the moon."

She smiled. "Why, that's very poetical, Mr. Winthrop. And thank you. Might I say you're looking radiant tonight, too?"

He gave a bark of a laugh. "There you are," he said. "You're an original, Miss Lowell. Face, form, and format. And though a lady ain't supposed to congratulate a fellow on his looks, I thank you."

She smiled at him. It wasn't hard to do. George Winthrop was a charming fellow. Tall, fair, with pale straight hair and light blue eyes, he was handsome enough in an unspectacular, but pleasant way, and very socially adept. That was also the problem.

He was so very fashionable she didn't know who he really was. He might be clever or stupid, it was hard to tell because he'd been educated, and his manners were so good. But it wasn't the fashion for a gentleman in his circle to appear too cultured, so his conversation, like that of the other men in his set, was sprinkled with the latest cant. He spoke like all the other dandified gentlemen, too, in accents just short of a yawn. The more she tried to shake him to see what his normal reaction would be to something she said that was outrageous, the more she pleased him. It wasn't what she set out to do.

But now she remembered her original mission: to find a husband for herself and another son for her parents. George Winthrop was pleasant enough, that would please her mama; and he was horse-mad, that might please Papa. If only she could find something to please herself—as least half so well as that liar and cheat she couldn't stop thinking about.

"Hot as blazes in here," George said. "Care to go for a stroll? Nice garden out back."

"Is that done?" she asked curiously. "It is hot. I'd like some fresh air. But you and I, strolling in the garden. Is that permissible?"

"No," he said, "but it ain't social suicide neither. Anyway, I'm shocked to find the unshockable Miss Lowell not game for any romp."

She grinned. "I had an older brother, Mr. Winthrop. That makes me unshockable, I suppose. But I won't be taken for an easy mark."

He laughed again. "Wise as an owl, ain't you, little Miss? So then?" he asked, offering her his arm. "Out to the balcony?"

She shrugged. "Why not?"

There were other couples out on the terrace behind the town house, and more she glimpsed as they strolled though the garden. It was damp, with rain coming on, but it felt deliciously cool in contrast to the stuffy ballroom. Julianne took George's arm, and they went out on the terrace, then down the little stair into the garden. They walked a few paces and paused under a tree. There was a fountain nearby; she heard it splashing, and she lifted her head and breathed in the sweet damp night air.

He lowered his head and kissed her.

It wasn't much of a kiss. Just a fleeting touch of his lips, neither pleasant or unpleasant; they felt cool and dry against her own. But she hadn't expected it, and drew back at once, flustered. He didn't pursue her.

"Your pardon," he said calmly. "Couldn't resist. Forgive me?"

*What for?* She wanted to say, but stayed silent. Because she was too busy being appalled at her reaction. She was disappointed! She'd been kissed, and it hadn't mattered. Where was the tingling, the sudden electric sting, the heat on her lips that coiled in her stomach and made her shivery with pleasure and anticipation? She hadn't wanted to throw her arms around this man's neck and drink deep at his mouth, or press her body against his. She didn't want this man in a darkened garden. She wanted Christian—or at least the man who called himself Christian Sauvage.

But this man seemed very pleased with the kiss, as well as with her obvious confusion.

He patted her hand. "Don't think I compromised you, Miss Lowell. But, tell you what. If you think I did, I'll be happy to make an offer."

"Oh, Lord no!" she gasped, and then, to spare his feelings, quickly added, "We hardly know each other. That wouldn't be right . . . or sporting." She gave a shaky laugh. "We'd better go back, before we are well and truly compromised by gossip."

"Heart of oak," he said with approval. "You're a brick, Miss Lowell."

She knew she'd been given high praise and saw his admiration for her in his eyes after he'd led her back into the house. She couldn't get away from him fast enough once she got there. She fled, leaving him with a smile as soon as she could, grateful that she'd already danced with him twice and didn't have to again.

Julianne danced with every eligible gentleman in the room that night, or so it seemed to her. But she only thought about the one man who wasn't there, and began to wonder if she'd been carried off by the Gypsy rover even though she'd never left with him.

"You were wildly successful," Sophie told her, as they went up the stair together when they came home from the ball. "Congratulations! Mark my words, you'll have an offer from Georgie Winthrop before another day passes."

"Well, I hope not," Julianne said crossly, "because that would be ridiculous. I hardly know him."

"You know enough, silly," Sophie said. "He's rich, decent, nice-looking, and he'll have a title one day."

"None of that matters," Julianne said wistfully, thinking of the man she'd yearned to dance with to-night. "Well, I suppose the decency does, but it's not enough to build a life upon. As for the rest, it's the man, not the money or the title that a woman must live with."

"Fiddle," Sophie began to say, but was cut off by a cool, dry voice that came from behind her.

"Such wisdom in one so young is admirable," Sir Maurice said. "What shall I say if young Winthrop comes to me, Miss Lowell?"

Julianne paused on the stair. Sir Maurice stood a step below her, but as he was so tall their eyes were on a level. She blinked hers in confusion. "Come to you?" she asked. "Why should he?"

"To ask to pay his addresses," Sir Maurice said.

"But I hardly think he will, sir," she said. "You're my host, to be sure, and head of Hammond's family, but you are not *my* family."

"Ah," he said, smiling. "Right, just so. One forgets. I'm pleased you didn't."

They went on up the stair in silence. Sophie waited until he'd bid them good night and gone down the hall to his rooms. Then she poked Julianne in the ribs. "Sly puss!" she whispered. "Just the right answer. There's no end to your cleverness!"

"What?"

"No, he's not a member of your family, but he could be, and you let him know it."

"Oh, Lord!" Julianne said, looking down the empty hall in the direction of the baronet. "You don't think I was trying to . . . ? Oh . . . blather! Not that again!"

But with a giggle, her cousin was gone, dancing down the hallway to her own room.

Julianne had a hard time getting to sleep, especially since it was so late there wasn't much darkness left to the night. But it wasn't the dawn stealing into her room that kept her tossing in her bed, or even the thought of her new young suitor, or the old gentleman she doubted was a suitor. It was the thought of the man who wasn't there. The thought and the vision of his face, and the remembrance of his kiss, and the vivid memory of the way his taut body had felt against her own.

When the sun rose, she slept at last. Because by then she'd decided memory wasn't enough. She had to know where he was and why she hadn't seen him, even if the knowledge was hurtful. Because she knew too well that longing was never enough.

"Bow Street. There it is, Miss," the coachman said, pointing with his whip.

"Oh," Julianne said. "Could you stop a minute?"

The coachman obliged. He stopped their carriage across the street from the plain gray house that was home to the Bow Street runners.

"Whatever do you want to see Bow Street for?" Sophie asked curiously. "No! Don't tell me!" She put a hand on her heart. "You've formed a passion that must be satisfied. You've lost your heart to an unsuitable man and can't bear not to see him."

It was a good thing Julianne was sitting. Otherwise, she thought she'd have fallen. All the blood felt like it drained from her head as well as her legs. She felt cold and weak and dizzy as she stared at her cousin.

"You've formed a passion for Mr. Murchison!" Sophie went on, now laughing so hard she didn't see the horrified expression on her cousin's face.

Julianne recovered quickly. "So I have. I've always liked older men."

"So I thought!" Sophie said shrewdly.

"Oh, bother!" Julianne said. "Will you learn a new song? I'm only joking. I scarcely remember Murchison—was that his name? All I wanted was to see a bit more of the real London, so I could tell them at home about it. Balls and parties are all very well, but there's more to the city than that. You may drive on," she told the coachman.

She sat back and took a deep breath. Her faint hope of somehow getting into Bow Street, finding the runner, and asking him about Christian, was dashed. She couldn't go alone. Not only was the place too open and visible, but a young woman of breeding couldn't go anywhere by herself in London. And she couldn't dream up a good enough excuse to go in with Sophie, because her cousin was all eyes and ears and speculations.

And though Mr. Murchison had seemed like a kind and reasonable man, the truth was she couldn't trust the runner not to go right back to the squire and tell him what she wanted to know. It had been a foolish futile fancy altogether, and Julianne was angry with herself.

"Don't sulk," Sophie said. "After the dressmaker's appointment, we'll go to the Tower again, and you can see the sights to your heart's content."

Julianne forced a smile. "Thank you," she said, and hoped she'd have some solitude there. Because she had to think of something else.

* * *

"Annie," Julianne asked, as her maid tidied up her room after her bath that evening before dinner, "do you know if any of the servants here ever go back to squire's house for supplies?"

"They do," Annie said. "And they're that eager to be the ones chosen, too. Because their families are there, and not all enjoy London like we do. Squire sends for supplies all the time; there's nothing like food from his own gardens, he says. And he's always sending instructions and getting reports from home, because he's a good manager of his land, and so say all."

Julianne tapped her fingers against the desk where she was sitting. Annie was her own maid. She'd known her for years, she trusted her as much as she trusted anyone in this world. "Is there anyone here, who goes there, that you would trust, entirely?" she asked softly.

Her maid stopped working and lifted her head as though she heard a far-off sound. Then she looked at her mistress, and nodded, slowly. "Aye, there is one."

Julianne took a deep breath. "If I sent a note, a very personal note, is that person one you could trust to deliver it, safely, unopened, to someone staying at the White Hart, the inn in the village near the squire's house?"

She held her breath. She didn't dare trust such a note to the post, not even in the care of His Majesty's Mail. The innkeeper could open it, it might be bribed out of the coachman's hands, who knew who might intercept it? Julianne had read a great many Minerva

Press novels and enough newspapers to know that truth was stranger than fiction, and the best fiction was often based on the truth.

Annie nodded, wide-eyed. "Rufus Smythe, the second footman, is going back this very week, and I'd trust him with my own life, I would."

Julianne cocked her head to the side. "Really?" she asked. "Then I may assume that one day you really might trust him with yours?"

Annie blushed rosily. "Oh, one day, who knows, Miss? But how did you know?"

"I hear you singing all the time now," Julianne said, smiling, "and I've known you a long time, and besides, I saw you talking to him the other day. No one could mistake the look on your face, or the one on his."

"And you don't mind?"

"Why should I? I'll miss you, of course, but I want you to be happy."

"Oh, I will be, Miss. He won't stay a footman forever," Annie said. "He's saving up to buy a share in a shop, one day. I know just the place, back home."

Julianne took a deep breath. "Good, and I wish you well. So. If I give you a note for you to give to him, to give to someone staying at the White Hart, it will get there safely?"

"He'll see that it gets into Mr. Christian's hands and no other," Annie said staunchly.

Julianne winced. "It is that obvious?"

"To me, Miss. I did see you coming home to squire's at dawn, and more than once. And I know

you led a horse out in the night . . . and there's not a
one who'd breathe a word of that, neither, because
there's that many who like you on staff, and what
their betters do is their own business, and so say all.
There's not much that goes on in a great house that a
good staff misses; but a servant who gabbles isn't
liked by anyone, and money can't buy friendship,
you know.

"And who else should you be going to see?" She
saw her mistress's expression. "I'd be a poor help to
you if I didn't know, wouldn't I? How can I sleep if
I know you're not home? I didn't go after you because I didn't think he'd do you any harm. I asked,
see, all innocent-like, and no one at squire's thought
any evil of him either—aside from some thinking he
was trying to pull the wool over their eyes, of
course. But where's the dire harm in that? A man
should try to better himself, all said. Some noblemen are wicked as can be, and who's to know who
is of the blood even in the best of families? And a
fortune is a fortune after all"

"Oh, Annie," Julianne said, feeling warm and protected, and stupid as a blind calf, all at once.

The note was very brief, but it took a day to compose.

"Dear Christian," it began, because a number of
versions starting "Dear Earl Sauvage" had been crumpled up. As had those starting, "Dear Mr. Sauvage."
Christian was the boy she'd known, she decided, and
she was writing to him. The rest was simple enough:

*You had said you would be in London, and you
are not. Nor have I heard word of you. Are you
in some sort of difficulty? Is there any way I can
help?*

*Your old friend,*
*J.L.*

Annie's footman took the note and placed it next to
his heart. He said he would bear it next to his heart
until he gave it into the hand of the man who called
himself Christian Sauvage. Rufus left London the
next morning.

In the next days Julianne went to balls and parties,
a concert and a tea. She flirted and laughed, danced,
and avoided offers and kisses, and she never once
stopped thinking of her note and the answer to it.

Some nights as she lay in her bed thinking about it,
she thought he'd answer her in person, braving the
baronet's wrath to ask her to drive out with him again.
Other nights she dreamed while awake of him coming up to her at a ball, silently offering her his hand,
and leading her into the dance. On darker, later nights
she imagined him coming to her without a word, taking her into her arms, and kissing her until she could
no longer breathe. As she could not when she thought
of it.

A week passed, then Rufus returned.

"He isn't there anymore, Miss," Annie reported
that very day. "Rufus said he cleared straight out after
we left, and no one's seen him since."

That evening Julianne was very pale and sat quietly

at the dinner table. No one seemed to notice because Sophie was so merry as she detailed the plans for her upcoming wedding day.

"And we shall dress the church all in white, which should not be difficult even in September," Sophie said, "because I saw the most cunning idea in a lady's magazine! We can use camellias and orchids, of course, but how charming if we also used daisies and meadowsweet."

"Charming," her mama agreed, "but not too many wildflowers, my love, lest people think you're being mingy instead of inventive. Surely a countess needs more roses than weeds, right, Hammond?"

Julianne's head shot up. She knew it would be the wrong thing to say, as welcome as a rainstorm on a picnic party, but she couldn't hold it in anymore. "But what of the man who said he was Christian Sauvage?" she asked. "What happened about his claim?"

They stared at her.

It was the baronet who broke the silence, his voice full of amusement and thick with triumph. "Why, did no one tell you, my dear? He's in Newgate Prison, and has been for a while, and is likely only to leave it in a coffin. So he need trouble us no more. I agree, Martha," he added, "a countess should have more orchids than weeds, to be sure."

# Chapter 19

decorative flourish

**J**ulianne couldn't ask more about Christian immediately. She didn't want to discuss it with the baronet, the squire, or his wife. She had to talk to Sophie. Though her cousin didn't share her concerns, she was at least the most approachable of the three. But soon as the dinner she couldn't touch was over, they were off to a concert. She sat in her box looking dumbly at the chorus, feeling numbed, too heartsick to bring the subject up even if she dared raise her voice enough to be heard above the music. She didn't discuss it at intermission because she couldn't get Sophie alone. And since Sophie and Hammond were permitted time alone because they were engaged, and took the opportunity to be private in the salon after the concert, that chance wouldn't come for Julianne until the next day.

Julianne woke after a restless night of interrupted sleep. She dressed, and sat waiting until noon, when her cousin would awake and dress. She went to her cousin's room the moment she saw Sophie's maid leave. Sophie was still at her dressing table. Julianne got straight to the point.

"He's in Newgate, awaiting trial," Sophie said in answer to her first question.

Julianne sank to a chair. "But, why?" she asked, when she found enough breath. "Is there new evidence that he wasn't telling the truth?"

"He wasn't, it's that simple," Sophie answered. "But that hardly matters now, unless, of course, he wants a silken rope instead of hemp. Sir Maurice said he'll be tried and hanged, and that will be the end of it."

Julianne gasped. "Hanged?"

"Yes, because Sir Maurice had Egremont inventoried after the tour he gave, and they found silver candlesticks missing—again! And an heirloom snuffbox and a silver candle snuffer as well. You'd think the fellow would have learned from the first time he was imprisoned, but I suppose he couldn't resist. The irony of it is staggering, just as Sir Maurice says, considering what the real Christian Sauvage was convicted of. It must have appealed to a twisted, criminal mind, like his—whoever he is."

"How do they know he took the candlesticks?"

"Why, they found them in his luggage at the White Hart, of course."

"But what about the proof that he is the earl?"

Sophie stopped adjusting the ribbon in her curls and turned from her mirror to look at her cousin. Her look was soft and pitying. "Poor Julianne. We do understand. You hoped against hope the fellow would be real, so that some way you could recapture your childhood and those happy memories of your dear brother. Sir Maurice said this would be hard on you, which is why we didn't tell you. But let it go, because regretting will only bring you sorrow. He was arrested for theft, and when the truth of his identity is known, he'd be hanged for that as well. And as no man can be hanged twice over, however much a villain he may be, either reason is good enough, or so Sir Maurice says. And he's right, as usual."

Sophie's voice became brighter. "Just forget it! You have enough to divert you. George Winthrop is dancing attention on you, and now that his friend Philip Reese is as well—and not just for competition's sake, I think—your dance card will be full. Sir Mark is sending flowers—although he is a pudding face, so I don't blame you for not paying mind to his attentions. And then there's Sir Maurice himself. Mama said it's clear he's very fond—aye! I'm mum," she cried, throwing up her hands.

"Pah. This ribbon will not do!" Sophie went on, as she looked into the mirror again. "White on blond is futile; I think a rose-colored one will do it, though I'd hoped for a new look. And as for Sir Maurice, you're right, or you might be. It may well be just fatherly interest on his part after all, or so Papa said. He reminded us that the poor man lost his only son and heir, and his son wasn't much older than you when he died. So that could be it, entirely." She swung around. "What are you wearing today—and then tonight?" she asked merrily.

"You haven't forgotten, have you?" she asked, when Julianne didn't answer. "We're promised to the Stantons for tea. And then there's the masquerade

ball at the Royces' tonight. Don't worry, we won't
need full costumes, a domino or an eye mask will do.
Luckily, Mama told me about the rage for masquerades, so I brought two eye masks with me, and a pea-
cock feather one, too." She eyed her cousin's pallor.
"But if you like, we can take a jaunt to the shops and
buy new ones."

"I'm not going out this evening," Julianne said quietly. "This has all been . . . a great shock to me. I
know you're right," she said at once. "As is Sir Maurice. And diversion would help me, but not just yet.
You must give me some time. Some people can lose
themselves in gaiety. I think I can—if I get a good
day's rest, then a good night's sleep."

"Of course, I understand," Sophie said. "You do
look heavy-eyed. Perhaps you're coming down with
something, too. Go straight to bed. I'll make your excuses, and entertain your beaux, and try to drive poor
Ham mad with jealousy while I do. As if I could." She
laughed. "Ham trusts in me, as well he should. Now
go, you're much too pale. Go to sleep, and in case you
can't right away, I'll send you some novels and fruit
and sweets, and tell everyone to let you be until you
feel better. Why, you'll soon be so comfortable you'll
never want to leave your room again. But you must.
There's that recital tomorrow night, then a late supper
at the Binghams'."

"Thank you," Julianne said softly. She rose and
went back to her room, still stunned, but relieved that
she'd managed to find a way to buy herself time
alone, so she could try to think of what to do next.

*  *  *

By late afternoon the baronet's town house was still. Everyone but the servants seemed to have left, except for Julianne. She had a tray of fruit and sweets and a stack of novels by her bedside, a note from Sir Maurice wishing her better health, and a promise that she wouldn't be disturbed.

"The squire, he's out looking at horses," Annie reported to her mistress. "His lady and your cousin and Mr. Hammond are still out to tea. And Sir Maurice went about his business and told the staff he wouldn't return 'til dinner. I can tell them all you're still sleeping when they get back, and they'll believe me, but oh, miss, I dearly wish you wouldn't!"

"I'll be fine," Julianne said. "Your young man delivered the note?"

"He did," Annie said anxiously. "Like I said. And like I already told you, Mr. Murchison read it and said, as best I can remember, 'Tell the young lady she's gone round in her head, and I'll have no part of it.' But he said you wasn't to worry because he'd keep his own counsel as always. So you see? If even a Bow Street runner don't approve . . . oh, please, Miss, don't do it!"

Julianne tightened her lips. "I wish I didn't have to. But I must. And I won't come to harm. Lord, girl, he's in *prison*! Under lock and key and behind bars. What can he do to me there? I must know the truth about him, and when I do, I'll be able to put it aside." She rose from her chair. "I'm ready. I've got a purseful of coins and banknotes that Mama gave me when I left home. Now, all I have to do is find whom to give them to in order to find a way into Newgate. If Murchison won't help me, I'll do it on my own.

"Now, remember," she cautioned her maid, "don't fall into a panic if I'm not home right away. It may be that I'll have other errands to run." *Because if he's innocent*, she thought, *I won't stop looking for help for him until I've seen every solicitor in Town.*

"But I should be with you!" Annie wailed.

"If you were, who would be here taking care of me in my sickbed? I need you right here," she added before Annie could protest again, "because so long as you're here, they won't suspect that I'm not. Don't let anyone in my room. I can do it on my own: I'll be heavily veiled, and I'll go in a hack, and I won't give my real name. If I have to, I'll tell them I've a maid waiting for me in the carriage. That way they'll think me a highborn lady on secret business." She remembered what Christian had told her about condemned men's last nights on earth at Newgate, and shivered. Though it wasn't to be his last night, what he'd said had given her inspiration for what she was about to do.

"I'm told they're used to that sort of visitor at Newgate," she said, and couldn't help shuddering again. Because it was a mad and desperate thing she was doing. She also knew that she had to do it, or never sleep easy again. The thought of him in chains, in doubt as to how she felt about what had happened to him, was too painful for her to bear, waking or sleeping. She'd been dancing while he had been taken away to rot in prison? She'd been flirting, laughing, living, while his very life was in doubt. Guilt and fear made her braver than she was. She had to do something, and immediately, no matter how much even the thought of what she was going to do frightened her.

"The only thing that may be harmed is my reputation," she told Annie firmly. "And you know that won't matter a snap to my mother and father, because they trust me and believe in me no matter what."

"But what about your cousins, and Sir Maurice, that nice young Mr. West, and all your other fine suitors?" Annie wailed.

"They don't mean a thing to me, any of them," Julianne said brutally. "They're just part of an experience, not my life," she added more softly. "And so if they find out, and forgive me, I'll be pleased. But if they don't, I won't really care." She looked at her maidservant and sighed. "Annie, don't you see? There are times when a woman must deal with her own life directly. She can't always be protected, if only because other people's plans for her life mightn't suit her as well as her own." She tilted her head and gazed at her maidservant curiously. "Surely you know that. You've always had to look out for yourself, haven't you?"

"Oh, aye, I have and I do," Annie said. "But sometimes, I think it must be grand to have someone else to watch out for you."

"So do I," Julianne said. "But that person must be someone I trust and believe in. And right here and right now, the only person I completely trust and believe in is myself." She squared her shoulders. "So, I'm ready. You go first to be sure no one sees me. I'll leave by the back door. The hackney will be waiting at the foot of the street and just around the corner, you said?"

Annie nodded.

Julianne took a deep breath, then hesitated. She had on her best day gown, low at the breast and trimmed with lace, the whole ensemble the color of ripe peaches and cream. She'd used floral water and powdered her bare shoulders. "How do I look?" she asked.

"Beautiful!" Annie said.

"Oh, what a fool I am!" Julianne muttered, her face growing pink. She whipped a dark cape from the bed, flung it over her shoulders, and pulled it closed, so that no one could see her fine gown. The she crammed on a veiled hat she plucked from her vanity table, securing it with the thrust of a jet pin. She used such force that she was glad she'd angled the pin, or she'd have done herself an injury. "There, I'm as good as invisible, see? Now go make sure the way is clear."

Annie cracked open the door to survey the hallway, then crept out to look at the stair and the hall below. While she did, Julianne pulled down the veil to cover her face, lifted her head, and marched to her door. She looked to her maid. Annie, white-faced, nodded.

Julianne took a breath, jerked the door open, and stepped out, before she could think of one more good reason not to.

A fine mist was trying to resolve into a soft rain, so there weren't any of the usual strollers out and about. The nannies and their charges were safe and dry indoors, the old ladies and gentlemen were sitting by their hearths trying to get the damp from their bones. Only a few servants scurried up and down the fashionable streets, but their heads were down as they went about their errands. It was a dim, clammy afternoon, perfect for her purposes, Julianne thought.

She almost wished it were broad sunlight, so that someone would see her, and she'd be forced to retreat. There was no shame in being bested by Fate. But no one noticed her as she hurried down the street. It was difficult to see where she was going. Her hat, one Annie had from the time when an uncle had passed, was black, with a heavy veil, made passably fashionable by the spray of brave jet feathers splayed on its crown.

The veil was of cheap heavy net, so it also trapped Julianne's breath and made her a little dizzy. At least, she hoped that was what was making her feel so lightheaded, and not the terror she was beginning to feel. But she was comforted by the fact that if she couldn't see out, at least no one would see in. She could, however, clearly see the only hackney carriage waiting at the foot of the street. As she approached, the driver nodded and saluted her by touching his whip to his hat. Julianne looked down, trying to see the steps on the little stair that had been let down from the carriage. She only hoped she wouldn't break her neck as she went up them.

She pulled open the door, ducked her head, bent double, and stepped in.

"Good afternoon," a masculine voice said from the interior of the carriage.

Julianne gasped, but before she could back out, the

man half rose, and, with one long arm, pulled the door shut. The hackney bucked and started moving. Julianne was thrown to a seat by the motion, and she sat down hard, one hand on her heart, trying to make out the figure sitting now opposite her again.

"Captain Briggs!" she breathed.

"The same," he said with a smile so wide and white she could see its brilliance even through her veil. "At your service, Miss Lowell. Literally," he added when she didn't speak. "Murchison told me what you asked him, and I'm here to help you."

"He said he wouldn't tell anyone," she said stiffly, her heartbeat slowing, but her heart sinking as she wondered who else the runner had confided in.

"No, he said you'd run mad," he corrected her, "and added that he'd keep his counsel. Which he did. But he wanted to help you, so he shared your request with me. Never put your faith in a man who's sworn to uphold the law, Miss Lowell, because the law has more holes in it than you have in your veil."

"Than I have in my head," she said bitterly.

"No, no," he said, smiling. "I really am here to help you, and I promise my lips are sealed. You want to see Christian. So you shall. Don't worry, I'm very good at such things, and I don't think you can do it without me. How were you planning on doing it, by the way?" he asked curiously.

"I was going to buy my way in," she said, answering truthfully because there didn't seem much point in lying.

"Really?" he asked with interest. "And how much money did you bring?"

She opened her purse and showed him.

He whipped the purse out of her hand and put it inside his jacket.

She gaped at him.

He laughed, and handed it back to her. "You see? I give it back. Whatever bloke took it from you at Newgate wouldn't have, and he wouldn't have done what you wanted either. What could you do then? Report him to the officials—if you knew where to find them—for *not* taking a bribe? He'd deny it, and where would you be? Or maybe report him for stealing your money? You'd have to give your name to make a charge against him, and then explain why you were there in the first place. Any way you slice it, you'd have been trumped, robbed, and dumped, all in an hour."

"But Christian said that women of means can come and go even in the condemned calls at Newgate," she said, her eyes wide.

"So they can, and so they do. But they're far more experienced in such matters than you are. They hire rogues like me to do their dirty work." He put up one gloved hand to stop her before she could speak. "But I'll work for you free. Because I think it would be good for him to see you. He needs diversion now. And I think you truly care for him, or you wouldn't be about this mad business, would you?"

"I don't know that I should be," she said wretchedly. "I don't even know if he is who he says he is."

"I know who he is, and I can tell you that he's his father's son. And that he didn't steal any candlesticks—not then and not now. He's sitting in Newgate because someone wants him dead—then, and now."

"Can you prove it?" she asked eagerly.

"I will. Until then, he needs all the help he can get. Are you willing to give that to him?"

Finally, it was all too much for her. Her head shot up. "I just sneaked out of the house," she said through her clenched teeth. "I lied to my cousins and my host, I was about to bribe the king's men and risk my neck and my name, *and* my body, by going to a loathsome jail! And you ask me if I am willing to help? My dear sir, if you don't think so, I don't credit you with much intelligence!" She sat back, fuming.

"My dear ma'am," he said, "I've seen more of the world than most men. Christian is a very handsome fellow, and he's a step from the scaffold right now. That's enough to make a certain sort of female lie, sneak, bribe, and cheat their own relatives, husbands, and priests, as well as all the king's men, in an effort to see him."

She fell still and looked at her knotted hands in her lap.

His voice came soft. "Forgive me. But that's the real world. Christian has seen it, and worse. I do think you care for him. And so if you do, please help him to forget all that, if only for an hour, will you?"

Her emotions had been so buffeted, she was so filled with doubt and fear, she didn't know what to say. That seemed to satisfy him.

"Now," he said briskly, "here's how we'll do it. Christian's being kept near the state side of the prison, which is a mercy. Common criminals stay in

the sties on the other side, and that's unbearable. But
he isn't in the best apartments. It was hard enough to
keep him out of the common pens. I only did it by
telling them he might be proved a nobleman still, and
by greasing every hand that was held out. But he isn't
in the best apartments either; they're all taken. So
we'll be going down some dark paths. You keep that
hat and veil on—how can you breathe, by the way?"

"With difficulty," she said, with a smile she
couldn't help.

His admiration was clear to see in his widened blue
eyes. "Damned if Christian wasn't always a lucky lad."

His smile faded, and he leaned forward, his face all
seriousness. "Now, listen well, because we'll be there
before long. When we get to Newgate's walls, I'll
leave you in the hack while I go in and take care of
matters. Then I'll take you in. Walk with me, don't
stop or say one word to anyone until I leave you alone
with Christian." He frowned. "You do understand that
I'll be leaving you by yourself with him, and the door
will be locked behind you two? If you're going to get
all missish about the proprieties and such, let me
know now.

"Think about it," he told her, his usual humorous
expression gone. "Whether or not you believe him to
be a criminal, I tell you one thing. This isn't some
giddy girlish lark your friends and family will soon
forgive you for. If you're discovered about this business, your reputation will be lower than a draggle-
tailed gutter wench selling herself for two pennies in
the streets outside of the place where you're going.
Do you understand that?"

She nodded and swallowed hard.

"Well, I'm thinking you won't be discovered," he said, sitting back. "I'll give you an hour with him, then I'll come back for you. So. What do you say?"

She didn't hesitate. She looked him in the eye. "What do I say? I say: Will you take me to him, please?"

# Chapter 20

Julianne was glad she couldn't see very well, it was bad enough that she could smell Newgate Prison. The reek was almost unbearable. It smelled of wet wood and clammy stones, stale food, human sweat, chamber pots, and worse. And although she knew it wasn't possible, it seemed to her that the nose-searing stench she tried not to breathe was also that of decades of desperation.

"Take a deep breath, no matter how it stinks," Captain Briggs whispered to her, as they walked down another dark corridor. "Then take another, and by the next you won't mind it half so much. Three more, and if you've lived through them, you won't notice the smell at all. The nose is very forgiving; how else do you think people live in such places?"

Julianne did as he said, and though it got better, she silently disagreed, because she never got used to the rank smell. Nevertheless, she kept walking, following the captain and the burly prison guard he'd produced to take them to Christian. She clutched her purse and kept her hands in her cape, but she was still cold. The stones of the walls and the floors of Newgate kept the winter in though spring rioted outside. Julianne thought that it would always be cold in here no matter the season.

Newgate was huge and sprawling, a city of punishment, a warren of corridors. It had been burned down twice in its long history, but Julianne thought there'd be no flame hot enough to cleanse the place of its ugliness.

"Don't fret," the captain told her. "It's not a Monday, so there's no hangings today. Just as well, we'd never get through the mob if there were. Nothing brings out the crowds like a good hanging, you know."

Julianne's stomach felt as cold as her hands and quivered just as much. Her courage had deserted her. She was too frightened to speak, or to run, or even to faint. She could only march on, trying to match the captain's slightly halt but rapid gait. She had time now, at last, to think of her folly. But her thoughts didn't go far, they only wound round and round in her head.

They passed through bleak stone halls and climbed a stair that led to a long hall. The air was a bit better here, but it was just as dim and dreary, and her thoughts were now even darker.

If she were caught at this, she'd be ruined. And she deserved it. Because she'd been rash, flying off to do something without carefully planning it. And because she'd been a great fool to sacrifice everything for love. That was what it was, she knew it now. She loved the man who claimed to be Christian Sauvage, and the more fool she, because she still didn't know who or what he was. She'd only her heart to go by, and at last, she doubted it and herself as much as she doubted him.

"'Ere we are," the guard said, stopping before a door that looked like all the others in the dark corridor. "You don't know how you got 'ere, nor seen me at all."

"True," the captain said. "But you'll wait and see me out when I call you. And bring me back within the hour."

The guard glanced at the veiled figure beside him. "And 'er?"

"She stays that hour."

The guard made a strangled sound that might have been a chuckle. "'E's set to swing, is he? Funny, I didn't hear that yet, 'cause when they're ready for the drop, they takes them to the other side, nearer the gallows . . . Aye, not my business," he said quickly, seeing Anthony's expression. "Go in. I'll come back for you, sir, in five minutes. The gentry mort can stay the night, do she wish, it's all the same to me."

He took a key from the mass of them he wore at his waist, put it in the lock, and flung open the door. "'Ere, you got company," he said. "Quick, quick," he told Anthony and Julianne, as he looked down the corridor to be sure no one saw what he was doing. The moment they were inside, he closed the door. They could hear the key creaking in the lock as it turned, and the sharp shot of the bolt falling back in place.

The cell was plain and simple, though bigger than she'd thought it would be. The stones of the walls were as thick and dark as they were in her nightmares. The one window was near the high ceiling, so small that only a glimpse of light showed through the bars over it. There was a bed and a table, a chair and a basin, and one lamp. And the man who called himself Christian Sauvage.

He rose from the bed and stared at them. "Damn you, Amyas!" he shouted. "Why have you brought her here?"

"She's wrapped like a parcel," the captain said. "How do you know who I've brought?"

"What other female in all England would want to see me? And who else would be naive enough to listen to you and come here? Did you think this would comfort me? It horrifies me. Julianne, go home!"

"She was on her way here by herself when I intercepted her. Aye," the captain said when Christian fell silent. "S'truth, on my life. Wouldn't that have been a pantomime? She'd hired the hack, and was waltzing off to Newgate alone, dressed like a widow and producing her money for anyone asking to see it. I brought her here, true. Would you have preferred I let her go by herself?"

"Gad," Christian said, running a hand over his hair.

"Or," the captain asked, "should I have spent the day arguing with her?

"She likely wouldn't have changed her mind," Christian said. "Always had to have your way, didn't you, Julie? But this is a bit different than a romp in the woods or a trip to a trout stream with the lads. We should have been less indulgent then, so you wouldn't be so reckless now."

She couldn't answer right away; she was too busy trying to fight back tears. He was changed. It wasn't because he was in his shirtsleeves, with no neckcloth, wearing only that shirt and breeches. Or that his boots were off, and he stood in his hose. But he still looked immaculate, as always, even with the new heavy discolored bruise on his cheekbone. She could see it clearly even through the heavy netting of her veil. It wasn't his injury or his half dress that made him look different to her.

She realized it was because of how edgy and distracted he was. He was usually so calm and self-assured. Now he seemed to vibrate with tension as he paced the little cell.

"Why did they do this to you?" she managed to say.

He paused, his head to the side. Then he reached her in three strides, and took her in his arms. She put her arms around him, laid her head on his chest, felt the warmth of him, and heard his rapid heartbeat beneath her ear. Now that she was in his close embrace, she sighed. He was her Christian again.

"Never a word of accusation from her," he said in a shaky voice, speaking over her head to Anthony. "Only what have *they* done. Was I right?"

"Yes, you're right. Again. As ever, it's sickening," Anthony said.

Christian released Julianne and stepped back. "Let's have a little propriety . . . gad! What am I saying? The woman's visiting a criminal in Newgate

Prison, with only another man as a chaperone! And he himself a . . . I'm not used to talking to a fishnet," he told her, quickly changing what he was about to say. "Since it's only you and I and Amyas here, do you think you might remove your hat?"

She reached up and pulled out the hatpin, lifted the veil, and took off her hat. She could see him more clearly, and he could clearly see the frown on her face. "Amyas?" she asked unhappily, turning the hat in her hands, looking from Christian to the captain, "I thought his name was Anthony."

"I must be more overset than I'd thought," Christian murmured. "But what's the point of secrecy at this stage? Julianne," he said soberly, "his name *is* Amyas. A proud old Cornish name, he says. We decided he'd be Anthony for a while in order to avoid discovery. He's my brother, you see."

"One of the brothers you and your father met . . . here?" she asked in astonishment.

"Yes. And he's been my brother in all but blood ever since. When we heard of the inheritance, he insisted on coming to England with me. There was a good reason for secrecy, believe me." Christian started pacing the cell again. "We realized being the earl of Egremont was a position with a certain amount of risk. Any claimaint to the title would be at an equal risk, and one with a criminal record at an even higher one." He showed a skewed smile as he added. "We trust the nobility about as far as they trust us. So Amyas came along to do some investigating of his own, to keep me safe."

"Much good I did," Amyas said bitterly.

"Much good you did do!" Christian corrected him. "I'll be out of here soon enough. I'm only on edge because of how I feel about this damned place. *On edge*." He laughed. "A fine euphemism for fairly insane. At any rate," he told Julianne, "you can see why we needed to change my brother's name."

"Yes, I do," she said, drawing herself up. "And *your* name?"

That made him check. He looked at her and smiled slightly. "A little late for doubt, isn't it? But I suppose it's earned. I am who I've said I am, Julianne. I've never lied to you."

"I see," she said stiffly, "but it isn't a lie if you choose not to tell me the truth?"

He nodded. "Some things aren't mine to tell. That's only truth. So, do you want to leave now?"

She took a deep breath. She could no more leave him now than she could fly out of Newgate Prison. "No," she said. "I want to help."

"That you can't do," he said. "We'll leave that to Amyas here, Murchison, and other friends. Yes, the runner's been helpful. And no, I don't know if he's playing two sides in this game, nor do I care."

"He's cautious and clever, and would take money from the Devil himself," Amyas said. "But he does have a heart. He was the one who told me Miss Julianne sent him a note asking where you were. He could just as easily have told the baronet about that, you know."

"He may well have," Christian said. "Be careful of whom you trust."

"You telling *me* that?" Amyas hooted. "Any road,

I'll be off now. There are some people abiding here I
need a word with. I'm hoping to have things resolved
before another day rises. I'll come back to collect you
in an hour, Miss Lowell, if that's all right with you?"

Christian was staring at her. "There's no need for
it. Thank you for coming, but you can leave now if
you wish," he told Julianne. "It's all right." She noticed that though his tones were casual, he held himself rigid as he waited for her answer.

"I'll stay," she said.

"I wish I could offer you somewhere else to sit,"
Christian said, when Amyas had left them, and the
door was shut firmly again. He indicated the bed with
a sweep of his hand. "But all I have is the bed."

Julianne promptly sat down. She winced as she felt
the unyielding surface beneath her. "Bed? It feels like
a rock." She laughed to hide her distress. "How can
you sleep on it?"

"Only a fool sleeps in Newgate," he muttered, and
began pacing again. "No sense lying, I'm glad to see
you. I'm also appalled. How did you get away from
your cousins? What possessed you to do it? Don't you
know the danger you're in?"

"As for how I did it, that was easy. I had my faithful Annie to help me the way she did when we met at
the White Hart. We said I was ill, and she's keeping
everyone away from my sickroom. It seems I have a
talent for deception," she said too brightly.

Then she frowned. "I'm not a deceptive person. At
least, I don't think I am. I never did anything so un-
derhanded at home. But I didn't have to." She put her

head to the side, considering it. "I suppose I don't worry about deceiving my cousins because I don't think they have my best interests at heart. After all, they tricked me into coming to them in the first place.

"And I don't think I'm in any more danger than I was those other times I met you in the night and was home by dawn. Maybe I am becoming an accomplished sneak, at that. I've certainly been a successful one. As for why . . ." She shook her head. "I couldn't bear the thought of you in here alone, thinking all your friends had deserted you."

He stilled. "Are you still my friend then, Julianne?"

She nodded, wondering why he'd doubt her.

"And nothing more?" he added, making her realize that he hadn't doubted her at all.

"I wanted to see justice done," she said, ignoring the undercurrent of meaning in his question. "I don't believe you're a thief, and I certainly don't think you stole any frippery candlestick," she said angrily. "Why should you? You obviously don't need the money, and you're not stupid. Why do the same thing they accused you of again?"

"Stupidity has nothing to do with it," he said conversationally, his eyes on the stones beneath his feet as he paced them. "Some men steal the way other men gamble or drink. It's not a thing they can help doing."

"Are you saying you're one of them?" she asked, her eyes widening.

He was beside her in seconds. He sat and took her hands in his. "No, I'm not saying that. But I have stolen. Bread, cheese, a link of sausage. I learned to do that here. It's how you survive this place. Amyas and his brother taught me—us. What was unthinkable becomes what you must think here . . . God!" he said with loathing, "I hate this place."

He sat so close she could feel the shudder that went through his lean frame as he said that. His speech was faster than usual; if she'd detested the way her fashionable suitors drawled, still she could hardly bear how rapidly Christian now spoke. His movements were jerky, his body tense; he was nothing like the calm, composed man she knew.

"This place," he said, looking around his cell. "It still has a grip on me. I *know* I won't be here long this time, but I can't seem to persuade my idiotic brain of it. I spent a year here when I was still a boy, and it seems coming back has reduced me to that state again. I remember it all too well.

"The thing is I can't stop remembering that first day," he said, staring off into middle distance as though he was seeing it again. "There are echoes, they keep reminding me. It was spring then, too. Such a contrast: my last taste of freedom and my first of horror. We'd had such a good day. My father seldom got a chance to spend an entire day with me, but it was such a glorious spring morning that he got an idea . . . Is it still spring outside?

"Stupid question," he said before she could answer, releasing one hand so he could slap himself on the forehead. "Stupid, meeching, pathetic question. Oh, pity the poor boy," he mocked in more of his old accents. "At any rate," he went on quickly, gripping her hands tightly in both of his cold ones again, "on that day my father took me with him when he went to the countryside to correct an error a rich client claimed he'd made on his accounts. The fellow had a manor house, and since it was a Sunday, said I was welcome as well. When we got there Father made a bargain with the stable master so we could ride when he was done working.

"We rode through green meadows, had a glorious time. Then we went home, happy and well pleased with ourselves. My father was kind as well as clever, always thinking about how to please his motherless lad. He hadn't married again because he'd buried his heart with my mother, and I know he felt guilty about it for my sake. That was one of the reasons he was so happy about my friendship with Jon. Your mother was kind to me. Remember?"

She nodded, but he was lost in his reveries and went on without waiting for her reply.

"We were weary, in that thoughtless way you are after a day in the sun. We were about to have dinner when a knock came on our door. Our maid opened it. Two men were there. They changed our lives, forever. They called my father a thief. When he protested, they put him in irons." There was no emotion in his voice, he might have been reciting a lesson. "I was terrified, I flew at them. They restrained me and put me in irons, too. Then as all the neighbors came out to gape, they loaded us in a coach like so much mutton for market, and brought us here, to Newgate."

He gazed around the cell, and his smile was bitter as his voice. "We weren't given such luxurious accommodations then. They threw us into a pen with twenty other men. It was lucky that I was literally thrown in," he added. "Because I skidded into another boy. I was too confused and angry to say anything but 'sorry' to him. And I certainly didn't want to say more after I got a good look at him. He was my age, ragged as a scarecrow and dirty as a sweep. But when he spoke his voice was reasonable, and whatever else I saw, I saw the pity in his eyes when he looked at me. That was Amyas. He told me not to worry. Then he went back to sit by another boy, his brother. But he kept watching me.

"A short time later, when my father had his back turned, a man put a hand on me. He was a monster of a man, dirty, unshaven, greasy, thoroughly terrifying to me. I think he was only trying to steal my coat; good clothes have to be fiercely defended here, most prisoners lose them the first day. I shouted. My father swung around, knocked the fellow to the floor, and warned him not to touch me again. My father wasn't a big man, but he was athletic and fit. The man he'd struck recognized a fellow who could handle his fives and crawled away without another word. That made Amyas sit up and take notice. A short time later he made us his offer.

" 'Look after us, my brother and me, like you do your son,' " he told my father, " 'and we'll do the same for you.' My father promised to watch out for him, and added that he needn't worry, because he didn't have to do anything for us in return.

" 'Do I not?' Amyas replied," Christian said, mimicking Amyas to perfection. "He asked if my father knew where to stand when they brought in the food?

He wondered if we knew where to put our shoes when we slept, so they couldn't be stolen. He put his hands on his skinny hips and asked if we knew which guards would do a favor for a penny piece, and which would take the penny and give back only a thump for it. Then his brother chimed in, asking if we know which men there would kill us soon as look at us and which only looked like villains?"

Christian's expression was as rueful as amused as he went on. "And while we thought about that, Amyas told us that he and his adopted brother Daffyd had formed just such an alliance, because they'd been practically raised in prisons, and had been in and out more times than they can count. They bragged that they know everything about Newgate. Amyas offered a bargain: If my father would protect them, he and Daffyd would look after us. They knew a lot, but they weren't grown men. They added they wanted to be, though. And since my father had a punishing right, and a son of his own to protect, they thought it would be a good trade.

"It was," Christian said. He smiled, remembering. "We became a fighting troop that night, my father and I and Amyas, and Daffyd. And so we stayed, to all our profit." His smile fled. "What profit, after all? The years have passed, I cheated Death so many times . . . and here I am again, on the brink of extinction again." He got to his feet and began pacing again.

"The pens where I was held are there," he told Julianne, waving in that direction. "Those for the condemned are farther down the passage. We were eventually held there, too. But we had enough money to ensure we stayed together, at least."

"But Amyas and his brother," Julianne asked, "surely they didn't put them in the condemned cells, too?"

He stopped, his smile was not pleasant. "Of course they did. Because they also had a date with Jack Ketch. The hangman," he explained to Julianne's puzzled look. "They were set to dance on the air for the crowds in Newgate square. Amyas had picked a pocket, and he was unlucky enough to have it contain a pound note, and his brother had held it for him before they caught him. Crimes punishable by death." One shoulder seemed to spasm as he shrugged it.

"Our cousin, the late earl of Egremont, heard of our misfortune and had our sentences commuted to transportation. We heard he didn't want a slur on the family name," he said with a twisted smile. "It certainly wasn't because of concern for us, because he never came to see us or hear our side of the story. I suppose he felt death in prison or a distant land was preferable to any taint of scandal because such deaths are quiet and quickly forgotten. Hanging's a matter of record. Father raised funds from his friends and used it to bribe the officials to get the same sentence for Amyas and his brother. We stayed together. We were sent to the Hulks to await transport to New South Wales . . ." His voice trailed off.

"That's the past," he said briskly. "The thing is, I know this will be, too. But I'm back in Newgate," he told her, pain and uncertainty back in his voice. "And try as I might, I can't forget it here and now."

His voice was by turns jaunty and dull with horror. He kept his expression serene by some incredible act of will, but his eyes were alive with terror and pain in that impassive face. Wide, bright, blazing blue, no wonder, she thought, that the young Amyas had taken him as a friend. She wanted to take him in her arms. She could almost feel all the blind terror that he was holding back with the main force of his will.

He turned and struck the wall with his fist. "By God, I'd give anything to forget this place; you can't know how hard I've tried. Most of the time, I can. But I can't get the hang of directing my dreams." He splayed his hands out on the wall and rested his forehead against it as he spoke. "Now, I'm awake, and I'm here again. It unmans me. I keep remembering what I've trained myself to forget. Such sickness and filth and degradation that there is within these walls, and no one cares," he muttered. "Men and boys, women and children went wailing to their appointments with the hangman, and the last sounds in their ears were the merry cheers of the good people of London celebrating as they died.

"That was merciful compared to what happened to others," he said, his voice low and haunted. "Men died in dark corners, and you didn't know it until the light came. There was no privacy for anything but death. Men coupled with each other in the night, and you knew it, even if both were willing, because of the noises they made. And sometimes there were those who were unwilling to die or to lie with anyone, and much good it did them. We couldn't protect the whole world."

He swung around, his eyes wild. "Damme for a villain! I shouldn't be telling you this. I've lost whatever control I had over myself, and I've kept such strict vigilance. Leave me. Go home! You're corrupted simply by being here with me. I'm not myself. I can't be here, this place lives in all the dark places of my soul, and there are too many of them. Go home, Julianne. I'll come to you when I can."

"How will you sleep tonight?" she asked.

"There's nothing wrong with staying awake. It's how you survive the place."

She sat quietly. He turned from her. The silence pounded against her ears, a deep silence born of the dark, buttressed by thick stone, meters deep in the earth. *So it must sound in your coffin,* she thought. There were no echoes here. The stone blunted sound and ate it up. The only echoes were in the mind, and so how much worse for him, who still heard all the old echoes of fear and pain?

"I'll be released in no time," he said after a moment. "Don't worry, and don't listen to me carry on. This is a good test of my character. I've endured worse."

He came and sat beside her again. He leaned toward her and breathed in deeply. "Perfume," he said softly, "Lord, but you smell sweet."

"Just soap, and lemon rinse for my hair," she said in embarrassment.

"Here, that's fine French perfume. Fah!" he said, pulling back. "And I must stink. Forgive me. But all they give me is a bucket of water. My years here gave me a deep appreciation of bathing, and I feel like a goat since they deprived me of that."

"You don't smell bad at all," she said thickly, turning her head aside.

"Weeping?" he asked, touching a hand to her cheek. "Ah no, Julianne. I never meant that. Be easy. I'll be dancing in the sunlight soon."

It was a bad choice of words. She got the sudden image of his lean body twisting in the wind at the end of a rope. "Oh, no, Christian," she cried, and embraced him. She buried her face in his neck. He didn't reek, he lacked his usual spicy scent but smelled faintly of soap, and his skin was warm and sleek. She raised her head. He looked at her, and then raised a hand, slowly, tentatively. He cupped the back of her head in one hand. And then he kissed her.

His lips were soft, his mouth was warm, his kiss tentative. And yet she felt all that he was holding back.

She kissed him back with all the art and passion, pity and love that she felt.

"Oh, this will never do," he said, when he raised his head.

"You don't like it?" she asked, so moved by his matching response that she trembled. She forced a smile. "You only like my kisses at dawn?"

"I like them too much at any time. Go home." He raised his head. "I hear my gentle jailer coming. Newgate never gives you value for your money, surely our hour isn't up?" He rose to his feet as the door swung open.

Amyas stood there, blinking, trying to adjust his eyes to the dimmer light.

"Ready?" he asked Julianne.

"No," she said, because she'd made up her mind. "Come back for me at dawn, please." And then, with a smile that was all sunlight, she added, "I'm used to leaving your brother at dawn, you know. It just wouldn't feel right to go now."

"Don't be ridiculous!" Christian snapped.

"If I'm caught, now or at dawn, will it make a bit of difference? Shall I have a shred of reputation left?" she asked. "I think not. In fact, I'd be more easily found out if I trotted home now, or even at midnight, because that's when my cousins are at their most active. I'll leave just before the dawn, when they're all sleeping," she told Amyas.

"Don't listen to her," Christian said roughly. "It's pity speaking."

"Pity feels, it doesn't speak," she corrected him. "I'm talking good sense. I've decided to stay to keep you from dreaming; I have a feeling you won't go to sleep with me here. Your manners are much too good. Come, Christian," she said seriously. "You know me, and I, at last, am sure I know you. I'm staying with you."

"A very good decision," Amyas said with a wide white smile. "Be ready to leave an hour before dawn."

He pushed the jailer into the corridor, backed off, and swung the door shut in their faces.

# Chapter 21

**T**hey were left alone, for the night, locked in a small cell together, with no one but each other for comfort and warmth. Julianne looked at Christian and held her breath, her courage born of the moment rapidly fading.

He sank to the cot and put his head in his hands. "Now see what you've done!" he said.

The tremulous smile slipped off her lips. "You really didn't want me here?" she asked.

"I really did not," he said.

"Oh!" she said.

He looked up at her. "I don't think you understand," he said in a slow, unhappy voice.

"Indeed, I think I begin to," she said, and now she was the one who began to pace around the cell. "I think I've been beyond blind."

He nodded. "So now you think that because I don't drag you into my arms and have my way with you that I have somehow betrayed you, misled you— worse, led you astray?"

"Well, yes," she said, "but that's not entirely your

318

fault. I had to believe you, didn't I?" She took another agitated turn around the tiny space. "I should've known that a man of your appearance, with your charm, having traveled so much as you have would naturally . . ."

He cut her off, as he said, wearily, ". . . Deceived and cheated you for my own vile purposes?"

"At least so much as to win me to your side," she agreed. "And I wouldn't go so far as to say 'vile' purposes." She swallowed down tears, and when she spoke again her voice was steadier, if a little muffled by emotion. "What a fool I was, am still. I ought to have known it was all for effect. At any rate," she said, stopping her pacing and faced him directly, "if you just call for the jailer, I'll be on my way. And don't worry—I won't say a word against you to anyone. This was between the two of us, and there it will stay."

"Sorry, it won't be so simple," he said. "The jailer was paid to make himself scarce until dawn, and he will. It's done, and I'm afraid you'll have to make the best of it. You can have the bed," he added. "I won't be using it anyway."

She just stared at him.

"I do have *some* honor," he said. "Don't worry, I won't touch you."

He rose from the bed, bowed, and swept his hand to indicate the empty cot. Then he stepped away and went to lean against the wall.

Head up, she marched to the bed, sat down, keeping her spine as stiff as a queen at a review of the troops. But she felt stupid, embarrassed, and shamed, too proud to cry and too hurt to speak.

The silence was deafening. Julianne heard the blood beating in her ears.

"You should consider yourself fortunate," he finally said, softly. "At least you're not ruined. If Amyas gets you back by dawn, no one will be the wiser, and there'll be no harm done."

She nodded.

"Come," he said softly, "don't hate me. This is for the best, you know."

She didn't answer.

"And I do appreciate your faith in me," he said, as though he too couldn't bear the silence any longer. "I'll never forget it. Honestly. That is," he added bitterly, "if you can ever think of that word in the same context as me."

"No, obviously you're honorable, in your fashion," she said dully. "I appreciate that. Not that it's any great effort on your part in my case, I suppose. I'd wish you'd not pretended otherwise before, but I understand the necessity. Thank you for speaking up at once and sparing me further humiliation. I just wish you'd let me know *before* Amyas had a chance to slam the door."

The silence beat on for a minute more.

"What the devil are you talking about?" he asked.

"I know you had to win me over," she said.

"It was helpful, but not entirely necessary."

"But . . ." Whatever she was about to say was stopped by a little choked sob that escaped her lips. Horrified, she threw up a hand. "Disregard that! I didn't mean it. Never mind."

He came to her, and knelt at her feet. "Julianne, Little Jewel," he said softly, "this is truly for the best. What can I say to help?"

"Nothing," she said on a shaky sniffle. "Just give me a moment to compose myself. I didn't expect rejection, you see, though I suppose I should have, considering."

"Considering what?"

She looked straight at him. Beautiful, she thought, that still solemn face is truly beautiful in my eyes. "Considering that you are what you are."

"And I am . . . ?" he asked, seemingly fascinated by what he saw in her eyes.

"You're so handsome, and charming," she said helplessly. "I suppose I've adored you since you were a boy."

He seized her hand. "You *still* believe I am Christian Sauvage?" he asked with wonder.

"Of course," she said. "Nothing you've done makes me doubt it. In fact, the reverse is true, because you always were honorable. I should have known you'd have found your true love by now. It only makes sense; you haven't lived in limbo all these years, as I have. I suppose I didn't want to contemplate the possibility. I know you had to show some ardor in order to win me over, but now that we're alone, I admire you for keeping faith with her—and me— whatever it might mean for your future. Although," she added on a wistful smile, "as I said, staying faithful to her wouldn't be so very difficult for you as it concerns me. Nor do you have to worry about what

I'll say. But you can imagine how sorry I am that I threw myself at you. Please forget it."

He frowned. "Let me be sure I understand you. You believe I rejected you because I'm being true to another?"

She nodded.

"Well, you are the greatest fool in nature," he said angrily.

In one swift move he rose, sat beside her, and gathered her into his arms. "How did such a wise child turn out to be such a fool?" he demanded, his lips against her hair. He didn't give her a chance to answer.

He drank at her lips as though he needed to in order to live. She clung to his shoulders, feeling his body tense and hot beneath the thin material of his shirt, and kissed him back, dazzled by pleasure, reveling in their closeness, refusing to think.

He raised his head to breathe, and murmured, "I tried, God knows, I tried to resist this; but Julianne, I can't, not anymore." Then he kissed her again. And again.

His hair was sleek and soft under her hands, his body lean and tensed muscle as he clasped her close to himself. His beard was growing in, and the contrast between it and his skin made her marvel once again at how smooth and fine that skin was. His mouth was soft, yet firm and insistent; it tasted of dark sweet liquors that made her drunk with desire for more of him.

He left off kissing her mouth and feathered little kisses on her neck. She arched her neck and shivered.

When he trailed his lips along her collarbone, she held his shoulders tight and trembled. When he moved her gown aside and cupped her naked breast, she gasped and held her breath, reveling in the wild thrill of it. When he put his hand beneath her breast and brought his lips to it, she closed her eyes to better feel the pure pleasure as it coursed through her.

Christian started to lower her to his bed. She lay back and reached for him. He drew back, and started to pull at his shirt, to be free of anything that would keep him from getting close to the smooth skin he'd felt. That was long enough to warn him. He didn't know how long it had been since he'd gotten drunk on her sweet compliance. But too soon, and almost too late, he realized how far they'd gone.

With a pang of frustrated desire so keen it was pain, he drew back farther. He opened his eyes, trying to free himself from the familiar, dark, relentless, mounting drive toward completion. He fought to return to sanity again.

Seeing didn't make it easier. He saw that his hands had loosed her hair from its ribbon, and so her face was framed by her soft dark hair. Her eyes were closed, her color was high, her lips were parted, and her gown was half off her shoulders. He was glad he was sitting, so she couldn't see the effect she'd had on him.

Her eyes slowly opened. She looked at him and saw the color on his high cheekbones, his eyes blazing blue as he looked at her, and she raised a hand to touch the livid bruise on his cheek.

He took her hand and kissed it, then held it, and forced himself to smile. "No," he said, "our first time, my lady, will be in a high soft bed, with sweet-smelling sheets and sunlight everywhere. You'll wear my ring on your finger, and nothing else. Nor will you feel shame because you'll be mine in heart as well as name, in every court of law in the land. I've wanted you for a long time. But if I could resist you before, it's even more imperative now. No hedgerow tumbles for you," he said, pulling farther away from her. "There won't be a union in a stinking little cell, either. Much as I long for you, I won't do it. And *that*, my clever girl, is why I tried to reject you, and will try and succeed through this night.

"I have no other woman," he said. "Though I can't in all truth tell you that I never did," he added with a crooked smile. "And all truth is what you'll have from me." He paused, as they both remembered what he'd said about the truths he could tell her.

"I adored you when you were a girl," he went on, "but I never thought of you as a lover then. You were, my dear, a charming pest. But now . . ." He touched her cheek with his fingertips. "Now you're my life. I pledge it, and whatever happens, so it will always be with me."

"But there's the point," he said seriously, his eyes steely as his voice. "I don't know what the future will bring. I can't take you as mine until I do. Fine thing to take you if I can't take care of you," he said, shaking his head. "I believe I'll soon be free. But no one knows the future, and Fate hasn't always been fair to me. So I have to tell you that in spite of all I want and hope, you may well have to marry someone else someday."

She opened her mouth to protest; he placed a long finger over her lips. "Ssh," he said. "Listen. If I touch you again, who knows what may happen? With all the care I could muster, still Nature is what she is. What I most wish to do with you now might burden you with more than my memory forever after. So rest easy and sleep sound. I won't touch you again tonight. Not because I love another but because I care for you too much to dare."

She smiled. She placed a finger on his lips, too, not to silence him but to trace and marvel at the purity of their strict classical lines. She shook her head. "Such a beautiful mouth to say such nonsense."

His lips quirked as he echoed, "Beautiful?"

"Yes, and such a pother, such a fuss you make over nothing," she said. "I love you entirely, and always have, and always will. At first I thought I was thrilled to see you again because you brought back my memories of my brother and happier times. Now I know it was because you brought back memories of yourself. You were the ideal male I always sought, and I never settled for less. What do I care about tomorrow? I've lived in the past too long. I don't trust the future at all. I believe in now, and now is what we have."

She didn't tell him she feared she might never see him again. Nor that she'd never have had the courage to offer herself if they weren't here, and he so overset, and she, so desperately sorry for him. But sorrrow had turned to desire, and desire to need, and that need, imperative. She'd tried to make him forget where they were. She'd forgotten that in his arms, and now that she was alone again, she could hardly bear it.

Julianne sat up, leaned forward, and brushed his mouth with hers. He sat still. She dared to touch his sealed lips with the tip of her tongue, and felt them begin to part, before he closed them tight again. She sat back and smiled at him.

"And now, my dear, honorable, upright . . ." She paused and glanced down at his lap. He was astonished to hear her giggle as she went on, "my dear so very upright love, I tell you that I want you, too. And I will not suffer to wait until we get into that high, soft bed. You said you don't like to sleep because of your dreams of this place," she said seriously. "I don't blame you. Let me give you new things to remember about this place instead."

He didn't answer.

She squared her shoulders. "You mustn't think only of yourself. I need you at least as much as you need me, you know. I've lived only on memories for so long, I need you to give me a chance to experience life. Because if anything *should* happen to your plans for freedom—heaven forbid—what would I have of you but the memory of kisses in a field at dawn and an embrace here? I need more of you. I believe you need me. I could be wrong," she said when he remained quiet. "I have been before."

He still didn't answer.

"Well!" she said, and blinked. "I won't beg."

She looked down at her gown, and flushed rosily. She drew up the neck of her gown and adjusted it. Then, head still down, she took a deep breath. She looked at the bed, then back at him. In the glow of the single lamp, he could see her eyes glittering with unshed tears. "It will be a long night, after all," she murmured. "So!" she said briskly, lifting her head high. "Do you perhaps happen to have a deck of cards?"

He gave a shout of laughter and pulled her back into his arms. "How can I resist you?" he asked again, as he rocked her back and forth. "Devil and imp, innocent and fiend, Julianne, you're my only love. And if you stoop to love me, I won't say no again."

"Good," she said, against his chest, "oh, good." She didn't say more. Because she wasn't half as sure as she pretended.

He knew that. But he needed her every bit as much as she thought, and more. He tried to show her that. "First," he breathed against her neck, "we must dispense with all these clothes."

She smiled as he pulled off his shirt. But as soon as he had done that, he frowned and looked around. He rose, went to the table, and, shielding the lamp with one hand, blew out the light.

It was suddenly so dark in the cell that she couldn't see him. But he was back at her side in a moment.

"I thought you wanted sunlight," she said breathlessly.

"Sunlight, yes, not lamplight, not here." His voice sounded pained, a little anxious. "If anyone—should glance in through any chink in the wall, . . . not that I know of any," he said quickly, "and I've looked, I promise you. But I take no chances. So," he said softly as his hands found and traced the shape of her, "you and I must meet in the dark, and our hands and lips will show us the light."

She smiled, and with his help, shucked out of her
gown and put it aside. Now her eyes were adjusting to
the scant light. She could see it was still late afternoon by the dim, gray, fading light at his high window, and so she could also see him as he bent and
stripped off his breeches and hose. He had wide
shoulders and a lean hard chest, but she'd known that.
She was pleased to see that shapely chest tapered to
a flat, well-muscled abdomen, and his hips were as
trim as they'd appeared in his clothing. Then as he
turned and bent to her, she couldn't see more than his
face, intent, his eyes filled with the reflection of the
last gleams of stony light, his stern mouth, smiling.
She closed her own eyes so she could better feel the
wonderful shape of him as he took her in his arms
again.

"Ah, Julianne," he sighed, and she needed no other
urging to relax and lie down in his arms.

They lay on his bed together. He made her forget
her surroundings, just as she'd said. But still, she'd a
moment to be glad of the feeling of her silken gown
beneath them, before she became more enraptured by
the feel of his smooth skin sliding against hers.

"Christian," she said, and he stopped, and waited.
"What?"

"Just . . . Christian," she said into his ear. "I like
saying your name."

She felt his smile against her cheek, then his hands
cupping and caressing her, as he turned her so that
she lay on the bed, and he above her.

She was thrilled not only with what he did, but
with the joy of who he was. She loved his long

hands, his slender muscular body, so different from her own, so perfectly suited to her. She touched him tentatively, and then with growing adventure and wonder. He let her explore, but lay with the lower part of his body against the cot, lest he startle her. But when he half rose, to turn so he could taste her other breast and begin to cover her, he brushed against her. She made a soft sound of surprise as her hands found his sex.

"I don't want to frighten you," he said gruffly.

"I'm a country girl," she said, "and know about such things. Although I haven't seen one when it's like this . . . and won't either, in this light," she added, sounding disgruntled.

Even muddled with desire, battling the need to complete what he'd begun, still he couldn't stop himself. He reared back and laughed. "Oh Lord, Julie," he breathed, "will you never stop surprising me?"

"I hope not," she said. "I don't want you to grow bored with me."

Her voice was breathless, and her heart was beating wildly. He was very large, and sleek with desire, obviously ready for what they would do. With all the excitement she felt and the joy of having him so close, and affecting him so strongly, still she wasn't sure of what was coming. She suddenly found conversation preferable to action.

Again, he knew. Holding himself up on his elbows above her, he bent and nuzzled her lips. "Let's go back to where we were," he said quietly. "And we won't go on until you're entirely sure, and absolutely ready. All right?"

She nodded.

He kissed her, long and deeply, his hands first tracing along the outlines of her body, then returning to those places that had made her sigh before. Then he found and stroked the other secret, wildly beating pulse she hadn't realized he knew she had. And then, finally, she stirred beneath him and gripped his shoulders tight.

"I shall surely die if you don't show me now," she told him.

"Oh, I can show you many things now," he said in a thickened voice, and pressed his fingers deep, withdrew, then stroked again, and whispered, as she gasped and began to rise against his hand, "Yes, that, and that, my love, and more, and more."

She caught her breath as she discovered a long dazzling spiral of pleasure that drew her out of rational thought, making her teeter on the brink of something cataclysmic, then whimpered in astonishment as she found it. As her body still hummed and buckled, and her mind spun, he rose above her. He moved her legs and settled between them.

"Yes," he said as he positioned himself and pushed down hard, "this, too. I'm sorry," he managed to grunt, low, as she froze in surprise. "But it will pass," he said in a hoarse whisper as he strained against her and finally moved within her. "Oh, Julianne."

He didn't say more as he thrust against her; he could not. She didn't do more than hold him hard, but when he fell against her at last with a groan, she still held him tightly.

"Thank you," she said, against his damp shoulder, when he finally lay still, breathing harshly.

He recovered his breath, and moved away from her, but only an eyelash length. "Are you all right?" he asked anxiously.

"Oh yes," she said. "It didn't hurt so much as sting and burn. After all I'd heard, I'm very relieved."

He chuckled. "Lord, but you're easy to please. But not for long, you'll see, I promise you." He rested his damp forehead against her shoulder. "Oh good Lord, Julie, I hope we have the time and space for me to teach you that. But I can't be sorry. Thank you, forgive me."

She didn't say anything as she took him back in her arms. But she turned her head so he wouldn't feel her tears against his face.

And so she never knew about his.

They washed from the tiny bucket, and since the toweling he'd been provided was already damp, he insisted on using his own shirt to dry her. Then they lay and spoke, low, about a dozen things they never would remember after.

"You have a scar," she finally said, when she felt comfortable enough with him to speak of difficult things. Though she'd given him her heart and her body, against all she'd been taught, she still was tentative with him because there was so much of him she didn't know.

"The one on my back, yes," he said. "You could scarcely avoid feeling it. It runs from my shoulder to my waist. A great knotty thing, isn't it? Does it bother you?"

"No," she lied, because she wanted to kill whoever had dared ruin the perfection of that strong, tapered back. "But it must have bothered you."

He shrugged, and settled her head more comfortably on his chest. "At the time, yes. It's from a whip. An overzealous guard on the *Orion*, a Hulk I stayed on, gave it to me. It never happened again. He learned. I had my father and my brothers and my friends to ensure that, you see." He sensed her confusion. "The guards are prisoners of their jobs, as surely as we are. If they want to survive, they learn whom they can or can't abuse beyond their right. Power is power, even in chains. They may kill you, by law. But they dare not bedevil you without reason—if you have friends."

She lay very still. She'd wanted him to talk about his demons and was glad he could speak of it now, but her heart hurt when he did. And he didn't seem to realize that when he did, he spoke as though he were still a prisoner. She felt cold when she remembered that he was, and splayed her hand over his beating heart, as though to shield it.

"Amyas has more scars, and deeper ones," he said conversationally. "I'm lucky to only have this. But you know," he said in wonder, "I'm even luckier, because now, here, with you, I can look back and see it all as past. You've erased Newgate itself. There's a miracle." He raised his head and tried to see her face. "Now, shall we see if you can make me forget the rest?"

She smiled and reached for him.

"You're sure you don't feel sore?" he asked.

She rose and bent over until she'd veiled him in a curtain of her hair. She kissed him.

"It might take a very long while to forget *all* the rest," he warned her in a thickened voice, as he touched her hair.

"Good," she said.

And it did take a long while, because he spent even more time preparing her and pleasuring her before he came to her again.

"I begin to see that there's more to this than I thought," she commented when they were done and lying spent in each other's embrace.

"Oh good," he said, "because I don't think I can show more than appreciation anymore, at least tonight."

They laughed, and murmured gentle praise and lovers' nonsense to each other. Neither wanted to end their meeting in something as mundane as sleep, not when they didn't know when, or even if, they'd see each other again. They chatted like old friends, and kissed like new lovers. But though they spoke of many things during that long dark night, they never once talked about the morrow.

# Chapter 22

The lovers lay entwined, exhausted, still astonished. The bed was hard and narrow, but she
rested against him, close as his next breath, her head
on his chest, her hand on his heart.

"I'm sorry," Christian said softly.

"I'm not," she said.

"I tried to take care," he said softly. "I was going to
leave you before I compromised you fully. Then when
I realized I couldn't do that, I was going to pull away
before I . . ." His voice dwindled. "But it turned out I
wasn't half as clever or in control as I wanted to be.
This place addled my wits, but you completely overwhelmed me. But I don't blame the flower for being
lovely enough to pick. It's entirely my fault, I'm sorry."

"I'm not sorry for anything," she said. "Except that
you are here."

He moved his hand over her back, then let it lie
there and closed his eyes. Without meaning to, he
slept. Lost, and found, and whole again, he drifted
away from his love in the place of his nightmares.

She heard the change in his breathing, and after

long moments of waiting she turned, carefully, so she could watch him sleep. She resisted the urge to touch him. She didn't move, not even so much as to ease a cramp in her leg, lest she wake him from what seemed to be easeful sleep.

She lay quietly, luxuriating in the fact of being with him, until she saw the texture of the black night outside the high, barred window begin to thin. Then she slowly and carefully eased herself out of his arms and edged off the bed. Her gown had fallen to the floor: She had only to give a gentle tug for the last of it to slide from under him. It was crumpled and wrinkled, but it was forgiving silk. She shook it out and quietly dressed.

When she picked up her slippers and sat gingerly on the bed again to slip them on, he woke in an instant and sat up sharply.

"Julianne?" he said. He saw her outline in the newly graying light, and sank back again, his arm crooked so it covered his eyes. "Is it already time, so soon? And I wasted it in sleep."

"Well, that's good. You needed it." She rose and paced to the door. "I hope Amyas comes before it gets too light."

"Tired of me already?" he asked from behind her as he slipped his arms around her.

She leaned back against him. "Never," she said simply.

He turned her and kissed her. She relaxed against him, feeling the now familiar thrill and growing languor his kiss brought to her. But then he stepped away, quickly.

"No more of that!" he said, as he went to the cot and scooped up his clothing. "I have to get dressed; Amyas is a man of his word. He'll be here in a minute, and I have my reputation around here to consider."

She giggled at his jest. "I wonder," she said carelessly. "If he doesn't come for me, does that mean I'll be an inmate, too?"

"Don't even joke about it," he said sharply as he dropped his shirt over his head. "Listen," he said, as he sat and pulled on his hose, "you're not anxious enough. You seem too contented, too pleasured, too pleased with yourself. I'm delighted, but it worries me. You told your family you were sick, please remember that. You must mind your behavior until I come for you. Suffer a little, please."

She laughed.

He rose and dragged on his breeches, then produced a flint, scratched it, and lit the lamp. Light bloomed again in the gray cell. He turned to her and saw her smiling at him. "Good gad!" he exclaimed. "Where's your veil?"

"Oh," she said, with another giggle, "I forgot."

He picked up her hat and brought it to her. She could see his troubled expression clearly. "Don't forget anymore," he warned her as he drew her cape over her shoulders and rested his hands there. "Don't speak a word until you're in the carriage again, then go home and straight back to your room. Let Amyas know that you got there undetected. Send a note to the runner by way of your footman, or let him know any way you can arrange with him, because I won't rest easy until I know."

Her expression turned serious, too. "And if I don't get there safely? If someone sees?"

"Then I'll have someone come for you, to take you from there," he said. "You don't have to experience a minute of their anger or accusations. I expect to be out by then. But even if I'm still here, I'll take care of you."

She smiled. "Don't worry. I can go home. My parents will understand."

His expression didn't change. He kept his two hands on her shoulders and looked down at her. "You're my responsibility now. Now, and forever, whatever happens to me. And I see to my debts."

She stilled. "Is that what I am to you?"

He finally smiled. "My debt, my reward, my heart, and my salvation. Do you think I'll let anything happen to hurt you?"

Her eyes filled with tears. He stood only paces from the scaffold, his own life was no longer in his keeping, and yet he promised her safety. And still, she believed him.

They both heard the key in the door. He plucked the hat from her hands, placed it on her head. She quickly put up a hand to keep it there, and pulled the veil down over her face. They swung around, in concert, as the door opened.

"Good morning," Amyas said. "Are you ready to leave?"

"We both are," Christian said. "But only she goes with you now," he added, as the guard stepped forward menacingly. "Take care of her, brother," Christian said, "as you would my own life."

\*   \*   \*

In spite of her worries about Christian and the new-found stiffness in unusual parts of her body, Julianne hummed a pretty tune as she slipped back into her bed at the baronet's house. "And no one suspects?" she asked Annie again.

"No one," Annie said, "so far as I know. I made sure they knew you were in your room. I had to tell them you were feeling a bit better, though, and would come down to luncheon today. I was scared they'd have called the doctor if I didn't. Because they were starting to worry, leastways, Sir Maurice, he was."

"You're a pearl beyond price," Julianne said on a yawn. "Wake me an hour before lunch, and I'll be fine. I'll have had just enough sleep to be able to make sensible conversation, but I'll be tired and wan enough to suit any story we told."

Annie stood by the side of the bed, holding Julianne's cast-off gown. She fidgeted.

"What?" Julianne said, opening an eye. "What is it? You were wonderful. I owe you favors in future, and you know I'll repay you . . ."

"It isn't that, Miss. We've been together too long for that. But are you sure you're all right? I can call the doctor, or even go there with you later, with no one the wiser."

Julianne sat up, looking worried. "Why? Do I look that bad?"

"No, Miss," Annie said unhappily. She held out her mistress's wrinkled discarded gown. "But see, there's blood on your pretty gown."

Julianne looked. There was, indeed, a darkened splotch on the back of her pretty peach-colored gown. Her cheeks flamed as she remembered how she and Christian had lain on it while they made love. And then she also remembered how tenderly he'd helped her clear her body of all traces of her first act of love, afterward.

"Being your personal maid of course I know your courses like I knows my own," Annie was saying, her color rising. "And they aren't due for two weeks."

"I . . . I know," Julianne said, ducking her head, her own face ruddy. "But I'm fine, I promise you. That's not it, nor am I injured. It's only natural, I just . . . we . . . that is to say . . ."

"Oh, Miss!" Annie gasped, her eyes growing wide.

"Oh, indeed," Julianne breathed. "It's all right, Annie, honestly, you see." She hesitated, and invented quickly, "You see I'm going to be wedded, and soon, and so . . ."

"Oh, Miss," Annie said, her eyes filling with tears.

*And why shouldn't she weep?* Julianne thought, biting her lip as she saw Annie's agitation. The girl was more than a maid. In the manner of servants of gentry in the countryside, she felt like one of her mistress's family, as well she should. And here she believed she'd helped her mistress steal from the house in the night so she could lie in the arms of a cheat and a scoundrel, a criminal, and a liar—and now, a seducer, too. But so, in the eyes of the world, Julianne realized, she had done.

Her smile vanished. Her newfound content shattered. All the doubts and fears she'd felt for days were back again, only now compounded by shame and guilt.

Julianne spent the next half hour reassuring her maid that all would be well and that she knew what she was doing.

And then she passed the next three hours sitting up in bed, thinking about what she'd done. Now, too late, doubts returned to plague her. Without Christian there to laugh them to scorn, without his smile to blind her, his voice to soothe her, his presence to reassure her, she worried again.

She wasn't promised to wed him. He'd made protestations of love, but he could have said what she wanted to hear. It was also what any clever deceiver would do, after all. She began to doubt his identity again, because she hadn't learned more about his past except for his time in prison. He hadn't told her about what he'd done since, or anything that had bearing on who he really was. She *had* learned ecstasy at his hands. But now that those hands weren't there to hold her, she wondered if she'd really understood what she was doing. She'd helped him, if only for a night. She might have destroyed her own future.

But she didn't worry about her reputation, she was wise enough to know that was futile. She had enough other things to trouble her.

Because he'd never explained about his "brother" Amyas before he'd had to when he'd made a slip of the tongue. And who knew if Anthony-Amyas had ever been a captain in the army at all? She'd been too entranced with Christian to think to ask more about

that. And later, on the ride home, she'd been too be-
mused, too full of memories of Christian's lovemak-
ing, to ask Amyas himself.

Now, too, she recalled that Christian had never said
he hadn't stolen more than a candlestick from Egremont, not really. She hadn't pressed him on that. She'd
been too busily pressing against him, carried away by
what she felt in his arms, at his lips. Julianne's head
began to ache, and she felt a sick disgust, remembering her own wanton behavior. He himself had said he
hadn't meant to go that far. She'd led him, letting him
go as far as he wanted—as she'd wanted.

She didn't blame him. She realized she'd taken
him, literally, on faith, and in love, without more than
what she felt in her heart—and in her traitor body.
She'd been moved by emotion when she ought to
have used her brain. Julianne put her head in her pillow but couldn't make it dark enough to escape the
light of dawning realization.

What if she had something more to remember of
this evening than a night of love? What if a child re-
sulted from it? Then she'd truly be an outcast, because even if her family forgave her, the world would
not. And he? Would he even live to know about it?
And if he did, would he care?

The worst part was that whatever he was, or
wasn't, did or didn't, she didn't know what would
happen next and had no control over whatever did.
And so she looked remarkably pale and drained when
she came to luncheon, which made everyone ask if
she was sure she'd been ready to get out of bed.

* * *

"Sir Maurice presents his compliments," the butler said, "and wishes to know if you would meet him in his study this afternoon, before tea?"

Julianne looked up, startled.

Sophie clapped her hands. "Of course she will. Isn't that nice of him?" she asked, when the butler had left the sunny small salon. "He probably wants to ask how you're faring. I was worried myself for a while, but though you're still pale and obviously not feeling up to snuff, you seem right enough now." She looked down at the embroidery she was holding. "But it's been a whole day, after all, since you came home at dawn with your gown trailing dew."

Julianne's eyes flew wide. She didn't even feel the needle as it stuck her thumb and not the cloth she was sewing.

Sophie nodded. "Oh, yes. I knew. My maid had it from a downstairs maid, who heard it from the scullery maid, who's always the first up in the morning and saw you creeping in. Don't worry, I won't tell anyone, excepting Ham, of course, because he and I share everything. He blamed us, you know. He always said you were too inexperienced and that we ought never to have used you as bait for the imposter in the first place. But what's done is done. Don't worry; even if it is locking the gate after the horse has strayed, we'll look after you. You won't be able to get so much as a yawn out now without someone knowing. But tell me," she whispered, bending close, "was it worth it?"

Julianne sat bolt upright, her face turning ashen,

her cheeks feeling hot. She heard a buzzing in her ears and was glad she was sitting down. "I don't know what you're talking about," she said. When Sophie smiled, she added, "Nor do I care what you think. I'm going home."

"I said I don't blame you," Sophie said petulantly. "The captain's one of the most dashing men I've ever seen, even if he is eccentric. Imagine, always wearing gloves! And he does have that crook to his nose. But it lends character, I think, and he has such a nice smile, and an impressively athletic form, in spite of that limp. He speaks well and acts respectably. My father wouldn't deal with a man who didn't; the runner is entirely a different matter, one has no choice in that. Captain Briggs has no money, I'd imagine, but maybe he has connections. Even so, I hope you think twice before you throw yourself away on him. You could do so much better, you know."

Julianne sat astonished, stricken with the urge to laugh as well as weep. But it was a reasonable conclusion, after all. Amyas *was* the man who had come home with her at dawn.

"There is no possibility of that," she said, thinking fast. "And a ride in the night is not a night of love-making. I have standards, Sophie, even if I do sometimes give my trust unwisely. After all, I never knew you had other purposes for me until I actually arrived and couldn't miss seeing them."

She was relieved to see her cousin's cheeks growing red. "One thing I can swear to on a stack of Bibles: I never made love to the man." And since that was the absolute truth, Julianne found breath returning to her constricted chest. "I just wanted to talk to him about Christian and what happened to him, and what other time could I do it with no one knowing? I know what you and Ham, and the baronet think. But I still believe he's really Christian Sauvage."

But since that was no longer strictly the truth, Julianne realized her voice lacked conviction. She was glad when her cousin merely shook her head.

"Poor Julianne," Sophie said. "You're too faithful and trusting by half!"

"I came to no harm," Julianne said. "Except for my reputation, I see. But I'll be going home soon." And so she would, she resolved, as soon as she heard what happened to Christian. She settled back with her sewing and relaxed. The interview might be embarrassing and difficult, but she thought she could get through it without too much lying. But first she had to write some letters.

Julianne went to her room and wrote three notes before she had to meet with Sir Maurice.

The first was to Mr. Murchison, to ask if he knew what was happening with Christian.

The second was to Amyas-Anthony again. She'd written to him the moment she'd reached home, to tell him she was safe. She frowned, realizing that hadn't been true. So now she wrote, simply and starkly, that he must never come to the baronet's house again because he'd been seen, and they all believed he was her lover. She looked at the little stack of banknotes she had left to her name, took out just enough for her seat on the coach home, and added,

"Use the enclosed, please, for him. Good men of law
are costly. Please try to find the best." Then she folded
the notes with the note. Whatever else the supposed
captain was, whoever he was, she sincerely believed
he was wholly for Christian—or whoever he was.

The third note was enclosed with the other two,
and addressed clearly. It said merely: "What is happening? At least, send word. You owe me nothing, believe me. But I worry."

And then she was ready for her interview with Sir
Maurice.

"My dear," Sir Maurice said, rising to his feet as
she came into his study. "How are you feeling? I must
say you look much improved, that color suits you. But
what hue would not? Please, sit down."

Julianne took a chair, glad she'd worn a gown so
rosy that it would make a dead woman look well.

The baronet came out from behind his desk and put
his hands behind his back. Julianne glanced round his
study, approving of the many shelves of books, all of
which looked old, valuable, and much read. It was a
neat and orderly room, very much like the man who
stood in it: expensively furnished and tasteful, and
filled with antique knowledge. And like him, everything in the room was in good repair, in spite of its
obvious age. Sir Maurice might be dry and pedantic
at times, and old as the hills, she supposed. But he
kept himself trim, and in spite of everything she
couldn't help liking to look at him, if only because
those unusually clear blue eyes so reminded her of
Christian.

He leaned back against his desk and folded his hands on his lean stomach. "I'm told you are not happy here," he said. He held up a hand before she could answer. "I can scarcely blame you. You're a country girl, my dear, heart and soul. Your cousin likes fashion, constant hubbub, and the nightlife of London. You do not, that's easy to see. Moreover, I'm told you want to go home."

He cast her a strange look, and cleared his throat. "But what have you got at home? Your parents, of course, and it's to your credit that you love and enjoy their company. But what sort of a future is that for you? They have each other. You are young; you need a life of your own, a husband, children. I'm also told that your opportunities for obtaining such are limited at your home. I have seen for myself that you are wise beyond your years, and so, too discriminating to settle for any of the fashionable fribbles who pay court to you here in Town.

"So I think I've come up with a neat solution," he said. "I am old, but not dead. I am rich, but not wed." He smiled. "A little romantic poetry. Are you surprised? Don't be. I've been thinking of this for a long while now. In short, my dear Julianne, I am much impressed with you, and would like to offer you my hand in marriage."

She stared.

"If I were younger," he said, "doubtless, I'd sweep you into my arms and profess my undying love. But I cannot pretend to be a prisoner of lust—a pretty sight I'd be if I were!" he said with a grimace. "And though I dislike thinking of it, it's plain to see my love won't

be undying. I'm not on Death's doorstep, but the likelihood is that I won't be with you for the rest of your
life. In fact, to be perfectly honest, I wouldn't have
contemplated this if it weren't for Death's presence.
I'm not a sentimental man, and my own marriage was
not a love match. But I have a strong sense of family,
as you know. My son was my future, and when he
died, I lost my chance for perpetuating my line. I remained in the north and tried to forget. It wasn't until
I saw you that I realized I could still ensure that my
name would not vanish.

"I am not too old to beget children," he said, watching her closely. "This is not an offer of love, perhaps;
but, rest assured, your life won't be bereft of it."

She said nothing. But her eyes widened as she
shrank back from him.

He nodded. "You're also a sensible woman," he
said in a cooler voice. "And to tell you the plain truth,
I think you should consider that mine might be the
only other respectable offer you're likely to get—
when the tale of your doings about Town are known,
that is to say. And be sure, they will be known."

He waited while that sank in, and added, "I don't
know what you did the other night with the good captain who was helping with our inquiries, nor do I
want to know. I would ask that we wait six months before we marry, so that I may be sure nothing lasting
comes of it. That, you will agree, would only be pru-
dent of me."

She shot to her feet and stood trembling, staring
at him.

He went on smoothly, "I'm also told you continue

to worry about the fate of the pretender to the earldom. That's a piece of utter foolishness and a complete waste of time. And money," he added with a sly smile that made her suddenly fear that her notes had already gone astray.

"I tell you right now, my dear, that the man who claims to be Christian Sauvage will never hold the title," he said firmly. "From prison he came, and there he will stay—if he's lucky. Well," he said, straightening, "I didn't expect an immediate answer. I leave it to you to think it over. If you consider, it is a generous offer. You'll be a very wealthy woman, even richer when I pass on. And who is to say?" he asked with a negligent wave of his hand. "Life is impermanent, who knows that better than I? One day, perhaps, it may even be that your child will be the rightful heir to Egremont. The man who claimed to be Geoffrey Sauvage's son is an imposter. Hammond is the last of that line.

"After him, of course, there's me," Sir Maurice said. "It's a thing few people have mentioned, perhaps because I am not expected to live much longer. So it is entirely possible, if not particularly probable, that our child could be master of Egremont one day. I've seen stranger things in my time."

"I have not!" she finally gasped, too shocked, angry at his presumption, and frightened for Christian's sake to be tactful. "The answer is no, it could be nothing else. I don't know what gave you the idea that I'd accept, I never encouraged you by word or deed." She paused, embarrassed for herself as well as for him. "I'm not what you think me, but that doesn't matter. Thank you for your consideration, but it would be impossible. Please forget this interview, sir," she said as she rose to her feet, "as I promise I shall. You needn't worry about anything I might say. I'm going home."

"And what about your friend, the imposter?" he asked smoothly.

She was on her way to the door but turned when he said that.

"Should you like to know what will become of him? Or perhaps know that if you were my wife, I might consider letting him leave the country in safety—on the proviso that he never return? I have that power, as well as the connections to make it possible. I don't really believe that the good captain is the object of your affections, Miss Lowell," he said coldly. "I never did for a moment. I saw your eyes when you looked at the imposter, you see. And I tell you, my dear, you can never deceive me."

She stood still and straight, trying to think of what to answer.

There was a tap on the door. "Yes?" the baronet asked in annoyance, without even looking that way.

"Sir," the butler said, as he cracked open the door, "you have guests."

"I invited no one. Send them away," the baronet said, never taking his eyes from Julianne.

"Yes, sir. But I believed you would want to see them."

"Indeed?" the baronet asked icily. "And why?"

"Because there is a man from Bow Street, sir, and a magistrate, and some other gentlemen as well. And they say they are here with the earl of Egremont."

# Chapter 23

Christian stood in the doorway. He was immaculately dressed; he wore his usual cool smile and looked as though he'd never been in prison, as though he'd never missed a minute of sleep.

Julianne caught her breath. She was about to take a step to run to him, then stopped, confused, remembering where she was and who was with her. Then she noticed that Christian wasn't even looking at her.

"What sort of joke is this?" Sir Maurice demanded.

"No joke, sir," he said. "Why should you think so? I have, after all, the papers to prove who I am. I presented them from the start: a record of my parent's marriage and one for my birth, as recorded in church registries. And fortunately, or unfortunately, I'm also in the unique position of having what few other men do to prove their existence: legal records of most of my adult life. Those are of my trial and transportation, every place I went, from Newgate Prison to the Hulks, to the ship *Retribution* and my arrival at New South Wales. And I have sworn depositions from those who encountered me everywhere down the line. Where do you see the joke?"

The baronet's head went up.

Christian's smile was not pleasant. "I am Christian Sauvage. But if it makes you feel any better, I am not the earl of Egremont, after all."

He turned to the doorway. "May I present the true earl and heir to Egremont? My father, Geoffrey Sauvage. Come in, sir, if you please."

"I do not please," the gentleman who strolled in through the doorway said as he stripped off his gloves. "But I do what I must."

He entered the room as though he belonged there, and he looked as if he did.

Julianne stared. The man was middle-aged, muscular, and obviously fit. He was dressed like a gentleman of means. As he handed his high beaver hat to the butler, it could be seen that his full head of brown hair was brushed back in the latest windswept fashion. His strong-featured face was tanned, and when he smiled, as he did now, his teeth were large, white, and even. His eyes were Christian's, to the life.

Geoffrey Sauvage didn't bow or extend a hand. He merely stopped, stared at the baronet, and smiled that broad white smile. "Sir Maurice," he said in a deep, rich mellifluous voice, "this meeting is a long time coming."

The baronet inhaled sharply. Julianne could see his thin nostrils pinching together.

"But I remember you well," the gentleman told him. "I saw you last on the docks, as we were being loaded onto the *Retribution*. You and that maggot, Sir

Gordon, who swore we'd robbed him, and perjured his soul—if he still had one. I heard he died a few years back. I'm sure you heard of that, too. In fact, it wouldn't surprise me if you more than heard. He was rich but of little account; no one ever investigated his sudden death. Choked on a bone, they said. Rather, *she* said, that sluttish housekeeper of his. But she'd have said anything for as little as a ha'penny." He shrugged. "It's done, little sense in unearthing that death, when there are so many others."

He kept his eyes on Sir Maurice, who stared steadily back at him. The only sign of emotion the baronet showed was a loss of color in his already pale face.

"It was foolish of you to come to bid me *bon voyage*," the gentleman told him. "And in the company of Gordon. Because he always dressed like a rainbow, and so I couldn't help seeing him and you when I took a last look at my homeland before I went below deck. I vowed never to forget your face or where I'd seen it before. I didn't remember until halfway across the sea, and little good it did me then. I suppose you were there because you wanted to make sure all ends were tightly tied up. You couldn't have expected us to survive. We ourselves doubted it.

"And this must be Miss Lowell," the gentleman said, his deep voice growing honey smooth and warm as he turned to look at her. "You're all grown-up and are as lovely as my son has said."

Julianne cocked her head to the side. A tremulous smile slowly bloomed on her parted lips. Her heart leapt so high she had to catch her breath. "I remember you. You weren't so tanned then, nor so . . . You were a thin man . . . but your voice brings it all back to me. I loved your voice. You're Christian's father, aren't you? Geoffrey Sauvage—I *do* remember you!" she cried.

He smiled. "Yes, I'm a bit larger all around and older than sin. But I'm back. If you'll forgive me now, child, we have work to do here. We can catch up later, if you'll be so kind. Proceed please, Christian," he said, sounding suddenly weary, "so we can have some peace and end this thing."

Christian nodded. "Sir Maurice," he said, "I think it's best we call your other guests in. The sooner we're done with this, the better for all of us." He gestured toward the door.

Hammond and Sophie and her parents trailed in from where they'd been standing in the hallway, looking wide-eyed and nervous.

"And let me introduce the rest of our party," Christian said. "My brother, Amyas," he said, as Amyas strode in.

Julianne heard Sophie gasp.

"And here is my brother, Daffyd." Christian said. A lean, handsome olive-skinned young man, dark as a Gypsy, Daffyd looked dangerous as he stared at the baron. But then he glanced over at Julianne, and she saw his strange and arresting blue eyes light with pleasure. He nodded to her.

"Mr. Murchison, you know," Christian went on, as the runner came in, "but perhaps not Mr. Turkell, chief magistrate for the district, nor Sir Eugene Clift, the noted barrister."

The men entered the room, and bowed, briefly, before they folded their hands and stood, staring at the baronet.

"Very dramatic, to be sure," Sir Maurice said in his usual dry tones. "And the reason for this little charade?"

Christian's smile was not pleasant. "The end of this charade, I'd say. We mean to end it, sir."

Sir Maurice stood very still.

"I originally came back to England to do just that," Christian said in even tones. "I was the one to receive the letter telling of my father's inheritance, you see. He was on a business trip. I was astonished at what I read and showed the letter to my brothers. Whatever we expected from the country that had thrown my father away, it was never notice that he'd inherited a rich earldom. But then, we never knew why he'd been falsely accused and sent away in the first place. But reading the letter, we began to understand."

"A very big mistake," Amyas said, rocking back on his heels. "Never try to deceive a criminal. Our minds work along similar paths, you see."

"We made some inquiries," Christian went on. "We may have been on the other side of the world, but we have resources here. That helped us discover a disturbing thing. Too many earls had died by too many accidents and in too quick a succession. In short, we realized that being earl of Egremont wasn't a secure position. Certainly not one we wanted to expose our father to."

"So I returned home to find two sons gone on what they said was an affair of business," Geoffrey Sauvage said, shaking his head. "They left a note telling me they were looking into a venture they couldn't afford to let wait. My other son was there to swear to it and try to allay my fears when they didn't return right away. How could you?" he asked Christian sadly.

"I told you," Christian said earnestly, "I was the natural one to come to England, claim the title, and try to sort things out."

"He *was* the next in line for the earldom," Amyas said. "I couldn't do it, nor could Dayffd. Christian could prove who he was if he had to, so they couldn't actually hang him for it. I came to watch over him though, Father, just as I told you."

"I would have, but I lost the coin toss," Daffyd said gloomily, scowling at Amyas.

"You were the youngest," Amyas said quickly. "Anyway, it was a good and fair way of deciding things."

"Oh, aye," Daffyd said bitterly. "Good and fair, coming from you, Amyas? Certainly. Still, I kept my part of the bargain as long as I could. But here he is. Try keeping back the rain."

"You did too well," his father said seriously. "There wasn't a moment to spare as it was." He stared at Sir Maurice. "My son was scheduled to be tried on Saturday and hanged next Monday. It couldn't be proved that he was a liar, so they tried to claim he was a thief."

"So, I suppose those items walked from Sir Gordon's house to follow you two home those years ago?" Sir Maurice asked with a mirthless smile.

"No, they were stolen," Geoffrey Sauvage said quietly.

"But we finally found out who the thief was," Amyas said, glowering at Sir Maurice, "with the help of a footman at Egremont."

"Helpful fellow," Daffyd muttered. "With a bit of encouragement, that is. He don't work there anymore."

"Lucky to work anywhere," Amayas growled. "To see what he did, and keep mum about it? He'll be lucky to work in hell."

"Newgate is almost the same," his father said, still looking steadily at the baronet. "That fellow will pay for his part in all of this, too. But his wasn't the major role; he only observed the theft and was paid for his silence. At least we can prove who the real thief is now. And though money can buy almost anything, it can only buy one judge at a time—your pardon, Magistrate," he added, glancing at one of the men who had come in with him. "But so it was, and that's why my son was clapped in Newgate again."

"He'll not be sitting at the next assizes," the man promised.

"My son was on his way to his doom," Geoffrey Sauvage said, "and only because of who he was."

Amyas nodded. "They'd never have done it though, not if I had to bribe the other half of the guards at Newgate, kill the rest of them, and burn the place down. Merely metaphorically speaking," he added as he saw the runner look at him. "I had Christian's papers in the hands of Mr. Clift," he added, tilting a shoulder toward the barrister, "even as my father's ship was sailing up to the dock in London. It would have made them think twice before they tied the hangman's knot."

"Again, I say it was too great a risk," Geoffrey Sauvage said.

"Again, it was one I chose to take," Christian told him. "Rather than you, sir."

"But it was *my* risk to take," his father said.

"No," Christian said. "That was the problem. They knew what you looked like, you must see that now. Whatever you told Julianne, you haven't changed that much. But no one could possibly remember me. If they weren't sure who I was, they were less likely to kill me right off. That bought us time to make inquiries, and discoveries."

"Time to throw you in Newgate Prison," his father said. "My God, Christian, how did you bear it?"

Christian looked at Julianne, and smiled. "Barely sir. But I did."

The baronet looked from Christian to Julianne. Seeing her trembling, growing smile as she gazed at Christian, he drew himself up. "So," Sir Maurice said coldly, raising his head, "we have a new earl of Egremont, is that it? An undisputed one, to be sure. And his heir is safely out of prison. All's well that end's well."

"Not quite," Christian said, putting up a hand. "There's the matter of the murders." He looked at the baronet, and Julianne was shocked to see sadness in his expression. "You heard that we found out the truth about our conviction, Sir Maurice. There's more. When we realized how close my father was to the earldom, if all the other rightful earls died before-time, it all fell into place. We've been working on it for months, and now have evidence about Charles's and Frederick's deaths. Statements from your hirelings, telling us how Charles's vertigo was made worse by being tossed off that cliff, and how Frederick, with his notoriously weak heart, happened to be startled by those highwaymen."

Christian shook his head. "You hired two men, the best, I'll grant. That's probably why you didn't exterminate them when their chores were done. Possibly you meant to use them again, who knows? In any case, our friends here knew them, as they know all the good criminals in London. Our friends are even better. Even better for us, they were very persuasive. When your men were made to understand that their fellow criminals were even more pitiless than the law, they told everything. It's all on paper now. And finally it all made sense. You were such a pillar of the family no one seemed to remember that you'd be heir to Egremont if all the younger ones died. And certainly no one imagined that you'd make sure they did."

Hammond made a hissing sound and stepped back, his face a study in confusion and rage. "You meant to exterminate me?" he asked the baronet, in horror.

Sir Maurice didn't reply.

"No," Christian said. "We think I was the one he was striking for. Though accuracy wasn't important, since you'd be next."

"Aye," Daffyd said. "So I was told. I've a few friends in that camp. The wench with the blade disappeared. She'll be found and dealt with, never fear."

"So you see, we've more than enough evidence. The only thing left to settle is the settling of it,"

Christian said wearily. "That's why these other gentlemen are here."

The baronet tensed and looked to the door. The runner stepped forward, as did Amyas and Daffyd. Geoffrey Sauvage moved quickly, putting himself between the baronet and Christian.

Sir Maurice did an unexpected thing. He relaxed, leaned back against the desk, and forced a smile. "Well, then," he said, "what is there for me to say?"

"You're right," Geoffrey Sauvage said. " 'I'm sorry' is hardly adequate. I'd been working on finding the reason for my conviction for years. Damme for a poor spirited fool, but I was so resentful of what had been done to us that when I had enough evidence to prove my innocence, I found I didn't want to return to England again. My hesitation meant many deaths. I never suspected it might, or I'd have swum back here if I had to."

The baronet shrugged. "They weren't deaths of any account," he said, "and some *were* stupid accidents. You see, the direct heirs to Egremont were unworthy. They were ignorant, wasteful men. They'd have beggared the estate and ruined one of the finest collections of art in the land, a treasure trove unlike any other, equaling the one the Prince is amassing."

His eyes glittered. "In fact, it was Charles's selling a few pieces of fine porcelain to the Prince to pay a gambling debt that made me see it. *I* was the one who had acquired them! *I* was the one his father had consulted to purchase new pieces for Egremont. If I could have afforded it, I'd have bought them myself.

But though I'm a rich man, my wealth couldn't equal Egremont's. So when Charles came to me after that, to find out how much the Bosch hanging in the front hall at Egremont was worth, I realized the necessity. He'd never stop gambling, and the riches of Egremont were in jeopardy."

"But why meddle in our lives?" Christian asked.

Sir Maurice gave him a pitying look. "A man must look at all aspects of a thing before he undertakes it. You might have become unexpected heirs. I was, after all, old even then. My son Simon would have succeeded me, had he lived." He looked toward the window, and said softly, "Now, that was a great tragedy. Simon was a biddable boy. He would have done as he was told, and the estate would have grown to a magnificence to rival the Rothschilds'.

"You, Mr. Sauvage," he said, looking at Christian, "and your father, were nearer to the succession than you knew, or obviously even guessed. And you had neither influence nor money enough to object to what happened, nor any reason to know the reason for it. You were easily put well out of the way. But your cousin, the old earl, didn't want the scandal of a hanging on the family name. I quite agreed after I thought about it. He solved it by having you transported. But as for Charles and Frederick? Don't waste tears on them. They were unworthy of Egremont. My Simon was," he said distantly.

"But Simon died," Christian said. "And yet Godfrey and his infant son, and Francis died after him."

Sir Maurice smiled. "You've no proof I'd any part in any of that, do you? Nor will you find any. But who better than I to be caretaker of Egremont, even if Simon was gone?"

"But what about Hammond?" Sophie cried.

The baronet gazed at her dispassionately. His silence was her answer. She shrank back against Hammond.

"The mistake was overreaching yourself," Amyas commented.

"The mistake was he didn't have the guts to do it himself," Daffyd growled. "He lacked the ballocks to grasp the moment."

"My brothers are both right," Christian said. "Some advice, Sir Maurice, although it's too late. The only way to kill cleanly is to do it yourself. You had the instincts of a killer but the manner of a nobleman. You refused to do the dirty deeds yourself. That, we learned early on, will never do if you mean to survive. So you botched it entirely."

"And so now you are going to kill me?" Sir Maurice asked pleasantly.

Julianne winced, and glanced at Christian. He looked troubled.

"My father, I think, should be the judge of that," he said.

"Here now, lad," Mr. Murchison said ponderously, "that's the job of Mr. Turkell here, and His Majesty's courts of law."

"But we both know better than that," Sir Maurice said, with a small smile. "Noblemen are seldom hanged. Arrangements can be made. And there's the matter of the family name. It saved you once." He glanced, in turn, at Geoffrey Sauvage, his sons, then Sophie and Hammond, and the squire. "Murder, especially sequential murder, is a heinous crime, one that would be long remembered if this were made public. After all, these weren't dustmen or Gypsies who were killed, but noblemen. Do you want your children—and grandchildren—to be met with cries of derision and laughter whenever their names are heard? 'Oh, you're a Sauvage, are you?' he mocked in a high, brittle voice, 'Whom have you killed today?' Children would say it. Their elders would think it. The broadsheets would be full of it. It would never be lived down.

"I'm old," he said on a shrug. "I haven't that much longer to live. Nor can I end any lives either. I am, after all, disarmed and discovered. I'd be willing to go to my home in the north and stay there among my treasures, until my natural end."

Christian looked at Julianne. She shook her head. She didn't want to see the old gentleman hang, but she knew she'd never draw one easy breath so long as he lived. Christian nodded, then looked at his father, who was watching them with interest.

"He's a murderer," Christian told his father. "They hang people for stealing a candlestick—as we know all too well. Should we let a murderer go free? And yet," he said, grimacing, "because I have lived in the shadow of the gallows, I hesitate to send any man to it. I'm glad it's your decision, sir."

"Mine?" his father asked.

"Yes, not only because you're the head of the family, but because you were most sinned against. Whatever you decide I will support."

"As for me," Amyas said, "I suppose I owe the old

man a debt. Because I'd never have met you, or long survived, if he hadn't had a hand in your fate. But I worry about him for your sake, sir, and would even if he were three years dead."

Daffyd nodded his agreement.

"This is irregular," the magistrate said, as he blotted his forehead with his handkerchief, "and should be decided by a court of law."

"But he's right," Geoffrey Sauvage said slowly. "You've seen this sort of thing handled privately before. My own order of transportation was accomplished without ever having seen the courts. A decision made here today will be as binding, I think."

The squire nodded to the magistrate. The runner looked up at the ceiling. And the magistrate fell silent.

Geoffrey Sauvage looked at Sir Maurice. "But it isn't so difficult. The answer's obvious. Forget having our name in the broadsheets and gossiped about all over Town. What's that to us, after all? We've lived through that, and you were the one who saw to it, and worse."

The baronet grew very white.

"But," Geoffrey Sauvage went on thoughtfully, "I will not have your death on my sons' consciences, nor will I have your continued life on their minds. I have a better solution. You'll get the same sort of charity we did. The solution the late earl of Egremont gave us shall be yours. Transportation instead of the noose."

Sir Maurice breathed out his pent-up breath. He cocked his head. "Yes, that will do, I think. I visited Italy on my Grand Tour, and quite liked the hills surrounding Florence. I can remove there and stay in solitude for my remaining days."

"No," Geoffrey Sauvage said. "You misunderstand me. I meant exactly the same sort of charity. The hills outside of Port Jackson, near Botany Bay. A house there, of your own not so grand, of course, because there aren't any grand ones there yet. Imprisonment, at least my people watching over you, for all your remaining days. You won't be able to stroll to the shore without them knowing. And I know them all. As the waters are filled with sharks, I doubt you'll go farther, unless you want a ride in their bellies."

"Mr. Sauvage!" Sir Maurice said sharply. "That will not do. My treasures, my collections . . ."

"Take what you can with you. But the thing's settled and equitably, I think. Do you?" he asked his son.

Christian smiled fully for the first time that day.

His father looked to the magistrate, who nodded, then to the barrister, who inclined his head.

"So it's done. And will be done with all speed, gentlemen, if you will. And," Geoffrey added, looking back at the baronet, who stood frozen and wide-eyed, "I remind you, sir, that I am the earl of Egremont, and so, 'Lord Egremont' to you, and not 'Mr. Sauvage.' But don't let your mistake trouble you, because there's no reason for us to ever speak again. Now, then," he told the others, "shall we leave Bow Street and the men of law to their work?"

Julianne didn't look back at Sir Maurice as she left the room. She couldn't. She didn't know if she could walk either because her legs felt watery. She didn't have to worry about finding the strength to walk away. A strong arm went around her.

"It's done," Christian said into her ear. "Now let's get on with our own lives."

She waited until they were out of the room and in the main hall, then hung back, so that they were out of earshot of the others, who were standing in a knot and chatting.

"Christian," she said seriously, "you mustn't presume that our lives are linked together from now on."

"Oh, mustn't I?" he asked, stopping, locking both arms around her waist and smiling down at her. "And everything we did, and said, is nothing now? Are you so light-minded? I didn't think so. Or did you think anything I said or did was done lightly?"

"It's not that," she said, avoiding his eyes.

"Maybe you think that now that I'm a certified heir to Egremont I'll change my mind about you?" He chuckled. "I had money enough before I came here, you know. And I'm not expecting to inherit anytime soon. My father, God bless him, is good for another generation. Literally, I hope. Because I'm hoping he'll marry again and have lots more heirs. Or is it that you wanted Egremont and are going to set your cap at him?"

She didn't laugh, as he'd wanted her to.

His expression grew serious. "*Were* you hoping for Egremont?" he asked, sounding hurt and surprised.

She looked up at his face. Her own convulsed as she tried not to cry. She shook her head and eased away from him.

He dropped his arms from her waist, and frowned. "Julianne?"

"It's not the money, or the title," she said, "but Christian, you didn't tell me half the truth."

"I didn't lie," he said seriously. "I told you that all the truth wasn't mine to tell."

"But you didn't tell me *so* very well." She raised her eyes and searched his. "And I never once withheld a thing from you."

"You're saying that you think I'd lie to you?"

"I'm saying that I wonder how often you'd think it was fair to withhold truth from me."

He took one of her hands in his. "My dear Little Jewel," he said softly, touching her cheek lightly. "You have reason enough to doubt me, and I'll spend the rest of my life trying to change that. But how do you expect me to go on without you?"

She bit her lip.

"I vow, on this place, and my head, and with all my heart, that I will never withhold truth from you again," he said solemnly. "And so if you ask me how you look when we are at a grand soiree, and think your gown doesn't suit you, and your hair's a disaster, why, if I agree, I'll tell you so. And if our firstborn resembles a frog when he arrives, as all babies do, I'll certainly tell you so. And if we're at your family home, and I'm asked if I like your mama's favorite recipe, I . . ."

She laughed and raised her hand to try to swat him. He danced away.

"Ho!" Amyas said, looking back at the noise they

made. "Look. She's abusing him already, and they're not even wed."

"As to that . . . ?" the earl of Egremont asked with interest.

Julianne looked at him and smiled. "My lord, you're much too premature. He hasn't even asked me yet."

"Slow top!" Amyas hooted.

"I *wish* I'd won that coin toss," Daffyd said ardently. "It's not too late, but if you'd give me time, fair lady . . ."

Christian gave him a hard look and dropped to his knees on the marble floor before Julianne. And there, in the main hall of the baronet's house, with his father and brothers, the squire and his wife, Sophie and Hammond looking on, Christian put one hand on his heart and held the other out to her.

"Miss Julianne Lowell," he said. "I implore you: Give me your hand and your heart and take mine forever, because I love you, and need you, and *damned* if I'll let you go!"

"Well said," Amyas told his father with approval.

"Well, it lacked a certain delicacy," the earl offered consideringly.

"It don't seem to matter to her," Daffyd said, sounding disgruntled, as Julianne pulled Christian to his feet, and he engulfed her in a fervent embrace. She returned it with enthusiasm.

"Damme," Daffyd said, "but I *wish* I'd won that coin toss!"

# Chapter 24

The music was faint and far away, but they heard enough to dance. They were alone and together, and didn't need music anyway. They had their own. And so the young couple waltzed round and round the inside of the great white rotunda.

"I'm so glad," Julianne said on a sigh.

"Glad? Is that all?" Christian asked, as he spun her around. "Then I'd better do something about that. I want you to be joyous, rapturous, overwhelmed with happiness."

She smiled as she looked up into his eyes. "That will come later tonight."

"No," he said seriously, "not just then. I want you happy always, my bride."

"I am," she said seriously. "I shall be, but Christian, we've only been married for a few hours."

"Then get at it, woman!" he said, and they laughed together.

They stopped dancing and strolled out of the marble rotunda, arm in arm, and stood looking at the ornamental lake. The sun was high, the water sparkled and danced, and from the distance they could hear the musicians playing at their wedding breakfast, which was still going forth on the great lawns of Egremont.

She rested her head against his shoulder. "It was good of your father to hold the wedding breakfast here on such short notice, too. Only six weeks have passed since he set foot in England again! My parents were going to have it at our home, but I think he was right. We needed this celebration to take away the bad memories of the place."

"He is a good man," Christian said. "But I promise you it was just as much for him. He has the place humming again, and he loves the company. He really does feel like a pebble rattling around the inside of a vast jewel box, as he said."

"Alone?" Julianne laughed. "Hardly! With Amyas and Daffyd there, and us, at least until our house is finished?"

"Alone," he said again. "Egremont is the size of four houses, and it does take some getting used to. Do you mind us not living there? He invited us, but . . ."

"But I prefer the idea of our own house, too," she assured him. "We're not far, we'll be visiting all the time. And I also love being near the sea as much as you do. Our house may not be an Egremont when we're done, but it will be big, and beautiful, and most of all, it will be all ours. An estate's a fine thing to inherit, but I think a home is something you must make for yourself. I daresay he won't be alone for long anyway. He's a very attractive fellow."

"Aha, I knew it," he said, wrapping his arms around her. "Already regretting your choice?"

She kissed him until he forgot the question. She did not. "I was half-afraid Sophie would set her cap at him, after all," she said as she laid her head on his chest. "When she told me she was convinced that she really loved Ham, I was delighted. So were her parents. They might have had their ambitions, but they didn't like the thought of a son-in-law their own age. They're not so bad, after all."

He didn't answer. He bowed his head in gratitude for the warm living joy of her in his arms, and held her close and thought about how nearly they had lost this bliss, because of ambitions.

She knew.

"Christian?" she said softly.

He looked at her.

She gazed back at him, enraptured. She couldn't get used to the fact that she'd see that marvelous face every day of her life from now on. He was and yet was not the same as when she'd first seen him; she seldom saw his cool collected expression when he was alone with her anymore. And yet she found him still as astonishingly handsome as she'd thought when they met. She raised a hand to trace the clean, hard contours of that beloved face. When her finger reached his lips, he seized her hand and kissed it.

"Your father said the baronet was ensconced in his new home yesterday," she said softly. "We need never fear him again."

She felt her husband's sigh. "Aye," he said. "No man escapes the burial vault. Who'd have thought that wicked old heart would have stopped ticking before it even left these shores? He was lucky. We never

sent him to prison, he never had to face those indigni-
ties. He died in his own bed, among his damned treasures, while still trying to decide which to take and
which to leave behind. He leaves them all behind
now, because no man can take them with him. My father's giving his collection to the Prince, you know."

"I'm very glad," she said with a shiver that made
him hold her closer. "I wouldn't want them, no matter
their value. Your father is very wise."

"Wiser than you know," he said on a chuckle. "I
hear our Prince is ecstatic, and already burbling about
new honors for the house of Egremont. My father is a
very good man of accounts. He never gives away
without some idea of what's coming back."

She grinned and took a deep breath of the air, perfumed by blooming honeysuckle. "I'm so glad we
married before the autumn came."

"I wouldn't have it any other way," he said. "I
didn't want to give you time to change your mind.
Nor did I want to risk any other gossip about us."

"Well, I wouldn't change my mind even if you
chopped off my head and offered me another," she
said.

"I'd never want to replace that wise head of yours,"
he said with a grin. He smiled wider when he saw his
embraces had set her wedding crown of woven fuch-
sia and daisies atilt on her curls. It made her look rak-
ishly adorable, and yet like a well-loved bride, all at
the same time.

"We did hurry the day," she said. "Are you sorry?
As it turned out, there was really no need for haste,
after all."

"Our wedding couldn't have come soon enough for me. As for how it turned out, we'll have to do something about remedying that. We'll need dozens of children to fill up our new home. We'll get some from London, as agreed, children already born and needing homes, even a few budding criminals to make life interesting. It's only fair to give back to Fate. If Father hadn't taken over responsibility for Amyas and Daffyd, my life would have been diminished, if not ended, and I can't forget it. But I'd like to grow some of our own as well."

"Me too," she said. "And I'm so glad we can finally try. My parents and your father kept me neat as a nun since we became engaged."

"Yes, and my wicked brothers were all morality when it came to you. They watched me like twin hawks. I think it was part jealousy and part pure pleasure in thwarting me. No matter, now we have the rest of our lives to make up for it."

They stood in mutual peace, watching the dancing waves glinting in the sunlight.

"I've very glad we stole off to come here," she finally said. "This is where I first realized that whoever you were, you were for me."

"So late in the day?" he asked. "I knew immediately."

"Did you?" she asked in pleased surprise.

"Well, no," he said. "I knew I wanted to bed you, of course, but I didn't hear wedding bells right away."

She stared at him. He smiled and touched a finger to the tip of her nose. "Your promise, love. The one you extracted from me? Remember? I said I'd never deceive you again. All you'll get from me is honesty," he said piously.

"Christian?" she said softly.

"Yes, love?"

"I think," she said, "that, after all, we'd be much better off with a few, well-considered and occasional, well-placed lies."

"Your servant," he said with a bow and a wicked grin. "It will be difficult for me, but I will try."

"So," she said with a matching grin, "do you really like kissing me, now that I'm your wife?"

He didn't lie, because he didn't answer, not in words.

But it was a very good answer. It was a while longer before they returned to their wedding breakfast.